The Cross of Shaphan

THE CROSS OF SHAPHAN

Kim Tong-ni

translated and with an introduction by
Sol Sun-bong

The Si-sa-yong-o-sa Publishers, Inc., Korea
Pace International Research, Inc., U.S.A.

Published simultaneously in KOREA and the UNITED STATES

KOREA EDITION
First printing 1983
The Si-sa-yong-o-sa Publishers, Inc.
5-3 Kwanchol-dong, Chongno-ku
Seoul 110, Korea

U.S. EDITION
First printing 1983
Pace International Research, Inc.
Tide Avenue, Falcon Cove
P.O. Box 51, Arch Cape
Oregon 97102, U.S.A.

ISBN: 0-89209-200-9

This book is a co-publication by The Si-sa-yong-o-sa Publishers, Inc.
and The International Communication Foundation.

We hope that this novel may stimulate foreign readers to take interest in Korean literature and Korean culture. We also hope that it may introduce them to other literary works by Korean writers.

Contents

Introduction

On his first reading of the novel, the reader, whether native or foreign, may ask: why did the novelist write a story that is so distanced from his own existential milieu both in terms of time and space?

Is it an interest in biblical history? Or, has he some other motivation more complicated either in a religious sense or otherwise?

In his Afterword to the publication of the first version of the novel, Kim Tong-ni explains how he came to conceive of writing "The Cross of Shaphan." What we can sum up as the most imperative motivation of his selecting such a material seems to be the fact that the novelist found an analogy between the Jewish tribulation under the Roman domination and the situation of Koreans under the Japanese rule and oppression. Kim Tong-ni was born in 1913 which means that he was at the height of his social and artistic energy toward the latter part of the Japanese Occupation which is noted for its repressive rigidity and consequent provocation of many humanitarian ills including the prohibition of the use of Korean language. Of this last, Kim Tong-ni relates in his Afterword:

> .... What suffocated us more painfully than the rest of their repressive measures was their decision to deprive us of our native language, both written and spoken. It is even said in the Bible that 'The Word is God' (John I, i). For both an in-

dividual and a people, language is life, spirit and soul. Their attempt to take speech and letters from us, therefore, was equivalent to a scheme to kill the national soul.

Kim Tong-ni goes on to relate how the prohibition of the use of the national language was even a harder blow on those who wrote by profession to whom the repressive measure on language was a double threat and constriction. He said that "no one but those who experienced it can know how it was like breathing death and darkness day after day."

Of course, the novelist did not choose his material and setting solely for the political implication it had for Koreans. There certainly was a religiously motivated incentive, also. Both in his Afterword and Preface to the revised version of the novel, Kim Tong-ni discloses his early exposure to, and an interest in, Christianity and religious habit of mind. As a child he was a faithful church-goer and attended a missionary school. But apparently his early Christian background does not fully explain such a complex and intense involvement of religious themes in the central plot of a story of a nationalistic struggle as we see in this novel.

In the Afterword, we find the following passage which may be a revealing clue to our question:

> . . . . My feeling at the time was that I could not allow myself to describe the despair experienced by a nation merely as such, that is, as a hopeless situation. I could not write a story about our national tragedy without somehow linking it with light, victory, and hope of salvation. Although vaguely, I believed that in the despairing condition Koreans were subjected in, Jesus was the only possible hope and salvation and this belief led me to set my story against the Jewish history of Jesus' time.

What we see here is a synthesis between nationalism and religious optimism. And between the nationalistic hero who was also symbol of despair and nihilistic abandon and Jesus who offered hope and salvation to men, the novelist confesses that he had at first chosen Jesus as the main protagonist of his story.

And yet, there occurred a change in the nationalistic and artistic consciousness of the novelist. It began with the awakening of a humanist impulse which found Christian ideal too unhuman and the-other-worldly. He felt that the light and victory promised by Jesus were not of this world and people living in it.

At this juncture, the novelist feels forced to either give up his belief and hope in Christianity or forsake his humanist awakening. He can do neither. Because if Christianity has its limitation in being too transcendentalistic and detached from human aspirations and happiness, the humanism that he discovered as a ideal of a society which saw the defeat of god and religion in their fight against man, is also an imperfect one. The gravest defect the novelist finds in it is the utter despair and nihilism on which the humanism of modern era is based. He feels that what it has brought to man after its victory over the Christian negation of human happiness and gratification of human wishes on the earth is perhaps even worse than lack of happiness and gratification of wishes on earth. What is brought about by humanism of modern times is only 'a season of nothingness' and 'a climate of anxiety and confusion.'

Surely the artist who could not accept the national despair even in the midst of a severest foreign domination cannot rest with such a solution because he cannot possibly believe that man can live on and find any kind of peace or happiness in that state. From this realization, he sets anew on his search for a more creative and constructive solution which is neither nihilistic realism nor transcendental optimism. And perhaps the result is what we find concocted in the character of the hero of the novel Shaphan.

In the character of Shaphan, we find that there is will to live happily as long as it is humanly and honorably possible. He loves many things of the world, wine, women, friends, and if allowed, worldly glory also. And yet, he believes in the spiritual meaning of human life and religious foundation of man's existence. Although he has failed to bring worldly happiness to himself, to his beloved ones, and to his people through his desperate fight against the Romans, even at the deathbed he experiences no disillusionment about his nationalistic conviction. Likewise, inspite of the fact that Jesus does not comply with his requests and at the end does not even save himself from the pain and ignominy of the cross, Shaphan avows to no loss of faith in spiritual heritage of humanity or in the existence of God. Although he dies without having succeeded in winning independence and freedom for the Jews, he dies peaceful in the conviction of his having lived right. We may even say that he dies in hope.

In his Preface to the Revised Version, Kim Tong-ni discloses that he had an uncle who, like Jair's uncle of "The Cross of Shaphan," was involved in the anti-Japanese nationalist movement who 'was always followed around by the Japanese police.' He relates that this circumstance sowed the seed of nationalism early in his life. He declares in the beginning of his Afterword that "Love for the country and fellow countrymen is like love of one's hometown and family." What we learn from this is not whether the nationalistic or the humanistic feeling was a prevalent factor in Kim Tong-ni's artistic impulse but the fact that in him nationalism and humanism were inseparably and ideally intermixed.

In fact, for Kim Tong-ni, intermixing of seemingly antagonistic forces for the ultimate good occurs more frequently than in many other writers of his generation. The penchant for dialectical thinking seems to have enabled the novelist to find a connecting point even between Christianity and oriental Shamanism. He says in his Preface, for instance, that he wanted to "make it clear that there is connection between Jesus' miracle-working, Hadad's astrological prescience and the theme of Shamanism that I deal with in some of my fictional works."

A short list of his more well-known works may throw some light on this point.

Although Kim Tong-ni made his debut on the literary scene as a poet (1934) (he still is a practising poet) and engages himself in literary criticism also, it is for his fiction writing that Kim Tong-ni is most sought after by the Korean reading public. The more important of his fictional works include short stories: "The Tableau of Shaman Sorceress" (1946), "Loess Valley" (1949), "Two Reservists" (1951), "Tungsin-bul" (Life-size Buddha) (1961), "The Cry of Magpies" (1973), and the novels: "The Cross of Shaphan" (1958, Revised 1982), "Spring and Autumn" (1958), and "Eulhwa" (A Story with Shamanist Heroine) (1978). Apart from his concern for the traditionally Korean themes, the list also indicates his partiality for what is known as literary regionalism or local color fiction. We need, however, only to remember his beginning words in the Afterword which we have already quoted to know the true and profound meaning of such a favouritism: "Love for the country and the fellow countrymen is like love of one's hometown and family." It may be specially noted here that it is for this preference of local color and traditional themes that Kim Tong-ni's literature holds its unique position in the mind of the Korean reader.

Sol Sun-bong

The Cross of Shaphan

Chapter 1

Those Who Look for the Messiah

The Jordan River that originated from Mt. Hermon and Mt. Lebanon flew from north to south between a dry desert on the east and Canaan, 'the land of honey,' on the west ending in 'the Salt Sea' or 'the sea of death' (the Dead Sea). Since the current was fast, the hills high, and the stone steps were steep, the river was not generally considered good for sailing. The three lakes situated upstream, however, were an exception. Especially, the Lake Chinnereth which was commonly known as the Sea of Galilee was usually well frequented by boats for fishing, for transporting freight, or for giving seaway passage to the inhabitants. Now that the rainy season was over and the season of suffocatingly hot wind (from April to October) began, there were not a small number of people who would spend their time on the water.

Shaphan and Jair who had been fishing or rather holding their fishing rod for over an hour near the southern part of the mouth of the river where the Sea of Galilee or the Lake Chinnereth joined the River Jordan perhaps belonged with this kind of aquatic tribe. One of them whose name was Shaphan was a broad-shouldered man of well over thirty and had a black moustache which gave a certain angry look to his face.

He had been looking into the dark water while his hand held the rod.

"Can you still not see anything?"

He asked his young companion who took the oar.

"I cannot see anything, Commander."

The younger man answered, stuttering a little. He seemed six or seven years younger than Shaphan and was quite tall. He had a well shaped straight nose and lips that were not heavy. On the whole he looked like an ingenuous young man.

"Jair!"

Shaphan handed the fishing rod to the younger man and took out a wine bottle. He took a swallow from the bottle and looked up. There were many stars in the sky and above the crest of Mt. Tabor hung the crescent. The very pale hue of the moon reminded him of the eyes of Baptist John from which a bluish glow seemed to flow out. John was now in prison. He had been imprisoned by Tetrarch Herod Antipas in the castle of Machaerus for nineteen days.

Maybe Baptist John was really a prophet. Maybe he was Elijah. Or, maybe he was none other than the Messiah himself. Maybe the two of them were sitting in the boat on this water with the fishing rod just to find an answer to these wonderings. One of the members had been sent to the castle at Machaerus where John was imprisoned to investigate this matter.

"I see a light, Commander," said Jair raising the fishing rod.

Shaphan looked up with the wine bottle in hand. There was a torchlight in the direction of Gadara far to the east from the mouth of the river.

The torchlight came closer and closer. As it came up, it moved three times to the left, another three to the right, and then raised itself straight in the center. There was no doubt that it was the torchlight of Thomas returning from Machaerus.

It was exactly ten days ago that Thomas left for Machaerus

after receiving orders from Shaphan in their headquarters, a cave on a high cliff in the hills of Gerasa to the east from the Sea of Galilee. Since the group had had a special concern for Baptist John, the news of his imprisonment was an event to which they could by no means remain indifferent. Besides, the group's hope in involving themselves in the affair in this way was to ascertain the identity of Baptist John.

What they wanted through this enterprise was to be able to decide once and for all whether or not Baptist John was the Messiah, Elijah, or if neither, a common fanatic that could be found in any number. Thomas who was among the wisest of the group had been selected to take out nine days to make the necessary research on the spot and find the answer to the general inquiry.

On the seventh day after Thomas departed, however, he sent back a member with a report about his encounter with the secret messenger of Aretas the Nabatean king. With this report, Thomas also sent a word about this messenger's wish to meet the Commander asking him to let him know of his pleasure. As there had been friendly, if in a somewhat vague way, feelings between the group and King Aretas, Shaphan answered that he would be willing to meet the messenger if the matter about which the messenger wished to see him concerned Baptist John. He even gave a date for the meeting and directed the manner in which the meeting should be brought about.

There was a second torchlight signal from the other boat, and Shaphan said:

"We had better give a signal also."

Thomas' boat drew up. In the boat were two strangers besides Thomas. One of them was a man in his forties with a magnificent beard and powerful eyes. The other party was a woman. The man no doubt was the secret messenger of King Aretas of whom they had been informed by Thomas beforehand. But of the presence of a woman aboard, they had heard nothing. The woman looked, at a glance, very young and pretty. She looked no older than thirteen or fourteen.

The two boats came almost close enough to touch each other. Thomas standing at the bow offered his ceremonial greeting to the Commander and Shaphan received it in his sitting position.

The two boats touched. After tying the boats together by the sterns so that the two boats were like one, Thomas introduced the male passenger first. He said:

"This is King Aretas' messenger Aquila of whom I have already written to you, Commander."

The stranger stood up and looking at Shaphan said:

"I am Aquila, envoy from His Highness King Aretas. I offer my respectful greetings to you, honourable Commander."

He spoke with an eloquence and urbanity fitting a diplomatic personage.

Shaphan was looking at the other stranger, the woman. He seemed to ask: who is this girl?

"This is daughter to Hadad and she came with us. As to the circumstances of her joining us on this trip, I will explain later on."

The girl sat perfectly still even while Thomas talked to Shaphan about her. With her kerchief wrapped around her head, the girl merely looked ahead of her.

(The daughter of Hadad!)

Shaphan exclaimed in his mind at the surprising revelation. He did not ask any questions, however, since Thomas had said himself that the circumstances of her visitation would be explained later. He turned to Aquila, instead, and said:

"I suppose King Aretas is well?"

"I thank you, honourable Commander. His Highness King Aretas is very well as far as the affairs of his domain are concerned. However, His Highness is not a little disturbed by certain affairs that occurred outside the kingdom."

Aquila answered glibly. This man whose eyes emitted quiet lustre and whose face had an elegantly oblong shape seemed to have a confidence in his skill with words. He continued:

"This also is an affair outside the domain, but the reason of my trip to this place was to see if we could work out some means of rescue for Baptist John. This is how I came to accompany respectable Thomas to your presence, honourable Commander. Here are the letter and gifts from His Highness King Aretas."

Aquila took from an inside-pocket a sealed letter and offered it to Shaphan along with the gifts.

Shaphan unsealed the letter and read:

I am sending my messenger Aquila with a purpose of rescuing the just man Baptist John. I hope you will see him in person and convey your honoured opinions to me through him. I am also sending a few products of our land as gift. I will be pleased if you receive them from me.

Gift: Gold ... Two Minae (about 1.4 kg.)
Gift: Sulphur ... One Bottle
Gift: Cheeze ... Three Boxes

The Second Day of The Month
of April
Aretas, King of Nabatea

To: Commander Shaphan

Shaphan placed the letter and the gifts in front of him and said:

"Tell King Aretas that the honourable writing and gifts from the king are my new honour. And now tell me what thoughts the king has about the rescue of Baptist John."

"What His Highness conceives of is, in case you, honourable Commander, decides to raise an army and come down toward Machaerus, we on our side would rise in the southeast and join forces with you so as to attack from both sides at the same time."

"I see. I will consult with the members and let you know until tomorrow night what we will have decided."

Shaphan said conclusively as if to stop Aquila's suave speech-making in advance. Aquila could do nothing about the situation for the time being, but if Shaphan were to downright refuse to cooperate with the king, he would completely lose face with King Aretas.

"His Highness seems to feel that what is happening to Baptist John today could happen to anyone tomorrow. I do not think that my King merely wishes to pay back his resentment toward Herod Antipas on this occasion."

There seemed no way to stop Aquila from adding one opinion more before they parted.

"It is well spoken. I will consider the matter with caution," said Shaphan and before Aquila could say one more thing, spoke to Jair:

"You had better wait on the guest and see to it that he sleeps in comfort.... To Capernaum...."

He said the last words 'to Capernaum' quietly, as if he were talking to himself. The reason he did not say it more distinctly was that Jair knew before he was told where he would be directed to take the guest. In all cases, it was either Capernaum or Dariqueyea that Jair would take the guests. Going to Capernaum meant going to Ananias while going to Dariqueyea meant going to Thomas who resided there. But if Thomas was away from Dariqueyea and with Shaphan as at this moment, it was only to Ananias in Capernaum that he could be expected to take the guest. He did not need to be told that. Shaphan had only lowered his voice in saying 'to Capernaum' by way of saying 'as you would know yourself.' Aquila, however, interpreted the change in the pitch of Shaphan's voice in a totally different way. His nerves seemed to wake up at this 'low whispering' and his eyes glared.

Shaphan saw the glare of suspicion in Aquila's eyes and said:

"It is a custom in the Group to accommodate first class guests like you in Capernaum."

"I thank your generosity, honoured Commander. But my true desire is to spend a night on your side and exchange thoughts and ideas freely. Nothing would give me more honor than this," said Aquila. He was indirectly protesting to Shaphan for trying to send him away from his presence as quickly as possible.

Shaphan answered, however:

"It is a wish I too share most sincerely, my honoured guest. But I fear that I may commit too great an error in hospitality if I were to keep you by my side because I lead too busy and hectic a life here. Jair, wait on our guest."

This left no more chance to Aquila for protest or maneuvering.

Jair had already gone over to the boat of Thomas while Shaphan and Aquila were exchanging words, and as soon as Thomas and the daughter of Hadad stepped into Shaphan's boat, he started rowing.

"I will make sure that this boat goes to Capernaum, Commander. And good night to master Thomas, too."

Watching Shaphan's boat that gradually disappeared into the darkness after Jair's parting words were said, Aquila asked:

"Where is the Commander headed for, now?"

Jair was confused. He did not know how he should answer that question. In the Group, Commander and the head-quarters were subjects prohibited for conversation. Instead of answering at once, therefore, Jair turned his head and looked toward where Aquila's eyes were fixed and finally said:

"I am not sure. It is too dark to see."

Aquila pretended to accept Jair's answer without suspecting the deceit. He then asked:

"Where is the headquarters of the Blood Contract Corps?"

He too adopted an innocent expression as he asked thus. Jair became angry and he answered gruffly:

"For us, wherever the Commander is is the headquarters."

In his mind, Jair hated this messenger of King Aretas who thought nothing of asking him questions such as where the Commander was headed for, or where the Corps' headquarters was, in short, the top secrets of the Corps. If he were to have his way with this man, he would kick him into the water, he thought.

Aquila asked these questions, of course, pretending not to know that they were such particular secrets with his hosts. But to Jair's simple mind, the delicate gesture Aquila displayed did not mean anything. Aquila, it was true, had an excuse as an alien who could be assumed to know nothing of the rules and customs of this country. But Jair's feelings were that even if one was an alien, he should know that these things were official secrets and were not to be probed into. He could not accept the fact that what were such very important secrets for him were no secrets for Aquila, and, therefore, if Aquila acted as if they were no secrets, it was only because Aquila underrated his intelligence, thought Jair and was made angry by this self-centered feeling of outrage he gathered up in himself. As things stood thus, Jair could have proved himself an unpardonably unkind and haughty host if his guest had been some good-hearted and noble person instead of the shrewd and cunning diplomat Aquila.

From the way Jair answered his questions, Aquila concluded that this young man who was leading him was not at all very bright but neither was he deceitful nor wicked. Therefore, he softened his voice further and, changing the subject, said:

"Ah, is that so? That proves that the Commander is as wise a leader as he is rumored to be. But what do you think, Mr. Jair.... I believe that's your name, isn't it?... about the recent affair of Baptist John?"

"That is a subject which concerns Thomas or Ananias."

Jair's answer was as gruff as ever.

"I see. With Master Thomas, I have had a good chance to freely exchange our thoughts during the trip. I could see that he is wise and also has a good heart. But tonight, since I am journeying with Master Jair like this, I would like to learn many things from you for our mutual understanding and friendship. I respect a person who has a straight and honest nature like you, Master Jair."

Jair said nothing. He did not speak partly because he did not know what to say but also because he was disgusted by the attitude of Aquila who pretended to have seen into his companion's character within such a short length of acquaintance. When Jair did not answer, Aquila opened his mouth again and asked:

"What is Master Ananias like? I have never met him and therefore I would like to have some preliminary information about him so that I may not be rude to him in any way after we meet."

"He is a person in Capernaum."

Jair's answer was very simple. Also it was a continuation of his previous gruffness and lack of hospitality.

"I know it, too. I asked about him only because you said a while ago that the affair of Baptist John concerned only Master Thomas and Master Ananias."

For a long moment, Jair kept on rowing without saying anything. But finally he opened his mouth:

"What I meant by answering in that way was that you may wait until I take you to Master Ananias to whom we are going now, anyway."

"Then, what do you yourself think about the affair?"

Jair did not answer. He said in his mind: Shall I say 'I am a person who do not know anything,' or 'I only run errands for the Commander'? But neither seemed good enough for an answer. So he did not answer. But more than this, an animosity toward the man who kept on asking questions he could not answer made him taciturn.

To Aquila, however, the taciturnity, and even more marked 'unkindness' and 'gruffness' of Jair were not at all disagreeable. On the contrary, he judged that Jair's reticence and unsociableness were more advantageous to him than the urbane loquaciousness and diplomatic kindness of Thomas. This wily and confident messenger of King Aretas, therefore, decided that what he should do was not to get into a quarrel with Jair but instead win his trust, somehow. He also decided that it was better for him to pretend as if he were freely confiding in Jair in order to attain that end.

"If so, I would like to tell you what we are thinking and doing about Baptist John."

Aquila attempted a new approach in this way.

Jair did not even seem to be listening to him but kept on rowing toward the north.

Aquila, however, was undaunted. He continued:

"About how great a prophet Baptist John is, I believe you yourself know better than I do. I will, therefore, not add any words to it. What I would like to tell you first of all is the fact that Herod Antipas is a faithful servant of the emperor of Rome. I do not wish to talk long on this subject because both Commander Shaphan and my King have suffered too much already because of this allegiance between the Roman emperor and Herod Antipas."

After saying thus, Aquila looked up and tried to read the expression on Jair's face. There was no change in his facial expression.

"Between Nabatea and Judaea...."

He continued.

Jair did not pay any attention to what he was saying but handled the oar more roughly than before so that there was more noise of water splashing. He himself was thinking, however, what he had heard about the complicated relationship between Nabatea and the house of Herod. He had heard these things more than once and in considerable detail from Shaphan and Thomas but, owing to his lack of interest in politics and diplomacy, had not retained in his memory very much of what he had heard. What he had heard and had kept in memory was like the following.

Nabatea was an Arabian nation which was separated from Judaea by a small river. Traditionally there had been an animosity between these two countries and the chief reason was that people of Judaea harbored a cultural superiority toward the Nabateans. The superiority that the people of Judaea had over the Nabateans was based on the fact that they had their God Jehovah, to begin with. They not only believed that their God Jehovah was the only God existing but looked down on the god of Nabateans as an 'idol' or a 'demon.' They even derived a theory of genealogical superiority from religious superiority. One old evidence of their self-adopted claim to genealogical superiority was that in the record of history they set down the Jewish people were represented as descending from Sarah the legitimate wife of Abraham while Nabateans were given as the descendants of Ishmael, son of the woman slave of Abraham. The Jews also felt superior to the Nabateans on account of the geographical advantage they enjoyed. The advantage mainly was that since Judaea was surrounded by Arabia on the southeast, the Great Sea (the Mediterranean) on the west, Syria and Phoenicia on the north, and across the Red Sea on the southwest, by Egypt, the Nabatean merchants had to pass Judaea on their way to sell their merchandise in other countries. This was not all, however. While the people of Arabia still lived in tents, the Jews who had bigger plains and more crops were living in houses and building fortress in many cities attesting to their economic stability. Especially in recent years, Judaea was made even more powerful by the favor they curried with Rome thanks to King Herod's sly diplomatic maneuverings.

From the point of view of the Nabateans, however, all of Jewish manifestation of superiority was nothing but fictitious and egotistic claims. They believed that their mysterious and profound religion along with their rich stock of Arabian jewelry, their camels, horses, and their oil were the objects of passionate envy for the sly and shrewd Jews. In national character also, the Nabateans felt that they were by far the better of the two nations. They thought that they were brave, faithful, noble, and straightforward, in all points superior to the Jews who were only clever and subservient.

In addition to these traditional disharmony and tension, there was added a new element of conflict to the relationship between the two countries, not too long ago. It was the arrangement and then break-up of intermarriage between the two royal houses.

King Herod (the First) came to suggest to King Aretas of Nabatea that in order to fortify themselves against the gradual aggressive approach of Rome, the two countries would do best by forming an alliance. Herod asserted that this was necessary in order to defend themselves against the Roman invasion and keep themselves as independent nations. As a practical confirmation of this alliance, he suggested that the daughter of King Aretas become his daughter-in-law. He had three sons then and he offered to take the daughter of Aretas as the first wife to the best of them, the second son Antipas.

"As you may know, great King, of my three sons, the second one Antipas would not be so undeserving as husband of your daughter."

There was nothing in King Herod's words or attitude that offended King Aretas' feelings. What attracted the king to the proposal of marriage was not the utilitarian idea of forming an alliance with Judaea so that Judaea and Nabatea may fortify themselves against the 'gradual aggressive approach' of Roman as King Herod put it, but rather the noble and kingly attitude and manner of speaking Herod displayed. He had at first thought of showing Herod who was noted for his extreme arrogance what strong national will Nabatea had, but after seeing Herod in person and finding the king quite different from what he had surmised him to be from hearsay, he had come to feel that maybe there was no need whatsoever for him to bear an antagonism toward King Herod. So he had said without reserve and even with not a little good feeling:

"I consider my meeting with you today has led me to a consideration of one of the happiest and at the same time most important decisions of my life. It is the law in our country, however, that the king decide not the marriage of princess by himself but make the decision in consultation with his senior statesmen. I trust you will understand this situation."

"Do not doubt it. But even the law exists after the country does, and the statesmen exist after the king does. If, therefore, you and I should accomplish this act for the good of the peace and self-defence of our two independent nations, there cannot be any senior statesmen who would hinder it."

"It is rightly spoken."

In this way the matter was progressed between the two of them in an unexpected spirit of harmony.

King Herod had his reasons for making most of his elegance and sociability instead of his age, political experience and power. It was that he well knew the fact that what had made it impossible up to then for Judaea and Nabatea to have any diplomatic relations was the pride of each country plus the unrealistic sense of superiority the Jewish people bore over the Nabateans. King Herod was originally from Edom and had himself a resentment toward the superior feeling the Jews had assuming themselves as 'the elected of the God' but had not cared to show it on the surface for fear of losing popularity and power with his people. He, therefore, believed that if a Jewish king were to gain any profit from a meeting with a neighboring royalty, he could do so only by giving up any pretension to the Jewish superiority and instead giving a full boost to the self-importance of the other. It was, therefore, the fact that he had originally come from Edom, a non-Jewish district that King Herod could win success from the tête-à-tête, indirectly at least. When looked at this angle, the elegance and courteousness King Herod displayed on his meeting King Aretas was perhaps not a pretension but to a considerable extent honest expression of what he really felt and thought. That is, perhaps it was not a sheer diplomatic tactic or staging for getting the better over his opponent. Not all of his words and behavior of this day, however, was sincere. It was true that he wanted the animosity between the two countries which was inexpedient and meaningless for both countries to be eliminated and a friendly relationship as well as amicable business trade to be developed between them. And it was also true that he saw there was not reason for their two countries that were under the threat of the aggressive intent of Rome to stand against each other as enemies.

What lay inside him aside from these thoughts, however, was the thought that in case a normal political and trading relationship would be established between the two countries, Judaea would be the country to hold the initiative.

His self-confidence in his political, or rather; diplomatic competence was absolute as was manifested by the calculation he worked out about this approach to King Aretas. Also, he had to think about the geographical circumstances his country was privileged to: Judaea was situated between the Great Sea which was like the thoroughfare of the Romans and the Arabians. Besides, he had already won the favour of the Roman emperor Tiberius. If only he could consolidate a relationship with Nabatea he would not only be able to use his friendship with Nabatea in dealing with Rome but also use his good relationship with Rome in dealing with Nabatea. He knew through detailed calculations that in diplomacy, military power, economy and politics, Judaea would have an incomparably weightier sway in its dealing with Rome if it were to have the Nabatean support on his side. He had also calculated that in order to intercede between Nabatea and Roman encroachment, Arabian horses and camels plus some amount of jewelry could be used quite effectively.

This minute calculating and far-sighted ambition, however, did not go any further than the realization of the marriage between the two royal houses. It was because Herod died before any further development of his plan.

As soon as Herod was dead, Rome who had interpreted Herod's approach to Nabatea as a beginning of his policy to form a united forces among eastern countries, turned Herod's dream in the opposite direction and enforced a strong division policy. As a result, the districts of Judaea and Samaria were brought directly under the Roman procurator and Herod Philip (younger son to Heord the Great) was made the tetrarch of the districts of Ituraea and Trachonitis while Herod Antipas was given the districts of Galilee and Peraea. And so, at first, Princess Anna too was moved to the palace in Tiberias which was closer to her home land.

It was not, however, because of the death of Herod the First or the political changes following his death that made Antipas enemy of Aretas. The enmity started as Antipas who was lustful took his brother Philip's wife Herodias and afterward paid no attention to the Nabatean princess Anna. To make the matter worse, Herodias in her own turn, schemed against Anna and contrived to take her life. But Anna who sensed this threat to her life managed to get away from the palace and escaped to her father in Nabatea.

The relationship between the two countries fell into an extreme tension from this time. Antipas felt that Aretas could invade his terrain at any moment and as a preventive had a fortress built in Machaerus, an already fortified spot on the borderline between Judaea and Nabatea, stationing an army of specially chosen soldiers there. Also, he himself moved to Machaerus along with Herodias. This way, he could give great pressure and threat to Nabatea than before, also.

The pressure and threat Nabateans received from Antipas turned up in many forms. To give one instance out of them, just this spring, the soldiers of Antipas came over the border to attack Nabatean merchants who were taking their camels to the north. The soldiers kidnapped the merchants and took away the camels. When Nabatean government protested against the act the Jews claimed that it was done by thieves and that they had no knowledge of it. There was no telling how far this audacity would carry. Instead of apologizing as they ought to, the Jews were paying back with more oppression and threat.

This was of course because the Jews had the Roman support at their back. Even so, if it had been the old days, Nabatea would never have suffered this harassment and mortification without retaliation. But Aretas bore it without taking any actions of proper revenge. The reason was that Aretas was by now too old and also that there was a feud inside the royal house itself.

It was just at this stage that Bapist John's imprisonment occurred. Baptist John had openly denounced Herod Antipas for living with his brother's wife while maltreating his legitimate queen Anna and chasing her out of his palace. He called these acts unjust and unfit for a king. From Nabatean point of view, Baptist John seemed to be just speaking for Nabateans and so they eagerly acclaimed Baptist John as their benefactor and hero. It was not for long, however, that Baptist John could act as Nabatean spokesman because Herodias even more than Herod was aroused by Baptist John's denouncement of Herod and herself and worked to have him captured and imprisoned.

To Jair, however, the commotion Baptist John's imprisonment was causing to Shaphan and Nabateans was incomprehensible. Since he too believed Baptist John to be a prophet or a just man, at the least, he had very bad feelings against Herod and Herodias who had been the cause of his imprisonment. Still, he could not understand why Shaphan and Nabateans were making so much fuss over it making all these trips back and forth, too!

"Do you then think that we should just watch Herod and Herodias do these iniquitous things without doing anything about it?"

Aquila asked Jair finishing his tale.

"Wait a little longer. You will soon meet Ananias."

"Whereabout are we now?"

"Do you hear the sound of the lute? That's where Bethsaida is."

"Which direction is Capernaum, then?"

"You see that light on your left? That's Capernaum."

"Are we not making a détour this way, then?"

Jair did not answer.

Instead of urging Jair to answer, Aquila said:

"What makes that lute sound?"

"That's water ghost."

"What is water ghost?"

"The ghost of one that drowned."

"Do you mean that a ghost is making that kind of sound?"

"Yes."

"That is a very strange thing. How can a ghost make that kind of sound? It sounds exactly like a lute music performed by a human."

". . . . . ."

"How do you know it's a water ghost?"

"It is said by the boatmen."

"I wish I could go there and take a look."

"Let's not do it. I hear there's no one who has seen it."

"Why is that?"

"Maybe it's because people are afraid they may be lured by the ghost into drowning."

"Is the water ghost a beautiful woman?"

Suddenly Aquila thought of the girl he had parted from a while back in the boat, the one who was said to be the daughter of somebody named Hadad. As he travelled these several days with Thomas and the girl, he had thought to himself that the girl was extremely pretty.

"I don't know. Nobody has seen it."

"Who is this Hadad that has such a beautiful girl for a daughter? Excuse me for saying so, but you too seem to have an exceptionally good look, Mr. Jair. Maybe the Commander means to arrange a marriage between you and the young lady."

Somehow, Jair felt a strange excitement by these words spoken by Aquila but he pretended not to have heard them and said instead:

"We will reach Capernaum very soon. It's just over there."

Saying this, he turned the bow in the direction of the eastern pier of Capernaum. Thus he could also stop Aquila from pursuing the topic any further.

At this same hour, the boat carrying Shaphan, Thomas, and the girl who is said to be daughter of Hadad was sliding slowly in the direction of Gerasa. The cave that they called their headquarters was in the hills on the eastern shore of the Sea of Galilee.

Shaphan poured a cup of wine from the bottle he was drinking from before Thomas arrived with his guests and handed the cup to Thomas.

"You must be tired after many days' trip," he said with affection.

"Thanks to you, Commander, I have had an enjoyable trip."

After thus answering, Thomas proceeded to explain about the strange visitor on their boat. According to what Thomas said, when he heard that Thomas was going to Machaerus, Hadad commented that it was a good thing to do and then handing a letter and some gold to Thomas had asked him to drop by his house which was in a village called Aroer near Machaerus and bring his daughter here as he returned.

"But what is his intent in calling a marriageable girl into the cave?"

Thomas answered Shaphan that he too did not know Hadad's reason or purpose.

Shaphan turned his eyes from Thomas to the girl and asked: "What is your name, young lady?"

The girl did not even take off her kerchief as she answered: "Zilpah."

Her voice sounded as cool as the water of the spring thrown on the back.

"Had you heard from Teacher Hadad beforehand?"

Shaphan asked thus but the girl did not say anything in answer. Shaphan decided that the girl was either an idiot or a very haughty one. As if to find out which of these two cases she was, Shaphan pushed the torchlight close to her face which was covered with the kerchief. Zilpah looked at Shaphan. Her eyes were like two jewels which were dug out from inside a great rock. They made a striking contrast with Shaphan's blood-shot big eyes filled with energy and ambition. Shaphan decided that the girl was not an idiot. But he still could not tell whether or not she was haughty. He put out the torchlight.

"From this part is a route in a cliff which is dangerous and covered with rocks, thorns and holes. If you fall, you will hit the water. We cannot have light as we pass here, moreover. Will you still go with us?"

Again, Zilpah did not answer. She seemed to be saying, however, that there was no need to ask her these questions because she would only do what she might be ordered to.

There was no choice but that the three of them stopped near Gerasa for the night. When the girl fell asleep in her compartment which was separated from men's sleeping quarter by a screen, Shaphan asked Thomas again:

"How could the mother let the daughter go to such an unfamiliar and lonesome place as this?"

"She acted as if she were merely obeying Hadad's orders."

"Even when the father has been away for so many years?"

"It seemed that Hadad had left words with them that when the daughter reaches the age of fifteen either Hadad himself would come to them and marry her off or would bring her to himself. I believe that is why the girl did not cry or make a scene but followed me after packing her things in a calm manner."

"That is really like a daughter of Hadad!"

"Yes, like father like daughter."

The two of them seemed to agree thoroughly on this point. After emptying his short knowledge of the girl Zilpah, Thomas started giving a report on what he had found out about the object of their main concern in planning this trip, Baptist John. What Thomas was about to tell Shaphan would also have its bearing on the answer the Corps would give Aquila to be conveyed to the Nabatean king.

It seems in order, however, to let known what it was that Shaphan wanted to find out about Baptist John through Thomas. This exposition will also disclose what sort of men belong to the Corps, what ideas they have, and what they are planning to accomplish. First of all, what is this Blood Contract Corps of which Shaphan is the commander and how was it organized?

It was when Shaphan was eighteen years old that he discovered a large cave on a cliff near Gerasa. Seven years after this discovery, that is, when he was twenty-five, Shaphan started organizing a society of men under the name of Blood Contract Corps and the cave he had found seven years ago became their headquarters.

The real name of Shaphan was Tobiah, and he was born in Gerasenes, a village to the north of Capernaum. His father was named Lucius and his mother Joanna. He had never seen his father's face, however. From what his mother told him, his father was a merchant travelling over Phoenicia and Alexandria, but three months prior to Shaphan's birth had disappeared out of their lives during one of these customary sales trips. He left from the Bay of Caesarea and never came back.

After the disappearance of her husband, Shaphan's mother seemed to have given birth to another child, a girl this time, although nobody concerned was entirely sure about it, in secrecy. The mother, it seemed, had wrapped the newborn baby in a blanket and took it to the river bank and left it there the night after the baby was born. The man who made Shaphan's mother give birth to the child — it was not certain whether he was from Judaea or Greece — seemed to have seen her now and then even after the event but from the year Shaphan became twelve years old never again appeared before them.

A marriage had almost been fixed for Shaphan when he became fourteen but because of his mother's misbehaviour already mentioned, the marriage proposal was cancelled.

Three years after that, Shaphan who was seventeen wedded a
girl in proper marriage. The bride fainted on their first night.
She was fourteen years old at the time.

The bride who had fainted on the first night recovered but
whenever Shaphan went near her, her face turned paper white
and on the whole stayed away from food and drink. She took
to bed often and within four months after the wedding she
died. It was about this period that Shaphan started his life
of a wanderer.

The area Shaphan wanted to visit in the first place was the
wide plains on the eastern shore of the Jordan River. He could,
however, not penetrate into the interior of Arabia and came
back home. He stayed mere two weeks at home and then left
again for Decapolis. He went by boat from Capernaum to
Gadara and from there went on to Dion of Auranitis. On his
way back to Galilee from Auranitis, however, he travelled
through Hippos, Gadara and Gerasa with an aim to look over
the mountains and cliffs that are situated along the mouth of
the Sea of Galilee. In a cliff facing the Sea, Shaphan came
upon a large and deep cave with a big black mouth resembling
that of an ominous beast. When Shaphan took a first look at
this cave, he seemed to be looking at something which he had
been dreaming of ever since he was a child. He felt so excited
and restless that it was hard to restore calmness. The cave
looked as if it had been waiting for him all these years and he
felt as if he had known all along that he would find this cave
here just the way he had. Shaphan made a torchlight with a
resinous pine branch and stepped into the cave. Just then:

"Who is that?"

Shaphan heard a metallic, dry, and low voice coming out of
the cave.

Too startled by this, Shaphan unsheathed his dagger me-
chanically. His adversary in the cave, however, did not seem
to be making any move. Shaphan pushed the torchlight which
he had moved to his left further into the cave and looked
inside. A middle-aged man with his hair and beard turned half

grey was sitting with his head erect and his body as immobile as a fossil.

"Who are you?"

This time, it was Shaphan who asked.

"I am one who live here," said the man in a very low voice.

"Is there anyone here besides you?"

The man pointed a finger as Shaphan asked this question. When Shaphan looked where his finger pointed, he could see the light of a fireplace that was a hole underneath something that looked like a wall. Shaphan could not tell for sure what sort of occupation this man was engaged in but he could at least feel that the man meant no harm to him.

"How long have you been living here?"

"I don't remember."

"How long are you going to stay?"

"This is a good place to stay in."

"What if I told you to go?"

"I am the master of this cave."

"That is a lie. I have been searching for this cave. I went to Arabia, and to Decapolis. But I could find nothing like this cave which is just like what I have thought about all these years."

"You are mistaken. There is a cave like this in Decapolis and another in Samaria."

"Are you saying you won't leave?"

Shaphan took a sharp step into the mouth of the cave as if he were giving a decisive stab of his dagger to an enemy. It was just then that the middle-aged man who had been sitting in the cave swished the sleeve of his right hand and threw something at Shaphan. A serpent which looked like a red belt fell on Shaphan's right arm. His opponent lost no time in throwing a thing looking like a weasel at Shaphan's left arm. Shaphan found a fox hanging onto his left arm by which he was holding the torchlight.

"What kind of a fiend are you, old man?" said Shaphan in alarm. But the man in the cave merely laughed and said:

"Put down your dagger."

As Shaphan dropped his dagger onto the ground, the old man said in a low voice:

"Retreat."

The snake and the fox slipped down from Shaphan's arms and disappeared into the clefts of the rocky walls on both sides.

"Would you like to stay in the cave?" asked the old man with a smile.

"I have been looking for a cave like this for a long time."

"You do seem to have been looking for this cave."

Thus saying, the old man stood up with a small bundle and a stick in his hands. He looked as if he were departing right away. Shaphan was startled once more and said breathlessly:

"Where are you going from here? If it is all right with you, sir, I would like to follow you." And he made a move as if to follow the old man out of the cave. The old man looked at Shaphan in the face for some while, however, and said:

"I will see you in six years."

He left.

After this, Shaphan spent three years practicing the arts of using the dagger, sword, spear and also the archery.

When he came out of the cave and went on a wandering trip again, he had become twenty-one in age. On this occasion, he travelled long and wide around Galilee, through Judaea, Samaria, Decapolis, Phoenicia, Trachonitis, Idumaea, Phaeris, Auranitis, and Arabia, in short, all the places where there was a fighting going on. Though Shaphan had spent whole three years visiting places of fight either as spectator or participant, he never saw a case in which Rome was not a victor. Shaphan himself had killed not a few Roman soldiers but in the end he had to flee from the battleground and not even once could stand up to the Roman army on his own. No matter how direct and exact he could throw his arrow or dagger, he could never defeat the Romans by himself.

It was when Shaphan had reached the age of twenty-four

when he returned to the cave. What he had in mind when coming back there was to collect whatever manpower he could and train it into a regular army through a collective disciplining.

When he reached the cave, however, he found out to his great surprise that the old man from whom he had parted years ago was again sitting in it.

"Do you wish to chase me out of here, again?" asked the old man in a low voice.

"No, sir."

"Why are you come back to the cave, then?"

"I come to borrow wisdom from you."

"You are quite grown now."

There was a smile on the old man's face. That night, Shaphan told the old man all about his past and also confessed to him about what he was planning for the future, that is, his plan for the organization of the clandestine army. The old man of the cave seemed to be listening to Shaphan's tale with interest. After Shaphan finished his talk, however, the old man said:

"I think I will read your future in the stars."

Shaphan then knew that the old man was an astrologer. His name was Hadad. But to Shaphan who had not yet felt the need to think deeply about such a thing as his fate the old man's offer to read his future did not make any clear and immediate sense.

The old man, however, spent that night with open eyes in order to study the stars. He spent three nights in like manner and on the morning after the third night said to Shaphan:

"You are born under a female star. A female star can act only when it meets a male star."

"But where is this male star now?"

"It is too far away from here right now. When that star comes near, other stars are bound to lose their brilliance by it. Both you and he are big stars."

"When would that star meet with me?"

"Seven years after now."

"What should I be doing during the seven years?"

"You can be engaged in your preparations. You will perish if you come out of the cave."

"Do you mean that I should only stay in this cave?"

"You may go out in the night. Only in the night. During the daytime, you may move about outside only by hiding your name and face, and by seeking shady and lonely places. You may not speak or act where there are many people."

It was then that Shaphan dropped his name Tobiah. At the same time, Shaphan changed his plan for the clandestine army to a plan for a more privately-based collectivization of manpower.

From spring of the next year, Shaphan started organizing his Blood Contract Corps. The First Members were Shaphan's friends through the years of his growing up: Ananias, Zechariah, Thomas, Jair, Gallio, and Judas. When these men gathered together in the cave, Shaphan pulled his dagger out of its sheath and ripping one of his arms with it had a bowl put under it to collect the blood. The six other men gathered all ripped their arms in the same way and collected their blood in the same bowl, which they afterwards offered up to Shaphan. Shaphan took a swallow out of the bowl of the blood and passed it to Ananias who then passed it to Zechariah. Zechariah passed it to Thomas who passed it to Jair. Jair passed it to Gallio and Gallio passed it to Judas. In this way they shared the blood that was collected from them all between them.

Ananias stepped forth then and declared before Shaphan:

"The six of us gathered here swear that we will live or die as our Commander Shaphan who wishes to free the people of Judaea from Roman oppression orders."

As Ananias raised his hand in indication of his allegiance, the five others raised their hands in accord to show their unanimous will and dedication. They said in one voice:

"We swear."

Shaphan raised his hand to the sky and said:

"There will be only glory in the rest of our lives. Otherwise, the death will guard our freedom for us."

Six men repeated Shaphan's declaration.

Next, Shaphan proposed that Hadad be elected the Corps Teacher. Shaphan stepped out to stand opposite Hadad and said:

"We would like to elect you to be our Teacher from now on."

"Maybe it was to meet you seven stars today that I left Arabia in my early years to come to this cave," said Hadad shaking his head so that his white hair fluttered. Shaphan told Hadad and six officers of the Corps what he was thinking of the main objective of the organization and what his beliefs were and what ideas he had about organizing.

First, Shaphan told them about how he had from childhood liked using weapons such as sword and spear and bow and arrows. He said that from eighteen to twenty-one, he had done nothing but training himself in these arts aside from praying in the cave. The reason why he had concentrated so much on developing the skill to use these weapons was, he said, that he realized that only a military force could end Roman occupation in Judaea which had been brought about also by a strong militarism. When he became twenty-one, he left the cave in order to put his self-training to a test. For three years, therefore, Shaphan travelled Samaria, Judaea, Decapolis, Phoenicia, Trachonitis, Ituraea, Peraea, Auranitis, and Arabia, in short, all areas around Galilee, and fought everywhere he went. He could never meet one, however, who could defeat him in an one-to-one contest. This did not give him much comfort because he had realized that no matter how skillful he was with his weapons, he could by himself never fight against an organized army.

Under the political circumstances Judaea was subjected to, organizing an army was impossible. Besides, even if a small-scale army might be gathered up, how could it fight against an

entire army of Roman soldiers? He agonized himself for a long
time with this question and it was to ask for an answer to this
that he prayed to the God for such a long time. What gave him
a new light in his dark fumbling was a new belief in the
Messiah. He came to realize that if only he worshipped the
Messiah and fought with Him on his side, he would be able to
even defeat Roman army. As proof of the greatness of the
Messiah's power, Shaphan enumerated various instances in
history such as Moses getting away from Egypt, Moses crossing
the Red Sea and defeating the great army of Egyptians, and
the fact that when Joshua, Moses' successor, crossed the
Jordan River to attack Jericho he only needed to blow his
trumpet as Jehovah directed him to for the solid rampart to
fall down, as well as Gideon fighting down one hundred and
twenty thousand enemy soldiers with mere three hundred
fighters on his side and Samson pulling down Philistine house
of worshipping all by himself. What Shaphan was empha-
sizing by telling all this was the fact that only with help of
Jehovah could the Jewish people win in their fight against
their powerful enemy.

Therefore, members of the Corps should guard against
following the examples of the Zealots Theudas or Judas and
Mathdias after him, said Shaphan. He also insisted that what
they must do was fortifying a clandestine network. By keeping
up with diligent training, the Corps would be able to stand up
bravely on the day of the Messiah, he said. This emphasis on
the necessity to be helped by the Messiah in their fight was the
decisive factor that won Shaphan the support and trust of all
the Corps members. It also showed Shaphan as having the
Jewish statesmanship and strategy.

It was true that Shaphan's linking of the Messiah and the
fight for the liberation of his country had its basis on the fact
that Shaphan was above anything a Jew. There was another
important and more direct motivation for this, however, and
it was the horoscope Hadad read for Shaphan. Hadad had
called Shaphan a female star and had said that there would

come a time when a great male star which was the female star's partner would appear before Shaphan so that the stars could shine each other in mutual illumination. Hadad had said that Shaphan should live in the cave in hiding until that star should come to him. When he first heard these things from Hadad, Shaphan had not thought that the great male star could mean the Messiah. After several days' pondering over the question, however, Shaphan had stumbled to the thought that maybe the great star he should meet was none other than the Messiah himself. It was from this thought that he seriously began to plan for a clandestine organization to be formalized under blood contract.

Lastly, he explained to the members what ideas he had about the structure and future activities of the Blood Contract Corps. He said that the seven members gathered there would be the First Members. Each of the First Members would form another seven-member core under him to be called the Second Members each of whom again would lead another seven-member junto that would be the Third Members, and so on. There was to be no communication, either horizontally or vertically, between the members from the Second Member level down unless there was a special reason for it. This was to maintain secrecy about the organization and activity of the Corps. It would be only the seven in the First Member group, therefore, that would know the overall objectives and activities of the Corps at all times and all below this line would be mere cellular existences. Shaphan made the First Members station themselves in different places, Jair in Gerasa, Thomas in Dariqueyea, Ananias in Capernaum, each acting as a fisherman, and let the three remaining ones, Zechariah, Judas and Gallio in Ophrah, Jerusalem, and Jobba respectively. Their main work in their stations was gathering information and supervising organization work.

Corps' operation funds came partly from voluntary contribution of wealthier members and also from the plundering by Shaphan's clique on rich merchants and caravans. Since Shaphan had issued a strict order that members should under no circumstances participate in plundering, the infrequent pillaging by the First Members was kept a secret from the rest of the Corps members. The Corps members were required to hold an occupation aside from their work for the Corps. This was to assure that the Corps activities would not be stopped because of financial difficulties, in the first place. But it was also an effective way for the Corps to spread widely and deeply in the world.

Consequently, ordinary members of the Corps belonged to the Corps only by existing as a minute part of the whole cellular network and so, looked at from outside, they were no different from other people. It was because owing to the fact that their organization was a clandestine one, each member needed to perform his duty as a Corps member publicly only once, that is, on the day of the Messiah. Their contract was that on this day they would rise up all together. Until each member would be notified about the coming of the day of the Messiah through their network, therefore, their membership and duty as a member could remain in secret.

The major task for the top officials including Shaphan, therefore, was in precise divining of the day of the Messiah and passing the knowledge to the members from the Second class downwards. The communication of the news from Second Members to the Third, and from Third to Fourth, and so on, was guaranteed by a long and assiduous training.

Under these circumstances, the news of Baptist John's imprisonment by Antipas could not fail to draw Shaphan's immediate attention. People were excitedly whispering about a man whom they called Baptist John who according to the rumor suddenly made his appearance on the bank of the Jordan River giving water baptism to the people and calling out for them to repent for the Kingdom of Heaven was upon them. This Baptist John, it was said, was afraid of no one, even high-ranking officials and called everybody a sinner. He was said to be different from any prophet that had yet appeared; some called him Elijah and others said he was the Messiah himself.

It was because of all this conjectures and excitement among people over Baptist John that Shaphan had sent Thomas to Machaerus to find out about him. And Thomas' report was:

— It was while John was baptizing at Bethany before he was imprisoned. One day, a group of Levites and Pharisees came up to him from Jerusalem. They were the investigation committee. They asked Baptist John who he was. To this John who understood the meaning of their question answered that he was not the Messiah.

"You mean he said that in person?"

"Yes."

Thomas continued:

— Then what are you, are you Elijah, they asked again. John answered again that he was not. Then are you a prophet, they asked. No, I am not a prophet, answered John. Then what are you? What shall we call you when we go back and make a report on you, they asked. I am 'a voice crying aloud in the wilderness to prepare a way for the Lord and clear a straight path for him' as the prophet Isaiah had spoken, he said. Then the Pharisees who had tried from the first to win advantage over John said: If you are not the Messiah or Elijah nor a prophet, by what right are you baptizing people? To this John merely said: The time is come. The one who can tell who I am comes after me and I am merely opening people's ears for him.

Although the Levites and the Pharisees were vexed by John who called crowds to him as if he had a great power on his side and labelled even the high-ranking officials sinners, they could find no good excuse to indict him because he did not claim to be anybody important himself but kept saying that the one who would come after him would be able to tell them who he was. The decisive blow came from elsewhere, however. It was that Baptist John had sometime ago denounced Herod Antipas for taking the wife of his brother Philip Herodias and called their relationship "unjust." This had angered Herod and Herodias into issuing an order of imprisonment for John.

At this point, Shaphan interrupted:

"We know all that. What we want to know is what signs John showed in prison, who is this one who John says will come after him, and whether or not John's only possible rescuers are King Aretas and our Corps."

Urged to arrive at the conclusion, Thomas said:

"I will answer those questions, then. First, Baptist John has not shown any sign while in prison that he is the Messiah. As to the one who is supposed to come after him and possible rescuers of the baptist...."

Thomas paused for a second, and then said he would now tell Shaphan the most important item in his report and added that it concerned 'the one who was to come after him.'

— It was the day after Baptist John had his confrontation with the investigating Levites and Pharisees. He pointed at a man who was crossing the wilderness toward Bethany on the bank of the Jordan River and cried out to his disciples: 'Look, there is the Lamb of God. It is he who takes away the sin of the world." He then continued: "This is he of whom I spoke when I said, 'After me a man is coming.'" As his disciples looked toward the man in confusion, Baptist John spoke again, "I myself did not know that he was the Son of God, at first. But when he came up to me and was baptized I saw the Spirit coming down from heaven like a dove and resting upon him and knew who he was."

On the next day the stranger was found still in Bethany and Baptist John again pointed to him and said: "Look, there is the Lamb of God." Out of John's disciples, Andrew and John from Galilee were the first to leave him to follow the stranger. In this way, the news about this strange man was spread wide from Galilee to the north and all along the Jordan River to Machaerus in the south. It was known by this time that this strange man was originally a carpenter named Jesus in Nazareth, Galilee.

Shaphan's blood-shot eyes lit at this new information and he asked briskly:

"Where is this man Jesus, now?"

Thomas, however, said that he had some more things to tell him which were more important. What he then recounted was that the strange man then had left Bethany to go up to Galilee. And a very strange thing had happened in Cana, a village near Nazareth. There was a wedding in one of the houses in the village and Jesus was among the guests. Seeing that there was no wine he had the servants pour water in the jars and, just by saying some prayers, turned the water in the jars into wine.

After recounting up to this point, Thomas said that maybe there was some reason to believe that this was the Messiah himself considering the things John was supposed to have said about his coming and also what supposedly took place at the wedding. He then told Shaphan that as to where he could be found at this moment, he did not know anything.

"Thomas, if all this was true, ..."

Shaphan's voice trembled a little when he said this. He continued:

"Then, it must be the Messiah. Because in Hadad's horoscope also, it is said that now is the time."

On hearing the name Hadad, Thomas threw a look at Zilpah and said:

"Let us look for him, then."

Shaphan said:

"Yes. I think we should do so. You go to Capernaum early in the morning and see Aquila. After that, leave at once. Go and look around in Nazareth and Cana. For my part, I will have Jair search through the west of the Sea and Capernaum."

"What then shall I tell Aquila?"

"You should tell him, of course, that we think it is not the time yet. You might tell him that we know of someone who insists that Baptist John is the Son of the God and therefore we wish to consult with him before we make up our mind about anything. It would be difficult for the Nabateans to understand our real situation. Our enemy is not Antipas but the Romans. We cannot afford to risk anything. Say what you think is proper to Aquila."

By this Thomas knew that he did not have to answer Shaphan's question about whether Aretas and the Corps were the only forces that could rescue Baptist John.

Shaphan spoke again:

"What would be the purpose of our rescuing Baptist John if we do rescue him? It would be to make certain that nothing happens to him who may be the one we have been waiting for. We would not be rescuing him for the good of Nabateans or the disciples of the Baptist. Isn't that so? If Baptist John's identity is what we now think it is, we would be fools to rescue him just to win the Nabateans and John's disciples on our side. It certainly is not an advisable thing to do until we should be ready to fight against the Roman army, anyway."

"You have reason, Commander. But if we were to flatly refuse to join in, the Nabateans are likely to go on with their plan, anyway, even by instigating Baptist John's disciples into coming into their force. If we stay away even then, we would be making them our additional enemy. I wonder if we could afford, at this point, to turn what has been a friendly relationship into an antagonistic one...."

"Even so, we cannot fight against the Romans until we join hands with the Messiah."

"Yes, of course. And that is the ultimate goal of our Corps, I know. But the question we face now is that the Nabateans and John's disciples are aware of the existence of our Corps and are wanting to have a friendly relationship with us. Our problem, therefore, seems to be in adhering to our basic objectives without turning them into an enemy."

"Turning them into an enemy...," said Shaphan to himself. The thought seemed to unsettle him a little. There were some among the disciples of Baptist John who had some knowledge of the Blood Contract Corps, and there were even some who were members of the Corps among his disciples. It was necessary, therefore, to avoid turning them into an enemy. He said:

"So you tell him to wait some time until we should find a proper occasion for action or something like that. We don't need to flatly refuse to cooperate as you put it. In the meantime, we can get in touch with this Messiah if he is one...."

Thus, early next morning, before it was light, Thomas took the boat and rowed to Capernaum where Aquila would be staying with Ananias. Shaphan and Zilpah left also. But their destination was the cave in the cliff, the headquarters of the Blood Contract Corps.

When Thomas arrived at the house of Ananias, it was late in the morning and sun was hot in the leaves of the fig tree in his yard.

Ananias came out to the gate to welcome Thomas. He held Thomas by the wrist and acted as though Thomas was his younger brother whom he had not seen for some time. There was an expression of affection on his face. His lips, however, were closed tight and only his two cheeks showed any indication of a smile. It was the custom among the members, especially the First Members, of the Blood Contract Corps to refrain from conversation even in the presence of their family but Ananias was one of the more typically taciturn of them all.

He opened his mouth only after he had led Thomas into his secret quarters.

"The man Aquila whom Jair brought to me stays in the annex."

"I come to talk to you about him."

"Jair kept his mouth shut about the guest and merely looking at me in the eye said you will come to explain to me today. Jair seemed a little disturbed about the man."

"I suppose the guest annoyed Jair on their trip here."

The two men smiled at each other for a second without

saying anything. Then Thomas started telling Ananias all he knew about Aquila.

After listening to all Thomas had to say, Ananias said:

"If so, the beginning itself seems to be somewhat at fault."

"You mean, I shouldn't have brought him here?"

Thomas sounded uneasy because if the beginning was at fault it meant that Thomas himself was to blame.

"That and the Commander's directing you to bring him."

"At the time, both I and the Commander thought that Nabateans meant to attack Machaerus by themselves first."

Upon these words of Thomas, Ananias made a vague smile and with his head bent did not say anything.

After a long silence, Ananias finally raised his head and spoke:

"They are now suggesting that we and they make the attack simultaneously but what they really want is for us to go first, isn't it?"

"The Commander also seems to see it that way. He seems to think that Nabatea would wait until we get up and make the fight. He thinks that they will merely provide weapons and supplies to us but avoid direct fighting as long as they could."

"If so, I don't think we need to give them any excuse. You had better tell him directly how we view the situation. I don't think they suppose us to be foolish enough to take their words at face value, anyway."

The two men then agreed to see Aquila without any more delay.

Upon seeing Thomas, Aquila smiled widely and said:

"This is going to be one of the most enjoyable trips that I have ever taken in my life. Commander Shaphan, the gentleman who took me here last night, and you two gentlemen here, all of you will remain in my memory as most remarkable persons for the rest of my life. Now I am ready to hear the wise decision of the Commander."

He seemed full of confidence and sure hope.

Thomas decided not to make the interview longer than

necessary. With this thought in mind he began:

"I am glad to hear that you enjoy the trip."

After this preliminary word of ceremony, he continued:

"Our Commander wishes us to have a closer and deeper relationship with His Highness King Aretas and you, Mr. Aquila. He wishes, therefore, to be of dependable assistance to him in his plans to attack the fortress at Machaerus. It is an inconsolable regret, however, that he cannot act as he wishes since his strength, different from the great military power of the kingdom of Nabatea, is merely that of a small group of men. His present intention is to wait until Nabatea commences the attack and then after the fight is begun, try to defend the area south of Machaerus along the Jordan River."

Thus, he promptly showed his adversary his mission in this confrontation.

A thin grey shadow seemed to pass through Aquila's face. However, he soon raised his head and said:

"I thank you for speaking with so much frankness. I believe that one needs to speak with absolute openness in a negotiation like this. With this belief, I would like to convey one more wish of my King to your honors. It is that in case your Corps decides to take a military action to rescue Baptist John, His Highness King Aretas will not only provide the entire weapons and supplies but also will be pleased to supply some force. Also, if the Corps should rescue Baptist John by some other means, His Highness will pay whatever reward you should find proper."

Neither Thomas nor Ananias spoke when Aquila announced this new proposal. After a while, Aquila continued:

"This does not mean that Nabatea will not do her part in the southeastern area. The above suggestion was offered merely because we feel that there should be established a clear boundary line when a joint military action is taken between two different countries, and from our point of view, it seems better for your Corps to take the initiative so that there may be no misunderstanding about how we stand to each other. I do hope you will understand the circumstances that prompt my King to make this proposal to your Corps."

With this, Aquila's diplomatic goal became quite clear.

To tell the truth, a secret organization like the Blood Contract Corps that had no financial foundation needed an assistance such as was offered by Nabatea quite badly. It was, however, out of the question, that the Corps should accept Nabatean proposal right away. Still, there was enough in it to hold interest of the two men negotiating with the Nabatean envoy.

"I think this is a matter that calls for a serious consideration," said Ananias politely.

"Does that imply by any chance that you doubt my King's intention or ability to keep the promise?"

"If I should speak with the frankness which your honor has had the kindness to commend, that is indeed part of the reason," said Ananias with a smile.

"I see. What if, then, we should hand over part of the arms and supplies in advance?"

Ananias hesitated a second at this new suggestion. Thomas felt it was his turn to step out. He said:

"Is this also the pleasure of King Aretas?"

Aquila did not seem annoyed in the least by this question. He said promptly:

"Yes, it is. It is one of the proposals His Highness ordered me to convey to you."

This time, Thomas also felt at a loss what to say. He could not possibly say: how can we believe it? After a long silence, Ananias opened his mouth and said:

"I think it is a fair proposal and I believe the Commander's attitude may change in the event that the content of the proposal be carried out in practice."

The negotiation seemed to have arrived at its end without disruption, for the time being, anyhow.

"I thank you. I am sure His Highness will recompense your honors for your trouble."

Aquila's face as he said these words and stood up seemed satisfied.

Hadad sat with his one hand on the back of the badger without saying anything or making any move as he watched Shaphan walk into the cave with Zilpah following. His face was sunken and yellowish. The prematurely whitened beard and hair made him look older than his age. Sun was rising in the east, but inside the cave which faced southwest, there was still not very much light and behind the old man one could see the charcoal fire burning red.

"Greetings to you, Corps Teacher."

Shaphan's voice as he greeted the old man sounded a little husky and thick.

"Oh, is that you, Commander? I am glad you came back safe."

Only after he answered Shaphan's greetings in this way, the old man looked at Shaphan and Zilpah. He looked them over as if he were examining them for something.

"Your daughter, Teacher," said Shaphan and took one step aside. Zilpah took off the kerchief with which she had been covering her head and stepped forward.

"Father."

Her voice was so clear that it seemed to spread bright ripples of spring river in the dark and heavy air of the cave.

"It was when I was seven years old that I saw you last, father."

"You have grown much, and become pretty."

Even before Hadad's dry voice died out, Zilpah stretched her slender white neck and put her lips on her father's cheek.

"You are going to live here. With me," said Hadad. Zilpah did not say anything.

"In this cave, there are only two rooms. This is one of them and I am using it. The other is farther inside and used by Commander Shaphan. You will be using this room with me for the time being."

Zilpah again did not say anything but merely looked at her father with a face that looked as if she had prepared herself for whatever may be ordered her.

The second room Hadad pointed to Zilpah was one made by digging into one side of the cave wall and hanging a blanket at the mouth to partition it from the outer space. After Shaphan organized the Blood Contract Corps and began to use the cave as its headquarters, the cave was dug out on the sides and also in the depth. As a result, two rooms were made, one on each side, and deep inside was made a space which could be used as a conference room for seven or eight people. Deeper inside, there was made another partition which was used as an armoury.

Hadad was originally an Arabian. He had followed his father out of Arabia to live in the east of Ariel at the age of twelve. He had married at fifteen and had his first son at sixteen. From seventeen onward, he lived away from home and wandered training himself as a Taoist master. His life of a wanderer continued to the present. Once in three or six years, he visited his home like a stranger and left quickly. His father looked after the family while he was young and after his father became too old to work, his son took over the responsibility. Hadad himself never shared the job of making a living for the family.

It was not because he had any definite purpose, however, that Hadad abandoned his family and lived a life of an ascetic and a wanderer all his life making a cave his home. Even the astrology to master the art of which he had dedicated such a great part of his life did not mean to him any means of making a name in the world or accumulating wealth. The only reason he studied astrology was that he had had the interest and habit of associating with the stars and also felt something like a mission to perform for his knowledge of the stars. Even on the rare occasions when he visited his family, he felt a scruple about conversing with his wife or children, and after three days' stay, would begin to feel positively guilty toward the stars for not being with them and studying them. His relationship with his stars of the entire sky was as close and intimate as any shared among family of a human home. To his eyes, the illness, or the temporary absence, or the slumber, or anger of some of the stars were as clearly perceivable as with humans. All the stars seemed to respond to him with feeling and individual characters. Thus when he took trips or changed caves, it was only to follow the advices the stars had given him and for no other reasons. His decision to bring Zilpah into the cave this time also was only his obeisance to the admonishments of his stars.

He did not tell these things to anybody, however. Nobody, therefore, knew at first why the old man had brought this beautiful young woman into the cave. Hadad made Zilpah clean her body and watch the stars in the sky every day. Seeing this, Shaphan decided that maybe the old man had called the girl in to teach her to be an astrologist.

(A woman astrologist....)

Shaphan could not help a grin when he thought of Zilpah becoming an astrologist like her father. At the same time, however, Shaphan thought that if Zilpah becomes an astrologer and succeeds her father, he would have her as Corps Teacher. It was first of all because he trusted Hadad. But it was also because of the strange strength that he could feel coming out of Zilpah that he had this thought. More than anything, her exceeding and mysterious beauty and crystal clear voice gave her a dignity and magnitude which were nearly supernatural.

In the meantime, Zilpah spent her days in the cave uncomplainingly. She seemed to be resigned to anything that might happen to her and merely obeyed Hadad in everything. Needless to say that she did not get much sunlight. And the room where she was destined to live was no more than a stone hole dug into a wall. She ate two meals a day which were no more than a piece of dry bread and a few raisins. There was hardly any building of fire to prepare a meal. In short, the life she was given to live since she came into the cave to join her father was one which no one but monks or ascetics could withstand. But here was a beautiful young girl as clear-eyed as a morning dew uncomplainingly living a life hardened for those who forsook all pleasures and comforts of the world. Observing her going through her trial with so much equanimity, the onlookers could not help exclaiming: "Like father like daughter!"

. At first, Hadad looked as if he were going to teach his daughter the art of astrology. He did not make her do any chores or works other than watching the stars with him on the flat top of a rock in front of the cave, his customary station of star-watching.

He usually did not say anything as he and the girl watched the stars but at times he mumbled something in his mouth by way of conversation. His teachings to her continued through the daytime.

Shaphan would hear him teaching his daughter as he passed by their room:

"If you have memorized the Twelve Palaces of the Yellow Road, you must next memorize the names of the master stars and their hours."

After the lean dry voice of Hadad, Shaphan could hear the clear cool voice of Zilpah:

"The master star of the Palace of White Lamb is Mars, the master star of the Palace of the Twins is Mercury. The master star of the Palace of the Lion is the Sun. . . ."

It was not often, however, that the father and daughter had their lessons aloud like this. This happened only once in several days when Hadad checked on Zilpah's progress of learning.

What Shaphan overheard thus outside their room, however, was enough to convince him that Zilpah was a person of exceptional memory and intelligence. Within a short time after she moved into the cave, she mastered the basic learnings of astrology concerning Ten Major Planets, the Twelve Palaces of the Yellow Road, the Master Stars and their Hours.

This was surprising to Shaphan since he knew that those

were things which neither he nor Jair could even begin to master although they had both spent many years exposed to all those learnings in the person of Hadad.

In the midst of Zilpah's learning of stars from Hadad, Thomas and Ananias who had completed their tour around the Sea of Galilee made their return to the headquarters. On the evening when they returned, Judas also rejoined the group.

Thomas made his report on his interview with Aquila first. The essence of the report was that Aquila did not accept Shaphan's suggestion about waiting for a proper time and that it was not found easy for the Corps to send him away with a downright refusal of the Nabatean request.

"Then. . . ."

Shaphan interrupted Thomas at this point. He seemed to wish to ask Thomas if it was because he lacked the decisiveness to give the envoy a direct answer that he could not conclude the interview as they had previously planned to.

Thomas sensed what was in Shaphan's mind. He therefore opened his mouth and said:

"What I find most delicate in this matter, Commander, is the fact that the Corps is so intricately interrelated with the disciples of Baptist John. If we were to flatly refuse to cooperate, we cannot be sure how the Nabateans would react to it in terms of involving Baptist John's disciples in the matter. What I mean is they may do what they can to incite his disciples to turn enemy to us."

"I see."

Shaphan's face changed its expression as he said this. How could he possibly ignore the importance of Baptist John's disciples whether from the view point of the Corps or otherwise? The fatal point in considering this matter, of course, was that many of them were Corps members.

"Besides, Aquila presented a new proposal. He intimated that if we should start the action, Nabatea would supply us with all the weapons and provisions."

"Is it not a thing he said extempore to save the situation, so to speak?"

To this question of Shaphan, Ananias took turn to answer:

"Thomas questioned him on this particular point, as a matter of fact. But Aquila said that this was one of the missions he had been ordered to perform by his king Aretas."

"What is the conclusion of the meeting, then?" asked Shaphan looking from Ananias to Thomas.

"We said that our attitude may change if Nabatea should send us arms and supplies in advance."

This answer was made by Thomas. In fact, Ananias had said to Aquila that the 'Commander's attitude may change' if those things should be made over to the Corps before the action. Thomas, however, gave a little variation to it and said 'our attitude' instead of 'the Commander's attitude.'

Ananias quickly noted what Thomas was doing and while thanking him in his mind for his tactful kindness, lost no time in assisting Thomas in his good office of arbitration. He said:

"In my opinion, we need not worry about being assisted by the Nabateans. If they should bring us arms and supplies in advance as Aquila promised, then I think we may be able to steer things to suit us."

"How do you mean?"

"We do not need to attack Machaerus with the entire force but can make those of our Corps members who are also disciples of Baptist John make one or two attacks by themselves. After that, we can either let Nabatea attack from the southeast or make an attack ourselves from the front as the circumstances will dictate us."

"What may decide the circumstances?"

"What I mean is, if we succeed in contacting the Messiah and obtain his promise of cooperation."

Shaphan did not say anything but slowly nodded his head several times.

If the Messiah of their long hope should appear before them now and promise to cooperate with them in their fight against the Romans, there would be no reason on the part of the Blood Contract Corps to hesitate to make the fight. On the other hand, in case the Messiah refuses to cooperate, the Corps cannot make an open and direct fight with the Romans but would have to just make a show of cooperation with the Nabateans by attempting a side attack or something if Nabateans should attack Machaerus from the front.

After the report on Aquila, the two men proceeded to report to Shaphan on this new character Jesus. Since Baptist John had made such strong declarations about this Jesus, Shaphan's emissaries could not help a most absorbing concern about this strange man.

The name of the owner of the house in Canan where Jesus was rumored to have turned plain water into wine was Manaen who was a remote relative on the mother's side to Jesus. There were six stone jars in that house and Jesus had let three of them filled with water. No sooner was the water poured into the jars than it turned into wine. Thomas and Ananias had asked the owner of the house if Jesus had not put some drug or uttered some kind of incantation but the owner of the house had answered that he had done no such thing. He said, however, that Jesus had looked up at the sky and then said: "Now you may fill your pitcher with it and take it to your guests." He did as he was told to and saw that it was wine that he scooped up from the stone jar in which there was only water a while ago. Moreover, the wine was so rich and fragrant that the guests had praised its taste very highly.

The two men had gone from there to Capernaum where they learned that Jesus had worked many miracles there two days ago and had left for another place the next morning. The two of them asked around among people about which direction Jesus had gone in. Since many said that they had seen Jesus going in the direction of Chorazin, they also went there. When they arrived at Chorazin, however, they learned that he had already left there, this time for Sukara. They had, therefore started for Sukara whereupon at a spot about ten *ri* (= 2.5 miles) on the way to Sukara, the two men found a crowd of over seven hundred people gathered in front of a village. Without asking, the two men sensed that this was a crowd following Jesus. They went close and found Jesus speaking with a leper surrounded by his crowd. It seemed that this leper who had a distorted face and was about thirty years old had come down from the hill on the left side of the road as Jesus was walking toward Sukara and kneeling in the middle of the road had said to Jesus:

"If only you will, you can cleanse me."

The voice with which he pleaded sounded indistinct.

Jesus looked at him with his eyes which were as deep and blue as the Sea of Galilee for some time. Thomas knew he was Jesus by merely looking at his eyes. There was hardly any need to ask bystanders if he was Jesus. His eyes looked so clear and lofty that they seemed to have the whole sky in them.

Finally, Jesus stretched a hand that looked as graceful as a wing of a white crane and put it on the leper's head. He said:

"Indeed I will; be clean again."

While the on-lookers were watching, the leper's face which had been distorted recovered its original shape and his two eyes shone with new light. The crowd who were surrounding him and Jesus burst out in exclamation when they saw this.

Now the leper with his new face and clear eyes called to Jesus:

"O, Lord!"

He could not say anything more because he was too overwhelmed with emotion and gratitude. Jesus said to him in a low voice:

"Be sure you say nothing to anybody. Go and show yourself to the priest, and make the offering laid down by Moses for your cleansing; that will certify the cure."

After saying this much, Thomas declared that he could not but believe that this Jesus was the Messiah for whom not only the Blood Contract Corps members but also all nation of

Judaea have been waiting.

Next spoke Ananias. He said that since he was at the time staying in Capernaum, he could follow Jesus from the synagogue on the Sabbath day to the house of Peter's mother-in-law and witnessed the miracles of Jesus with his own eyes. Ananias who was tall with yellowish complexion and a sonorous voice did not employ any rhetorical expressions in his narration but presented facts as he himself saw and experienced in a straight and concise manner.

When, in the synagogue in Capernaum, Jesus said that the Pharisees, Levites and lawyers as well as other sinners should all have their sins cleansed and be saved, a man named Linus who had not spoken a word with anyone for years suddenly raised his voice and said:

"What do you want with us, Jesus of Nazareth? Have you come to destroy us? I know who you are—the Holy One of God."

Jesus looked at him and said:

"Be silent and come out of him."

Then the man fell on the ground in front of the people as if he were thrust by something. A little while later the man stood up by himself but showed no sign of being hurt by the fall but instead started to look healthy and fresh. When the crowd saw this, they said that the one they saw before them had the power to order the unclean spirits to go away.

This was why people followed Jesus when he went with Simon (Peter) and others to his mother-in-law's house. Simon's mother-in-law was running a high fever and her life was in danger. As Jesus went up to her and touched her with his hand, however, the fever left her at once and the crowd saw her walking to her kitchen.

At sunset, all the villagers had heard this news and they gathered in front of that house bringing with them all kinds of patients. Ananias was not there himself but heard from people who had been there about how Jesus healed all ailments and diseases there. It seems Jesus left Capernaum and from the fact that Thomas saw him to the north of Chorazin after that Ananias figured that it must have been two days after the Sabbath day that he saw Jesus.

After the two men finished their testimony, Judas began his report. Judas was a young man in his late twenties. He had shrewd eyes and narrow chin and as he began to speak he smiled slightly.

"Master Thomas and Master Ananias have just recounted the miracles Jesus performed such as turning the water into wine or healing the sick, but for my part, I would like to tell you about how Jesus made a dead person live again," he said. He seemed pleased that what he was about to tell the audience exceeded in wondrousness whatever Thomas and Ananias had so far mentioned. His story was as follows:

It was when Jesus came back from Gerasa to Capernaum. He was at the lakeside when one of the presidents of the synagogue named Jairus came up to him and prostrated at his feet saying:

"My daughter is dying; but come and lay your hand on her, and she will live. Please come and save her."

Seeing that Jairus' entreatment was sincere, Jesus went with him with the crowd following. On the way, they met another man who said to Jairus:

"Your daughter has just died. Therefore, you need not trouble the Rabbi any further."

When Jesus heard the man say this, he turned to Jairus and said:

"Fear not. Only have faith."

Jesus took only Peter, James and John out of his disciples as he went into the house with Jairus. In the house, he found flute players and people making a lot of noise thinking the girl was dead. Jesus said to the crowd:

"Be off! The girl is not dead. She is asleep."

The crowd laughed at him.

Jesus went into the room where the girl was lying dead with just the girl's parents and his three disciples. There he took the girl by the hand and said:

"Rise."

The girl rose from the bed at once and started to walk. She was a pretty girl of twelve.

Jesus turned to her parents and said:

"Let no one hear of this, and give food to the girl to eat."

Then he left the house.

Judas said that making the dead live again was the biggest miracle one could think of and from this he knew that this Jesus was the Messiah and no other. Then he proceeded to tell them another story as if to fortify the one he had already told them.

Baptist John also heard about the miracles Jesus was performing and thought in his mind that he must be the Messiah. In order to hear directly from Jesus himself, however, he sent some of his disciples to Jesus. They sought out Jesus and said to him as directed by Baptist John:

"Are you the one who is to come, or are we to expect some other?"

Jesus answered at once:

"Go and tell John what you hear and see: the blind recover their sight, the lame walk, the lepers are made clean, the deaf hear, the dead are raised to life, the poor are hearing the good news — and happy is the man who does not find me a stumbling-block."

After saying this much, Judas commented that through these words Jesus meant to let John know the fact that he was the Messiah.

When Judas was finished, Shaphan asked with a smile:

"Being far away, how could you find out so much about what Jesus did?"

Judas' eyes shone at this question and he said proudly:

"Is it not a matter of utmost importance from the point of view of our nation, our Corps, or myself as an individual whether we meet the Messiah or not?"

He spoke quite in the manner of an orator and Thomas and

Ananias smiled contently thinking Judas had made much progress in thought and deed lately, but they did not say anything outwardly.

As if encouraged by the taciturn approval of his elders, Judas went on:

"As you know, I am in charge of the district around Jerusalem and therefore am closer to Samaria than Galilee. And I inquired about in Samaria, also, and found out about an incident which is that Jesus knew everything that had happened to a woman whom he had never met before. From this, the people in the district are sure that he is the Messiah."

When he finished listening to all three of them, Shaphan asked them where Jesus was now. Thomas said maybe he was either in Sukara or Jarun since he had seen him and his followers move in the north as he was leaving them.

Ananias, however, said that since it was in Capernaum that the house of the mother-in-law of Simon who was the closest of his disciples to Jesus was and also Simon's brother Andrew and Zebedee's sons James and John were all from Bethsaida which was close to Capernaum, he thought that they would come back to Capernaum or Bethsaida soon.

"Listening to the three of you and thinking of what our Corps Teacher Hadad had once told me, I am convinced that there is a need for me to meet this man named Jesus by all means. All of you say that you think he is the Messiah, and Hadad's reading of the stars says that the time of our long waiting is now come. I had better find a way to see him at once. This is no time to idle in hesitation. And I think I can guess what it was that he is said to have uttered to Nicodemus in Jerusalem or to the woman in Samaria. If he is the Messiah, he should speak in a different way from us, should he not?"

It was arranged then that Thomas and Ananias would stay in and around Capernaum in watch and as soon as they learned of Jesus' appearance in the district would send a word to Shaphan. Shaphan, in the meantime, would stay by the water (of the Sea of Galilee) near Capernaum and Bethsaida.

Chapter 2

The Robber and the Water Ghost

Shaphan decided to move out to the vicinity of Capernaum and Bethsaida and wait for further news from Thomas or Ananias about Jesus. The reason why he decided on this spot was that many of Jesus' disciples and their relatives and friends lived around this district. He had often come out to the Sea of Galilee or the villages on the lakeside leaving the care of the headquarters to Hadad and Jair, but he had chosen mostly Capernaum or Magadan (Dalmanutha) or Dariqueyea at most for his sauntering and rarely any other places. For some reason, he had always avoided Bethsaida and its neighborhood. People around Shaphan thought among themselves that this was probably because he had no woman in that district but this did not seem to be the correct guess. To tell the truth, Shaphan did not have any special women in Capernaum, Magadan or Dariqueyea, either. It was no problem for one to get women in fairly big villages where there were bound to be one or two taverns. No one, in short, knew why it was that he had never gone near Bethsaida up to now.

This time, however, it was between Capernaum and Bethsaida that he chose to stay while he waited for the reports to come from Thomas and Ananias. Jair took the oar while

Shaphan drank wine from a bottle. Overhead, a full moon of the Fifteenth was looking down at the lake. Every time the oar hit the water urging the head of the boat to cut through ahead, the moonlight scattered in many directions throwing ripples of little laughs all around. When the boat leapt over a wave with the help of fresh wind, the moonlight fled ahead showing whitish on the dark water like the belly of a big fish.

Shaphan bent back his head and looked up at the sky. The moon looked always friendly no matter how many times he looked or how long. When he looked at the moon, he felt cool and pleasant in the heart as when he held a desirable woman in his arms. Maybe it was for this reason that the pagans worship the moon, thought Shaphan. Maybe he had come to have a similar feeling toward the moon living the kind of life he had, in the shadow of the world, so to speak. In any case, he drew boundless solace and happiness from the moon and before he met Zilpah he had always gone to women on nights when the moon was as bright and pleasant as tonight.

As Shaphan's boat drew near to the shore of Bethsaida, the sound of a lute playing came toward the boat from the olive grove the sloping lakeside connecting Bethsaida and Capernaum. The sound was as agreeable as the moonlight that was now frolicking with the breeze that blew over from the olive groves and the ripples of the lake water.

"Do you hear that, Jair?"

"Yes, you mean the sound of the lute?"

Jair stopped rowing and listened to the music intently for a while. It was the lute music of the water ghost that everyone who passed here in the night heard.

"Do you also believe that to be the music played by a ghost?" asked Shaphan.

"Yes, Commander," answered Jair unhesitatingly.

"Would it be really a water ghost?"

"Of course. Don't we all know that that is a place where the water ghost appears from time begone?"

"What would it look like? Would it be a woman or a man?"

"A woman, of course."

"How do you know? Has anyone seen it?"

"That's what people have known from time begone. Maybe, a ghost needs to have a woman's body to be able to lure the people, do you think?"

"Why does a water ghost have to lure the people?"

"It is natural. Water ghost is one who drowned. And because of it, it wants other people to drown like itself. Out of resentment, that is. That is why it lures people into the water."

Jair was a simple character that believed most of the things that have been believed by most people from the old time.

"Strange! Would a water ghost be able to make that kind of sound? A sound as friendly and agreeable as that? And on a beautiful night like this, too. . . ."

Jair did not say anything.

"What if we went and saw with our own eyes, Jair?"

"You mean we should go there of our own will when other people flee far and fast when they hear that sound fearing they might be lured into drowning?"

"Aren't you curious how the water ghost looks?"

"One gets lured because of curiosity."

"What is we get lured? If being lured is all there is to fear, we only need to stand on guard not to be lured. Do you believe that a water ghost would be cleverer and stronger than us?"

". . . . . ."

"I have never met Jehova. But a mere water ghost cannot frighten me, I am sure. I am afraid of no ghost or man. Let any man or ghost that is willing to fight me come out. I will teach him, subdue him and make him obey me."

Shaphan's confident voice hit the back of Jair's neck like a whiff of hot wind. Without looking back, Jair knew that a fearful light would be flowing out of his eyes. Jair seemed to see Shaphan's face in close-up.

Jair slowly turned his head toward Shaphan and said:

"Commander, are we not working for a cause that would

decide whether Judaea would be saved or not? Suppose you do not get lured by the water ghost into drowning, what would we gain from the risk?"

"You speak correctly, Jair, but the reason we want to save Judaea is because we love her. What is Judaea, then? Isn't this sea (lake) Judaea? Don't you love this sea and those hills on its shore? If you love these, don't you wish to know every corner of this water? Are you content to just believe that there is a water ghost in one of its corners and keep on avoiding that part of the sea? People are often very foolish and cowardly. As for us, we will meet this water ghost, and if there is such a thing as resentment in its heart as you mentioned, we will help it find a recompense, shall we? I am sure it will be friendly toward us. Come on. Let's go."

"Do you really want to?"

"Yes, I do, and don't you worry."

Shaphan's voice and attitude all this while were so naturally calm and confidence-inspiring that Jair could not tell whether he was unawares drawn into Shaphan's adventure by the hypnotism of his voice and personality or he was going because of his sense of duty which was protecting Shaphan in all danger. Whatever may be the stronger reason, he headed the boat toward the foot of the hill from which the sound came and slowly rowed the oar.

When he finally brought the boat to their destination, Jair said:

"I think you had better stay in the boat for now, Commander. I will step up first and take a look."

Jair then unsheathed the dagger from his waist and leapt out of the boat. With his hands on his hips, Shaphan watched him run up the slope of olive grove.

A while later, the voice of Jair came from the shadows of the olive trees:

"Commander."

"What is it?"

"It's a woman."

"Is it a human or a ghost?"

"I do not know."

"Bring it here."

After a rather long while, Jair's voice sounded again:

"It would not go, Commander."

Shaphan at once jumped out of the boat and went up the slope. He, however, did not hold a weapon in his hand the way Jair had done.

The woman sat on a rock with her lute held to her bosom. Although her back was covered by the shadow of an olive tree, her knees on which the weight of the lute was resting and part of her face were exposed to the moonlight. Shaphan went up close to her and asked in his somewhat husky thick voice:

"Are you a human or a ghost?"

". . . . . ."

The woman did not answer.

"Are you a water ghost?"

"No."

The woman's voice was low but soft.

"Are you a human, then?"

"I am a woman."

"A *kisaeng* (geisha)?"

As the woman heard this question of Shaphan's, she started to giggle. It was, however, not a happy giggling but one that was quite hysterical.

"Follow us down to our boat."

"No."

"If I forced you to?"

"It will be regretted."

"By whom?"

"By you."

"Who am I?"

"It does not matter who you are. You will regret it."

"All right, then."

Shaphan bent down and lifted the woman easily.

"Jair, carry this woman's lute."

"No. I will hold it myself," said the woman calmly. With the woman in his arms, Shaphan walked down to where the boat was.

"Will you enter the boat with your own feet or do you wish me to throw you overboard like this?"

"It doesn't matter."

Shaphan put the woman down on her feet on the top of a rock. The moon fell on her whole body. Her hair was shiny black as if it had been just oiled and combed and her face was as pale as the moon. Her two eyes seemed filled with passion and remorse. She was watching Shaphan look her over with a thin nonchalant smile on her lips. As their eyes met, Shaphan felt that he had seen her somewhere. He could not remember where, however, and as he was searching in his memory for some clue, the woman said:

"What did you stand me here for?"

The woman's voice sounded defiant although the smile was still on her lips. Her voice rang his heart in the same way her lute music had a while back on the sea.

"I wanted to know."

Shaphan's voice had changed from what it was when he first addressed the woman. It was tender and carried feeling. His voice when changed in this way was somewhat similar to the voice of the woman. Especially to Jair's ears, the two voices seemed to have the same heart-moving tenderness in them.

"What did you want to know?"

"I wanted to know your face, name, address, and occupation."

"Does a water ghost have such things?"

"You are not a water ghost. I know it because I have carried you from up there down to this place with my own arms."

Shaphan did not say, however, that he had found it out from her weight and body temperature.

"If I am not a water ghost, then how am I different from one?"

"In this you are different from it. In that you have this body."

Shaphan held the woman by the shoulder and shook her a little as he said this.

"No, you are wrong. I am a water ghost. At least, I am a woman possessed by the water ghost. Otherwise, why would I come out to the seashore every night and play the lute? What other woman would do that?"

"I want to know it, too. How had you come to be possessed by the water ghost and what is being a water ghost like?"

At these words of Shaphan's, the woman again burst into a giggling in that hysterical manner she had giggled up on the slope.

"Let me go back, now. I will not consider what has happened tonight up to this point as a disaster."

"All right, but I want to know you. My wish to know you is stronger for the reason that I feel I have seen you somewhere."

Shaphan's voice now sounded almost exactly the same as the woman's aside from the fact that it was lower and thicker than the woman's.

The woman merely smiled vaguely, however, and did not tell him anything to help him in his search for recognition.

"Why don't you say anything? If you want to go away, tell me your name, address and occupation quickly."

"It is useless."

"Useless? Why?"

"How do you know I would tell you my name or address correctly?"

"You cannot make it up. You would not deceive a person who wants to know so much as I do."

"You remember you are the person who brought me here by force just a while ago, don't you?"

"It is not the same now. What you are talking about belongs to the past."

"But not a far one."

"True. But you are not the same person as you were then.

Neither am I the same person that I was that time however short a while back it may have been."

When Shaphan said this, the woman stopped smiling and looked straight in his face.

Shaphan spoke again:

"I believe that you will not deceive me. Although nothing can be done about it if you would."

"Let me go now. I do not know you just as you do not know me. It is fair, isn't it?"

Shaphan was somewhat alarmed when the woman said this. What would he do if the woman started asking him his name, address, and occupation? What defense does he have against the woman? Is it not only in bodily strength and the use of a weapon that he can be said to be stronger than the woman? He cannot, however, possibly take the life of a fellow countrywoman on such a trifle account as this.

"Are you a woman who has secrets to keep?"

Shaphan's voice even trembled a little as he asked this question.

The woman began to giggle again.

"I will play the lute here again tomorrow night. Why would a woman who has secrets to keep play an instrument in a place like this?"

"Then promise me that you will come out here and play the lute tomorrow night also."

"I will do so if I don't escape. I am not called a water ghost for nothing."

Next night, the woman played the lute at the same place as she had promised. Shaphan was alone this night and he had no other engagement, and so he stayed to the end of her performance by her side. The woman, however, did not tell him anything to give away her identity.

"If you are not going to tell me where you live, you must come down to the boat with me."

The woman turned down this suggestion also, and then Shaphan picked her up as he had done the night before and carried her down to the boat tied at the shore. He put the woman inside the boat and took the oar. Neither of them spoke until the boat reached the middle part of the lake. Shaphan laid down the oar. The woman kept her eyes down on the surface of the water as if she were looking at the reflection of the moon on the lake.

"In this part of the lake I can throw you into the deep of the water without anybody interfering."

Shaphan uttered these words almost to himself while looking at the pale profile of the woman. She did not raise her eyes from the water but merely started that hysterical giggling again.

"All right, then. Shall I throw?"

Shaphan made a move as if to lift up the woman.

"Do you think I would be afraid of this water?" said the woman with her eyes still fixed on the surface of the water.

"You would be more afraid of dying than being thrown into the water."

"I like the water. Would a water ghost fear the water?"

But the woman still kept her head away from him.

Shaphan moved away from the woman and with his back against the sideboard, looked up at the moon. He knew in his heart that this woman would not tell him anything even if he asked questions like the night before. He turned his head and looked across the water. All he could see was a few fishing boats in far distance. He could be certain that the woman would not easily attempt to escape.

He picked up the wine bottle. It would be better to drink the wine than wrangling with the woman, he thought. It was just as he drank up the second cup of his wine. Suddenly he slapped himself on the knee without knowing what he was doing. It was that all at once he remembered.

He went up to the woman with the wine bottle and held out the wine cup to her. Unexpectedly the woman did not refuse it but took it in her hand. He poured the wine for the woman and said:

"I just remembered. Hadn't you been in Gadara last spring?"

There was a slight change in the way he spoke to the woman now. His style had turned somewhat more honorific, for one thing. The woman looked at Shaphan a long while before she answered:

"Yes."

"Were you in company of someone at that time?"

The woman did not say anything but merely made a vaguest gesture of nodding with her head. It meant 'yes', anyway.

Shaphan also fell silent. He stared long at her face with fearsome eyes. More silence passed. It was the woman who first opened her mouth:

"It was a Roman soldier. He died. He was killed by an unidentified arrow . . . ."

"Was the culprit arrested later?"

Shaphan's voice had changed once more.

"Many suspects were caught. A few of them were found guilty and turned over to the law. Even so nothing certain had been established, it seems. That, I suppose, is why any man who associates with me is suspected by the Roman army even now."

"You must have suffered much."

"I was put in prison for six months. They insisted at first that I had been an accomplice. Later they decided that it was an act of revenge committed by a rival and demanded me to give up the names of all the men I had had anything to do with. But where could I get names of so many men, anyhow, when I had hardly known any other man than my husband who was dead? There had been another, but he too had gone far away . . . . In the end, they condemned an innocent man from Gadara and put him to death, I think."

"Is this man from Gadara one whose name you had given them?"

"No. They made up a case against him on the basis of some connection or other in the course of their investigating."

"Had they not asked to testify?"

"They did. But I testified that I had never laid my eyes on him. It was true."

"Even so he was condemned guilty."

"I could not testify he was not the culprit, either, because I could not see anything that could offer any clue to the identity of the culprit. It all happened so fast, you know. An arrow flew in from somewhere and stuck in his (the Roman soldier's) chest, and he fell. But I fainted as soon as I saw him fall. So all I could say at the court was that I had never seen the man before."

"If the man whom they could establish as the murderer had been executed, what is the reason they still bear suspicion toward you?"

"They want to harass me, I suppose."

"Is that what you meant when you said last night that I would regret it if I get to know you?"

"......"

The woman did not say anything but gave a light sign of assent with her well-shaped chin.

Shaphan looked up at the moon for a long while and then turned his head saying:

"How are you called?"

His tone sounded more grave now.

"I am called Mary."

"Is your home in Bethsaida?"

"It is in Magdala."

It was only for form, however, that Shaphan was asking her these things now. If this was really the woman, he knew all such things as her name or where she lived. And it was no wonder because it was Shaphan himself who had shot that Roman soldier with an arrow. It had not been a premeditated act, and he had never known Mary. That is why he could not easily recognize her here in the moonlight three years after the event. As to certain facts about her, which he had found out from hearsay and through inquiry, he had kept a pretty good memory.

Early in spring three years ago, the Festival of Dionysus was held by the Greeks in the city of Gadara (A Greek city in Decapolis). During this festival season many people gathered in the city not only from different parts in Decapolis which was heavily populated by the Greeks but also from such other districts as Galilee, Samaria or Paraea in order to enjoy the music and drama performed by the Greek artists. Shaphan had decided to join this crowd of pleasure-making not so much for the entertainments the occasion promised but because he judged that it would be wise to make use of such a crowd-gathering time to meet Members or to raise the Corps fund. He took the boat at Gerasa and started for Gadara by the sea. On the way he met a Roman centurion coming from the direction of Tiberias in company of a pretty-looking Judish woman. His boat was also headed for Gadara, it seemed. Shaphan had no plan to kill him then, however. It was on his way back from the festival that he killed him. It happened while Shaphan walked to the shore of the Sea of Galilee in Gadara in order to get aboard. Shaphan hid himself in a hill by the road near the quay with his arrow and bow set ready to shoot. What he had in mind was to kill one of the rich or the powerful if any chanced to pass that way. It was near sunset. Shaphan saw the Roman centurion whom he had seen rowing to Gadara in the morning walking toward the quay again in company of the pretty Jewish woman. He had his arm around her as he walked. At that instant the arrow left the bow and was stuck in the Roman soldier's chest next. And just then an unexpected scene occurred. Suddenly six or seven men whom Shaphan could not identify as members of the Blood Contract Corps appeared from nowhere and, picking up the body of the centurion and the woman, started for the hill on the other side of the road. Shaphan wanted to go after them, but seeing other Roman soldiers and crowd approaching the quay, he ran down to the water before them and getting into his boat, returned home. According to the rumor Shaphan heard later, when they knew they were being pursued by the Romans, stationary in Gadara, the unidentified men had abandoned the body of the Roman centurion and the woman on top of the hill and fled somewhere taking with them just the one arrow that had been stuck in the Roman soldier's body.

"Then the man from Gadara who was said to have been executed as the culprit must have been one of those who had fled carrying you and the body."

"I think that's how it was. It seems the man was found with an arrow which the Romans found unfamiliar."

"But how was it proved that it was the very arrow that killed the Roman?"

"I don't know. But anyhow, the arrow was the only evidence, it seems. The Romans claimed that the arrow came elsewhere than the Roman armoury."

"What did the man have to say, do you know?"

"He denied everything at first, it seems, and said that he knew absolutely nothing about what had happened to the Roman soldier. When they questioned him about the source of the arrow, however, he confessed first that it was indeed the arrow that had killed the Roman and then, it seems, he confessed to the deed, also."

"How did you find out all this?"

"I heard it in prison. People whispered, you know."

Shaphan was relieved when he heard this answer of the woman. Because if what she told him was the truth, she would not know where indeed that arrow had come from. Shaphan had known about the man from Gadara who was executed undeservedly. He was one of the Third Members of the Blood Contract Corps residing in Gadara, and when he was caught with an unidentified arrow (that actually came from the secret armoury of the Corps) and discovered that the one the Romans secured from the dead body of the Roman centurion was also from Corps armoury, he had decided to confess to the killing so that another Corps member might be saved.

"Where would the man from Gadara have gotten that

arrow, then?" asked Shaphan mainly to hear what Mary would say to that.

"It seems at first he said he had picked it up in the streets and then said that it had come from somewhere in Arabia. In any case, he didn't tell them the true source of the arrow until he was executed. Although he was asked about his friends and associates, he never gave away any names, they say. Under the circumstances, the Roman army had very little to help them. So they contented themselves by arresting and punishing a few whom they could convince themselves as being related with the man from Gadara somehow. It is quite apparent however, that the Romans did not think that they had tracked the accident or crime to the end."

"In your opinion, would I be a suspect in the eyes of the Romans if I were to follow you around like this?"

"I think it is quite possible. That is why, I believe, no one that used to know me would come near me now."

"Do you live by yourself, then?"

"Would I roam about in this kind of a place in the night, otherwise?"

"Are you still thinking of the man, the Roman?"

"How could I forget one who died on account of me?"

"Were you two in love?"

"He captured me with power at first, so I hated him for a time. But...."

"But?"

"I lived with him for two whole years. I couldn't hate someone who is dead, anyhow, could I?"

"So that's how you got lured by the water ghost and got in the habit of coming out to the seashore in the night with your lute...."

".... . ."

She apparently did not wish to answer. She had her eyes fixed on the surface of the water as she had done before.

Shaphan brought out a new bottle of wine and invited the woman to a second cup. She declined it, however, and began to pick on her instrument. Then a rich melody that seemed to be filled with all kinds of human emotions flowed out of the lute penetrating into the deep of Shaphan's heart.

After drinking the wine by himself for some while, Shaphan approached the woman again and said:

"Mary."

" . . . . . . "

She stopped playing the lute and turned her eyes to Shaphan.

"Who are you thinking of at this moment playing your lute?"

" . . . . . . "

Without answering the question, the woman looked at Shaphan with an expression that seemed to challenge him to guess who it was she was thinking of.

"Can it be I?" asked Shaphan pointing with his finger at his own chest. The woman, however, did not answer and merely smiled.

"I guessed right, didn't I?"

"Do you think it is possible? And I don't even know your name...."

"What importance does a name have when an actual person is there before your eyes...."

"Do you then have the same feeling toward me now, when you know so much about me, as yesterday when you knew nothing?"

"No, Mary, it is not so. My name is Shaphan. Do you wish to know me?"

She stared at his eyes and then nodded with her head.

"Will you not run away from me even after you find out who I am?"

"Do you intend to seek me even after tonight?"

"Of course, Mary. I have never met any other woman whom I found as good as you are."

"It is dangerous. You will regret it."

"We can meet at night like this, can we not?"

"What about the daytime?"

"Can you go about in the daytime?"

"Can I . . . ?"

The woman stopped herself in the middle of her sentence which she said under her breath, barely audible.

Shaphan kept his eyes on her face which was as pale as the moonlight as if he were intensely waiting for her to continue, and finally she opened her mouth again:

"I cannot go about in public in the daytime. That is why I became a water ghost."

Her voice was low as she continued to speak:

"Do you know how the people treat me after the accident? Do you guess why it is that I could not return to my home town Magdala but stayed in this spot closer to Bethsaida?"

Mary then took the bottle which Shaphan held out to her and, after pouring some in her cup and sipping from it once, continued:

"It has been five years since I left Magdala. I lived two years in Tiberias with the centurion and then lived half a year in prison. For this reason, people looked at me as if they were looking at an unpardonable witch or an incorrigibly retarded person. I had no other choice but burdening myself on the household of a sister of my mother's in Bethsaida. I have been living there since. And just think, how would I walk about under the sun? who would befriend me? It has been such a long and lonely period of self-exile that I am not sure if I am in my right mind. Even the people at my mother's sister's house where I am staying now think I may have been lured into being a water ghost and I myself feel that maybe I am. Why else would I come out to the sea every single night with the lute in my arms? If I were to have my lute snatched from out of my arms now, what is there for me to live for?"

"My lovable water ghost!"

Shaphan picked her up and put her on his knees.

"I felt all this as soon as I saw you last night. I knew that we had the same voice."

"I am a woman unhappier than anybody. My past is such that I dare not speak of it to you now."

"Mary, I am a robber."

"A robber?" asked the woman with an unbelieving voice and then asked again in a whisper: "How did you come to choose such a profession?"

"What else could I choose? I could not stay with such boring work as farming, selling or fishing, and working as Roman agent or tax collector was a worse job than being a robber to me. Also, I could not live as Sadducees do on the tithes collected from their sale of the holy temples, or, as the Pharisees do, live off the law and the church...."

"What profession can be worse than that of a robber, though?"

"You said a while ago that you could not tell me all about your past. It is the same with me. I cannot tell you how it has been with me. But tell me, are you going to report on me?"

"No, I don't think so. Even if you now hated me."

Shaphan embraced her passionately and said:

"Live with me, Mary! I like you very much. Let us speak to each other with our low husky voice like the owls do and let us live together."

Ever since this night, Shaphan made it a rule to go to see Mary whenever he left the cave for his customary excursions. In the course of time, he came to know about what she called the past she dared not disclose to him. What she referred to as her 'past' seemed to be her life before she came to live with the Roman centurion.

It was when she was fourteen years old that she was first married. But her first husband died and she remarried at the age of seventeen. She remarried two years after her first husband's death and so it was barely a year that she had lived with her first husband. With her second husband also she lived no longer than a year and then left him. She said she had left him because he had an uncurable disease but that people would not excuse her for leaving him whatever her reason was.

Accusation and slander began to pile on her from this time onward. At first, it seemed, there were quite a few men who wanted her. But none of them were in a position to marry her and for this reason she would not have anything to do with them. Then she seemed to have met the Roman centurion, and the accusation and slander of the people around her became more profuse and malicious. And it was still the same way.

Mary who had thus told Shaphan about her past did not ask him back to tell her about his any more than he had already told her. Neither did she ask how he had happened to see her in Gadara the other night or how he could have remembered her through all this time. She only appeared to be endlessly happy about having been acquainted with Shaphan.

Seeing that Shaphan stayed out at night frequently after he came to know Mary the water ghost, Hadad spoke to him one day:

"Have you forgotten, Commander, that the great star is approaching you?"

"No, Teacher, I have not. I am still waiting for the day when I would have the honor to meet the great star."

"The great star, however, would not come nearer while you are so deeply occupied with wine and women."

Saying thus, Hadad stared at Shaphan with his deep-sunken shiny eyes.

"......"

Shaphan looked back at Hadad's face with his blood-shot big eyes without saying anything. Hadad opened his mouth again:

"I suggest that you, Commander, stay in the cave for three days on from today and abstain yourself from wine and women."

"I will do so if it is your order, Teacher."

"And prepare to have the Meeting of Seven Stars at the headquarters on the third day. You will then let the other six stars know about the approximation of the great star."

The 'seven stars' Hadad meant were the seven First

Members of the Corps.

"I will do as you say, Teacher."

Shaphan obeyed Hadad in everything. He therefore kept away from wine and women for the next three days and in the meantime gave himself a spiritual disciplining in the cave.

On the third day, Hadad came to him bringing with him Zilpah. He then said to Shaphan:

"This is my daughter Zilpah. I have been studying the stars about you and her and lately arrived at the conclusion that you two are predestined pair that could achieve great things together. I have, therefore, brought her here so that she may as your wife support you from the inner side of your life. Please accept her."

After speaking thus, Hadad looked at Shaphan with his skinny yellowish face.

Only then did Shaphan realize what it was that Hadad had ordered him to stay away from drinking and women and keep to the cave for three days for. He could also see from this instance again how devoted Hadad was to Shaphan himself and the Corps as a whole. But even so, he did not think he could easily settle down to a matrimony doing away with his burning passion and desire.

If Hadad had thought to put an end to the flames of desire that perennially burned in Shaphan's heart, it had been a miscalculation, thought Shaphan. And it was not right for him to accept Hadad's offer of his daughter in this state. He said, therefore:

"I thank you for your most generous offer, my Teacher. But I feel that my life is too rough and disorderly to welcome a noble young lady such as your daughter into it."

Shaphan looked from Hadad to Zilpah with those huge blood-shot eyes of his as he said this. He did not, however, really mean to decline the offer as his words made out. He had already been not a little attracted by the girl for her mysterious eyes, water-clear voice, trim white neck, and the small round shoulders. And so, in his heart he was quite pleased with the offer Hadad was making to him. Only when he thought of the special esteem Hadad was held in by himself and by all the other important members of the Corps and the relationship in which he stood with Hadad did Shaphan feel a need to at least make a show of declining for courtesy and delicacy. Also, it was possible that he was making this gesture by way of making excuse for his later behavior.

Hadad, however, seemed to be seeing through Shaphan's inner thoughts already. He said:

"The time has come. You are one that would be a king and my daughter is one destined to be a queen. Your union, therefore, is by no will of yourself, Commander, or mine, or of my daughter. It is by the will of that star."

His attitude was now more domineering.

"I will then gladly welcome your daughter as my wife just as you command, my Teacher."

Shaphan did not feel like hesitating even for form when Hadad spoke of his daughter as a future queen. He did not feel that it was proper to say many words about it if the matter stood like that. Besides, he was pleased by Hadad's mentioning him as a king-to-be. Shaphan had heard such things as 'a big star,' 'a great female star' or the coming of 'time' in connection with his own fate, but this was the first time that Hadad said anything about his becoming a king and it surprised him and made him happy and proud of himself. The reason he was so gratified by this intimation was that his becoming a king meant that the Messiah would descend on them in a near future and the Romans would retreat from Judaea and the kingdom of the Israelites would be founded. In short, it meant the realization of their long-cherished dream. He had never thought about, or wanted, being a king. What he had ceaselessly thought about and wanted was merely that his country Judaea be not ruled by Rome, Syria, Egypt or worship Zeus, Jupiter or any other pagan gods instead of Jehovah. If Jewish people get freed from being slaves to other nations and become independent people of Jehovah with their own Jewish dream and pride allowed, Shaphan himself would be content to be fishing in the Sea of Galilee for his living for the rest of his life. And now Hadad was revealing to him the advent of that wonderful time when this dream of his would be realized and moreover he was telling him that he would be king in that new world. How could he help being moved by the news!

"We will then hold the ceremony of wedding at sunset time (from six to nine) tonight."

Hadad withdrew after saying this.

That night, Hadad made Shaphan and Zilpah kneel on the rock in front of the cave. He looked up at the sky for a long time and then finally said in a thin dry voice:

"The two stars have just met."

He pronounced the words one by another as if it were difficult for him to speak. He then called the two by their names and ordered them to make an oath of union.

First Shaphan said:

"Zilpah."

His voice was low, but thick and forceful.

Next came Zilpah's clear voice that always carried the coolness of the spring water:

"Shaphan."

Her voice trembled a little as she called thus.

Now Shaphan said turning himself to face Zilpah:

"Zilpah, I Shaphan will welcome you as my wife and will love and keep you until I die."

Zilpah turned to Shaphan and said:

"Shaphan, I Zilpah will welcome you Shaphan as my husband and love and respect until I die."

This oath had been made by Hadad to be used at the weddings of the Corps members.

When the two people finished saying their oaths, Hadad turned to Shaphan and said:

"Your word is your soul and it is your name."

He then turned to Zilpah and said again:

"Your word is your soul and it is your name."

These were repetition of the same sentences but Hadad said them not as mechanical repetition of fixed words but in the manner of saying separate incantations, each of them of grave special meaning.

After saying the 'incantation,' Hadad turned his head up toward the sky again. Shaphan and Zilpah, too, looked up. They turned their eyes at the same spot as Hadad was staring at. There they saw two stars which they had not noticed before touching each other. Shaphan was surprised to see that these stars had wings that looked like the wings of a dragonfly. He had always thought up to now that all stars looked like little flowers.

From a forest nearby, song of night pigeon drifted over.

Turning his head back from the stars, Hadad helped Shaphan to stand up first and then Zilpah. It was the end of the wedding ceremony.

Next day, Shaphan held the meeting of the First Members at the headquarters. It also turned out as the celebration party for the wedding.

The First Members with the exception of Gallio of Joppa began to arrive at the headquarters from early in the morning. As for Gallio, he could not attend because of the great distance between the headquarters and his place of residence. It was arranged that Judas of Jerusalem would convey the outcome of the meeting to him later. During the meeting, Shaphan did not mention what he had heard from Thomas about the arrow that was in the keeping of the Nabatean king Aretas. He was afraid that mentioning it which may be taken by some of the members as Aquila's strategic thrust might endanger the amicable relationship between the Corps and Nabatea as it stood presently.

He told the members that the most important news of all was the appearance of one who might be the Messiah they had all been waiting for. He told them the name, place of birth and deeds of this man as he had heard from Thomas and

Ananias.

Lastly he suggested that the members keep a thorough watch over the man's (Jesus') whereabouts and deeds and devise ways to have access to him and also to help establish a practical basis for cooperating with him.

When Shaphan's last words were spoken, all five of them swore obeisance and loyalty to him by touching their heart with their hand.

When the meeting was over, wine, goatmeat and chicken meat were served. Although this was a feast that followed every First Member Meeting at the headquarters, more wine and meat were prepared this day to celebrate the wedding of Shaphan and Zilpah. For this same reason, Hadad and Zilpah joined the party at the table today. The dark outer garment of the old man and the snow white garment Zilpah wore made good combination with the blue and red clothes the members were wearing.

Raising his wine cup high, Shaphan said:

"Teacher Hadad called his daughter here because he knew that the Time is come."

By this, he let the group know that their marriage did not end by being personal affair but had deeper and broader meaning which concerned them all and more. All at the table raised their cups and shouted:

"Long live the Blood Contract Corps! Long live Commander Shaphan! Long live Madam Zilpah!"

Wine cups made fast rounds as the party became livelier and more exciting.

Jair and Zechariah of Ophrah were the two most outstanding in military arts. Now Zechariah raised his hand and, pointing to the armoury at the back of the cave, said with emotion:

"Our meager stock of weapons will now show to the world how they can chase after the Romans!"

"Until we defeat Rome, Egypt and Syria and establish the Kingdom of Israel on earth!"

When Shaphan exclaimed like this, they all shouted: Long live the Kingdom of Israel.

There was one man, however, who did not appear gay or excited. It was Jair who unlike his usual self looked melancholy tonight. He kept his eyes on his wine cup and did not contribute much to the joy-making. He threw a hot glance toward Zilpah now and then but as if recovering from a temporary inattention he returned his gaze back to his wine cup.

"What is the matter with you, Jair? Has anything happened to you today?"

Zechariah moved closer to him as he spoke to Jair.

Jair started at this question and said hurriedly:

"No, no. Nothing is the matter."

He then drank the wine in his cup in one swallow to cover his embarrassment.

"Jair."

It was Shaphan this time. He approached Jair and held out his cup to him.

"Thank you, Commander."

Jair drank up the wine in the cup he was handed by Shaphan in one swallow like before. Then he got up and went outside. Zilpah's eyes, which shone like jewel men found hidden inside a great rock which they broke to get the jewel, unexpectedly shot a glance at the back of Jair as he went out of the cave.

Within that night the members returned to their posts but Thomas was given the task of following Jesus for some time to find out more about his thoughts and deeds. Thomas, therefore, did not go back to Dariqueyea where Judas was made to keep a watch while making trips to his post Jerusalem.

Jair's post was in Gerasa. So his boat was always floating on the water near the shore of Gerasa. His role was to stay on water pretending to be fishing. His first duty was to see if anybody was watching their headquarters. Another important duty he had to carry out was conveying messages between Shaphan and other First Members. The members did not stop in at the headquarters unless there was specific business for it. They usually gave their message to either Ananias of Capernaum or Thomas of Dariqueyea who then handed it to Jair to be relayed to Shaphan. The position Jair kept at the Corps was thus a very important one and the trust and affection Shaphan bore toward him also were very special. Of course, his loyalty to Shaphan and the Corps was no less. He had not known anything except working for Shaphan and the Corps and had never thought about anything else. Although Shaphan not infrequently went to women, Jair had been indifferent to the matter. (He had believed that Shaphan's private life and the work of the Corps were two separate affairs.)

But now suddenly Jair's eyes were open to the sight of woman. He saw Zilpah. And he found her so beautiful that he could hardly keep his eyes open before her. Zilpah! How can such a beautiful person have come to this cave and possess both the cave and Shaphan all at once? It all seemed like a dream to Jair. Did they perhaps get caught by Aquila's black magic?

Jair was afraid to visit the cave, now. He even thought that maybe some devil would tempt him into damnation if he were to go there and get caught by him. It was also possible that Zilpah and Hadad were both servants to the devil.

But look how Shaphan was behaving! He seemed to trust Hadad and Zilpah thoroughly. Otherwise, he would not have accepted Zilpah as his wife. It was true Shaphan was fond of women and when it was a woman of such unbelievable beauty as Zilpah there was perhaps no question of refusing. Still. . . .

He could not betray Shaphan and the Corps for anything. No. Even the thought was too horrible for him to harbour. Maybe, he was already won over by the devil. How could he otherwise even think of betraying Shaphan though it was for less than a second? He was a soul that would have been dead long ago if it had not been for Shaphan.

Six years ago, that is, when Jair was twenty years old, Shaphan had saved him from being slain by a Roman sword, or dying on the cross as his uncle had died earlier.

It had been when he was only four years old that his uncle Judas (Judas of Galilee) led a group of young patriotic Galileans in a battle against the Romans. They had been attacked by the enemy forces in Galilee, Samaria, and Decapolis and were massacred. Young though he had been, he had resolved then that he would avenge his uncle's death and the suffering the Jewish people were made to endure by the Romans. He ground the daggers and scraped the arrows and made associates while he trained and waited for the day of reckoning to arrive. His name, then, was Simon.

In the year when he reached his twentieth year, he heard the news that the commander of the Roman army stationed in Ophrah was going to travel to Tiberias by the invitation of Herod Antipas. He had heard the news from his sworn associate Zechariah. Jair got in touch with other sworn associates, and it was decided that they would attack him on the way between Cana and Alpaerea. The Commander's party was scheduled to pass there between the cool hours (between 3 to 6 in the afternoon) and the Zealots as Jair and his sworn associates called themselves had been hiding among the rocks and trees in the valley along the road. They were to fall upon the Romans at a signal given by Jair. Jair himself, however, did not know how big the enemy force passing that road would be. He had hopes that it would not be a very big party since the Commander was answering a private invitation. He estimated that the Commander would travel with a few of his senior adjutants and bodyguards only.

Around noon, however, Zechariah sent a word and said he wanted to see Jair in a hurry. He had brought with him a man who looked about thirty (actually he was twenty five years old at the time) who had broad shoulders and glaring big eyes. He introduced the man to Jair. The man's name was Shaphan.

Zechariah told Jair that he had just that day met Shaphan for the first time through Thomas, his good friend, but felt as if he had known Shaphan for a long time as a close friend.

Shaphan took Jair by the hand and said that he learned from his sworn friend Thomas and Thomas' friend Zechariah about something important. He then said that he wished that Jair would cancel the plan to attack the Romans that day. His reasons were first that he had heard from Zechariah that Jair was not in knowledge of the size of the enemy force against which he and his followers were going to fight. Another reason was that from what he had found out, this plan had somehow already reached the ears of Herod Antipas' agents. The third reason Shaphan mentioned was that even if Jair and his friends succeeded in killing the Roman commander and his followers, it would not greatly contribute to chasing the entire Roman force out of their land Judaea.

Jair's reaction to what Shaphan said was not only unenthusiastic but also nearly antagonistic. He told Shaphan that he could not change a plan which he and his sworn associates had already made up their minds to carry out. He further said that he was almost sure that since the Roman commander was going to Tiberias in answer to a privately arranged invitation, he did not think that much military force would be escorting him on this trip. And even if their plan had been known to the enemy, it was still better than attacking Ophrah or Tiberias from the front. He also told Shaphan that although as Shaphan pointed out he and his friends might not be able to make the entire Roman army and administration retreat from their land, it would not matter to them so very much as long as they could carry this plan through.

"Simon."

Shaphan took Jair's hand again as he called him his name. Jair saw that his shiny two eyes were burning with passion.

"I also have felt the way you feel now. From the age of twenty-one to twenty-three, I had that kind of feeling toward my country and behaved accordingly. Not a few Romans fell at my sword, dagger or arrow and went into the deep of the Sea of Galilee. Have faith in me, my friend. Make use of my experience."

Jair felt in Shaphan's somewhat husky thick voice a manly authority and sincere friendship. Even so, Jair pulled his hand slowly out of the grip of Shaphan's hand and said:

"I feel I can respect you as a person and as a fellow patriot. But I cannot forsake my duty toward my uncle. This is where you and I are different."

"Simon, I have already heard that you are nephew to Judas the brave, but what I mean is your life is too valuable to be used in just avenging an uncle. Please reconsider."

"I do not wish to let go a good opportunity to save my life out of petty calculation."

Saying this last sentence, Jair moved as if to leave Shaphan.

"Simon, do not destroy yourself and your friends by such a thought. If you want it, I will by myself stick an arrow in the heart of that Roman commander within three days from now. Do you know what this is?"

Shaphan raised an iron cudgel that he had been holding in his hand the way one would hold a walking stick. It was blackish and bent.

"This is that bow."

Shaphan took out a bow string from his back pocket and bending the stick by its two ends tied them with either end of the string. Then he reached to his back with his hand and pulled out an arrow.

"You see, with this bow and arrow, I have never failed to hit anyone or anything I wanted to, so far. And all the dead bodies have gone down into the water. I have never done such a reckless and wasteful thing as killing a few men while losing ten or a hundred at the same time."

Shaphan's voice was angry and he threw his bow and arrow at Jair as he finished his speech.

Jair was dismayed. He felt that if he were to resist or raise objections, it might end up with somebody getting hurt of critically wounded.

More than that, he felt an unresistable awe and, strangely, something like an affection toward the bow and arrow Shaphan had thrown at him. Out of Shaphan's eyes, fire seemed to flow out. At that instant, Jair felt an impulse to throw himself in Shaphan's powerful arms. He picked up the bow and arrow deferentially and offered them back to Shaphan.

That day, the party of the Roman commander and his followers going to Tiberias did not appear on the road, after all. Early next morning, troops of about five hundred men put out an unexplained demonstration parade between Ophrah and Tiberias.

It was from this time that Shaphan and Jair became close associates. Soon after, the Blood Contract Corps was founded and the name Simon changed to Jair. Jair became one of the key members of the Corps and even among them he was the one person Shaphan had most trust and affection for. And ever since, he had been working for the Corps in the capacity of Shaphan's aide-de-camp while pretending to be a fisherman on the water along the shore of Gerasa.

Jair knew every movement Shaphan made. It was partly because Jair had more contact with Shaphan outside the cave than anybody else among the important members of the Corps. But it was also because Shaphan did not hide anything from Jair. During the six years Jair had spent near Shaphan, there had been about a dozen women Shaphan had associated with. Especially one Gadaraean woman named Ruhamah had been visited by Shaphan for six years, that is, ever since the Blood Contract Corps was first organized, as far as Jair knew. And now Shaphan had committed himself to still another woman, and this time in bond of marriage. Jair did not mind it because he thought Shaphan was demeaning himself morally by doing so or was in danger of losing guard on himself. Jair had never seen Shaphan in all his association with him losing control over himself or undoing a work on account of women. No. The trouble was in Jair himself. With all those women Shaphan had been acquainted with within his knowledge, Jair had stayed thoroughly indifferent. It was not the same, however, this time with Zilpah. Toward her, he could not help a feeling that burnt his inside like an angry flame.

Five days after the meeting at the headquarters, Shaphan took the boat and headed for Bethsaida. Part of his business there was to see if he could hear any more news of Jesus, but it was also to see Mary.

As Shaphan's boat slided in toward the hill of the olive grove, the sound of lute that had been drifting down from up the hill stopped. When Shaphan anchored his boat at the foot of the hill, Mary who had been sitting on the hill ran down to the quay with her instrument hugged in her arms.

"Let me go in there, please."

Mary said to Shaphan imperatively looking fiercely into his eyes.

Shaphan helped her into the boat. Until the boat left the hills behind and pushed toward the center of the lake, Mary's face kept its angry expression.

Even when Shaphan put down his oar and embraced her, she kept her head back away from him although her body was given up to his embracing. Shaphan disengaged one of his hands and started caressing her hair. Suddenly the woman said in her husky low voice:

"Hold me tighter. More."

Shaphan embraced her again holding her tight in his arms.

"Put your chest against mine. I have such soreness in my chest."

"What if I crushed you on the chest doing that?"

"It doesn't matter. It's better than feeling this soreness in me. More, more...."

The woman dug into Shaphan's chest wildly as if she had turned insane. Shaphan's black beard that had an angry look blocked the woman's nostrils and her cheeks were wet and sticky with tears. Shaphan relaxed his arms and looked her in the face. She burst out into a violent sob. Shaphan brought out the wine bottle and poured her a cup saying:

"This is the medicine for such a disease. I know it from experience. . . ."

"Give it to me."

The woman drank up the cup of wine in one swallow and gave back the empty cup to Shaphan.

"Give me another cup."

She emptied the second cup in the same way.

"Again."

Shaphan did not pour wine into the cup when the woman held it out to him.

"Now it's my turn to have a cup," he said and poured wine for himself.

"Shaphan."

She called him in a low voice which now had affection and longing in it instead of anger.

"Have you ever longed for a person so much that it ripped your heart?"

"Man and woman are different. Man can always go to his woman."

"I am afraid."

"Of what?"

"Of loving a person. I am afraid of waiting for someone. There cannot be any punishment more horrible than that."

"Is this the first time?"

"Yes, the very first. Maybe I have not known what man is until now. Also, I have not known that love is such a dreadful thing."

"It is all because you are pure gold, Mary. I knew you were pure gold from the first time I met you."

"What do you mean by 'pure gold'?"

"It means a woman who has a past like yours and yet has the purity of mind and body just like a virgin."

"You say my 'past.' But I have not done anything wicked in

my past. Once, the man died from sickness, and the next time it was a disease that made it impossible for me to stay with him. Was it my fault? And the next man, that Roman, I did not go to him of my own accord, how could I when he was an alien, but he captured me with power. And yet, people curse me and avoid me. They seem to think that my wickedness was the cause of all those deaths."

"That's why I became a robber. I did not want to have anything to do with those."

"Shaphan, you have such understanding for a person's heart! You must be a very noble and wise man. But if you don't come to see me for so many days as this time, I think I will lose my mind. I can't bear it. My heart would tear into so many pieces. . . ."

"Didn't I tell you beforehand that I would be absent for some days this time?"

"But I can't stand it for more than three days. I am sure I will go crazy if I have to wait longer than that. It is true."

"But when there is business. . . ."

"What business? What is the business that would take you away from me for seven days?"

"What business. . . ."

Shaphan did not finish what he started to say. Because he suddenly saw Zilpah's face in his mind. He could not possibly tell Mary that he had been with another woman who was as mysteriously beautiful as Mary was in another way attractive. Zilpah had beauty and fragrance that no other woman in the world can be expected to have. But there could be no one that could give one the kind of absolute satisfaction as Mary did and put a body on fire in such a pleasant way as Mary could. In this sense these two women were both indispensable and inseparable for his happiness.

Mary's seductive attraction and passion along with the ripeness of the body of a woman in her twenties made a perfect and ideal contrast with Zilpah's cool clear voice and mysterious jewellike eyes. But he could not tell Mary these things. Although it was not in his nature to keep devious relationship with anyone, he decided that it would be wiser to keep these things from Mary for the time being.

"Does anyone ask a robber what kept him busy?"

Shaphan's voice sounded thick and low.

"Don't talk like that. I am sure you have been occupied with something far nobler."

"Something nobler. . . ." mumbled Shaphan as if to himself.

"What kind of people would occupy themselves with noble things, do you know? Are there such people?"

"Yes!"

Mary's answer was firm and decisive.

". . . . . ."

Shaphan looked at Mary with uncertain eyes.

"There is one called Jesus."

Mary's voice came out strained as she said this.

"Have you seen him, Mary?"

"I am wanting to."

"So you have not seen him yet."

"Have you forgotten that I am a water ghost? That I cannot walk about in the sun? How could I go near him when he is surrounded by so many people? They may point a finger at me, spit at me, or maybe they will throw stones. How could I go to see him?"

"How do you know then that he does noble things?"

"I have heard all about it."

"From whom?"

"From my cousin."

"Your cousin?"

"He is son of the aunt with whom I am staying now. He is twenty-two this year and a good man."

"So this cousin of yours, has he seen Jesus?"

"He certainly has. He follows him around along with Andrew and Simon next door. They are so excited about him they seem nearly crazy."

"So where is this Jesus now?"

"It seems he has just entered Capernaum. My cousin, too, came home this evening. He said that he had travelled quite far with the man."

"Why does your cousin think he is great?"

"It seems Baptist John called him the Messiah."

"Did your cousin hear it in person?"

"He seems to have heard it from Andrew."

"He did not hear it himself, then."

"But there are many things he has himself heard and seen."

"Such as?"

"He saw that the man healed an insane man and Simon's mother-in-law who was ill with high fever, and also he is said to have healed a leper somewhere."

"Don't you think it is some kind of black magic?"

"If it had been magic, he would have seemed to cure the diseases on the spot but the sicknesses would have returned right away. Or he would have destroyed the people he pretended to heal. But the people who were cured by this man never got their illnesses back. Even if he used magic, as you say, isn't it great that he can cure diseases by saying a few words merely?"

"That alone does not prove that he is the Messiah."

"My cousin seems to believe that he is. Can anyone except the Messiah work those kinds of miracles? And it is not all. He also sees through people's minds as if he were looking into a mirror. Even if a person has been accused by the people as being wicked and depraved, he sees what truly lies in the person's mind and give a fair treatment."

"Then I had better meet him myself. Shall I?"

"It is a good idea. Even if you are a robber, he will know everything. He will know that you are in fact a very noble person. It is true. I am certain that you are noble. You had better meet my cousin first. And ask him where you might see him."

"I think it is better to do so."

Shaphan headed the boat north.

Shaphan absented himself from the headquarters often and went to Capernaum. His main purpose was to maintain contact with the members gathering information about Jesus and also to watch for opportunities to meet him personally. But he had another purpose. It was seeing Mary. For this he would turn his boat from Capernaum in the direction of Bethsaida.

Jair knew this well. He knew that Shaphan's business in Capernaum was an official one of finding an access to Jesus while his errand in Bethsaida was a private one, that of seeing Mary, that is, a pursuit after pleasure. Jair also understood that this kind of diversion was one needed by a person in Shaphan's situation. The only thing that bothered him in this was the fact that Zilpah would be spending a lonesome time during Shaphan's absence at the headquarters. Jair could not help being perplexed by the fact that Shaphan would neglect Zilpah whose beauty seemed to excel that of the most precious and rare jewel of all Arabia to seek Mary who was in Jair's eyes no more than a lustful wild woman. If Zilpah should find this out? When he asked himself this question he found himself getting angry with Shaphan. Because how can he deceive a person so angellike as Zilpah? But what could he do about it when it was Shaphan that was in question? Even if he might die from agonizing, he could never do anything to betray Shaphan or the Corps, that was for sure.

Still he wanted to do something that would console Zilpah while Shaphan was away from the headquarters (playing with Mary). And it was from this thought that he brought a falcon to the cave in a cage and hung it in front of her room in the cave. He thought of doing this because he decided that if Zilpah like her father was fond of star-watching she would also be fond of birds and animal the way Teacher Hadad did.

The bird was even more warmly welcomed by Zilpah and Hadad than Jair had expected. Zilpah spent a long time by the cage getting acquainted with the bird and soon she and the bird were friends to each other. Hadad was no less enthusiastic. With the easy way he had developed through study and contact toward wild things, he soon began to train the falcon.

"This is a very clever bird," said Hadad to his daughter. When Zilpah assented with her eyes, he went on:

"Jair has done a good thing both for the Corps and for us."

It could not be said that Zilpah fully knew the meaning of the words he had just said. She knew, of course, that by 'for us' her father meant that the bird gave them diversion and pleasure, but she did not understand how Jair could have acted 'for the Corps' by hanging the bird cage in the cave. She said to her father, however:

"I am also very pleased with this new member of our family, father."

"I know you are. And this fellow is going to run an errand for me across the sea in a short time."

Hadad was even smiling as he said these words which was a rare thing for him to do.

Jair was very glad that Zilpah and Hadad had welcomed the bird into their family so well and were deriving much pleasure from its company. He thought he would do a thing harder than catching a falcon if it would make her any happier. He was looking into the water in which countless stars were reflected and he thought he would like to scoop up a basinful of stars and bring them to Zilpah.

As he was sunk in thought about these things, suddenly he heard a boat approaching toward his boat from a short distance away. Quickly, he pulled out his dagger and stared at the boat that was coming close. In the boat, he saw only one man besides the boatman that was at the oar. Jair held the fishing rod with one hand and, with the dagger in his other hand, continued to stare at the suspicious-looking boat.

"Excuse me...."

Man on the other boat spoke first.

"......"

Jair did not answer. The other man spoke again:

"Are you Master Thomas or Master Ananias by any chance?"

Jair still did not say anything.

The other boat came closer.

"Oh, you are Master Jair, are you not?" said the suspicious man and Jair could not tell who he was even then.

"Who are you?"

"I am Aquila. I travelled with you to Capernaum some time ago, do you remember?"

Then Jair too remembered. But what was this man doing in this dark water by Gerasa all by himself? What was it he was seeking?

"If you are Mr. Aquila, I would think you were back in your own country."

"It is natural for you to think so, and as a matter of fact I had been back there until I left it again a few days ago. I hope Commander Shaphan and everybody else have been well since I saw them last."

"......"

Jair who was still disturbed by the sudden appearance of this man here at this time of night did not answer. And the other man continued:

"I am glad to have come across you like this. I have been hoping to meet either Master Thomas or Master Ananias by rowing out here like this. No, I will be more direct. In fact it was Commander Shaphan himself whom I had hope to meet somewhere here because there is a matter that calls for the Commander's prompt attention to it."

Still Jair kept silence. And Aquila continued:

"It is because of the order I received from my King that I am in such a hurry to see him. This is an extremely important business not only for our King but also for your honored Corps."

"......"

"So, now, would you be so kind as to lead me to the Commander?"

"I do not know where our Commander is now."

Jair's answer was markedly uncivil. It was not clear how Aquila was interpreting Jair's attitude. He said:

"How regretful! Then please receive the royal letter and royal presents that my King has charged me to convey to Commander Shaphan and the higher members of your Corps and distribute them as fit, later on. I am really sorry that I am burdening you with this chore but...."

"If you came on such an errand, I think, you had better see the Commander in person and do the distribution yourself."

"Would you then arrange for me to see the Commander and other high members of the Corps?"

"......"

Jair did not know how to answer. All he knew was that it was better for him to exchange as few words as possible with this man and make him leave this place as quickly as possible. Just then Aquila spoke to him again:

"Don't you get to see Commander Shaphan often yourself?"

"No, I don't."

"How about Mr. Thomas? Does he get to see the commander any oftener?"

"No, it is the same with him."

"Then, how would you be able to contact him? I can come to see you everyday, myself. It is no trouble for me, but...."

"It is better for you to let me know where you could be found. We will come to you if anything is arranged."

"Would it suit you better? All right, then. I can be reached at the inn near the quay of Dariqueyea. But maybe I will row out like this again even before you seek me because I will be restless until I hear the definite word, you know."

Just then, even while Aquila was finishing his sentence, Jair was assailed by a compulsion to kill the man there and then. Unawares he brought his hand to his dagger.

"I think Commander Shaphan would be pleased when he

hears the proposals my King is pleased to make to the Corps. They are beneficial to both countries (he said 'both countries' for some reason), to be sure."

Jair restrained himself. It occurred to him that he could wait until he could hear Shaphan's words on the matter even if the man were to be done away with.

"Time is gold, as they say. The quicker you can establish contact the better and more beneficial to both countries. . . ."

"Goodbye. . . ."

Jair turned his boat before the other man finished speaking. Then he started rowing the boat in the direction of Tiberias so that Aquila might not guess the location of their headquarters.

The news that Aquila made his return to these areas and was trying to see Shaphan, however, reached Ananias at Capernaum within that night and until next day it was conveyed to both Shaphan and Thomas as well.

Chapter 3

Shaphan and Jesus

Jesus who had returned from the district of Sukkara to Capernaum was staying at the house of his disciple Peter's mother-in-law. Peter was taking care of all important things of daily living for his mother-in-law's house since his father-in-law had died early and there was only an eleven-year-old boy, Peter's wife's brother, at the house beside the old woman. Peter's position in that house, therefore, was more that of an older son than that of a son-in-law. In short he enjoyed the rights of an elder son at the same time that he performed the duties of one. Since he was by nature chivalrous and open-minded, and cared to look after other people's problems before his own, the fact that he took responsibility for his wife's mother's house did not oppress or annoy him.

Another reason why Peter stayed with his wife's family was that Capernaum was the fish trading center and Peter was the representative of a cooperation of fishermen formed by James, John, Philip and Andrew whose job it was to take charge of the fish they had caught among them and dispose of them.

Peter's mother-in-law who had a wart on a lower cheek was in her forties. Since she thought of Peter as a most remarkable person in the whole world, she considered Jesus who was master to her wonderful son-in-law and moreover had cured her from high fever by saying just one incantation, as a most welcome and honored guest of her house.

"Master, our Simon has boundless respect for you and I myself look up to you along with Simon with highest respect."

When Peter's mother-in-law spoke thus to Jesus, he had said:

"You have my blessing, and you will see the glory of heaven along with Simon."

He raised his hand and gave Peter's mother a blessing.

After he stayed at her house one night, it was discovered that news of his arrival had spread overnight and a crowd was gathering around Peter's mother-in-law's house from early morning. Many of them were sick people who came to have their diseases healed by Jesus, but many more were those who came to have a look at this Jesus who were supposed to have worked so many miracles. The curiosity these latter shared had two sides. One was that harboured by the group of people who wanted to find fault with Jesus' way of performing his 'miracle' or to put him to test. Then there was the other kind of curiosity that rather sought to find more wonderful things about Jesus so that more respect and faith might be grown in people's minds for Jesus. The group who came there out of this kind of curiosity wanted to find out about whether or not his deeds were true miracles or a make-belief, from whence his power came, and whether or not he was the Messiah. If general public belonged to the latter group, Pharisees and the lawyers formed the former. The division was not very clear, however. Even the Pharisees and lawyers that belonged to the first group had in some corner of their minds a suspicion that this man might really be a new prophet, and in the psychology of the general public who had not come there to criticize or test Jesus, there was an element of suspicion that still did not quite accept the miracles Jesus performed as true miracles.

Jesus was sitting in the only room of their house while crowd stood around in the yard that was surrounded by a hedge.

Only the Pharisees and the lawyers sat in the room with Jesus asking him questions as if they were the representatives of the general public.

It was just then that four strong-looking men pushed through the crowd in the yard with a stretcher on which lay a patient. Although they pushed hard, they could not get through to where Jesus was. They then went back out with their load and, turning around the hedge, went to the back of the house where the ground rose considerably forming a kind of a mound. They claimed up this mound from the height of which it was possible for them to reach the roof. They hoisted the stretcher onto the roof and started removing the hardened mud and reed from one part of it. Finally, when they could make a hole in the roof, they tied ropes to the stretcher and swung it down into the room below.

So a paralytic patient desended in the room from a hole made in the roof. The crowd that stood in the yard shouted in excitement as they saw what was happening and Jesus himself moved off a little on the floor.

The men who had let the stretcher down from the roof now looked down into the room and implored:

"It is our nephew. Please cure his disease for us."

"He is paralized. Please make him well again."

They kowtowed many times to Jesus.

The patient was a young man of about twenty-two or thereabout. He moved a little on his bed on the stretcher and made a move to bow himself to Jesus looking at him with big beseeching eyes.

Pharisees and the lawyers seemed to think that the time to test Jesus was come and looked from Jesus to the patient with much interest. Outside, the crowd made so much noise that the house seemed to be buried in boiling water. Everybody seemed to have a say about whether or not Jesus would be able to cure the patient.

Jesus looked at the frightened big eyes of the sick young man for a long time and then said in a lucid voice:

"My son, your sins are forgiven."

The Pharisees and the lawyers became angry when they heard this. Unless Jehovah descended on earth in person, no one, even the most holy prophet could ever say a thing like that. And one did not even know whether this Jesus was actually a prophet or a mere fanatic. Under the circumstances, it was unpardonable that he who was only a son of a carpenter, after all, dared to give forgiveness for sins. What blasphemy!

As they were getting furious in their insides, Jesus who saw through this spoke to them:

"Why do you harbour thoughts like these? Is it easier to say to this paralysed man, 'Your sins are forgiven,' or to say, 'Stand up, take your bed, and walk'?"

The Pharisees and the lawyers could find no answer to this question. It was not just that they were stupefied by the fact that Jesus had the power to see into their minds. They could accept that, they thought. But they were bothered by something in the question Jesus raised to them that seemed to be a trap to catch them out. The basis of Jesus' question was that he was acting with the power given by God both when he forgave sins or when telling a paralytic to pick up his bed and walk. But this was a premise the Pharisees and the lawyers could not fully accept. From their point of view, healing a disease or an ailment could not always be taken as sign descended from God. And even if they take it as such, it does not justify a prophet or a rabbi that can work in that way to forgive sins on their own. It is true that they could grant that maybe Jesus was actually one of the prophets and in a small corner in their minds they even had an inkling of suspicion that maybe he really was the Messiah. But no matter what thoughts and suspicions they had, it was utterly beyond their imagination to think of Jesus as an incarnation of their god Jehovah whom all Jewish people had been seeking and worshipping for thousands of years. As matters stood in this light, it was not easy for them to make an answer to the question Jesus had thrown to them. The main trouble was that they did not know how they should interpret it. Even so, their inner feeling was that things might appear differently to them if this Jesus would actually make the patient stand up from the bed. For how could they help connecting that kind of wonderous happening with the might of their god Jehovah? They seemed to decide, therefore, to wait until they could see how this operation with the patient would work out before they would give their answer to the question.

When he saw that the Pharisees and the lawyers would not answer his question, Jesus turned back to the patient and looking intensely into his eyes said:

"I say to you, stand up, take your bed, and go home."

The patient's two eyes seemed to flash brightly once, before he put his left hand on his forehead, and then, he got up from the stretcher. He picked up his bed as Jesus had ordered to and walked slowly through the excited crowd and went out of the house.

The Pharisees and the lawyers in the room and the crowd outside were all spellbound at what had just happened. A work like this which was beyond human capability belonged to the range of Jehovah's power.

And just then the Pharisees and the lawyers who woke up from their spell of the first moments experienced a strange conflict in their minds. It was that seeing what they had just seen, they could not keep on totally denying a connection between the deed performed and the power of Jehovah, but at the same time they could not downright join the common crowd in calling this man Elijah or the Messiah (the son of God) for the background out of which Jesus emerged was too different from the one foretold by the prophets and also his condition of life was too humanly similar to their own. If he had been predestined to come to the world authorized by Jehovah to use his power and to forgive sins, why would he be born a son to a carpenter in Nazareth of Galilee and why would he look just like everybody else, and most of all, why would he be sitting in such a miserable house of a common fisherman as this?

It was better to wait for some more time, however. This was only a beginning and there would be a sequel that would clarify who really this Jesus was. This was the conclusion the Pharisees and the lawyers who had come there that day arrived at.

Next day, Jesus went out to the waterfront early in the morning. There he had hoped to converse with his God in view of the water of the Sea of Galilee which he loved. He stood at the water's edge looking toward the south in calmness when he felt that someone was looking at him from behind. Turning his head, he found that there was a man by the side of a custom house nearby looking intently after him with sunken eyes. Jesus raised his hand and beckoned him over to his side. The man looked startled when he saw this but ran over at once and knelt down before Jesus:

"I am a sinner, my lord. I am Matthew, the tax-gatherer."

The man said and looked up at Jesus with a face that showed he was a generous and open-minded person.

Jesus held out a hand and raised him from the ground saying:

"Follow me."

Matthew was moved by this command and said in a trembling voice:

"Do you bestow so much glory on such a sinner, Lord?"

That afternoon, Matthew prepared a meal and invited Jesus and his followers to his house. He had decided to give as big a feast as he could afford to commemorate the glorious event of yesterday and also to thank Jesus for his grace. It was not just because Jesus had granted such a great opportunity to serve him and God to a mere sinner, a tax-gatherer, that Matthew felt so overwhelmed with emotion and gratitude. It was also because from the instant when Jesus told him to 'follow' him, an indescribable happiness took hold of him. He wanted, therefore, to find some way of showing how happy and grateful he was.

The above was part of the report Thomas made to Shaphan about the things Jesus said and did in Capernaum lately. Of Jesus' followers, Thomas mentioned Peter, Andrew, John, James, and Philip who never left the side of Jesus.

At Matthew's house, however, more people were with Jesus. It was because the important members of the Blood Contract Corps had made Ananias arrange for them to be invited to the feast. The news that Jesus was to dine at Matthew's house that afternoon was conveyed to Shaphan by Philip, the cousin of Mary of Magdala. Philip had met Shaphan through the mediation of Mary the night before and had been requested by Shaphan to look for an opportunity that would enable Shaphan to meet with Jesus. When Philip learned that Matthew had invited Jesus to dine at his house the very next day, Philip was overjoyed.

Hearing from Philip about the party, Shaphan at once went to see Ananias in Capernaum. Since Ananias was residing in Capernaum with a special mission from the Blood Contract Corps, his name came to be known widely in the town and he had come to enjoy a certain power over the townspeople in the course of time. He lit his eyes when Shaphan told him what it was that he had come to see him about. Slapping himself on the knee, Ananias told Shaphan that there was nothing to worry because Matthew was one of the Second Members under him and therefore, would think nothing of inviting a number of senior Corps members as extra guests to his party. Aside from Shaphan, Ananias, Thomas and Judas could be with Jesus at the feast.

Matthew lived in a house adjacent to the custom house. It had a fairly high hedge wall around its yard. From the lake (the Sea of Galilee) which one could look out in the south from the house came a cool wind and the three well grown fig trees made ample shade along with the grape vine, which was covering nearly half of the yard.

Matthew had pitched a clean tent amongst these fig trees

and grape vine so that about twenty guests could sit together. Jesus sat with his disciples on both sides facing the south, and Shaphan sat opposite him with Matthew. On the left and right of them sat the rest of the Blood Contract Corps members and also some men from the custom house.

Matthew had a plenty of fish, pigeon meat and mutton brought out to the table and pouring wine for Jesus told him that from the first instant that he came to know Jesus, he felt like a new man cleansed from all troubles. He said that when he first looked at Jesus from behind, his heart felt a strange elation. And when Jesus turned back and beckoned to him he felt as if he were floating up into the air and he had run to Jesus in a daze hardly realizing that his feet were touching the ground. He said at the end:

"I pray that you would grant the same grace on those of my friends who are with me here today."

Jesus turned to Matthew and said:

"Matthew, I have come to help men in trouble and that is why I am sitting here with you and your friends."

A tax-gatherer who was sitting next to Matthew, when he heard Jesus say these words, thanked him in his mind for calling the like of him 'men in trouble' instead of 'sinners.' He said to Jesus:

"Lord, you do not speak like the other prophets."

Jesus turned to him and said:

"You said right. Truly I tell you that I have not come as other prophets or teachers to condemn the people but to save them from their sins."

At this point Shaphan opened his mouth for the first time. He said:

"Rabbi, are you the one we have been waiting for?"

Shaphan was by this time almost convinced that he was the Messiah but wished to hear what he himself would speak about it to make things more certain.

Jesus turned as he heard a voice which had a note different from anything he had been hearing in people's voices as they spoke to him. He looked at the other man in silence for some time because in look, also, he was different from any other man Jesus had been seeing lately. This man had strong shoulders, broad chest, big blood-shot eyes, and a beard that twisted angrily. All at once, a light cramp, barely noticeable, passed through the translucent pale visage of Jesus.

"Man, if your waiting is for a thing of heaven, follow me."

People at the table did not understand at once what the meaning of these words was, but as he heard them, Shaphan felt a sharp pang in his heart and at the same time began to tremble inside. Jesus was still looking into his blood-shot eyes with his clear lake-blue eyes.

"Rabbi, we live on the earth. Let what was sown in the earth bear fruit on the earth."

Shaphan's husky thick voice sounded to people at farther end of the table somewhat like the roaring of a wild animal because of the trembling that was in the voice now.

"Listen to me, man. Man is on the earth so that he may bear fruit in heaven. If man binds himself with man, he will die with man, and if man binds himself with the earth, he will perish with the earth. Truly I tell you that only by binding itself to heaven, man's life will enjoy the eternal life and glory of God's kingdom."

The clear voice that came out of Jesus penetrated into the hearts of men at the table as if it were a very strong perfume. Hearing him assert to the end that things of the earth must be bound to heaven, however, Shaphan felt perplexed and began to think maybe this was not the Messiah, after all. He said again:

"Rabbi, Israel is a land that is bound to heaven and the people of Israel are also bound therewith. Let Israel stand on earth."

Jesus said with a somewhat sad expression:

"Listen to me, man. It is because Israel is bound to heaven that I am here with you now. I came to help you receive the glory and happiness of the kingdom of heaven."

"Rabbi," said Shaphan in a voice that had turned pathetic:

"Our great ancestor Moses led our people from Egypt to this land. Wasn't it to make Israel stand on the earth that he led the people on such a long and difficult journey? Can we now say that Moses did wrong by that?"

Fire seemed to sparkle from Shaphan's big eyes as he said these words and his angry-looking black beard and bared teeth reminded one of a fierce animal of prey about to snap its jaws on a fleeing rabbit.

"Son of man," called Jesus and raised his wax-white long hand up. Suddenly, Shaphan remembered Thomas' phrase: a hand that looked as graceful as a wing of a white crane. As he looked at the white, slender fingers stretched in erect gracefulness, Shaphan had an illusion about seeing a rainbow arching itself over them. Jesus' penetrating clear voice was heard again:

"Truly I tell you. If Moses had not helped Israel bind herself to the heaven, the Son of Man would still not be here. Though you call the name of Moses you do not know what fruit Moses bore."

Thus Jesus twisted Shaphan's questions from the first to the last. The things they were seeking were fundamentally different. Shaphan felt that there was no point in putting to him any more questions. As Shaphan turned his eyes from Jesus and started looking over his disciples at his sides, Thomas who had been silent opened his mouth:

"Rabbi, I saw the miracle you worked with my own two eyes. With the power you used in doing it, rescue the people of this country and her holy temple from the hands of the aliens."

"Thomas, if you follow me you will see that the glory of heaven is greater than anything you can have on earth."

"Rabbi, the aliens have in turn stepped on us. If we lose our temples to the aliens and worship Jupiter instead of Jehovah, how would we be able to serve Jehovah as our God."

Although the questions Thomas asked were more or less a repetition of Shaphan's questions, Jesus did not seem to find it

bothersome but rather looked with sympathy at Thomas as he
told him:

"Though all the countries and powers of the earth pass
away, the kingdom of my Father will never pass. Therefore,
you need not worry about Israel but think of the kingdom in
heaven. Truly and truly I tell you that though all the countries
aliens build will fall one after another, the country I have built
will never perish."

Jesus touched his forehead with that white long hand of his
when he finished speaking to Thomas.

Now Matthew spoke to him again:

"Lord, let me help build your kingdom."

"Matthew, you are already bound with me."

"Rabbi, I too wish to enter your country."

It was Thomas who said this.

"Thomas, I know who you are."

Judas was about to repeat what Thomas had said when
Ananias who was sitting next to him restrained him. Ananias
felt that they as members of the Corps were not in the position
to choose their abiding place following personal inclinations
and moods. This question, however, came up again as soon as
they left Matthew's house.

Shaphan, Thomas, Ananias, and Judas, all those who had
attended Matthew's party went straight to Ananias' house
after they left Matthew's. They all felt that they needed to
have a discussion about the experience they had at Matthew's
house.

Shaphan had kept a gloomy expression on his face for some
time after his dialogue with Jesus at the feast. Now he opened
his mouth and asked Thomas:

"Thomas, do you know what is meant by 'the kingdom of
heaven' or 'the country I am building' as Jesus put it? He also
used the phrases 'glory of heaven' or 'happiness of the kingdom
of heaven.' Do you know what it all points to?"

"I think all of them mean the same thing."

"What would it be?" asked Ananias this time.

"It means that just as Moses led the people of Israel out of Egypt, he is going to lead us into a new country. This is how I understood it, any how."

"Does that mean that we would give up this land of Judaea and again go into the wilderness?"

There was anger in Ananias' voice as he said this.

"I don't think so. I think what was meant was that Jesus did not wish to have a direct collision with the Romans but will find a way to establish a new country in which we will be able to worship our God Jehovah to our hearts' fill."

"Do you mean that we could live on in this land occupied by the Roman army and yet would build a new country in it separately?"

"Well, that's how I understood it."

"It is a dream talk," said Ananias gruffly.

"Thomas," Shaphan called him again.

"I heard Jesus mentioning specifically 'the heaven.' He said 'the kingdom of heaven,' 'my father in the heaven,' 'bound to heaven,' and so on. I think what Jesus was talking about was that sky up there. I don't think he meant wilderness or this Judaea."

"I think so, too. And how can one who lives on earth build a country in heaven? And even if he could, what good would it be for us? I was annoyed that Thomas was so moved by words which were so vague in meaning and asked to be his disciple."

Ananias spoke out what had been seething in his mind ever since the party. Thomas, however, was not offended or distressed by this. He said, instead:

"I myself feel sorry about that. But I don't think it is right that we criticize him or resist him just because his way of thinking is not the same as ours. It is because I saw how he worked a great miracle with my own eyes and also have a faith that he is the Messiah or one who is just as great as the Messiah. I felt that even if we could not understand him fully, we would do well by following and staying by him and endeavouring to know him better," Thomas said. And what he was saying sounded as fluent as the flowing water. Ananias, however, stopped him saying:

"Even so, could you not have waited until we should have met by ourselves and shared words?"

"I thought of that, too. But I decided that it would be very hard for us to see him in that intimate way another time. And unless we showed our respect in some such way, we would look in his eyes no different from the lawyers who come to him for a test. It would be different if we are decided not to cooperate with him. But in so far as we still think of joining hands with him, I thought that it would be better to establish some such relationship with him, if only for the cause of our Corps."

Thomas' explanation of his conduct at Matthew's house was faultless and his attitude was calm and dignified. Shaphan felt that he had better play the peace-maker in this debate.

"Now that we have Thomas' reason for his conduct, I don't think there is any more need to discuss it further. Rather, we should think about how we will hold ourselves toward Jesus from now on. Will Judas speak first?"

Judas who had a pointed chin and gentle longish eyes smiled pleasantly to hear his name called.

"To tell the truth, I was going to ask at that feast table a while ago to be allowed to work for the new country. I was stopped by Ananias and I let it go. I agree with Thomas on his feelings about these matters. We had discussed about his being the Messiah at our last meeting at the headquarters and as long as we feel that he is probably the Messiah, I think that it is better for us all to become his disciples."

Judas was tougher than he looked. His firm words seemed to have touched the ears of Ananias with a thorn and the latter kept his mouth shut and did not make a retort as he did to Thomas. Judas continued:

"As Thomas said, if Jesus says he is going to build a new country in heaven, our duty is to find out what he means by it. It really may have been a metaphor for something else so that

Romans may not suspect anything."

Judas looked at Shaphan in the face when he finished speaking. He seemed to be asking Shaphan to give the last word. Shaphan began in his low voice:

"What Judas says has a sense, but to tell you honestly I felt right on the spot that there was something fundamental that made it impossible for him and us to work together. When we talked of the earth, he spoke of heaven, and when we mentioned today, he mentioned tomorrow which we could not see. When we talked of living, he talked of dying. It is true that I cannot say I understood his words sufficiently, but I had an almost sure feeling that he had something that was fundamentally different from us. That's why I did not ask him any more questions."

Shaphan paused a moment here and as if encouraged by what Shaphan had just said, Ananias opened his mouth again:

"I think the situation is exactly as you see it, Commander. He brought out such things as happiness of the kingdom of heaven or the glory of heaven while we were asking him to say something about our country that is suffering from the trespassing Romans. How could we find sense in what he said, then?"

"I think what we do need to do now is to decide about the practical tactics we should use toward him. In my opinion, having a more active contact with him as Thomas and Judas suggested is not a bad idea. My reasons are, first, that he is undoubtedly a being specially gifted and, second, that, whether his new country or heaven is a metaphor or not, what we need to concern ourselves about is not interpretation of his rhetoric but what can practically be brought about through application of those metaphors to actual situation."

"If they should bear no practical results?" asked Ananias unable to keep silent.

"Then he will swallow his own phrases and go away."

"We will have wasted ourselves in the case."

"The miracles he has worked and the words he has spread

are already enough to compensate for our trouble, don't you think?"

Shaphan's voice had become softer and his attitude was calmer than it had been at the beginning of the discussion.

This was how it was decided for the members of the Blood Contract Corps to follow Jesus.

That night Thomas went to Dariqueyea where Aquila was waiting and Shaphan returned to the headquarters.

In the meantime, Jesus was getting surrounded by a great number of people as he was leaving tax-gathered Matthew's house. All of them wanted to get close to Jesus and they began to push and pull creating a big confusion all around.

Jesus saw that the confusion was too great for him to control and so he ordered Peter to put out the boat and stepped aboard. Even when the boat left the lakeside and moved toward the center of the lake, the crowd did not disperse but, remaining by the water, kept on making noises and confusion.

As the boat neared the middle part of the làke, the noise of the crowd became more quiet. Jesus who had his back toward the crowd from the first was sunk in thought. His face looked a little tired and his eyes were turned up to the sky. Just then Peter came up to him and said:

"Lord, the Pharisees are asking us why our master eats with tax-gatherers and other sinners."

Jesus turned to him and said:

"It is not the healthy that need a doctor, but the sick; I have not come to invite virtuous people, but to call sinners to repentance."

His voice was low as he explained thus.

Philip who was at the oar said thinking of Shaphan and his followers:

"Lord, who are those that sat opposite us at Matthew's house?"

Jesus looked up at Philip's face for a while and then said:

"Philip, which among us would know who they are?"

Rebuked thus by Jesus, Philip at once confessed:

"Lord, forgive me. I know one of them whose name is Ananias. He has lived in Capernaum from his father's time and has given up his big property to do good for his country. Of the other three, I know nothing."

Jesus did not rebuke him any further.

"Philip, I know that you are speaking honestly when you say you don't know the rest of them. They are not the same as the Pharisees or the lawyers, but they are not ones that are destined to go the way you are going to go."

Jesus seemed hesitant to speak more openly about those men.

"Lord, what is the work they are doing?"

It was Peter who asked this time.

"Didn't you two hear them exchange words with me when we were at Matthew's house? The Pharisees blamed me for eating with the tax-gatherers and the sinners, but what did they call those when they were sitting with me?"

After asking this question, Jesus sat in the boat and leaning himself forward against the sideboard of the boat, dipped his hands in the water as if to cool them. With his hands still left in the water, he looked across at the far southern sky and whispered:

(My Father, save me.)

The words came out as softly as a sigh.

His disciples felt that their master was different today from any other day they had known him. For one thing he ate with the sinners and taught them things in such a kindly way without rebuking them even when they were in the wrong. Also the way he dipped his hands in the water and whispered as if in agony was something they had never seen him do before. They decided, therefore, as for now they had better not trouble him any further with foolish questions and began to talk in low voices among themselves.

When he realized that his mouth had whispered the words: "My Father, save me," Jesus felt as if what he was holding with his hands now was not water but the heart of Baptist John. The reason why he turned his eyes in the direction of Salt Sea (the Dead Sea) and thought of Baptist John was not only that he had at first taken 'the sinners' he met at Matthew's house this afternoon as Baptist John's disciples. Another reason for his having this kind of mood was that the insistent questions about Judaea and the Jewish people those men asked this afternoon had turned his mind to his younger days when those matters were cause of his misery and agony, also.

It was when he had turned five years old that Jesus first thought of such things as the country of Judaea or the Jewish people if in a very vague way. It was also the beginning of his realizing that he was someone chosen by Jehovah. As he reached the age of ten, these two realizations began to take a more or less definite shape and when he was twelve he was as convinced in his mission as to call the temple of God in Jerusalem 'my Father's house.'

His thoughts about his country and his people also had become more mature by this time. He knew well the meaning of Roman Empire and Roman governor to his land and people. He also understood the historical fate the Jewish people had been subjected to and the realistic position of Jadaea and her people at the time.

For him, these two missions he felt, that of saving Judaea and the people from Roman oppression and that of following Jehovah's will on earth, went well enough together without one getting in the way of the other. He believed that his Father Jehovah had sent him to the earth to save Judaea and Jewish people from oppressors. He would therefore rise up on the day when his Father would call him and rescue his country and his people. Never for a moment did he doubt the legitimacy of this mission.

(There the angel of the Lord appeared to him in the flame of a burning bush. Moses noticed that, although the bush was on fire, it was not being burnt up; so he said to himself, "I must go across to see this wonderful sight. Why does not the bush burn away?" When the Lord saw that Moses had turned aside to look, he called to him out of the bush, "Moses, Moses." And Moses answered, "Yes, I am here." God said, "Come no nearer; take off your sandals; the place where you are standing is holy ground." Then he said, "I am the God of your forefathers, the God of Abraham, the God of Isaac, the God of Jacob." Moses covered his face for he was afraid to gaze on God. The Lord said, "I have indeed seen the misery of my people in Egypt. I have heard their outcry against their slave-masters. I have taken heed of their sufferings, and have come down to rescue them from the power of Egypt, and to bring them up out of that country into a fine, broad land; it is a land flowing with milk and honey, the home of Canaanites, Hittites, Amorites, Perizzites, Hivites, and Jebusites. The outcry of the Israelites has now reached me; yes, I have seen the brutality of the Egyptians towards them. Come now; I will send you to Pharaoh and you shall bring my people Israel out of Egypt." "But who am I," Moses said to God, "that I should go to Pharaoh, and that I should bring the Israelites out of Egypt?" God answered, "I am with you. This shall be the proof that it is I who have sent you: when you have brought the people out of Egypt, you shall all worship God here on this mountain." Then Moses said to God, "If I go to the Israelites and tell them that the God of their forefathers has sent me to them, they will never believe me or listen to me; they will say, 'The Lord did not appear to you.' " The Lord said, "What have you there in your hand?" "A staff," Moses answered. The Lord said, "Throw it on the ground." Moses threw it down and it turned into a snake. Moses ran away from it, but the Lord said, "Put your hand out and seize it by the tail." He did so and gripped it firmly, and it turned back into a staff in his hand. "This is to convince the people that the Lord the God of their forefathers Jehovah has appeared to you.")

This scene never left his mind and he thought to himself that one day the Lord his God would call his name as He had called the name of Moses and give him the sign of the Chosen One.

He had lived for twenty years waiting for this moment like a bride waiting for the arrival of the bridegroom. When he was younger, he helped his father Joseph with his work of a carpenter, and after Joseph died, he helped his mother Mary to raise his younger brothers. But all the time, his innermost thought was about Jehovah calling him on the chosen day ordering him to rise up and rescue Judaea and the Jewish people from the hands of the aliens.

Then one day — he had reached the age of thirty by then— 'the Word of God' came to his ears in wilderness.

"Repent. For the Kingdom of Heaven is upon you."

This was 'the voice in wilderness' that was spoken by John the Baptist who wore clothes of camel's hair with a leather belt around his waist and ate locusts and wild honey for food. And this Baptist John was calling out to the people to repent their sins baptizing them in the water of the Jordan River. A horde of people from Jerusalem and many other towns and villages surrounding the Jordan flocked out to the riverside to be baptized by this man. And the Pharisees and the Sadducees also came. When John saw this, he shouted in a voice full of anger:

"You viper's brood! Who warned you to escape from the coming retribution?"

He continued:

"Already the axe is laid to the roots of the trees; and every tree that fails to produce good fruit is cut down and thrown on the fire."

Baptist John's warning shouts shook the entire land of Judaea. What he shouted was simple and clear: Repent. For the Kingdom of Heaven is come upon you. This was all. He did not speak about Judaea and the problems the Jewish people were facing. Neither did he say a word about Roman Empire or its governor or any other things of the alien nation.

His cry, however, was as pervasive as 'the wilderness' itself.

And the word, 'the Kingdom of Heaven' rang powerful to the ears of Jesus who had waited for thirty years for the call from his God. When he heard the word from Baptist John's mouth he felt so jubilant that his mind leapt from earth up to heaven at once. It was the 'revelation from Heaven' that he had heard in the voice there and then. It was something that began and ended in one second. But it was a final one. He felt as if he were hit by lightning on the head, on the chest, and in his blood.

Had he not heard the word 'Heaven' until that time, then? Of course it was not so. He who was born the Son of God cannot have avoided knowing about the 'Kingdom of Heaven.' Had he had special esteem, then, toward Baptist John thinking that his teachings were impeccable or had he found John with some definite sign from the God? It was not so, either. Why was it then that the one word cried out from the mouth of Baptist John caused him such a decisive spiritual conversion? He knew. It was because the cry of Baptist John was not a cry of a mere human. It was the 'Voice in Wilderness,' and 'the Voice of God.' The voice of God or the revelation from God had been sent to him through the mouth of Baptist John in wilderness. And this was a voice and word which only one who had waited twenty years in hot tears and ardent prayers for an opportunity to rescue Judaea and her people from Roman fetters could truly understand. Are the problems of Judaea greater, indeed, than Moses with his power to separate the Red Sea in two could solve? Isn't Rome of today a huge empire which cannot be compared with Egypt of Moses' time? He asked himself. The only reason Jesus could wait for so long without utterly despairing was that he believed in the boundless might of his Father Jehovah. Although the condition Judaea and her people were in was so hopeless that no wisdom or power of man can change it, Jehovah would bestow on him such power and light that he could do the impossible work on the appointed day, he had thought.

It was true that up to then it had never occurred to Jesus

that the earthly problems arising from the relationship between Judaea and Rome could cease to be the problems that had to be solved realistically on earth and become the problems that could be eliminated by God's will. But all this was changed as soon as his ears caught 'the Voice in Wilderness.' And at the same time, his soul was filled with holiness.

On account of these circumstances, Jesus was not in the frame of mind to make light of the work of Baptist John and his particular service to himself. For even if it was not John but God who had spoken through John's mouth in wilderness, still his role in it was too important not to be considered with appreciation. But since 'the voice' did not belong to anyone, not even John, it could not be thanked or paid back with something. Therefore, when he felt as if he were holding the heart of Baptist John with his hands dipped in the water, it was not because he felt particularly warm in his own heart toward John. Rather it was because he was perturbed by a remembrance of his younger days' passion which was kindled by his encounter with these men who had asked him so persistently about the land and whom he had almost taken for Baptist John's disciples. As he came out farther out to the center of the lake, the water of the lake that was connected by a belt of a river with the Salt Sea — where there was the fortress of Machaerus of King Herod — he was unawares thinking of Baptist John. The Jordan River of bygone days had let John baptize him in its water, but the Salt Sea of present day was shutting John up in a prison by the water. It was indeed the Dead Sea, a name appropriately suited the present situation.

(My Father, save me.)

Jesus whispered again this phrase which he used to say when he was burning with a passion of freeing Judaea and the Jewish people from Roman bondage. Now, thinking of John suffering in prison, he said these words which he had said before he had heard 'the Voice in Wilderness.' It was also a prayer which he repeated out of his sympathy toward those 'sinners' he had met at the house of Matthew whose agony he could well remember from his younger days.

So, the next day and the day after it, he welcomed 'the sinners' as they came to him one by one, Thomas and Judas including.

Shaphan whose têt-à-tête with Jesus had not turned out quite successful asked Hadad to read the stars again to divine the fate of the Corps as soon as he returned to the head-quarters.

Hadad looked at Shaphan with his shiny two eyes that were sunken deep under his dishevelled white hair that reminded one of the head of a ghost. He kept on looking at Shaphan until the latter said:

"Tell me, my Teacher, when the time would come for me to repay you for all your generous kindnesses to me."

Hadad replied:

"Oh, Commander, I have never taken my eyes off your stars ever since you went away."

". . . . . ."

Shaphan could barely restrain his restlessness but he did not open his mouth again but looked straight at Hadad's face in silence.

Just then, the falcon in the cage hanging from the ceiling of the cave fluttered his wings. Hadad opened his mouth again at the same time:

"Commander, your star is just at this moment shining face to face with the great male star."

Is this Jesus then the Messiah, after all, Shaphan asked himself and this thought made him the more restless.

"Is the time to repay your kindnesses near, then?"

Shaphan asked Hadad bringing his blood-shot eyes almost to the tip of Hadad's nose.

"Oh, Commander, your time is come."

"Is the great male star going to give light to me to the end? Or, could I continue to give light to the other star?"

"Oh, Commander, you are yourself that great star."

Shaphan took more and more courage as his interrogation with Hadad continued. Now he said:

"Respected Teacher, the two stars you have seen have already met and found out that their thoughts and words are not the same."

Shaphan made this confession, painful though it was for him even to think of it. Hadad, however, did not seem to understand what was said by Shaphan. He merely said again:

"Oh, Commander, you and he are even now giving light to each other."

This was the same thing in meaning as what had already been said by him.

Shaphan was at a loss how to take Hadad's words. Hadad never lied to anybody or for anything. There was no need for him to. And since he had done almost nothing but studying the stars and reading them, he never misread or misjudged as far as Shaphan knew. If so, maybe it was not in the way Hadad read the stars but in his own judgment about realistic matters that the fault lay.

If this was the case, should he then not try not to reach a hasty conclusion about his meeting with Jesus. Should he not make another approach with more stubbornness and force? And maybe, this applied to his attitude toward Nabatea also, he thought.

"Respected Corps Teacher, I will endeavour with more patience and force and obey your commands."

After bowing to Hadad, Shaphan went to Zilpah. Zilpah was absorbed in watching the bird cage when Shaphan went near. Then she turned her face that was as bright and pale as a star to him.

"Oh, beautiful Zilpah," said Shaphan and embraced her.

"Shaphan."

Zilpah's voice was as cool and clear as ever.

"Yes, Zilpah."

"I am your wife."

"I am your husband. Your father bound us together."

"So, I am yours. I want to know what you have been doing and where, and whom you have met. I must ask you about all these. I wish you would tell me before I should ask."

Shaphan was a little staggered by this. All of a sudden, Zilpah who was so much younger than he was and was no more than a tiny girl appeared more mature than Shaphan himself. He decided, soon, however, that this had nothing to do with her mental maturity but her pagan blood and mustering up courage he said:

"I will tell you, then."

He looked at her jewellike eyes once again and continued:

"I went to Capernaum and met a man named Jesus. He calls himself the Son of Jehovah and has proved himself to be a man of extraordinary gift."

"Did you work with him?"

"No, he wants to build a country in heaven. But my plan is to build a country right here in Judaea so that the Jewish people can live together among themselves without the Romans. Our thoughts were not the same."

"Did you have a quarrel with him, then?"

"No. We did not quarrel. But Thomas and Judas decided to follow after him and see clearly the things he does."

"That was well decided. I wish to meet him, too. He seems to be extraordinary."

"You will see him in future."

"Promise me, then. That you will let me see him."

"I promise."

"Who else did you see?"

"Who else?"

Shaphan hesitated for a while whether or not he should tell her about Mary of Magdala and then decided to tell her because he could not keep this away from her knowledge forever.

"Next I saw a woman who is called Mary of Magdala," he said.

"Who is this woman?"

Zilpah asked looking straight into Shaphan's eyes with those clear jewellike eyes of hers.

"She is a woman I sleep with when I am away from home."

Shaphan looked Zilpah straight in the eyes as if competing with her for defiance.

"Let me meet her, too, then. I wish to see her very much."

"All right."

Shaphan embraced her once more and put his lips on hers saying:

"Zilpah, you are the most beautiful woman of the world and my most wonderful wife."

Shaphan's voice came out a little husky and thick.

While Shaphan was caressing Zilpah in her quarters, Thomas was seeing Aquila at Dariqueyea. When Thomas handed the receipt of the gold which he said was written by Shaphan, Aquila looked glad.

"Then, does your Commander agree.to my King's proposal?" asked Aquila and looked across at Thomas. What he meant by 'agreeing' to his king's 'proposal' was that the Blood Contract Corps would start an attack on the fortress at Machaerus upon receiving the two talents of gold and that when this would be confirmed Nabatea would send over arms.

But it was not Shaphan's plan. His idea was to accept the gold first and, after observing the situation further, think of a way to carry out his part of the promise by getting help from Jesus—if it could be worked out—or make a show of attacking while avoiding a direct collision with the Roman army, or, again, let John's disciples who were also Corps members make sporadic attacks in the style of a guerilla warfare. This Shaphan had not made clear even to Thomas. He had vaguely told Thomas that they would act according to how the situation would develop. However, Thomas was not unaware of this. He thought that Shaphan was making it intentionally vague for fear that he might make a slip in his interview with Aquila. He could not of course tell these things to Aquila. But the gold had to be secured.

"Your Commander would not have written a receipt like this if he had no intention of taking action, I should think."

Thomas mumbled something which vaguely sounded like an assent to it. Aquila, however, did not seem to think that Thomas was being intentionally vague about that part of their negotiation. So he now said:

"I think everything is settled, then."

Aquila took out the bundle of gold which he had kept hidden behind a screen. He put the bundle down in front of Thomas and picking up the receipt paper said:

"An action like this is best quickly undertaken. Even tonight, if possible. . . ."

This was to emphasize the condition in their proposal that they were to go into action 'upon receiving' the gold.

"Mr. Aquila, you yourself are in an important position of governing a country. And yet you talk as if you did not know anything about what a delicate thing it is to plan a military action. Attacking a fortress is no simple thing. Even though ours is not such a very big organization, still we would need at least time to gather our men and weapons together for the attack."

Thomas spoke in a tone which he calculated would put down Aquila's demanding manner. It was of course intentional.

"I understand, Mr. Thomas. I had forgotten the fact that the Blood Contract Corps was a very widely spread and complex organization. But even so, I would like to ask you to see to it that no more than a day and a night is added to my estimation."

Thomas left with the bundle of gold without even saying anything to Aquila's last words.

Chapter 4

Zilpah and Mary

Three days later, Shaphan left for Capernaum again. His purpose in going was to find out about the deeds and moves of Jesus after their confrontation and also to hear from Thomas his report on seeing Aquila in Dariqueyea.

Thomas' report ran as follows.

The main concern of Aquila at present seemed to be finding out the location of the headquarters of the Corps and whereabouts of Shaphan. The reason for these interests seemed to be the following two. One was that Nabatea wanted to prepare against the Corps' failure to keep its promise with King Aretas. The other reason was that the Nabateans genuinely wanted to know where the center of the Corps could be found in preparation for further deepening of their cooperative relationship with the Corps. Thomas told Shaphan about how he had tried to draw his attention to Gadara and Magdala so that he might have no chance of finding out about the true objects of his interest. Thomas also told Shaphan about his pretending to row in the direction of Gadara to distract Aquila after they were parted from each other. When he thought further into the matter, however, it seemed to him that the Corps and Nabatea had not a little interest to share between them. He, therefore, did his best to prove himself as a well-intending ally to Aquila instead of offering him occasion to become suspicious of the Corps' motives or attitudes.

"Aquila brought out that event of three years ago, the one in Gadara. He implied that the arrow that was found stuck in the chest of the Roman centurion was from the Corps armoury."

"So?"

"He said that when he returned home after his diplomatic failure with us, some radicals in his country had come out with the question of the arrow. That is, they proposed that Nabatea blackmail the Blood Contract Corps with the arrow."

"What did you say to it?"

"I said that we don't know anything about the arrow on our side. I told him that it was not a wise thing to do to suspect another party on account of an arrow that has some resemblance to the arrows used by that other party."

Thomas seemed to feel good about having moved Aquila about at will. He now brought out the bundle of gold in front of Shaphan.

Shaphan first picked up a folded piece of paper that was lying on the inner bundle after the outer wrap was removed. He read: Gold... Two Talents.

He shot a glance at Thomas with his blood-shot eyes and asked briskly:

"What made the old man send us so much gold as this?"

Shaphan seemed to have forgotten the fact that Aquila had reached some sort of an agreement with Thomas and Ananias as he was leaving for his home after his last visit with the Corps. Even while he wrote the receipt for Thomas to take with him, Shaphan was unaware of the concrete details of the agreement.

Thomas spoke slowly:

"Nabatea had offered to send us arms and materials in case we should agree to attack Machaerus and they offered to make a side attack in answer to our initial attack. This gold, therefore, is being paid in place of the supplies they promised."

Shaphan seemed to remember now. He said:

"That's right. It had been the agreement that they would send us the weapons and the supplies in advance. Is this gold price of the arms and supplies put together?" he asked.

"I do not know for sure. At the time, we had thought that Aquila would probably not return. We had interpreted his talk of negotiation as a diplomatic exercise and did not confirm about the items and quantity of the supplies and weapons they were to send."

"Did you not ask him about it?"

"I could not open the letter because it was a personal epistle from King Aretas to you. So, I had no way of knowing what I was to ask him before I left him. I brought the gold after giving him the receipt. He told me to see to it that the answer to the king's letter be conveyed to him within two days."

"Things were well-arranged."

Shaphan praised freely and continued:

"Our time to go into action is drawing near anyway. This means that we need to secure arms by any means. The situation is such that we may have to go out to loot the weapons. Under these circumstances, why should we not accept what has been offered us. Again, things were well-arranged."

"The trouble is we must comply with their request and the condition of their request is that we take arms immediately."

"We will delay by all the means we can think of. And in the meantime, we will ask them to send us the arms. We will take the gold as the price of mobilizing the men."

Shaphan seemed determined to get all he could out of this negotiation with Nabatea. But Aquila too was not the kind of man that would suffer himself to a loss in this kind of a negotiation, no matter how diplomatically shrewd Thomas might try to be or how determined Shaphan was to make the most out of it. For one thing, Aquila had fortified his position by spending a huge amount of money on infiltrating his information agents into numerous circles of Jewish community from whom he was gathering new data and contacts all the time.

It was true that Aquila, as Thomas reported to Shaphan, disappointed and even angered King Aretas and his higher courtiers when he went back home without carrying out his diplomatic mission successfully with the Blood Contract Corps. And it was also true that there was a radical segment at the court who demanded that the arrow be used as bait for catching the Blood Contract Corps. It was not an easy work for Aquila to ameliorate all of these discontents and antagonism and again bring off a new proposal that needed a great amount of expenses. This was a proof of Aquila's diplomatic adroitness. His first basis for mediation was a theory that annihilating the Blood Contract Corps meant ten losses and no gain to Nabatea. Secondly, if they brought law on Shaphan, it would also incriminate themselves by the logic of events. Thirdly, the cause of Shaphan's delay in attacking Machaerus was not a sign of his disrespect toward King Aretas or lack of sincerity but a factor that lay with the necessity of the political and strategic network of the Corps itself. What Nabatea had to do to profit from their contact with the Blood Contract Corps, therefore, was to give it more time and get them to cooperate by and by.

He suggested that Nabatea make a double-edged approach to the Corps to prompt their action. First of all, he said, they would do very well by sending them weapons and materials beforehand to show them their enthusiasm for this war. Secondly, Nabatea would, through investigation about the organization and the location of their headquarters and armoury, force them into a hot situation from which they cannot escape without keeping their promise with Nabatea. For the first project, they were to send half the required number of horses and amount of weapons and supplies to the Blood Contract Corps to be used at the time of their attacking

Machaerus. The second project could be promoted by infiltrating agents and actively gathering information from other sources, which could progress in step with the carrying-out of the first project.

The first step Aquila took for this new diplomatic enterprise was to draw Baptist John's disciples to the Nabatean side. In fact they were the ones that had made it possible for Aquila to make his contact with Thomas and now they came in conveniently in his plan as they had their duty to report to their master Baptist John about Jesus and his deeds, and had to travel up to Galilee at all times in order to meet Jesus or his disciples. When Aquila realized that through the disciples of Baptist John who could easily get access not only to Jesus and his disciples but also to the members of the Blood Contract Corps, he could operate an excellent intelligence network, he was boundlessly pleased by the thought. On the part of the disciples of Baptist John also, it was a fortunate thing that they could earn their expenses for their necessary trips up and down the Jordan River and this for doing something which could really contribute to rescuing their master Baptist John from prison. They did not believe, as Aquila tried to convince them, that the Nabateans' purpose was merely in rescuing Baptist John, but was also in securing the Blood Contract Corps' cooperation and in their scheme for chasing Herod Antipas, with whom King Aretas stood enemy on various accounts, further to the north.

Baptist John's disciples became busy going after Jesus' disciples — especially Andrew, Philip, and John — with whom they were already acquainted and Thomas, Judas, Ananias and some other members of the Blood Contract Corps. What they did at these meetings was to give them current news of Baptist John in prison and gathering data and information about Jesus and the identity and activities of the Blood Contract Corps. They gave the results of their investigation to Aquila.

That Shaphan was out in Capernaum meant that he intended to gather more information about Jesus and decide about the tactics to be used toward the Nabateans. But on a private basis, it also meant that he could see Mary if he wanted to.

At the time, Mary was staying in Chorazin where the house of Shaphan's mother was. As Chorazin was right next to Capernaum, Shaphan usually spent his nights there with her unless he was called to other places for special businesses.

Shaphan did not, however, let her know yet anything about the Blood Contract Corps or Zilpah. He decided that this could not go on. He chose to speak of Zilpah, first.

As soon as he opened his mouth, however, Mary stopped him:

"I don't want to hear about it."

She then looked at him with her fierce angry eyes.

Since Mary's reaction to his words was too sudden and un-expectedly violent, Shaphan kept silent for some time. Soon Mary started to sob.

"Mary, trust me."

". . . . . ."

Mary did not stop crying.

"Mary, what is the cause of your anger? What makes you cry? Am I not a robber and you a water ghost? A robber and a water ghost are both sinners and good-for-nothings in the eye of the world. If you are crying because you don't get the respect and love from the people of the world, your crying is much outdated. For myself, I don't pity myself in the least. And I have no regrets, either. If anyone should say he would change me into one of the Pharisees or the lawyers, no thank you! I will refuse it for double seven times. This life can be lived and enjoyed even if one should throw away all regard for the world and the people. Even so, there is hope. Why are you angry? Tell me what it is that makes you angry."

". . . . . ."

Mary persisted in silence and merely looked at Shaphan with those wild fierce eyes. When Mary's eyes looked wild and fierce, the pupils rolled up leaving the whites to cover most of her eyeballs. She did this with her eyes now and then.

"Tell me. What is it that makes you angry? What relation does your anger have with your crying?"

"I did not want to hear that story. I did not want to know." Mary's voice was husky and pathetic.

"Mary, from the first, our paths in life have been different from those of the other people. Why are you acting like this at this point?"

"The people do not matter. I cried because of myself."

"I don't understand. Do you mean you hate me, now?"

"No, it is not that."

"Do you hate my being a robber, then?"

"I don't like you to be a robber. But it had nothing to do with that, either."

"I can see you don't like associating with a robber. But who but a robber would love a woman who is possessed by seven demons?"

"That's why I am crying."

"Why would you start crying about it after all these years?"

"But what if I can't help it? I would rather become the water ghost that I used to be than loving you half."

After declaring thus, Mary covered her head with her kerchief and went out of the house. She was away from home for seven days. From what Ananias told Shaphan, she began to play the lute at the lakeside in Bethsaida as she did before.

Shaphan went out in boat near the shore of Bethsaida the very night he heard this news. He looked for Mary in the same olive grove where he had found her that time. Mary stopped playing the lute when she saw Shaphan tie the boat at the quay and start to climb up the slope. Shaphan stood silently before her with the moon at his back.

"......"

Mary looked up at him in silence with her hands on the instrument. Her face in the moonlight shone pale. Two of them remained in silence without moving.

"Mary."

Shaphan's thick husky voice broke the silence first. Next instant, he bent down and gripping Mary by the wrist pulled her up. She stood up without resisting. Until they climbed down to the boat and until they rowed toward the middle of the lake, they remained in silence again.

"Mary."

Shaphan called her name again as the boat reached the center of the lake.

". . . . . ."

Instead of answering, Mary glared at Shaphan with those wild fierce eyes of the other day.

"I want to ask you one question. What did you mean when you said you could not love me half?"

The woman remained silent hanging her head over the water. She was fingering the lute at random with her right hand.

"Do you know how many times I wished to throw you into this water?"

Suddenly Mary raised her head. There was a strange smile that was hard to describe on her face.

"Did you think that I would be afraid to go into this water for your sake? Do you think I am afraid of doing it even now?"

"Why did you say such a thing, then?"

"Why? Is it not clear enough to you? It is because you love two women."

Mary said these words distinctly.

"Why does my loving two women make you love me half only?"

Shaphan asked smiling. He seemed really curious to know.

"It is because you only love me half."

"I don't know what you are saying. Mary, believe me. Honestly speaking I don't know what love is. But it may be said that I am very fond of women. I believe it is not much different from what you call love. Because even if I am very fond of women, I don't like just any women. Some women I dislike even. And there are women I like only a little. But the women whom I like very much, so much that they seem like part of my destiny, those are only you and my wife Zilpah."

"So you love me only half, don't you? Or, you don't love me at all. Even if we talked about liking and loving as the same thing."

"That's because you think of me as the same kind of person as yourself."

"That is not true. There is a limit to the power of love. If one person were to love two persons at the same time, that love has to be divided in two and no other choice there is to it."

"That is what you think, and only you. And that is only how you feel. But it does not apply to me, you see. In my case, not only is there no division of love into two halves but also there seems to be a deepening and enriching of love because of my loving two women equally and at the same time. This is my honest testimony to my actual experience. If I had loved just you, I feel that there may have come a time when my love would have been exhausted. But just because there is also this other woman apart from you, I seem to be able to know you completely and like you unlimitedly. I know this because it is what I feel in my own mind. And I can say exactly the same thing about my relationship with her. If I were loving each of you as much as seven pounds' worth now, I would love you each only five pounds' worth in case one of you were to be lost to me."

"If so, it would not be love."

"I am not sure if I know what love is myself. But I am convinced that you and I cannot be separated in this world no matter whatever may happen."

"Even so, it would not be love."

"I don't think I would care. I am not so particular about calling it love, anyway. The only thing is you mustn't leave me. I desire this of you and I order you to obey me."

As soon as he said this, Shaphan abruptly moved up to

Mary and embraced her powerfully.

In three days after she had been taken back to Chorazin, Mary felt as if she were really his woman whose sole wish was to obey him. By this time, she had already consented to a confrontation with Zilpah which she would have objected to in fury only ten days ago.

"I hope she would not be rude to me," said Mary as if this were the only consideration that might still detain her from meeting Zilpah.

"I will be responsible for it. If she were to act rudely toward you, I will restrain her. If you were to treat her rudely, however, I will restrain you instead."

Shaphan seemed sure of what he was going about.

The reason why Mary changed her attitude and obeyed him and, more over, accepted the difficult conditions he proposed was partly that she felt overwhelmed by his knowledge and creative way of thinking against which she felt herself utterly incompatible but it was also, if not more, because of some imperceptible power that emanated from his personality which presented itself chiefly as a sense of sureness about what he was doing as pointed out before.

Upon receiving word from Shaphan, Zilpah arrived at Chorazin escorted by Jair. She had taken the boat after it became dark, it seemed.

Although it was in the dark of the night that she arrived, the jewel-bright eyes and water-clear voice of Zilpah attracted special concern and curiosity of people there.

One strange fact was that Shaphan's mother did not receive Zilpah with the cordiality with which she had met Mary although the former was a far more good-looking and well-bred woman than the latter. Shaphan's mother was a tallish woman of about fifty who had a slim waist. Although she was wrinkled in the face, there still was much energy in her and she made herself hard-working and active. But for some mysterious reason, this woman seemed to distrust Zilpah from the first. She treated Zilpah as if the latter were an unwelcome guest to the family. This feeling of alienation was forgotten for the most part when Zilpah presented her mother-in-law with a coat on the next day. It was clear, however, that the older woman kept herself more aloof to Zilpah than to Mary.

The morning after Zilpah's arrival at Chorazin, the two women met. On their first meeting, Zilpah was the first to greet Mary in her voice clear as water spring:

"I have come to this place so that I may meet you. My lord Shaphan graciously granted me my wish."

Mary who was older than Zilpah by ten years and also bigger and more mature physically did not know what to say. She only managed to stammer:

"I. . . I, too, have heard from Lord Shaphan."

Why Mary who was so much older and domineering in physique let herself be swayed by this slim young woman was hard to explain. Could it be because of the striking beauty of the younger woman? But in that respect, Mary herself had never felt inferior to anybody so far. If one compared the delicately square face of Zilpah with its clear complexion to a rare jewel, one would think of a lotus blossom when looking at the graceful and attractive face of Mary. There was also a tragic touch in the latter's beauty as can be felt by one from looking at a lotus blossom opening and closing in a forsaken pond. It was not face alone that was strangely attractive about this woman. She was also endowed with a body ideal by any esthetic standard; her posture, height, volume, neck, shoulders, and waist formed a perfect balance and harmony.

Above all, her rich and soft voice was so enchanting that whoever heard the voice, especially men, felt as if intoxicated by a strong perfume. If Mary with all these female advantages felt overpowered by Zilpah, what power did the latter have over the other? And if it was the power of beauty, for beauty was certainly one form of power, what was the source in Zilpah's beauty from which the power that dominated Mary come? The power of Zilpah's beauty lay in its elevated and noble stature, and this was symbolized by her crystal-clear eyes, clear complexion, and voice that had the clarity and coolness of a water spring in it. Compared with this kind of beauty, the beauty of Mary that was characterized by a tragic evocativeness that one felt from looking at a lotus blossom gained power when it was faced by a man but did not have so much power over a woman. Seeing Mary embarrassed like this, Zilpah talked to her again in a voice that had the tone of an older person speaking placatingly to a younger person:

"Just as I thought, you are a very beautiful and fine person."

Mary seemed more embarrassed when Zilpah said this. Unable to find adequate words to say in answer to Zilpah's generous praise, she said:

"You are welcome here and I think you are very beautiful also."

Zilpah looked straight into Mary's face and said:

"I am very glad, and now I would like to present you with a present."

She then took a small box out of her travelling pack and, opening the box, issued a pair of gold bracelets decorated with big pieces of ruby and handed them to Mary.

Mary seemed not to know whether to take them or not. She threw a glance at Shaphan who was standing apart from them as if to ask him what she should do, and then took the bracelets from Zilpah's hand as if she didn't know what else she could do. But again, she found it hard to find proper words to utter. So she said:

"I suppose a fine treasure like this is a rare thing."

Then, she left the room abruptly with the bracelets still in her hand.

Later, Shaphan said to Mary:

"She came from the east and is somewhat different from the people in these districts."

His words sounded as if meant to console Mary and Mary felt all the more embarrassed and humiliated for it.

Then, all at once, she was very angry and she said to

Shaphan pointedly:

"Have you given up to her what you have stolen up to now?"

"I have not given up anything to her and only stored whatever there is in the place where she is. It may be that I will decide to store my things at your place if the occasion should direct it in the future. But this has nothing to do with her or you directly."

"Why is it so? Is there anybody in this world who would not like to have jewels or money?"

"But we are not going to live one or two days and then die. For the time being we should be content to be able to just eat and live. The time when we can have treasures and money will come much later. When everything is straightened, there will be enough jewels. You will have as many jewels as you wish when that time comes. But nobody has anything really at present. If anybody has a few jewels it is only that he or she has them as temporary charge. Moreover, if there is anything I have stolen, you, just like her, would not wish to have it even as a temporary charge."

"I don't care if it is a stolen thing. As long as there's your heart in the thing, I would like to have whatever you can give me. I will not be afraid to take it even if I get captured for owning it. Let me have the jewels, also. Let me have big ones. I want to give her a memento too."

"You don't have to repay her right away. It is better that you give her something when you two meet next time. I will find some jewels and give them to you before that occurs."

"No. I want to give her something right now. If you don't give me some jewels now, I will return these bracelets to her."

"It would be rude and you promised not to do anything rude, didn't you?"

"I don't like to receive a present and not give anything back in return. I cannot bear it."

Declaring thus, Mary went into the room where Zilpah was and said to her:

"I would like to give you a memento, too. But I don't have anything as fine as this. I will, therefore, give this back to you as my present to you."

She handed the bracelets to Zilpah. Zilpah, however, did not seem in the least surprised or perturbed.

"No. It is my present to you. I liked you from my heart and for that reason wanted to give you something that I found pleasing enough. I have lived a lonely life in a dark cave in company of a sole falcon and I was so overwhelmed with joy to be able to be acquainted with a lady so beautiful and nice as you are. Even now, I am so very happy to look at you and speak with you like this. Please accept the bracelets as a token of my happiness."

There was dignity and elevation in her clear calm voice as she said these words.

Mary felt she could not persist in refusing the present without making herself rude and vulgar. But she did not know how to continue the conversation. After a while during which she tried to find words to say to Zilpah, she managed to say:

"I will then leave this with mother, and I will bring back a present for you."

Leaving the room, she went to the mother (Shaphan's) and entrusted her with the bracelets.

Although Zilpah took many pains to show friendliness and good will to Mary, the latter could not help feeling alienated and burdened by the relationship. She could not feel a natural affinity toward the other woman as toward a sister or a friend. Two days later, Mary left for her home in Magdala without even letting Shaphan know of it.

Zilpah, too, could not stay on in Chorazin. One reason was that Shaphan's mother kept an unfriendly countenance toward her, and another was the two days after Mary left for Magdala, Zilpah received an unexpected order from Hadad for her to return to the headquarters immediately. According to what Jair said to Zilpah, Hadad wanted her back because he read in the stars that Zilpah who ought to be in the southeast by astrological divination was in the northwest, directly opposite to what the stars directed. Hadad's plan seemed to be that he would make Zilpah return to the headquarters first and then perhaps send her on to her home in Aroer. Jair added, however, that about sending her to Aroer, Hadad seemed to be intending to consult Shaphan on his return to the headquarters since it would be a matter of not a little gravity. Shaphan's feelings, on the other hand, were that it might not be a bad idea to let Zilpah visit her home since it had been quite some time since she had left it, and as long as she was planning to do so it would be wise to make the trip before the rainy season started when travelling over a long distance would become very difficult. If she were to be sent to Aroer, it was better to send her now as Hadad seemed to be thinking of. But who would escort her on this long journey? And after she gets to Aroer, who will be there to protect her, he asked himself. The reason why Zilpah had been safe in Aroer before she came to Hadad was that she was then too young to draw much attention and besides she had spent all her time inside her house so that hardly anybody had seen her face aside from her family. But if anybody should have a chance to look at her face either on the way or after she arrives at Aroer, there will be no safety guaranteed for her, thought Shaphan. He therefore decided that they would have to think more about sending Zilpah to Aroer. He sent Zilpah to the headquarters with his words to the effect that he thought the decision to send Zilpah on to Aroer would require a deep thinking.

In the meantime, Aquila who had waited for six days after Thomas took the gold from him and yet not heard any news of military action on the Blood Contract Corps nor any word from Thomas, decided that he had been intentionally deceived and the gold embezzled. Aquila felt that he could not sit and wait any longer. In fact, he could not afford to, since there had been some serious opposition from a faction in Nabatean court about Aquila's taking two talents of gold to an unknown underground organization like the Blood Contract Corps. He had nearly staked the whole of his political career in this negotiation with the Corps. Under the circumstances, he needed to utilize all methods available to him in order to meet the situation without a total loss on his part. First of all, he had to have something that could be used as leverage against the Corps. And in order to achieve this end, he had to find out where the headquarters of the Corps was located and also where Shaphan resided.

The disciples of Baptist John and a number of Nabatean youths—these were the soldiers disguised in civilian clothes—began to penetrate into various towns, streets and waterfronts of the Galilean coast. The towns that were thus infiltrated at first were Gadara, Gerasa, Bethsaida, Capernaum, Magdala, Tiberius, and Dariqueyea. But the surveyance network concentrated into five towns from the initial seven: Gadara, Gerasa, Capernaum, Bethsaida, Magdala, and finally it was active only in three towns: Gadara, Gerasa and Capernaum. Also, on the water of the Sea of Galilee, there was no time when a secret patrol boat was not afloat to watch for the torchlight signals of the Blood Contract Corps members.

That Aquila made the Nabatean patrol boat only watch out for the torchlight signals of the Corps, however, proved to be a grave miscalculation, because except on special occasions the Corps did not use the torchlight signals. Therefore, Jair and other members could travel in fishing boats or freight boats without the Nabatean patrols suspecting it. The discovery by one of Baptist John's disciples of Zilpah and Jair on their way to Chorazin had not been through any spying of the patrol boat but was a rather accidental happening. Zilpah and Jair who travelled as her escort had come to Capernaum and then before they continued their journey to Chorazin had dropped in at Ananias' house and it was at the latter's house that they had been seen by a disciple of Baptist John's who was watching that neighborhood. It seemed the report found its way to Aquila but not because the man thought the discovery had any importance. It was only when Aquila heard the report that the event of discovery acquired gravity. That a tallish and ruddy faced young man of around twenty six or seven who had the look of a Corps member had visited Ananias in company of a young woman who had a jewellike beauty certainly did not appear as harmless to Aquila as it had seemed to the man who made the report of the discovery.

"What? Did you say a jewellike beauty?" asked Aquila to the disciple of Baptist John.

"Yes, that is what I said, sir. I did not know of it until she stepped onto the carriage in front of Ananias' house because it was only then that the kerchief with which she had covered her face was loosed for a second. But the face, when it was thus exposed, shone bright like a jewel although it was a smallish face. I was hiding in the olive tree that stood in front of the house and could see her face clearly if it had been only for such a brief second. It was as if her small face and two eyes were positively emitting light."

"What was she dressed in?"

"It was a white cloak that looked as distinguished as those worn by a princess or a noble lady."

When Aquila heard this much from the man, he knew instinctively that the woman was no other than that beautiful girl from Arabia or thereabouts who had travelled in the boat along with Thomas and Aquila himself as far as the Sea of Gerasa. And the tallish young man with a ruddy face was certainly Jair. From meeting Jair several times lately, Aquila knew the characteristics of the other man's face and physique quite well. He had also learned the fact that Jair was the Corps member Shaphan trusted most. And so if the young beauty were being transferred somewhere under Shaphan's direction, Jair would have been the most natural choice as her escort.

Aquila at once sent the disciple of Baptist John to Chorazin with a direction to watch the woman and her escort closely and to report whatever he would find out back to Aquila

himself. At the same time, Aquila ordered two boats to lie in
wait in the sea near Capernaum and Gadara-Gerasa district.
In each boat, he posted five armed Nabatean soldiers. They
were to receive a signal as soon as Zilpah and Jair would get
afloat in boat. The order was that they attack the boat upon
receiving the signal and killing the man throw him in the
water while capturing the woman carefully and sending her to
Nabatea without any delay.

There were calculated reasons on the part of Aquila in
making this kind of risk.

The first reason was that he had taken a formidable amount
of money and manpower from the king on this mission. And if
the negotiation should fail as it now looked likely to, he Aquila
would face a grave danger. Sending a beautiful woman to
him, therefore, was a clever thought because King Aretas liked
beautiful women in his old age as much as he did in his prime,
and Aquila felt from his knowledge of the king's character and
past precedents that this scheme would probably work to
mitigate king's anger toward himself.

The second reason was that through the woman they might
be able to find out all the secrets of the Blood Contract Corps.

The third of Aquila's calculation was that under such
circumstances Shaphan would have no other choice but taking
immediate action as originally settled in their negotiation.

Aquila's plan, in short, was killing three birds with one
stone.

Four nights after, the boat carrying Jair and Zilpah was
sliding in the dark, leaving Capernaum behind and setting its
course in the direction of Gerasa. One of the two boats that
Aquila had stationed was waiting in the middle of the lake
while the other was afloat on the sea near the coast of Gerasa.

The first to detect the boat of Jair and Zilpah were the men
in the patrol boat stationed in the middle of the lake. Taking
care not to be detected by Jair they headed their boat in the
southeast. Their plan was to get to the sea of Gerasa ahead of
Jair and Zilpah and, when they should get there, attack them

from one side while the other patrol boat that would already be there attack from the other flank.

As Jair's boat pulled in toward the coast of Gerasa, there was a signal from an unknown boat that was floating about. At the same time, another boat slided in at full speed from the direction of Gadara. Jair pulled his dagger from his side. Even if the men in the other boats were armed, he knew he could fight down two or three men by himself. When the boats came nearer, however, he saw that there were at least five men in each boat and they all had spear and sword. There seemed to be some with bow and arrows, too. From all this, Jair decided that these were robbers that were assailing them with a plan. Jair was taken aback. He decided that what he should do was to push the boat toward the land by any means. But a boat that seemed to have been waiting right at the spot came in and blocked the way to the coast. None of the men spoke and only their sword and spear shone white in the darkness as the boats drew close to Jair's boat.

"Who are you?" asked Jair in a high and authoritative voice.

They, however, did not answer.

Jair had only three daggers with him at the moment. It was no problem for him to throw them one by one and kill three men in succession. But what would he do afterward? He could not possibly fight all the rest of the armed men with his two hands alone. And then he could not just wait and do nothing. He had to take some action before the second boat came up closer. He let the boat slide toward the boat that was blocking the way to the coast and at a point threw one of the daggers toward it. The dagger flew in the night air and hit one of the men in the other boat. He fell down causing a big swaying movement to the boat. Taking advantage of the commotion caused by this, Jair threw another dagger at the same time that he bumped into the other boat with his. Another man fell. Still the boat would not move out of the way. In the meantime, two daggers had flown into Jair's boat from the other boat and one of them hit Jair on the upper part of one leg. Pulling the dagger from where it was stuck in his leg promptly, Jair said in a gentle voice to Zilpah:

"Bend yourself further, Madam."

By this time, the second boat had come up close enough to touch Jair's boat. From it two men tried to jump into Jair's boat. One fell into the water, however, being struck by Jair on the head with the oar. The other grabbed Jair's oar with both hands and would not let it go. Just at this instant, Jair felt something like a sheet of ice touching him on the back. It was another dagger thrown by an enemy. Still, Jair did not give up. He believed yet that he could keep on fighting even now. He, therefore, pushed hard against his oar and as the one that had held onto it fell behind, he made a quick turn around. But two men who had jumped over from the other boat had stuck two more daggers into him one on his side and the other on his right arm by this time.

"Ohoy," Jair seemed to hear somebody shouting from afar as he fell on the bottom of his boat bathed in blood.

Aquila was relieved when he heard that a number of Nabatean armed men had kidnapped Zilpah while wounding Jair severely, but at the same time he was suddenly uneasy and afraid. It was because the Nabateans had failed to throw Jair into the water as had been planned and so even though he was much wounded there was no telling when Jair would recover strength and retaliate. Another cause of his worry was that the report said that a large-sized fishing boat had come upon them in assault while the Nabatean men were busy dealing with Jair, and so they had fled after hurriedly packing Zilpah into one of their boats. And what was the identity of this large-sized fishing boat? What did its appearance on the scene mean? Aquila could not help feeling uneasy about it all.

Since the Nabateans were all disguised and spoke almost no words during the operation, there was not much chance that Jair would be able to identify them even if he should recover consciousness. But there was such a thing as human insight and moreover there was this fishing boat that was reported to have followed the Nabatean boats persistently. If so, it would have found out something about the Nabatean boats, that is, where they were headed for and where they belonged. No. Aquila could not sit back and rest in peace.

In spite of this uneasy feeling he had, Aquila as yet did not know who exactly the young woman was and how risky it had been to attack the boat with her in it. He did not know what great danger he was facing on account of this happening. What he was thinking now was that the Blood Contract Corps might be forced into taking a military action for the rescue of Baptist John. If not, he thought, he would perhaps put an end to his diplomatic activities at this point and return to Nabatea. He would explain to King Aretas that Nabatea would do better by waiting for a better time. Even then, it would not mean a one-sided loss for Nabateans, he thought.

The next morning after breakfast, Aquila visited Ananias at his home and asked him with an innocent face when Thomas was expected to be back in Capernaum.

"Why do you ask? If you have anything to speak to Thomas about, you may speak with me," said Ananias with an expression in which Aquila could not read anything. It was obvious that he had not heard anything yet.

"No, don't bother. I have something to consult with him in person."

"Oh, is that so? I won't ask you to tell me, then."

"Well, it is a fact that any personal talk can have public meaning and conversely a public conference can be biased by personal feelings. And then with Master Thomas, I have maintained a relationship as if he were your Commander's spokesman. In fact I have suffered quite a bit of inconvenience for that reason. It seems I am staying here when there is nobody willing to accommodate me."

"It is not quite true. And whatever you may think, I am also in a position to speak for the Commander. Thomas is charged with dealing matters involving diplomacy because he knows how to speak for the Corps in a clever way. Otherwise, I am not any different from him in the capacity of the Commander's spokesman."

Ananias spoke without reservation, gesticulating with his hand.

"I see. I will then dare trouble you when I cannot speak with Master Thomas from now on. And I would be grateful if you would tell Master Thomas as soon as he comes back that I should like to see him immediately."

Aquila went back to his lodging after these words, but as soon as he got there, he began to be assailed by uneasiness and worry again. He feared that the news of the kidnapping might have reached them even in the interval between his visit to Ananias and now. His uneasiness and fear grew as time passed.

He packed his things ready for any sudden departure. But he could not help hesitating because if his opponents really hadn't got wind of anything yet, his leaving like that would be the same as confessing to the deed. He made his spies find out if people were talking anything in the streets. Most of them reported that there was no unusual thing talked about in the outside world. A few of them came back with the stories that said either that Jair seduced Zilpah to go away with him and they both disappeared, or that Jair threw Zilpah into the water after raping her and, failing in his attempt to commit a suicide, had fled in the direction of Gadara. In short, they came back with stories which Aquila himself had spread.

Three days after the kidnapping, Aquila visited Ananias again. Since it was impossible for the Blood Contract First Members not to have heard anything about the accident until this time, Aquila resolved to find some clue in the talk or expression of his host before he should leave his house that day. He felt that this might be his last day in Capernaum and made preparations for an immediate departure before he left his lodging to go to see Ananias.

Ananias seemed pleased when he saw Aquila. He shook the latter's hand eagerly and said:

"Why have you been staying away from my house these last few days?"

His long muscular neck looked the longer as he said these words and bent toward his guest this day.

"You mean you have been waiting for me? What an honor!" said Aquila with exaggeration and innocence.

"Have you then not heard the news yet?"

Ananias' voice was as natural as could be when he said this.

"What news?"

Aquila's face also was as innocent-looking as ever.

Ananias looked at Aquila's face intently but for a very brief while, and then began to recount the story in a low voice. The story was that Jair who had long had his mind fixed on Zilpah tried to force her to elope with him as they were travelling together in a boat three days ago. When Zilpah refused to comply with his wish, he killed her and threw her into the water. And then after wounding himself on several spots with his dagger found himself a place to lie in. He was insisting that they had received an attack of pirate boats in order to cover his crime. He was also saying that he had fainted in the midst of the turmoil.

Aquila could not decide whether Ananias believed the story himself or just pretending to believe it to see how he, Aquila, would react to it. The facial expression, attitude and voice of Ananias were so natural that Aquila could not find any clue there.

"How do you know if Jair is not telling the truth?"

"For one thing, he has acted strangely toward our lady from the first."

It was a slip of tongue Ananias made perhaps owing to his nature which was not as shrewd and cautious as Thomas'. The slip he made was the phrase 'our lady.' And Aquila heard it. My goodness! He thought. Because if the woman was 'our lady' to Ananias, she could but belong to Shaphan! The reason that he had not associated the women with Shaphan up to now was not only because of what Thomas had told him about her. Thomas had said that he had taken the girl to her father Hadad. The stronger reason than that was what he himself saw when Shaphan and the girl had met the first time as Thomas had taken her and Aquila himself in his boat to meet Shaphan. From the way they all acted, Aquila had thought that what Thomas was telling him about the woman might be true on the whole. He was as yet ignorant about in what kind of relationship Hadad and Shaphan were to each other. Aquila tried not to show the shock he received on the outside. Assuming a natural voice, he said:

"Oh, I don't know what to say! It is too unfortunate. And how grieved Commander Shaphan must be!"

"Yes, it has been a great blow on the Commander, especially since he had had a special feeling and trust toward Jair. I believe that is why he in person went out on a search for Jair."

"I am very sorry about everything. I hope you know that what your Corps suffers is the suffering of Nabateans also."

Aquila got up to leave but before he did so he added one more word:

"I am all the more sorry for the Commander since he has come to lose two precious ones at the same time."

He looked at Ananias after risking this bold insinuation. Ananias, however, did not react to it in any significant way. As if sunken in some thought, he merely gazed at Aquila in an absent-minded manner and answered vaguely:

"Quite so."

With the situation standing thus, Aquila thought, it would be too much of an adventure for him to stay on, no matter whether or not the other party suspected him of anything. As soon as he returned to his lodging, therefore, Aquila re-inspected his luggage packs which he had previously packed with care, and he waited for the dark to come. When it was dark enough, he sent his luggage out to the quay before him and then left the lodging trying not to draw attention as he walked toward the lakeside.

As he went around the foot of a hill on his way down to the quay accompanied by a seaman, however, Aquila suddenly saw three or four men appear from nowhere. They seemed to have followed Aquila and his company from the lodging. But Aquila had no time for further thought because they hit the seaman with an iron cudgel on the head and made him fall down on the ground. Next, they bound Aquila with a rope and dragged him away with them. (As a matter of fact, the seaman had been armed, too. But he had no chance to defend himself since the assailants fell upon him too fast. They dragged away the body of the fallen seaman, also.)

The place where the gang took Aquila and the seaman seemed to be somebody's warehouse at a spot a little way to the northwest from the outskirts of Capernaum. Although it seemed to be used as a storage place, it was not a regular building but a cave room with a door at the front where the cave opened to the outside. The gang pushed Aquila into this cave warehouse and with his arms still bound tight to his body, they left him there locking the door to the cave room from the outside.

The door was opened next morning and two men who seemed to belong with the gang that bound him up and dragged him there came in and checked to see whether nothing was amiss with the binding. Then they began to search him all over. Finding a dagger and a few jewels along with some papers, one of them growled:

"You ruffian, what else have you stolen besides these?"

Aquila raised his head and looked at the face of the young man who was speaking so unceremoniously to him. He had guessed from the first moment that he was attacked last night that it was the deed of the Blood Contract Corps. But as he was being questioned by this young man about what he had stolen, he thought that maybe this was some robbers' gang instead of the members of the Blood Contract Corps. At this thought, his hope revived and he said:

"This is all I have with me. I had taken the other things to the boat ahead of me."

"Who is the other robber who was with you?"

"Oh, he is just a man who worked with me."

"What are the things that had been taken to the boat?"

"Oh, they are various. I can bring them to you right now if you will let me go."

The two men did not ask any more questions. They left the room taking with them the things they had found on Aquila's person.

When it was almost noon, the door opened again, and this time it was Shaphan with his blood-shot eyes that looked in. Outside, several other men were talking between them about something.

Coming into the cave, Shaphan looked at Aquila's face for a few seconds without saying anything. Then he said:

"You are Aquila, aren't you?"

Aquila was distressed. He rolled his eyes to the left and right in confusion and then said weakly:

"Commander Shaphan! What brought you here?"

The angry-looking beard on Shaphan's face seemed to move a little as Shaphan said:

"Tell me in straight words what you have done lately."

"Honorable Commander, please unbind me first. I could not speak as freely as I wished to when I am bound up in this way."

Shaphan called a man into the cave and had him unbind Aquila. Even after his binding was undone, however, Aquila kept his head bent down without saying anything, as if he were sunken in some deep thought.

"You mean you won't say anything even if you were to lose your life?"

There was uncontrollable anger in the voice with which Shaphan said these words although he kept his voice low.

"Oh, no, no. Not at all. The reason I couldn't speak right away was because all this is so unexpected and absurd from my point of view."

After these preliminary words of self-explication, Aquila went on telling Shaphan the same made-up story that Shaphan had already heard through Thomas.

"Aquila, I have no time to gossip with you. And your lying will do more harm to yourself than trick me. Answer me briefly. Where is the woman whom you kidnapped?"

"The woman I kidnapped?" repeated Aquila as if he could not even understand the meaning of those words.

"Do not try to wrangle with me. Just make a confession of what you have done wrong."

"I, as a matter of fact, visited Master Ananias even today, no, excuse me for my old age forgetfulness, it was yesterday that I had visited him. Anyway, I had visited Master Ananias and heard that how Master Jair had behaved toward your lady from some time ago, and...."

"Aquila."

Shaphan's blood-shot eyes were angrier as he stopped Aquila.

"You do not need to tell me anything about Ananias, or Jair, or any other person whomsoever. Where is the lady now? Answer me just this question."

Again Aquila was silent his head bent forward a little. He sat like this some time as if he were thinking about something intently. And then he said, raising his head:

"My honored Commander, I will tell you all I have heard about the whereabouts of the lady and I will tell you just what I heard and nothing more. And in fact this was why I decided to leave Capernaum, too. I mean I wanted to go to this place where you lady is rumored to be myself and then let you know what I would have found out. Now the story I heard is the same story that Master Ananias told me yesterday, I mean the one about the pirate boats. It seems several of my men witnessed a gang of pirates seriously wounding Master Jair and kidnapping your lady. They had chased after the pirates as the latter rowed toward Gadara. There seems to have been a battle between the pirates and my men, at the end of which the latter forced the pirates to escape leaving the lady behind. My men then escorted the lady to safety. She is now in Nabatea, they say."

"When did you hear this?"

"Yesterday evening, Commander. I was very surprised and shocked by the news and made up my mind to go to my country at once and see with my own eyes how things stand. My plan was to bring the lady back here."

"Is the lady in Nabatea, then?"

"Oh, yes. I think so."

"Where in Nabatea?"

"I believe she is being protected in the palace of King Aretas."

"Then your life is tenable only so far as you can bring her back here. You should never lie or try to get out of this by any other schemes."

"I understand perfectly. But I am right now too weak from being bound up, beaten, and famished to the boot."

"I will arrange it so you will be freed, not beaten and get food and sleep. Only you should do what you can to save a precious life. You can start by writing a personal letter to King Aretas telling him to send her over immediately. You can tell him that it would be the only way Nabatea and the Blood Contract Corps to work together. Write him that there will be only deaths and perishment if he does not do so. You will have your life back when that letter becomes valid."

"I understand perfectly. As you know I am one who have spared no effort to make the cooperation between the Blood Contract Corps and Nabatea bear fruit. Even if the misfortune you have suffered on account of that iniquitous gang of pirates is unfathomable, do not turn your back on my loyalty to our friendship."

Aquila wrote a letter addressed to King Aretas that very day and offered it to Shaphan.

To His Highness King Aretas who is the Lord of the kingdom of Nabatea and the father of the tribe of Bedwin, Aquila bow two times and beg forgiveness. A month has passed since this servant left the presence of His Highness carrying His command. Even during that time I have seen His Highness' royal fame and the prosperity of our kingdom shining brighter every day. By His Highness' royal authority bright as sunshine and His Highness' grace as bounteous as sea, Aquila has kept up a close contact with the commander and members of the Blood Contract Corps in order to bring the common goal and friendship of the two countries to a fruitful end. Pray be assured, my lord, of my constant loyalty and determination to devote my whole for the fulfillment of my dreaded responsibility.

The occasion of my present writing is to beg His Highness' graceful mediation in a matter that concerns a lady who had been rescued from the kidnapping pirates by a group of Nabatean subjects who had fought valiantly with the said pirates and taken to Nabatea in order to be protected in safety. What I would like to humbly report to His Highness is the fact that the lady is no other than the lady of Commander Shaphan to whom I personally feel a highest esteem and with whom I am constantly consulting about our great affair. Assuredly, it was a happiness in misfortune that the lady could be rescued by our men. If I were so bold as to suggest my humble opinion about the matter, I think the action we Nabateans should take at hand is not so much the search and punishment for those evil kidnappers but to send the lady safely back to her own country so that our kind allies here including the honored Commander Shaphan could rest their minds at peace and concentrate on the rescuing of Baptist John as has been agreed between our two countries. I pray that His Highness would deign to understand my motive in writing this letter which is no other than repaying His Highness' boundless grace even if it should break up my flesh and bones. Lastly I touch the ground with my forehead with the prayer that His Highness' fame would spread through the seven seas and that His Highness would prosper through ten thousand years.

> The Third Day of the Month of Tammuz
> From Your servant Aquila

Shaphan had the clause "who had fought valiantly with the said pirates" struck out from the letter and then had it handed to a disciple of Baptist John to take to Nabatea without delay.

It was over two days and nights after that Shaphan heard of this criminal deed from Ananias, who had himself heard the news on the very morning of the kidnapping but could not get in touch with Shaphan because he had gone after Mary out of Chorazin. The person who had first informed Ananias about the accident was a young man that belonged to Jair's group. According to what he reported, they—the Corps members who belonged to Jair's group—were aboard a freight boat leaving Tiberius for Hippos when they noticed a suspicious scene near the eastern coast between Gerasa and Hippos. Although there was some distance between the freight boat and the spot where this questionable scene was taking place, they hurried there at full speed. The ruffians that were aboard two boats picked up only Zilpah and fled since they had no way of knowing who were on the boat that thus chased them. If the other party had decided to fight the new comers, they would have come out the winner because the men on the freight boat were not armed.

Shaphan had left Chorazin three hours before Ananias arrived there with this urgent news. He had gone to Bethsaida to look for Mary. When nobody in Bethsaida could tell him anything about Mary, he went on to Magdala. He had to spend a whole day in Magdala to placate Mary who was in one of her obstinate and hysterical fits. It was only the next night that Shaphan could come back to Chorazin taking Mary with him. It was only then that Shaphan heard the dreadful news from Ananias.

Shaphan knew instantly that this was Aquila's doing and gave out an order for Aquila's immediate capture. He also ordered a horseman to be sent after the kidnappers. Shaphan had three reasons to believe it to be Aquila's work. One was that the Blood Contract Corps had not kept their promise to take military action for the rescue of Baptist John. Two.

Aquila had not just waited for the Corps to rise up but had kept himself busy gathering information that could be used against the Corps in case of necessity. Three. The Nabateans were known to have kidnapped beautiful women of aliens to be offered up to their king. Moreover, Aquila had already met Zilpah in the boat when he had first come to see Shaphan accompanied by Thomas. And Jair had caught him hovering about Gerasa in order to find out the locality of the Corps headquarters and the residing place of Commander Shaphan.

Ananias agreed with Shaphan on principle but suggested that they postpone the capture of Aquila until they could have more definite evidence of his culpability. He suggested this because although Aquila was clearly the first suspect, he did not think it wise to take such a definitive action as capturing without an absolute evidence against him. Ananias also suggested that Aquila be watched constantly and if he should make a move to escape they capture him at once. He said that it would be more sensible than taking an action that might prove to be too hasty.

And as to letting horsemen go after the kidnappers, it would be difficult to catch up with them unless they had best quality horses, and even this, only in case their opponents had not taken advantage of carriages or speed horses. Also, unless Shaphan himself would go, how could one or a few horsemen cope with an enemy who was estimated to be no less than ten armed strong men. Also, since King Aretas was now an old man, he would not easily take an abusive act toward Zilpah after knowing to whom she belonged. Ananias' feeling was that the crisis might be gotten over with just Aquila writing that letter.

Shaphan told him that he had thought about all that himself but had not been able to decide what was the best thing to do under the circumstances. Ananias had never seen Shaphan indecisive like this in a grave situation. Shaphan seemed to be distracted on account of Mary also. Then too, the fact that his close followers such as Thomas, Judas and Jair were not with him and Hadad too was absent seemed on this occasion to have its effects on him. Shaphan spoke to Ananias again:

"Then, I will leave it to you to decide how and when Aquila should be captured. I only hope you don't lose track of him."

Shaphan volunteered to go after the Nabatean kidnappers in person.

He told Ananias to procure a horse and prepared himself for the trip which was actually no more than getting himself armed.

Mary tried to stop Shaphan when she learned of Shaphan's leaving. She listened to Shaphan while he explained how things stood and then said conclusively that in her mind Shaphan's course of action was nothing but a reckless adventure.

"If you will persist in this determination, I have a thought of my own," said Mary obstinately.

"Suppose you were in her position and she in yours," said Shaphan in a blunt and rough tone and stared at Mary with his blood-shot eyes that looked as if they were fire-lit. Still Mary was unafraid.

"I know that. You mean if I had been she, I would have told you to go at once and rescue her no matter whatever may happen to me. But I am not she. And I cannot do what she might have done."

"All right, then. It is your fault that you cannot do what she might have done and so I will not do as you wish."

"It is the same with me. I cannot do as you wish. I cannot let you take the foolish risk. I am cleverer than that. I cannot live without you."

Mary stood at the doorway as if to block it. She seemed ready to die rather than let Shaphan go.

"Get out of the way, will you?" growled Shaphan. He looked violent enough to make his way by force.

"Kill me," said Mary, her mouth twitching.

Shaphan glared at her with anger and hate for a few seconds and then said:

"You are a devil of a woman."

". . . . . ."

Mary merely glared back at him without saying anything.

"You deserve to die. You are a wicked woman of no worth."

"I can put up with even that kind of harsh talk. Anything is better than giving you up to the man-killers."

Mary's voice was calm. Shaphan realized that no cursing could have any effect on this woman. This realization somehow made him sad. He went closer to Mary and said in a tone much gentler than before:

"Mary, do you wish to ruin me? Is that what you want?"

"No. If you really have any such thought, you may kill me right away. The only reason I am stopping you is that I know too well that this is too late for you to be following after the kidnappers and that your disadvantage in making this pursuit is too obvious. I am afraid that you are perhaps making this unwise risk because of some sentimental feeling toward your wife. I mean perhaps you are so set upon taking this dangerous risk out of your remorse about having gone to Magdala after me thus losing time in pursuing your wife's kidnappers. I am not stopping you because I am jealous about you valuing her life so much."

"Oh, Mary, you are a woman. You don't know the world of men. I am three times faster than they are and can use bow and arrow ten times better than they can. You are afraid for me because you don't know these things."

"Even so, unless they were napping on half-famished horses, they would have reached their destination by this time. And in their country, those would be the ones who got chosen for quickness."

Shaphan seemed to find some logic in this argument. He spoke after a moment of thought:

"Mary, do not interfere in my important affairs too much. It is dangerous."

His voice was even gentler now.

". . . . . ."

Mary did not answer. She decided from the softened tone of his voice that he had come around to at least suspending the decision about his going.

"I will consult with the men who work with me about this matter," said Shaphan and went out of the house.

Shaphan went to see Thomas in Dariqueyea.

"There is no question that our Commander should not go after those murderers. Is not the Corps more important than Madam Zilpah? How can you leave the country when matters stand at such a critical point as now? Of course, it is too late, too. But it is only part of the reason why you should not go. The more important reason is who will guarantee your safety on the way."

They ended up by sending two men out of the Second Member rank who were outstanding in military arts. In case they could not catch up with the Nabatean kidnappers on the way, they were to go deep into the capital of the kingdom and collect information that might be useful in case of an attack.

Shaphan decided to wait out the time back at the headquarters after paying a visit to Jair in Gadara.

Jair was being treated by a Greek doctor practicing in Gadara. Although his face was sallow and cheeks sunken, he had completely regained consciousness. When he saw Shaphan, he said in his gentle voice, tears in his eyes:

"I am sorry, Commander."

"Do you remember what happened?"

"Yes," answered Jair and his face became angry with the memory of the hideous act he had witnessed and suffered. "The ruffians were all masked and did not speak. But I seemed to recognize a disciple of Baptist John among them. And judging from the fact that the ruffians knew my route, I am sure it was Aquila's wicked scheme."

"Don't worry yourself, Jair. We have that one in our hand. You guessed right. It was he who schemed everything."

When Jair heard this, he shuddered.

"I almost killed him once. Thomas stopped me from doing

so. And my judgment was right.... Where is Madam Zilpah, now?"

"It seems they took her to their king. I had our men go after them. We will hear something pretty soon."

After spending some time with Jair, Shaphan left for the headquarters. It had been quite some time since Shaphan had been back there. When he arrived at the headquarters, he saw Hadad sitting with the falcon on his knee. It seemed he was teaching him some lesson.

"How have you been, Corps Teacher?"

As Shaphan greeted him thus, the old man raised his head with its white hair and responded with words that were exactly the same as other times.

"Oh, Commander. Have you been well?"

There was nothing different in his attitude and voice.

"Have you heard about Jair and your daughter?"

Even to this question, Hadad merely answered without emotion:

"Yes. A member was here the day after the event."

Shaphan remembered what Hadad had conveyed to him through Jair about Zilpah's horoscope. He had said that Zilpah ought to be in the southeast.

"Please tell me if Zilpah is safe at present."

Hadad looked up at Shaphan without saying anything for a few seconds and then said:

"She is tired both in mind and body, but there is no change in her voice and color."

It was as if Hadad were talking about a stranger. Turning his head toward Hadad's room, Shaphan saw that the bird's nest was empty.

"When was the bird taken out?" He asked.

Hadad picked up the bird and put it on his knee and then he said:

"Say hello to the Commander."

Hadad held down the bird's head as if to teach him to offer greetings.

"When did you train the bird to play out?"

"I had not thought of it when Jair first brought this bird to me. But on the night of the event, I heard a strange sound coming from the bird cage and remembered that Zilpah had been partial to the bird. I got up and looked up at the star and saw that it was invaded by evil air. Since I have known to associate with living things like this, I at once took the bird out and started training him."

Hadad seemed more interested in the bird than in the news of Zilpah and Jair. Three days later, Shaphan left for Capernaum again.

One of the men whom Shaphan had sent after the kidnappers returned and reported that by the time they caught up with the kidnappers, they had already gone quite deep into the Nabatean domain and guards checked on the men in chase at regular intervals making it impossible to pursue further.

The report said that one of the Corps members was on his way to see King Aretas representing both Commander Shaphan and also Aquila. He would also be checking on the men who went into the palace taking Zilpah with them.

A week later, a disciple of Baptist John conveyed a letter from King Aretas addressed to Aquila.

I order my ambassador Aquila to do the following.
One. Make Commander Shaphan take an immediate military action for the rescue of Baptist John.
Two. Come back at once and give an explanation about the woman whom you requested by letter to send back there.

Aretas

Aquila was greatly disappointed when he learned from this letter that things were not going as smoothly as he had hoped that they would. He begged Shaphan to allow him to go back to Nabatea so that he might do what he could in order to rescue the lady. He said that he would consider it as gaining a second life if he be allowed to have this try. But Shaphan would not listen to his entreaty. He told Aquila that it was what he thought now but once he were back in Nabatea nobody could say for sure that he would come back. He told Aquila that the only way he could save his life would be for Zilpah to come back in safety and so the best thing for Aquila to do under the circumstances was to cooperate with them in rescuing Zilpah. As an evidence of his cooperative spirit, Shaphan made him write down in detail all military secrets and draw a map of the palace of King Aretas.

Chapter 5

The Hot Wind of Nabatea

Zilpah fainted twice on the horseback during the trip to Nabatea. When the travelling party went within seventy *ri* (= 17.5 miles) from the palace of King Aretas, she was transferred onto a wagon. As the wagon pulled into the front gate of the palace, however, she fainted for the third time.

When Zilpah opened her eyes, she found herself lying on a bed covered with a fox fur blanket. The ceiling was high and the air was fresh, and her nostrils could smell the strong fragrance of perfume.

"Are you awake, lady?"

The one who asked this question was young woman with blue ribbon. She looked like a waiting woman. She smiled as she talked to Zilpah. The language she used was the Arabian that sounded very familiar to Zilpah's ears.

"Where am I?"

Zilpah wanted to ask but found that she could not produce any sound. It was because she had not had anything but a few mouthfuls of water throughout her trip here. Seeing Zilpah moving her lips, the waiting woman offered her milk in a jade cup.

Zilpah, however, could not sit up or take the cup in her

hand to drink. After a meager attempt to raise her arm to take the cup, she gave up and let her arm fall back on the bed.

"You had better not move, lady," said the waiting woman and started to feed the milk to Zilpah with a small spoon. After taking the milk from the spoon several times, Zilpah closed her eyes again.

From the next day on, Zilpah started eating eggs, raisins, oranges, and from the third day on, she ate a small amount of pigeon meat and lamb, too.

"Look in the mirror, lady. You look quite healthy, now."

There was a stone mirror the size of half the human body hanging on a marble pillar to which the waiting woman was pointing.

Zilpah had never seen such a large and fine mirror up to now, and she felt her heart pounding from excitement as she looked at her face in the mirror.

"Thank you for showing me that," said Zilpah to the waiting woman.

"Oh, no. This mirror has been hanging in this room for some time," explained the waiting woman with a smile.

After a week, Zilpah's health was almost completely recovered. The waiting woman brought an embroidered robe to Zilpah and told her to change into it.

"What is this?" Zilpah asked with a little alarm. The waiting woman smiled and said:

"This is an embroidered robe made with Persian silk. If you put this on, you become the mistress of this palace."

"The mistress of this palace?" asked Zilpah in a greater alarm.

"Yes."

"Why would I become the mistress of this palace?"

"Because you will be the queen of our King."

"The queen of your king?"

Zilpah's eyes opened wide.

"Why do you speak like that? Are you not glad to be the queen?"

" . . . . . . "

Zilpah sat dumbfounded for a second and then said:

"I cannot become the mistress of this palace. I will return this robe."

Zilpah shoved the robe toward the waiting woman.

Just then another waiting woman came into the room and said:

"It is the order of the Head Attendant to the King that you change into this quickly and come out at once, lady."

Zilpah turned to her and said:

"I do not wish to change into this robe, and I cannot become the mistress of this palace."

The second waiting woman seemed a little surprised at what Zilpah said.

"It is not so, lady. You do not become the mistress of this palace just because you put this robe on. This is an attire one who is found pleasing to His Majesty wears when she meets His Majesty for the first time," said the second woman. At this the first waiting woman opened her mouth again and said as if to placate Zilpah:

"When I said that you would become the mistress of this palace when you put this on, I was only saying what was in my mind. It was no more than that. So, please change into this robe now."

But Zilpah's attitude was adamant.

"Even so, I do not wish to change into this robe. If I am bound by law to meet the king, I will see him in the clothes I am wearing."

The two waiting women consulted between themselves in whispers and then one of them went out of the room. A little while later the Head Attendant came in. He was a tall man with a decorated helmet on his head.

"Lady, why don't you change into the new robe?"

The Head Attendant's black moustache twitched as if they were bird's wings as he said this.

Zilpah watched his face without saying anything and then

said in her cold, spring-water voice:

"I never asked for a new robe."

"Even if you did not ask for it, you must wear it since it was His Majesty who gave it to you."

"I never said that I would change clothes." Zilpah spoke in an even tone.

"I ask you personally, lady. Please change into this robe."

" . . . . . . "

Zilpah pretended not to hear him. When the Head Attendant repeated what he had said, Zilpah said shortly:

"It is not mine."

The Head Attendant looked at Zilpah with angry eyes for a while and then left the room. The waiting women went and came for several times until it was conveyed to Zilpah that she could come out to the presence of the king even as she was, in her own clothes, that is.

Attended by four waiting women, Zilpah went to see King Aretas. King Aretas was an old man with grey beard, a crown decorated with strings of yellow jade and pearl, and a long staff of white amber in hand. He was sitting on his throne covered with the tiger coat from India.

"Oh, you are far more precious than all other treasures I already have," said the King with pleasure when he laid his eyes on Zilpah.

"But why is it that she is not wearing the silk robe I bestowed on her?" He asked the Head Attendant. Embarrassed, he said:

"Er. . . , it happened this way, my Lord. That is, owing to her young age, the lady did not wish to soil so valuable a robe by putting it on."

"It is a praiseworthy attitude," said the king although there was no way of knowing how he understood the quick lie the Head Attendant gave him.

"Prepare a bath water of milk and perfume, and escort the lady to it."

This was an usually generous entertainment on the part of

the king.

Zilpah returned to her room again escorted by four waiting women.

There was a great commotion in the palace when Zilpah refused to take the bath which the king had ordered at such a great expense. The Head Attendant came to Zilpah many a time to entreat and threaten because it was upon him to make this woman take the bath and wait on the king in his bed. Every time, he came, however, Zilpah gave him one short icy answer: No, I do not wish to.

Finally, the Head Attendant called in the soldiers and said:

"Take this woman to the dungeon. Lock her up and watch closely until I give you another order."

Zilpah was led by the soldiers to the dark, cold, and damp dungeon. The floor, although it was originally paneled with wood, was now covered with so much dust and filth and was so damp that there were all kinds of bugs and insects crawling over it, and it was impossible for Zilpah to sit or lie on it. The air, too, was so rank and foul that she could not breathe. Zilpah spent the night without any sleep.

About the noon next day, Zilpah was taken to the presence of the king again.

"Listen. I will order a bath water of milk and perfume once more today. What do you say?"

" . . . . . . "

"What do you mean by saying nothing, is it no or is it yes?"

" . . . . . . "

"If you do not obey me here, you will receive a bad treatment."

As soon as the king said this, Zilpah was again taken to the dungeon.

When this was repeated for three days, Zilpah had become so weak that she could not control her body. She let herself fall on the foul and damp bug-ridden floor. Just then, however, she was again taken to the room with the large mirror on the marble pillar and was lying down on the bed covered with the fox fur blanket. It was made known to her that this would be repeated endlessly until she should change her mind.

It was when Zilpah was taken to the dungeon for the third time. As she was turning a corner of the marble-floored corridor, she saw a soldier walking toward her from the opposite direction. He looked about thirty years old, had a square face, and was wearing a soldier's uniform on which many stars were shining.

"What are you doing?"

The soldier said sharply to the soldiers who were leading Zilpah.

"This is the order of the Head Attendant."

The man looked at Zilpah with sympathy when he heard the answer and then asked in a voice lower than before:

"Who is she?"

"It seems she is a Jew."

"Why is a Jewish woman here?"

"We do not know, sir."

"Why are you taking her to the dungeon?"

"It is because she disobeyed His Majesty."

". . . . . ."

Again the man looked a long while at her face and then went past without saying anything more.

Five days passed after this. It was the day when Zilpah would again be taken to the dungeon. Zilpah was lying on the bed with the fox fur blanket when the waiting women came in and whispered meaningfully among themselves. Zilpah was by nature indifferent to gossip but she now listened to what they were whispering because their strange attitude attracted her curiosity.

— The prince and the Head Attendant had a quarrel, they say.

— It was not just a quarrel. I hear that they even pulled their swords.

— When do you think the prince saw her?

— In the corridor the other day, it seems.

— The prince too must have gone for her completely, the way things stand.

— Besides, the prince and the Head Attendant never agreed with each other.

— Even so, he should not meddle with a woman whom his father the king took fancy to.

— Who would the king take side with, do you think? Will it be the prince or the Head Attendant?

— I say the Head Attendant. When the elder prince caused displeasure to the king on account of a woman, the king had the Head Attendant kill off the prince, don't you remember?

— But the Head Attendant is only a nephew to the king while prince is his own son. I doubt that he will take side with the Head Attendant and have his own son killed.

— But the prince dared covet a woman whom the king wanted.

— Do you think this will end peacefully this time?

— It all depends on how the king will take it. Come to think of it, the king is now a very old man. He may take the matter benevolently.

— No, I don't think so. They say man gets more particular about women as they get old.

— Do you think then that the prince will die this time also or escape from the kingdom?

— Maybe that's guessing too far.

— Yes . . . and besides, the prince has quite a few soldiers on his side. He may not be beaten so easily this time.

The waiting women did not seem to care whether or not Zilpah heard. Or, they seemed to be whispering like that as a means of giving a hint to Zilpah. They threw quick glances toward Zilpah as they whispered on.

Suddenly Zilpah was afraid uncontrollably. The fright seemed to shake her from inside her heart.

"Why do you tremble like that, lady?" said one of the waiting women coming closer to Zilpah.

"I am afraid."

Zilpah's lips trembled as she said this in a low shaky voice. The waiting women stopped whispering all at once when they heard Zilpah and looked at each other.

Just at this moment, the door of the room opened abruptly and the Head Attendant rushed in with a very angry face.

"I will kill you if you don't listen to me this time. I would kill you even at this moment if it had not been for the command of His Highness. I will give you just one more day's time of repentence. Now, get up at once and go to the dungeon."

The black moustaches of the Head Attendant twitched on for a few seconds after he finished speaking. And after that, the soldiers came upon Zilpah and took her out of the room.

On this night, however, Zilpah heard outside the room where she was locked up a shuffling sound of people in fight and then she heard the door of the prison room break and several men disguised in black leap into the room. Then she was being carried away into the darkness hurriedly. Zilpah could not grasp much of what was happening. But from the vague impression she could gather, she seemed to have seen or felt fire flames rising and many people fighting and then she thought she heard many a woman screaming as they were hurt and some hard things broke.

It was a tented compartment of the same palace but quite a distance away from where Zilpah had been that the men took Zilpah to. The fighting still seemed to continue outside. There were shriekings, sounds of stone walls falling, wagons running, arrows swishing, metal things hitting against each other, high trumpet sounds, and the booming of drums. This continued throughout the night and even after the dawn came the sounds came intermittently.

It was only after the sun rose high that the fighting stopped. Then there was the sound of the trumpets and the soldiers parading. After this there was the sound of cheers.

"Our victory! We won! Long Live His Highness!" cried one of the soldiers that were watching Zilpah.

Although she had heard the waiting women whispering the evening before, Zilpah did not know that this was a fight between the prince and the king for which they both staked their lives. Moreover, she had no way of knowing that over the night, the king, his Head Attendant, and all the subjects and soldiers on their side, fell in blood and the palace now belonged only to the prince.

Three days later, Zilpah was moved back to the room with the stone mirror on the marble pillar where she was residing in the first place. Soon after, the square-faced man in soldier's uniform whom she had met in the corridor some time ago came into the room. After entering the room, he looked at Zilpah's face without a word just as he had done the first time he saw Zilpah. Then he went out of the room.

The prince appeared again the next day. He stood at the doorway and said in a low voice:

"Zilpah."

". . . . . ."

Zilpah raised her head without saying anything.

The prince walked up to the bed on which Zilpah was sitting up.

"It was when you were being taken down to the dungeon that I first saw you. After that I set out at once to find out how you came to be here in this palace, why you were being taken to the dungeon, and also who you were. My first entreaty to the king my father was that he send you back to Galilee. I saw how beautiful you were and yet I wanted you to be sent back to your husband Commander Shaphan because I thought it was important for the good of my country Nabatea. When the king refused to listen to my entreaty and became angry with me, the Head Attendant schemed to kill me. So I killed the king, his Head Attendant, and all of their followers. It was to save Nabatea and myself. When I saw your face again after all this happened, my heart changed about sending you back to Galilee. I am going to make you my second queen. I know that you refused the bath of milk and perfume. I also know that you refused to put on the silk robe that would have made you the mistress of this palace. I will therefore kill you when you don't obey me, the way I killed my father, his Head Attendant and all their followers."

The prince kneeled himself in front of Zilpah as he finished his speech.

"Do not kill me."

Zilpah's voice trembled as she said this.

"That is my very wish. And that is why I am on my knees like this."

The prince took Zilpah by the wrist. Zilpah shook his hand off, however, and said in her spring-water voice:

"I am wife of Commander Shaphan. I cannot become your queen."

The prince got up and went out of the room even before she finished her words.

That night Zilpah was moved out of the room with stone mirror and the marble pillar to a tented compartment different from the one she had been taken to before. And it was there that prince made Zilpah his queen regardless of the words and movements of resistance Zilpah put up.

Next morning, the prince said to Zilpah:

"It was last night that I killed you. It is a thing of the past. You must live as my queen from now on."

He called in the waiting women and ordered them to wait on Zilpah as on the queen.

Zilpah was moved to the inner palace that very day. There were a ceiling more gorgeous, a marble pillar more magnificent and a stone mirror even larger than there were in her former place of temporary residence. Also, the bed on which she lay the whole day after being moved there was decorated with all kinds of valuable things of luxury.

In the evening Zilpah let herself persuaded by the waiting women to take bath of milk and perfume and also ate oranges and eggs. Then she went, succumbing to the waiting women's lead placidly, to join the prince in his bed. And, moreover, she now did whatever the prince or the waiting women wished without resisting. (This attitude was adopted by Zilpah from the moment she was derobed by the prince for the first time.)

From her facial expression or behavior, she seemed no longer resentful or sorry about what happened to her. This is not to say, however, that she showed any sign of contentment or satisfaction.

The prince, however, seemed to long to see a happy face and an attitude of content on her.

"I did not take from my father the kingdom of Nabatea. I took just you."

The prince said these things at times when they slept in the same bed. But Zilpah never showed even a shadow of a smile.

"Aren't you glad, even now, to be the queen?"

The prince (or rather the king) asked her once only to hear Zilpah say in her spring-water cold voice:

"I am not a queen."

"What are you, then?"

"I am the wife of Commander Shaphan."

She seemed prepared for the worst when she said this to the prince.

"That part of you is dead already, isn't it? You now live as the queen to the king."

"It is something I do not know."

"Do you mean to say, then, that you are not mine? Do you say that you are not my queen? What is it that you know, then?"

"I am the wife of Commander Shaphan. It is a thing decided by my father. From the teaching of the stars...."

"The teaching of the stars?"

"I cannot become your queen unless my father decide it for me. That is what I know."

The attitude with which Zilpah responded to the prince in this conversation was most natural and dignified.

The prince did not take offence at what Zilpah said and said with an expression which could be called a happy face rather than an aggravated one:

"It is not important."

He then laughed heartily and said again:

"You are a fine queen. You have excellent qualities of a queen."

He showed his respect and attention by holding her by the hand for a while and then went out.

Time passed in this way and then one day, the palace was again thrown into a turmoil. There were armed soldiers, horses, trumpet sounds throughout the palace and courtiers gathered around the king (or the prince) and talked among themselves. The waiting women too looked alarmed and continuously looked out of the windows. Zilpahwanted to ask them what it was that happened. She had made it her practice, however, not to ask anybody anything or speak unless she was spoken to. (This was something she started after she was forced into becoming the queen.) So she now controlled her desire to find out what was happening and contented herself by making some conjectures on her own. She had at first thought that the former followers of the former king and the Head Attendant had risen up in rebellion against the prince and his subjects. But her thought soon changed its course. It was because she seemed to hear from the whispering voices of the waiting women the name Shaphan once or twice. Would it be, then, Shaphan, who came to rescue me with his men, she wondered. Still, she kept her mouth shut and did not venture a question.

That night, the king came to her and said:

"Commander Shaphan has come to take you home. Do you wish to go back to being the wife of a robber, queen?"

"I am the wife of Commander Shaphan."

Zilpah's answer was the same as so many other answers she

had given the king up to the time.

"Would you go back if I permitted?"

"Yes."

"Do you think I will let you go?"

". . . . . ."

"Tell me if you think I will let you go."

"I think you will."

Zilpah did not hesitate as she answered. But the king turned suddenly angry and said:

"Would I return my queen to a robber? The queen that I had taken from my father the former king by force? You whom I have made mine by killing my father, his Head Attendant, and numerous other men?"

Zilpah did not seem perturbed, however, and said:

"You said yourself that you had asked your father to return me to Galilee, did you not?"

"I have changed my mind after I could make the country and you mine. Besides, when I first suggested your return to your home to my father, I may not have meant it really. I may have wanted, even then, to own you for myself. Maybe I had already made up my mind when I saw you first in that corridor."

"Your mind is your own, prince. But I gave my mind in the presence of my father, to Commander Shaphan. That is the only mind I know I have. I cannot, therefore, become your queen until Commander Shaphan agrees to it in the presence of my father."

"Unfortunately, however, the robbers have all retreated. They were pitiably chased by my horsemen. I think you will be happy as my queen yet."

The king seemed to deride Shaphan by saying this. But outside the palace wall, the fighting seemed still to be going on. The sound of horses rushing and people shouting and moving about did not cease. Also, from time to time, one could hear the swishing sounds of arrows flying somewhere close enough to the palace. The ones outside the wall did not come over the wall, however.

From the next day, the fighting seemed to abate during the daytime.

A strange thing happened about this time, however. It was that her food was getting poorer by the day. When about a week passed in this way, the faces of the waiting women were sunken into an unconcealable gloom and uneasiness. It seemed the supplies for living had become scarce even within the king's palace. It seemed that supplies could not be gotten from the outside.

Shaphan along with seventy armed men had infiltrated into the domains of the kingdom of Nabatea after well over a month had passed since the kidnapping of Zilpah. Shaphan had seven teams consisted of seven men each watch different passways around the city and led the remaining twenty one men for an attack against the city itself. The reason that Shaphan decided on having twenty one men join him for the attack was merely that he wanted to find out the goings on inside the fortress and not to make such a bold attack with so small a force. This was why they made a quick retreat when they had first made their attack on the western gate and were chased back by the cavalry. When they succeeded in making a part of the stone wall fall, also, they had not pursued the attack but came out back. This was all because they had found out how large an army and supply of arms there were inside the fort.

Shaphan had the men dig caves and holes in the mountain slopes and the hills around the city and let them stay inside them for the most part during the day. Then during the nights, Shaphan led the men into an attack or a number of attacks. The aim of this strategy was to cut the passage in and out of the city. By this way, Shaphan thought, they could stop the supply of daily necessities into the city and by so doing threaten the life and energy of the fighting force inside the fort. Shaphan knew well enough even if his men who numbered only about a hundred were outstanding in every way, they could not fight against the whole army of a kingdom through any outright and quick method.

It was not only in the number of men that Shaphan's army was inferior to the Nabatean army. One grave handicap they faced was the fact that there was not any forestry aropund the Nabatean capital to hide several dozens of horses. The result was that Shaphan had to have about twenty horses perform the duties of guarding, collecting information and liaison work.

After some time passed, the characteristics of both armies were clearly perceivable. The Nabateans' advantages were that they had their own fortress, large army and horses, while the strong points of the army of Shaphan were that each man was outstanding in military arts and that they had much mobility. The Nabateans had about thirty horsemen attack the enemy during the daytime and Shaphan had his men meet this attack from various hiding places in the mountains and hills from where they counter-attacked the approaching enemy. Nabateans did not try to pursue their opponents up the mountains or hills because their initial attempt to do so had failed miserably. At that first attack up the slope to reach the enemy hiding place, their advance cavalry of five or six had fallen by the very first arrows shot by Shaphan's men. Then the rest of the horses and men had turned back hurriedly and made a retreat. It was on this occasion that Karhams, the most valiant of the Nabatean soldiers asked to fight a man-to-man battle with Shaphan. He had got off from his horse and raising his sword high in the air declared:

"I am Karhams, the Commander-in-Chief of Nabatean cavalry. Which of you will fight me in a one-to-one sword match?"

Shaphan had responded at once in a high tone:

"I will fight ten of you at one time," said Shaphan and stepped forward. He was stopped, however, from going any further toward his enemy by Zechariah of Ophrah who was standing beside.

"Leave a man of that sort to me," he said.

Zechariah then pulled his sword and went out to meet the enemy Commander without time for any one to stop him.

The two men fought on a lower hill while the Nabatean soldiers watched from the road and foot of the mountain and Shaphan's army looked down from their places on the mountain. Karhams whose height was six feet and three inches seemed disappointed to find Shaphan's second man so small-boned and puny as Zechariah looked. He bellowed:

"Send out your Commander. I cannot fight with a weakling like you."

"Wouldn't my Commander come out if you should beat me? Don't talk gossip but get ready at once to take my sword."

Karhams seemed to change his mind about not fighting Zechariah when he heard what the latter had to say in his cool provocative voice. He took the fighting pose as if he were going to dispose of Zechariah quickly and proceed to fight Shaphan as Zechariah had advised. Their swords met about ten times without any serious result and from this point on Karhams seemed to lose control visibly.

Zechariah was next only to Shaphan among the members of the Blood Contract Corps in the art of sword fighting. When the swords met for the sixth or seventh time, blood flowed from the arm and shin of Karhams and he dropped his sword on to the ground. At the same instant, he stepped back and threw his dagger over to Zechariah. The dagger was stuck below Zechariah's left shoulder. Karhams tried to pick up his sword from the ground counting Zechariah to be inactive at least for the second. Before he had time to put his hand to the sword on the ground, however, the tip of Zechariah's sword pushed into his side and he fell. Just then Shaphan's voice was heard from up the mountain:

"Do not kill him off."

Zechariah then turned his face toward the Nabateans down the hill and shouted:

"Take your commander back."

Zechariah returned to his post on the mountain after this.

The Nabateans did not pursue the army of Shaphan up the hill or mountain side after this event. Also they avoided a battle of infantry.

The fight turned gradually to one over the supply of food and materials. The Nabateans had to have several dozens of men secure the passage of the supplies into the city and almost all the trading businesses of the kingdom were in a paralyzed state. It was because Shaphan's army that had captured all the higher terrains surrounding the city watched the passes to the city closely and interfered with the traffic.

This kind of warfare continued about a fortnight, when Thomas came to see Shaphan along with Mary who carried the falcon in her arms. Thomas explained first the business of his visit. He said that he had come to inform Shaphan of the recent news of Jesus and then to see how the Corps members were faring in Nabatea. Shaphan stopped Thomas with this question:

"Was it Corps Teacher Hadad who sent that bird?"

"Yes, it was. He did not say anything except that he wanted you to bring the falcon back with you when you return."

Shaphan did not seem to understand. He stared at Thomas' face inquisitively for a while and then said:

"I have no choice. You had better put him on a branch of the oak tree back there."

Shaphan seemed to find the appearance of the falcon bothersome. He remembered Hadad's order to bring back the bird when he returned, however, and along with Mary, took the trouble of taking in the bird into his abode and getting acquainted with him so that the bird would not go away.

The falcon flew up several times a day and disappeared somewhere but returned to his branch of oak tree again.

Mary said that the reason she came with Thomas to Shaphan was that she wanted to help Shaphan in his fight against the Nabateans. The basis of this motivation seemed to be that in the time before she went around with the Roman centurion, Mary had frequented the palace of King Herod (Antipas) as a woman performer of lute. King Herod had not yet gone completely over to Herodias and still had something to do with Queen Anna who was daughter to the former king Aretas. Mary was somehow favored by this queen and according to the subtle insinuation Mary made to Shaphan, Herod himself was not indifferent to Mary's charms. Since Herod was already gone over to Herodias from Anna for the most part, Anna seemed to take Herod's interest in Mary as a favorite sign because it would mean pushing Herodias back from Herod even so much. Queen Anna, therefore, acted as Mary's protector in her relationship with the king. This plan failed, however, because of Herodias' watchfulness and the appearance of the Roman officers on the scene.

Even after this, however, the friendship between Anna and Mary continued, until Anna was chased out of Herod's court and returned to her father in Nabatea. Mary said that Queen Anna would be glad even now to see her. Since Queen Anna was said to have supported the prince in his taking of the throne if indirectly, she would have a say with the new king, and Mary might be able to help Zilpah out of their hands if she should negotiate through Anna, Mary said. Even if this plan should fail, said Mary, she would be coming back with all sorts of information about the inside things of the palace and the city, and therefore there would be no loss to be suffered on the part of Shaphan.

When Shaphan heard Mary out, he commented with eyebrows knitted in displeasure that in his opinion all that was a dumb thing to try.

"Why do you make light of another person's ability? Why are you so stubborn?" protested Mary.

"What ability? Who can be sure that you too will not be caught by them?"

"Why should I be caught by them?"

"When they find out who you are. . . ."

"Even among the members of your Corps, only two men know who I am. How, then, can these people would know? Even if, as you fear, there are some among the disciples of Baptist John or Jesus that suspect our relationship, we are very far from them all, are we not? As it is, we are in a different world from where they all are."

"Even so, I cannot let you go because it would mean more risk than possible gain."

"The risk is small and possible gain is very big. Suppose I get caught by them. Do you think I would be acting their queen?"

"What if it is forced against one's will?"

"In the worst situation, I will choose death. I will stick a knife into the throat of the prince, set the palace on fire and escape as well as I can. If it fails, I will merely kill myself."

"But for me to lose you would be a loss greater than any gain I could have by the death of the prince or burning of the palace."

"That's why I said in the worst situation. But we do not need imagine only a worst situation. Please allow me this once to do as I wish. I am not a woman who would lose in this kind of a dealing. Besides, think of the fact that all this may not have come to this extremity if you had not followed me over to Magdala. I do not love her but I will take her back to you no matter how difficult it is so that you may have your courage, hope and victory. And I am also duty-bound to do it."

Shaphan could not argue with her any more. Although he was averse to the scheme from the bottom of his heart, he did not say so but told Mary that he would think it over again.

The next day (Thomas had already left for Galilee by this time), Shaphan heard a very bad news. It was that the Roman army stationed in Jerusalem were on their way to Nabatea in order to suppress the 'gang of robbers' that had invaded the kingdom. (The gang of robbers was of course the Blood Contract Corps.) Shaphan's face darkened at hearing this news. He became extremely fretful. His one great fear was that they should be made to fight against the Romans right here and now.

"You see. You should at times listen to me, too. Anna still thinks I am a close friend of the Roman soldiers. If I should ask to meet Anna at a time like this, what kind of reception would she give me? The Nabateans will beg me to put in a good word with the Romans and make them come here quickly. Don't you think so?"

Mary's eyes shone with imagination as she talked thus to Shaphan. This time, Shaphan seemed to find her persuation somewhat sensible.

"Try what you can, then. But do not forget these three things. One. Do not let them suspect your relationship with us. Two. If you cannot take Zilpah with you, collect what information you can, as you yourself suggested, and pull out as quickly as possible. Three. Do not be too subtle or confidential with Zilpah because although she is a very bright woman, she is also very straight. In short, you are to be a superb actress and should under no circumstances go slack in your performance."

"I understand. Now give me a dagger. I want to carry one inside my clothes just in case."

"Forget about the dagger but carry that falcon. I think Hadad sent it for her daughter. You can say you are bringing it to the queen as a present. It will sound natural enough."

"That is a very fine idea. It will also help me in my acting."

Mary was suspected of being a spy of the Blood Contract Corps by the Nabateans right from the time she met a group of cavalry outside the city wall. She told them she was from Judaea and then exposed her relationship with Anna and explained the purpose of her visit to Queen Anna after such a long time. The cavalry seemed to think all this suspicious. They called her 'a strange woman' or 'a dangerous guest' when they sent her on to the police headquarters.

"Where do you live?"

"Magdala, district of Galilee of Judaea."

"You come from the same place as the Blood Contract Corps, then."

"Blood Contract Corps? I have never heard the name before."

"What made you come here from Galilee?"

"I came with my husband who was taking one of his business trips."

"Who is your husband?"

"A Roman soldier."

"His rank?"

"Centurion."

"Name?"

"Titus Lupas."

"So, where is your husband?"

"In Arabia."

"Why are you here?"

"To see Queen Anna."

"How did you come to know Queen Anna?"

"She was very kind to me when she was in Tiberias of Galilee as Queen of King Herod."

Mary's attitude was resolute and dignified. There seemed to be only one thing to be done: to arrange a meeting between her and the queen. But the police postponed it yet. And it was rather because they were thinking that what Mary was saying was true for the most part. What bothered them was the fact that she was Jewish and that she came from Galilee. Also the fact that she was so unusually beautiful seemed to have some story behind it. They could not, however, lock a person up for many days just because she came from Galilee, in so far as there was no specific evidence that she was related with the Blood Contract Corps. They decided to keep Mary under their custody for the night and arrange a meeting between her and Queen Anna in the morning.

Mary was led out of the dark place where she had been kept overnight to a bright and clean tented compartment. She was asking for something to feed the falcon when Princess Anna came in. She was a shortish woman nearing her forty with a yellowish complexion and was quite charming. She came in, attended by two waiting women. As she looked on Mary, her round and pretty face shone with delight.

"Mary, what brought you here?"

She seemed overjoyed to see Mary. She came closer to her.

"It has been a long time since I last had the pleasure of waiting on you, Your Highness. I have come here because I have long wanted to know how you were faring." Mary said holding the falcon with one arm.

"Oh, how charming! But why did you not come to me directly?"

Before Mary had time to answer Anna, however, the soldier who had questioned her whispered something into Mary's ears. Seeing this Anna said in a high voice:

"Stop it. What right do you people have to detain my guest from seeing me? You did wrong."

"Forgive us, Your Highness. This happened because we are in war right now. I pray you overlook our mistake with generosity."

Although he was thus apologizing in meek words, the suspicion he and the others had for Mary did not go away. They gave Mary up to Anna but issued an order to restrict Mary's activity within the inner palace and to watch her day and night.

After presenting Anna with the blue jade ornament she had prepared in advance, Mary bowed to Anna formally and said:

"When I heard that your ladyship had moved from Tiberius to Machaerus, I wished to go there and see you. And then, to my surprise, I heard that you went back to Nabatea."

"It was very nice of you to think of me in that way. There are no people as endearing as Galileans."

A simple and unsuspecting person, Anna seemed overwhelmed by Mary's friendship. She began to recite the names of the people she used to know in her time in Galilee as well as she could remember and seemed to feel nostalgic about her life in Galilee in general.

"The wife of Chuza too is a kind person. Although she never said a kind word about you, Mary. Salome too is not as vicious as her mother."

Mary wanted to ask Anna about Chuza wife not saying a kind word about herself but decided not to because it was a thing past. Above all, Mary wanted to hear from Anna's mouth the news of Zilpah as soon as possible.

"Your Highness," Mary started in this way without quite knowing how she was going to bring it up. "What is the Blood Contract Corps, do you know?"

"The Blood Contract Corps?" asked Anna in an alarm.

"The police asked when I was with them last night about the Blood Contract Corps. They seemed to think I am from the same district as this Corps — they said so when I told them I was from Magdala in the district of Galilee — and asked me if it was not so."

Suddenly Anna drew Mary to her as if in an embrace and whispered in her ear:

"We are in war now."

"In war? Are you then fighting against King Herod?"

"No. We are fighting against this Blood Contract Crops from Galilee. ... It was for this reason only that you were detained by our police yesterday."

"What a pity! That you should be having a war with Galileans!"

Hearing Mary say this Anna embraced her anew and said:
"And it is all because of a woman."

"Because of a woman? Is she a Galilean also?"

"It seems she is wife of the leader of this Blood Contract something, or rather the gang of robbers."

"What did she do? How could this woman start a war?"

"It seems our soldiers had stolen this woman for my father the late king. And then her husband has given up so much to take her back."

"Oh, is that how things stand? I did not dream that anything like that was happening and came here with the sole wish to see you again, your ladyship."

"How very kind of you! And you suffered so at the hands of our police!"

"It was nothing. I was detained only for one day."

"But you must have suffered much."

"No, I didn't. But I am worried about this war. Why can't your soldiers chase back this gang of robbers?"

"Oh, no. That's not how it is. They fight twice as well as our soldiers. How can we chase them out of this kingdom when they are such good fighters?"

"Is there a gang of robbers who are as reckless as that? Why don't you hand them back this woman, then?"

"Would the king listen? The First Queen is doing her best to get rid of the woman on this occasion but the king shows no sign of giving up."

Mary woke up at the word 'the first queen' because she seemed to see hope there.

"The First Queen?"

"The queen before this one, I mean. The relatives of this first queen has much power in the palace right now."

"Couldn't they talk to the king, then?"

"They dare not because they are afraid they would cause the king's displeasure by talking to him against his wish."

"Does the king love her that much?"

"Don't men act alike when they lay their eyes on a pretty woman?"

"Is she that good-looking, then? I would like to meet her."

"It is not difficult. I will arrange for you to meet her."

Anna seemed ready to arrange such a meeting right away. Mary was distressed. It was because she would be ruined in case Zilpah whom Shaphan called 'straight' should let it known that she and Mary knew each other by greeting her or in some such ways.

"I am quite tired now. I would not wish to meet anybody for the present. I would be grateful if I could just rest beside your ladyship for a couple of days."

"Please do that. I will arrange the meeting for later."

Anna had her servants prepare a room for Mary and even gave her a waiting woman to attend.

Mary asked the waiting woman that was alotted to her in a sweet voice.

"What is your name?"

"I am called Abiral."

"Abiral, it's a pretty name. Let us be friends, all right?"

Mary took out a jewel from her bosom and gave it to the woman.

The waiting woman exclaimed when she held the jewel in her hand:

"Oh, princess, this is too good for me to have."

She stood in a daze for some while with the jewel in her hand.

"Abiral, you please me but you should not call me princess."

"But you are more beautiful than our princess. Are you a queen, then? Maybe, you will become a queen."

The waiting woman talked by herself in excitement.

"How can one become a queen that easily?"

"Oh, yes, one can. One can become a queen if she has a beautiful face. And you are more beautiful than many a queen."

"Oh, that reminds me. I heard from Her Highness Anna a while ago about the new queen. Is she really that beautiful?"

"Oh, yes. And that is why the prince killed the king his father. To take her from him, I mean. Not that she is glad about it, either.... Oh, but even she is not as beautiful as your ladyship."

"I am too old and not much to look at, anyway. But your new queen seems to be quite a beauty. Her Highness Anna said she would arrange a meeting between me and the queen. But I would like to see her somehow on my own."

"Shall I go and ask her?"

"Oh, no. I would rather prefer to send a few words to her in writing. Writing a letter may make her curious about me the way I am curious about her."

Mary tried to sound casual and nonchalant as she talked to the waiting woman in this way.

"Give me the letter then. I will take it to the queen at once."

"All right. I think it is the best thing to do. But not now. I am too tired now. I would like to rest for a while."

That night Mary composed a letter to be sent to Zilpah.

I came here to rescue you. Pretend to meet me for the first time. If my identity is exposed, I will lose my life at once. Do not show this letter to any waiting woman but burn it at once.

Mary

Mary, however, did not give this letter to the waiting woman. She kept it inside her bosom and spoke to her again.

"You must have heard from Queen Anna, but on my way to see her, I was captured by the police and had a bad time. It was explained to me that this happened because it is a war time here now." "It seems Queen Anna punished the soldiers severely for that."

The waiting woman sounded as if she too had a resentment for the soldiers.

"Well, maybe it was because of that. But they went quite far, you know. In fact, that is why I hesitate to send the letter to the new queen. Because in case the soldiers find this out, they are sure to raise another racket like the other time."

"One does not need to go around among the soldiers to ask for permission. I will take it to her without anybody knowing...."

"But things of this world are not that simple. The waiting women in that quarters may ask you questions. They would like to know whose and what kind of letter it is. Then the story may leak out somehow and the police may come to me with an accusation. They may find fault with me for sending suspicious letters — because they would find everything suspicious — and end up by locking me again in their prison room."

"I will take it personally to the new queen. And I will keep it a secret from everybody."

"But it is so difficult to keep a secret. Suppose you tell Her Highness Anna about it, unawares, that is, and through her ladyship it may reach the ears of the police. Not that her ladyship would ever tell on me. But she just might mention the letter to somebody without knowing it may harm me."

"That is quite likely. But it all depends on my determination. If I decide to keep a secret, it stays a secret."

"I am glad to hear that. So, we will keep our little secret between ourselves, all right?"

"Do not worry."

"Oh, I am so glad. What prize should I give you this time?"

Mary gave the letter to the waiting woman that night. Two days later, Princess Anna had a food table prepared in her quarters and invited Zilpah and Mary.

Mary was surprised to find Zilpah whom she had not seen for a few months looking even prettier than before. Part of the improvement could be the fine clothes and jewelry Zilpah was wearing as a queen. But even so, it was more correct to say that her inborn beauty and nobility suited this kind of elegant outfit.

"I am so honored to meet you, beautiful queen."

Although Mary meant to offer her the customary greetings, she could not help a smile which could have been taken as sneer.

Zilpah, however, did not seem to be interested in deciphering the complex psychology or meaningful smile of Mary. She merely looked at Mary with a face devoid of expression. Zilpah played dumb from the first to the end of this interview.

Anna seemed to interpret this attitude of Zilpah as natural. She seemed to think that Zilpah was acting dumb and maintained an expressionless face in order to keep her dignity as a queen. Mary, on the other hand, thought that Zilpah was putting on this act because she had asked her to pretend not knowing her. She could not guess that this was Zilpah's constant mood after she was per force made a queen.

When the feast was over and Zilpah was getting ready to go back to her palace, Mary offered her the falcon.

"This is my offering to Your Highness. Please accept it as a token of our meeting."

"Oh, thank you."

This was the first time she spoke throughout the meeting. She seemed quite surprised to see the bird. Only then, her expressionless face seemed to become somewhat more alive. Then while the waiting women were not looking, she turned herself to Mary and whispered:

"Rescue me."

"Don't worry." Mary, too, said in a barely audible whisper.

That night, Mary talked with the waiting woman about Zilpah.

"Your new queen is like an angel. I wish I could see her even just once a day."

"That should not be too difficult to arrange."

"It is difficult. So I want you to go in my place and offer her greetings for me."

Three days after, Zilpah invited Anna and Mary to a feast. This time there were the new king and a war captain related with his first wife named Dimon present. (Mary had requested Zilpah to arrange their presence at the feast.)

Mary's beauty was such that it showed up in a company of many people like now. (Maybe this was because her figure was better than those of Anna and Zilpah.)

Dimon, the war captain, and uncle to the First Queen, as Anna explained to Mary, came close to her and said:

"I hear your husband is now travelling in Arabia." He seemed eager to have a conversation with Mary. He had in fact heard from Anna about Mary's husband being a Roman centurion.

"Yes, he obtained two weeks' leave."

"Do you think he will visit here on his way back?"

"He will do so if his trip does not take too long. If not, he will just pass by, I think."

"Then your husband does not have any business in Nabatea, is it not so?"

"Yes. This was a trip of purely personal business."

The conversation stopped for the moment here. It was because a clamourous sound of cymbals followed by the sound of flute typical in Nabatea flowed out. Mary opened her eyes wide and looked in the direction from which the sound came.

"You too play the lute for us," said Anna turning to Mary. But Mary did not seem to have heard Anna. She fixed her eyes on the band of musicians and sat as if enraptured.

"Mary plays harp and lute excellently," said Anna this time to Dimon.

"She looks as if she had some such special talent. And she is very beautiful, too."

Dimon smiled confidentially as he said this to Anna.

"Oh yes. You know, at first I was drawn to her beauty and talent, but later on, Herod too got interested. . . ."

"Oh, is she acquainted with King Herod also?"

"She certainly is. And had it not been for Herodias. . . ."

Anna seemed moved by this reminiscence and she stopped speaking in the middle of her sentence.

The flute sound ceased and Mary turned an excited face to Anna.

"I have never heard that kind of flute music in Judaea. It is really wonderful. I feel as if the hot wind and cool moonlight of Nabatea were rushing into my heart all at once."

Her voice came out excited, too, as she said this.

"Thank you for praising it. Flute music is one of the prizes of this kingdom," said Dimon.

Anna added:

"There is nobody even in Nabatea who can play the flute as well as that player, you know."

The company began drinking more wine as the music stopped. And Dimon, now somewhat drunken, turned again to Mary and said:

"Did you happen to hear from your husband that Roman army is coming down to Nabatea?"

"No, I don't think so. In any case, my husband does not talk to me about his military duties or the affairs of the army. . . . But come to think of it, maybe his trip in this direction this time has some connection with that you are saying, don't you think?"

Mary's manner was natural as she went on like this.

Dimon seemed to take a great interest in this conjecture Mary was making.

"When you see your husband again, do tell him to bring the army over here as soon as possible. This situation must be ended quickly. Under the circumstances we cannot even entertain our guests properly."

"But I have no concern for men's affairs, you see."

After diverting Dimon's attention this way, Mary brought up another topic.

"I have heard from her ladyship Anna that Her Highness the queen has some longing for her original home. Or did I hear right? I am so inapt in this kind of a thing. . . ."

"Sh. . . ." Dimon stopped Mary from going on.

"If that kind of talk should be caught by ears of the king. . . ." Dimon touched his neck with one hand.

"I am not one of his subjects, am I? I am merely talking as a stranger and besides I am having my conversation with just you."

"But that is not my position, you understand."

Dimon pointed at his chest with a hand and made a meaningful face at Mary. He seemed to be saying: If there were only you and me. . . .

Just at this moment, Anna came into their conversation.

"Mary, General Dimon is right in that. I am also of the same feeling as he, but we must all watch our mouth in the palace."

There seemed to be even more meaning in what Anna said. Dimon, however, made a slight nod to Anna and walked away toward the band.

When Dimon was gone, Anna whispered to Mary bringing her mouth close to the other's ear:

"My father the former king died a tragic death because he liked women too much. The new king is a remarkable person if he is my own brother. If only he did not seek beauty so much. . . ."

As she got more familiar with the atmosphere of the palace surrounding Zilpah, she decided that getting herself onto the side of Dimon would be the quickest way to rescue Zilpah. But she knew that she had to avoid being suspected by any means because she could not afford it. She made herself known from the first to the last only as wife of a Roman centurion. She judged that it would be best if she acted as guest of Queen Anna in the negotiation she would be participating in. For this, she had to make her waiting woman her absolutely loyal servant. Mary had given her many jewels besides the one she had given her in the first place. So by this time, Abiral was so devoted to Mary that she would jump into the deep water if it was for Mary.

Abiral found out for Mary that the Western Gate and the Southern Gate were now being guarded by the soldiers that were followers of Dimon. She also told Mary that one of her close friends who was now waiting on Queen Zilpah had her lover in the camp of General Dimon.

Abiral seemed to have decided in her mind that what Mary was doing was chasing out the new queen in cooperation with Dimon. This was, of course, maneuvered by Mary. She had led Abiral on to thinking that way. Abiral also thought that the reason Mary wanted Zilpah out was that Mary herself wanted to step into her shoes with the assistance of the general. If all this turns out according to plan, I, Abiral, would be the head waiting woman of the queen enjoying her trust and affection in one body, she said to herself. Nothing could be more welcome than that from Abiral's point of view.

"General Dimon's followers hate the new queen so," said Abiral.

"If they hate her that much, why don't they chase her out? Why do they keep her here?"

"But one cannot let such a feeling known in this palace. If one is known to harbor such a thought, he is sure to lose his life even if he was a high ranking courtier."

"Do you think so?"

Although Mary spoke calmly and indifferently it was not how she felt inside.

(If that is the situation. . . ?)

Mary tried to think ahead somehow.

As Mary was sunken in thought trying to find a way to connect the Dimon's faction with the Blood Contract Corps, Abiral whom she had sent to greet Zilpah came back with a sealed envelope.

"The queen wanted me to give this to you," she said.

Mary took the envelope nonchalantly. But as soon as Abiral went out of the room she hurriedly opened it. This was the first time she was receiving either a message or a letter from Zilpah. And the content of the letter was also very surprising.

> The falcon which you had taken with you came back here after six days. The bird comes here everyday and perches itself on the branch of the oak tree. I believe it flies here from the palace where she is now. It goes away at dusk everyday and then comes back here next morning to spend the day on that branch. If this letter reaches you by some fortune, write to me in the same way that I am writing to you now.
>
> He-Owl

There was enclosed in the envelope a letter from Zilpah also. Shaphan had signed himself as 'He-Owl'; a name Mary could guess at. He must have done that to prepare against accidents, thought Mary.

I am sending you Lord Shaphan's letter which reached me hidden in the falcon's feathers. At first, I discovered that there was a tiny piece of cloth tied to a leg of the falcon with Lord Shaphan's name written on it. Next morning, as I fed the bird, I tied a piece of cloth with my name Zilpah written on it. Then on the next day, the bird came back with a message: in the feather. So I looked in the feathers and found this letter from Lord Shaphan which I am enclosing in this envelope now. I believe he hid this letter in the feathers to avoid attracting people's attention. I would like you to write the answer to his letter this time. I will send it the same way his letters come. And be sure to rescue me, Lady Maria.

From Zilpah

When she finished reading the letter, Mary was totally confused. This was not so surprising considering the fact that she had had no occasion to know that kind of person Hadad was. Then all at once the suddenly brightened face of Zilpah when Mary gave her the falcon loomed up before Mary's eyes and from this Mary could gather that maybe the falcon had been acquainted well with Zilpah before she was taken here. And also the thought that maybe this Corps Teacher Hadad is a kind of a magician dawned on her. Come to think of it, she said to herself, there was something magical about Zilpah, also. In any case she wrote a letter to Shaphan losing no time:

My beloved Shaphan, I see you have communicated with queen Zilpah many times through the mediation of the falcon. But I will not mind it. I am here to rescue your Zilpah, am I not? Among the Nabateans, General Dimon is the only one who may prove useful to you. He is said to be the uncle to the First Queen, and commands the guards at the Western and the Southern Gates. But I do not think that you will succeed in breaking into the castle even if you should approach it by the Southern Gate. Because the guards there have not yet received any words about such contingency. I will try to bring Zilpah to a place where you could easily find her as soon as I get connected

with General Dimon's faction. But you must wait for some
more time. And I would like to tell you that it was a wonderful
wisdom on your part to make me carry the falcon rather than a
dagger in my arms. I would have been thrown into a grave
difficulty if I had come with the dagger on me because I was
captured by the police on the outset of my journey here and
was examined thoroughly. I have many more things to tell you
but I will not write more for fear that it may be too heavy for
the falcon to carry.

Your Mary

Next she wrote a letter to Zilpah. But this time, it was a far
shorter letter than the one she wrote to Shaphan.

Dear Madam Zilpah, I have well received the envelope you
have sent me. You have in no time turned the falcon I have
carried here into your message boy. I envy you your sagacity
and feel a little jealous for it, also. But there is nothing that can
be done about it. In any case, believe that I am here to rescue
you by the wish of Lord Shaphan and that the maid Abiral is
one you may trust.

Mary

When she finished writing these two letters, Mary sealed
them in an envelope and gave it to Abiral to take to Zilpah.

Abiral met her friend Ceres several times a day on average
performing errands for Mary. Ceres was waiting on Zilpah now
but was betrothed to a warrior under the direct command of
General Dimon and the wedding was not far away. Under the
circumstances, Ceres knew quite a lot about what was
happening in the camp of General Dimon.

According to what Ceres told Abiral, General Dimon was
such a person as would give his absolute loyalty to the new king
if only he would send Zilpah back to where she came from and
get along with his First Queen. The proof of this was that
Ariste who was now the chief member of the faction of the

former king had for many times approached General Dimon through messengers about supporting him onto the throne if only the latter would stand up against the present king, but was turned down every time and with very severe words of reprimand, too. It was clear from this that Dimon's loyalty toward the present king was firm enough but that it was perhaps too much for the general to bear to see the king give himself from top to toe to Zilpah while shamefully neglecting his rightful wife, the First Queen. The new king also seemed to trust him for his sincere personality and loyalty.

Mary could gather from all of this that General Dimon and his followers merely wanted to alienate Zilpah from the king and as long as Zilpah could be gotten out of their way would continue to be loyal and faithful subjects of the king. After listening to what Abiral had to say with attention, Mary said:

"If the things stand that way, wouldn't it be sensible for someone on this side to send a word to the Blood Contract Corps to the effect that if they would come to get Zilpah, people on this side would close their eyes to it?"

It was only for playing game with words that Mary said this but Abiral jumped up saying:

"Do you think one did not suggest it?"

"What did they say to that, then?"

"When I said that, Saraknas, the betrothed of Ceres, said that he would do so if he were in a position to do it but that he did not think General Dimon would go along with a plan like that."

"Would he not listen even if he is convinced that doing so would be beneficial for his country and himself all at the same time?"

"General Dimon seems to think such a thing as betraying the king."

"What betrayal? It will only do good to this country and also to the king!"

"I said the same thing to Ceres. But she too seemed uncertain about letting General Dimon into this plan. She actually suggested that I bring this up directly with her betrothed, Saraknas.

"Did you do so? What was the reaction of Saraknas like?"

"Saraknas said that he did not think it wise to risk so much for a stranger. So Ceres went back at him saying what kind of warrior he was if he only thought how to protect himself from the harms? She asked him if he thought it an unfit duty for him to do something that meant a great deal for his country. Then Saraknas told her that was exactly what he was debating with himself about."

"This is all so very rare. You must have unusually wonderful persons here. Your friend Ceres, too. She must be as fine a person as you yourself are, Abiral."

"She is the closest with me among all the court ladies. I gave her one of the jewels you gave me for memento."

"Oh, really? I will give you another to make up for that one," said Mary and gave her one of the jewels Shaphan had sent her by way of the falcon.

"No, I am content with the garnet your ladyship gave me in the first place."

"But isn't one garnet too little to keep?"

Thus saying Mary caught one of Abiral's hands and put the jewel into the hand. Abiral looked down at the jewel that had been placed in her hand with curiosity for some time and then suddenly raised her head and said:

"Oh, I forgot. Tomorrow is Princess Anna's birthday and we waiting women have prepared an entertainment for her ladyship with songs and dances. And also we had included your lute playing in the program without asking for your permission. Princess Anna seemed to take in all this with pleasure. But then this morning, she showed a strange change of mood. She declared that she did not wish any birthday celebration. It seems somebody named John or some thing died."

"Somebody named John?"

"I think that's what they say it is. I seem to have heard that he too was from Judaea."

"A Jew? Called John?"

"Yes, that's what I heard. At all events, won't you go and talk to Queen Anna about the birthday celebration, I mean, talk to her so that she would permit us to celebrate. . . ."

"I have not even dreamed about it. I surely will go to her ladyship and put in a word by all means."

Thus saying, Mary went to Anna's compartment which was only a few paces from her own quarters. Anna, who was having her waiting women massage her lying down, seemed delighted by her visit.

"We were just talking about you, my dear," said Anna raising half her body.

"Is tomorrow really your ladyship's birthday?"

"Yes, it seems it is. And these girls brought instruments in like that for celebration, you know."

Anna pointed at the instruments that were stood up in one corner of the floored compartment adjacent to the room where they all were. There were harps, lutes and many other instruments besides them.

"But what is the meaning of this rumor, my ladyship, about a certain John who has just died?" asked Mary turning her face to Anna. And then Anna replied as if she had been waiting for this one question:

"That foxlike woman, Herodias, finally had Baptist John killed, it seems. I heard it only last night myself, you know."

According to Anna, Salome, daughter of Herodias, had danced in celebration of the birthday of Antipas (Herod). And then very delighted with her performance, he had asked her how he could recompense her for her performance. Just at this juncture, Herodias who had been all that time meaning to get rid of Baptist John somehow, made her daughter ask the king for the head of John. And that Salome did upon which Antipas, although he was hesitant in his heart, felt that he could not with grace fall back on his own words, and so decided resolutely to do as she or her mother wished. He had his men behead Baptist John and bring the tray with his head on to Salome, whereupon Salome took it to her mother Herodias. Salome was a daughter Herodias had from her former husband Philip and so was originally niece to the king.

"I believe Herodias would have the heart to have even a very just man killed like that," said Mary when she had heard out the story.

"If the former king had been alive, he would have found means to save this just man," said Anna with a deep sigh.

Anna looked sad as she reminisced in this way. And then she added:

"Salome, was friendly with the wife of Chuza, too. Those two were the best among that clan in the fox hole."

And then Anna spoke again as if to herself:

"Salome was friendly with the wife of Chuza, too. Those two were the best among that clan in the fox hole."

Anna seemed really absorbed into reminiscing. All at once, however, Mary remembered what Anna had said about the wife of Chuza when they had met first after so many years. She had said: "The wife of Chuza is also a good woman, although she never had a kind word to say about you, Mary."

"What did you mean, your ladyship, when you said that the wife of Chuza did not have a kind thing to say about me?"

"Oh, that. Yes, that. I believe I will have to explain that to you, after all. And now is as good a time as any other if not better. And you may stop massaging, now, girls. All of you go out to the other room. I have things to talk about with just Lady Mary."

Anna opened her mouth again after all the waiting women had gone out of the room.

"It was on the occasion of a palace feast. Maybe it was winter. It was constantly raining. Do you remember, at all?"

"I think I do. I seem to remember playing the lute for the second time in the palace on a rainy and stormy day. And I remember there was the wife of Chuza, too."

"Yes, yes, that's the day. It was when your lute playing was cheered by all the people gathered there most enthusiastically. And on that day, the wife of Chuza talked to me about you. . . ."

Anna paused for a while when she came as far as this.

". . . . . ."

Mary did not say anything but sat with eyes that seemed to urge Anna to go on with her story. Anna spoke again:

"I think even the good wife of Chuza with all her nice qualities got jealous of you when she saw so many people praising and cheering you. In any case she brought her mouth close to my ear and then said: 'That woman there was born illegitimate. It is only I and that woman's mother who know this.' I asked her what she meant by that and she said that your present mother had picked you up when you were very young. I protested that, even so, that kind of a thing cannot be kept a secret a long time and that, if so, why was it that you did not know anything about it. And then the wife of Chuza said that you did not know because you were really young when you were picked up by your present mother and also that she had treated you not a bit differently from what would have been if she had been your real mother. And so you had no way of knowing, she said. So I asked her how she came to know about it. And she said that she and her family had lived next to your house and so there was no hiding from her and her family what was happening there in your house. Do you yourself know anything about it at all?"

Anna looked at Mary with her affectionate eyes as she finished speaking.

". . . . . ."

Mary had been looking at Anna with an absent-minded expression all the while the former continued her story, but as soon as it was ended, Mary put the lute down on the floor and made a move as to raise herself up. But before she could get up she fell back on her bottom and said:

"No. No. It is not true."

She even shoved her hand wildly as she said this. Then next

moment, Mary went limp and her head fell sideways on her shoulder as if she had been hit with a heavy hammer.

Anna thought Mary was acting very strangely and started regretting that she had told her the story.

"Mary," called Anna in a low voice.

Mary raised her head as if she were waking up from a dream and then said in a barely audible voice:

"It must be so. Maybe... it was not possible that I have anything warm which I could call mine. I cannot have such a thing as mother or father. I cannot have anything like that... anything."

Mary went on like a person with a fever.

Anna was seized with an uncontrollable pity for Mary. She went up to Mary and holding her by the hand said:

"Mary, please calm down. I was a fool to tell you what the wife of Chuza said out of malice. Forget everytrhing if only for the sake of me, Mary."

Anna's voice came out thick from too much emotion. But Mary's eyes which were filled with unfathomable sadness were fixed on the wall and did not move.

Anna had her waiting women bring some wine.

"Here. Drink this. It will be good for you."

Mary refused the wine, however, and said:

"Your ladyship, I would like to take leave of you, now."

After saying this almost in a whisper for lack of strength, Mary returned to her room.

After coming back to her own quarters, Mary lay down in the bed. Eyes closed and immobile, she looked like a dead person. Out of her closed eyes, however, the tears flew constantly.

When she had lain like that for about an hour, Mary got up and started packing her things.

"Why are you packing, your ladyship?" asked Abiral.

"I must go. There is something urgent I have to tend to."

"Tomorrow is Princess Anna's birthday. Would you go away even without celebrating?"

"I must. I will explain to the princess."

"Wait just a while. I believe the things we brought up with Saraknas too will also be concluded in a short time."

"No. I must go at once. You had better talk to the new queen about it for me."

Mary acted as if she were possessed by some ghost. She seemed extremely dismayed and restless. After packing hurriedly, Mary went to say farewell to Anna who surprised at such a sudden notice tried all she could to change her mind. Mary was adamant, however. She did not seem to have any good reason she could give for going away so hurriedly. Merely she repeated that she had to go at once. She said the same thing to whoever tried to detain her. Anna cried holding Mary by the hand. To her, Mary was now somewhat frightening. She could not understand how a person could change so just because she heard something rather unpleasant.

"I will go now, your ladyship."

Mary left with these words.

After Mary left the palace in this way, Abiral did not seem to have any reason to pursue the scheme to chase the new queen out of the palace. She just went to Queen Zilpah's palace and told her and her waiting woman Ceres what had happened. But Ceres did not seem to feel the same way as Abiral. For her it did not make much difference whether Mary or the First Queen took the place of Zilpah after the latter was gotten rid of. If it had been Mary, it would have been good for her best friend Abiral. And if it is the First Queen, it would be good for Saraknas, her future husband.

And Saraknas' position was also different from that of Abiral or that of Ceres. His position was that getting rid of Zilpah meant necessarily restoring the First Queen to Zilpah's place. And even if this could not be realized there would be an end to one of the big causes of trouble in the court. In any case, he had no special reason to include Mary in the plan. Therefore, Mary's leaving the palace in that way did not affect his plan in any way. So even on the night Mary left and on the next night, he kept himself busy with the plan to chase Zilpah out of the palace.

It was the fourth day after Mary left. One of his men who was in charge of liason work with the remaining officers of the former king came back to him and conveyed the suggestion made by them. The crux of the matter was that the Remaining Faction of the former king and the Blood Contract Corps would make an attack on the Eastern Gate and Dimon and his followers were not to join them there but keep a guard on the Western and Southern Gates. If they would do so, the rest of them would break in through the Eastern Gate and carry Zilpah away. The only thing the Dimon's party should do was placing Zilpah somewhere near the Eastern Gate where she could be spotted easily. If the work is done in this way, Dimon and Saraknas would not be suspected of conspiring with the enemy, they argued.

But now was the turn to analyze what difference there was between this new proposal and the old ones. The proposals that have been made so far was that Dimon and his followers would open the Western and Southern Gates to the Remaining Faction of the former king if the latter should start and attack. The Remaining Faction of the former king then would come in and either just carry away Zilpah or kill the king at the same time and give the throne to Dimon. But these suggestions were turned down by Dimon as already explained before this.

What was different in the new proposal was that the Remaining Faction joined hands with the Blood Contract Corps. And also the fact that the attack would not fall on the Western and Southern Gates that were guarded by General Dimon's men. This was an undeniable improvement on the old ones.

"Would there not be impure motivation behind this co-operation between the Remaining Faction and the Blood Contract Corps?"

"No. I don't think so."

"What is the reason, then, that the Remaining Faction joins

hands with the Corps?"

"According to what they say, first, it is to make the Blood Contract Corps go away. Second, they wish to obtain General's favour by doing this since they do not now have any footing at the Nabatean court."

"Is there not a chance that they will make unnecessary disturbance and damages after coming into the palace?"

"They were saying that they would not feel any need to do such a thing and neither could."

"Why is it so?"

"That they would not feel the need to means that the Blood Contract Corps' purpose is solely in carrying Zilpah away and nothing more. That they could not even if they wanted to means that the soldiers under General Dimon would not let them and they would be no match against the General's force."

Saraknas told Aquillabo, the liaison officer, to go and rest and went to see Ceres. He asked her if she could make Zilpah come near the Eastern Gate.

"I won't have to make her do anything. The queen herself has been wanting to go back to the Blood Contract Corps, has she not? The only important thing is that the king be not in the inner palace at the time."

Saraknas thought for a second and then said:

"I think that can be arranged."

Saraknas nodded his head as he said this as if to himself.

"How?"

"We could make it so the king would be talking about military affairs with General Dimon. Don't you think this will work?"

Saraknas seemed quite proud of his own idea.

Shaphan met Ariste, the commander of the Remaining Faction of the former king Aretas for the first time one day before Mary returned from the palace. Ariste had brought with him a letter written by Thomas. He told Shaphan that he had been away in the south to appeal to the Roman army about the unlawful political happening in Nabatea asking the Romans to come to their assistance and dethrone the present king. Although his negotiation did not succeed fully, he was certain that he had been at least instrumental to keeping the Romans from coming to Nabatea to suppress the Blood Contract Corps in spite of repeated requests from the present government.

Just then, Ariste heard the news about Baptist John getting killed by King Herod and in order to find out details of the event he travelled down to Machaerus where he chanced to meet disciples of Baptist John. He said he even went around observing the miracles Jesus worked. In the course of his conversation with the company about Baptist John, Jesus, and Nabatea, he heard that among the disciples of Jesus, there were members of the Blood Contract Corps. As he expressed his wish to meet some of them, one of the disciples of Baptist John arranged a meeting between him and one of the Blood Contract Corps men and this was no other than Thomas. During his conversation with Thomas, said Ariste, some common interests for the Remaining Faction and the Blood Contract Corps were found. Among the things Ariste had put out to Shaphan as his conditions was one condition which he did not tell Aquillabo, the secret messenger from Saraknas. It was that Ariste asked Shaphan to free Aquila who was kept in imprisonment in Chorazin. Other conditions were: One. That they should rescue Nabatea from the present regime. Two. That the Dimon faction render the Remaining Faction their favor and protection. But what he really meant to pursue by all means was the rescue of Aquila, said Ariste to Shaphan. And it was not merely because Aquila was one of the important courtiers under the late king but also because he was a very close friend of Ariste.

There was something else that Ariste did not tell Aquillabo, not because he intended to keep it a secret but because he did not wish to bring it up unless the other party was especially inquisitive of it. It was the manner by which they were dividing work at the time of the attack on the Eastern Gate between the Remaining Faction and the Blood Contract Corps. Ariste had proposed to open the gate and keep Dimon's army from coming out and asked the Corps to take care of the soldiers at the Gate and take away Zilpah.

When Ariste had finished making his proposals, Shaphan said:

"Do you think you have enough force among the Remaining Faction to break through the Gate?"

"Frankly, no. Not yet, anyhow," answered Ariste as honestly as Shaphan's question was straight.

"Then, how are you planning to open the Gate?"

"......"

Ariste did not answer at once. Then,

"I would have liked to say do not ask how but wait and see what happens on the night of our great undertaking, but I will tell you how because you will find it difficult to trust us if I didn't. This is how we are going to do it. There is a waterway that flows from a branch of River Zeresh into Borura, the capital of Nabatea. As it is covered with stone slabs and earth, one cannot guess by just looking that there is a waterway underneath but the depth of the tunnel is one and half a body length on average. And this waterway goes through between the Eastern Gate and the Southern Gate. We can therefore follow the waterway into the palace and coming up just inside the Eastern Gate will be able to bribe the guards to open it."

"How deep is the water?"

"It is about a quarter of a body length on average. And on account of the fact that there is stone slabs and earth covering it, the inside of the tunnel is completely dark."

"How long is the waterway?"

"About five *ri* (= 1.25 miles) from the starting point."

"How could you people travel through this long waterway when it is so dark and the water is that high?"

"The depth of the water could be made to go down low if we draw the water sideways at the upstream and there are places at adequate intervals where the stone slabs could be raised up for light. There will be no problem because it was my grandfather who had supervised the construction of this waterway."

Shaphan's face brightened when he heard these last words and he said:

"How many soldiers would there be guarding the Eastern Gate?"

"From two or three to something more than a dozen. Maybe there will be seven of eight. But at night, only about two or three are likely to be awake and others would be sleeping until their shift comes."

"I see. But I will have about a dozen of my own men join the party travelling through the waterway to make sure. These men are all excellent warriors and, also from having lived on water so much, could swim or dive if necessary."

"That will be very reassuring," said Ariste with satisfaction. Now there was only the negotiation with Saraknas left for final decision.

Then just one day after Ariste had been to Shaphan's quarters for the secret negotiation, Mary showed up all of a sudden. On her pale face, there was a strange anger.

"Mary, I am glad you are back. I was just about to call you back." Shaphan seemed happy to see her. But she said abruptly:

"I will go back to Galilee."

Shaphan thought that this was one of her customary hysterics and so he said, "Mary," in a gentle voice and tried to catch her wrist. But Mary leapt backwards as if she were about to be bitten by a poisonous insect shaking his hand off fiercely.

"You can stay here and get your Zilpah back. You can live with her or die fighting. But I am going back to Galilee. Don't look for me ever again."

Mary stood up abruptly.

". . . . . ."

Shaphan sat without saying anything and merely watched her behaviour. Then Mary spoke again:

"The more I think of it, the angrier I get. Just look at you going through all this merely to get her back. You throw away men and fortune just for that one purpose. Only for her. Do you know how far this is from Galilee?"

"Don't you think I would have acted just the same if you had been placed in her situation?"

"I can believe that. But that is why I am so angry with you. If it had been me, I would have told you to give me up even if they should kill me. . . . I should have drowned that time. Why did you make me the kind of mad woman that I am now?"

Mary sat down again and covering her face with both hands started sobbing so violently that her whole body shook. Shaphan, however, still thought that Mary was having one of her fits and did not try to look into the matter any more seriously. He just sat and watched her cry. And so, when on the next morning, while he was out to command the fighting, she left without leaving a word, he did not suspect anything. He thought even if she would go back to Galilee, he would be able to find her again once the fighting was over and they could go back home. Even so, she should not have acted that waywardly when everybody was staking their lives in this war. She is an uncurable water ghost, said he to himself.

Two days after Mary left, Shaphan received a letter from Ananias in Capernaum:

Respected Commander Shaphan,

I am forced to write this letter knowing fully that you are very busy and troubled. The reason I write like this is that our Corps is faced with a serious crisis right now. The heart of the matter is that a few days ago, an unidentified man from Nabatea sent a letter to the headquarters of the Roman army stationed in Galilee. The content of the letter was that the person who had shot a Roman centurion with an arrow three years ago was a man named Shaphan who is commanding a secret organization called the Blood Contract Corps that has its headquarters on the eastern coast of the Sea of Galilee. The letter then proceeded to say that this commander Shaphan was at present doing his robber's job leading his followers. And so this was a best chance to attack their so-called headquarters and turn it to dust, said the letter. The letter even pointed to the fact that our headquarters was located between Gadara and Gerasa. If you think you cannot recover Madam Zilpah quickly, maybe, it is better for you to postpone the undertaking for another time and return at once.

Ananias

The Second Member who brought this letter to Shaphan supplied more information which Ananias' letter had omitted. He said that at the time of the incident of the death of Roman centurion, the Nabateans under Aquila's command had infiltrated into the district for an intentional kidnapping of beautiful women or money. Although Aquila was at the time a high ranking government official in charge of foreign affairs, there was one man under him who led a gangsters' organization called the Band of Strong Men. They had already had their eyes on Mary and was looking for a chance to kidnap her when they saw an arrow flying to her companion, a Roman centurion, and make him fall. At the time they had thought that it was done by one of them and picking up the body of the centurion and Mary, fled up to the mountains. They were caught up by the Roman army soon enough, however, and were forced to leave the woman and the body of the centurion behind and flee with just the arrow they had had time to pull from the body. But they had no idea where that arrow had come from. When a man from Gadara was caught by the Romans carrying the same type of arrow that had killed the centurion and confessed that he was the true culprit, however, the gangsters knew that the arrow belonged to the Blood Contract Corps and that Commander Shaphan must be responsible for the death of the Roman centurion for the most part. They guessed this because they knew that this man from Gadara was one of the members of the Blood Contract Corps. They decided that this man chose to die for the sake of the Corps and the commander. (Shaphan too knew by the time that this man from Gadara was one of the Second Members under Jair who was working at the armoury.) The young man who came as Ananias' messenger said that this was all that Ananias upon receiving news about the secret letter informing on the Blood Contract Corps, had gotten out of Aquila by interrogating. However, Aquila himself did not seem to know any more about the gangsters' whereabouts or the letter.

"This will make us busier," said Shaphan after reading the letter. It was true that he had to go back at once if such was the situation there. But how could he leave this place when the success of their long effort was only two days and two nights away?

Not knowing what else to do, he wrote an answer to Ananias telling him to hold out just a little while longer because the victory would be theirs after only two more days. He did not forget to give an order about digging deep traps around the headquarters, and to consult carefully with Jair and Corps Teacher Hadad about everything and act with utmost caution. He also asked Ananias to keep an eye on Mary.

Two days passed after Shaphan received Ananias' letter and it was the night of the great undertaking. It was a dark night. In fact, they had waited two more days to get this darkness. If it had not been for the fact that Shaphan had to go back immediately, the undertaking probably would have been postponed one more night so that they might have the darkest possible night for their work. As it was, however, they decided to make the attack without any more delay.

The Corps members that joined the party to travel by the waterway were fourteen in number including Manaen, Sachaeus, Cleopas, Uzziah, Gana Judas, Timeus, and Parmenas. Together with the twenty Remaining Faction men led by Ariste and Ariste himself, there were thirty-five of them.

The water which they had made to flow away from the waterway from early evening was far shallower that it would have been ordinarily and reached only up to lower shin. But it was very cold. Men kept hitting themselves against the walls of the tunnel or fell down to the water because of darkness and slipperiness of the cold water. The clothes of the men were almost all wet.

"Do not loosen attention because the water is shallow. There are three places where the water is quite deep. It will come up to your waists. Ones with shorter heights should be especially careful since they may drink in the water."

The one who gave these directions was Ariste who was walking ahead of them all. He spoke again:

"But you won't have to walk through that deep water for long. It will be no more than six to seven steps at a stretch."

Shaphan's men who were taking up the rear did not seem to care whether the water was shallow or deep. They were rather worried that Ariste may not be able to detect the spot of their destination in this darkness. The men of the Remaining Faction, however, seemed to worry mostly about the water getting suddenly deep on account of some unforeseen mistakes on the ground level.

"If they should stop lower end and open the upper end, we will be turning to fish," said one of the men of the Remaining Faction. Then another of them said:

"The upper end is nothing to worry because it is in the hands of our men."

"What if they should stop the lower end?"

"Even so, I don't think the water will get so deep so suddenly. But if anything like that happens it would mean that our plan has been exposed, in which case we will be dead soon enough any way. What's the difference whether we die underground or on top of it?"

"Do not talk in that way, man. It sounds cowardly. I don't

know about drowning, but once we are out on the ground, why should we be beaten so quickly? We will fight, won't we?"

"I only meant we should be careful."

As the two men were talking away in this manner, Ariste shouted back:

"It's the deep part. All of you be careful! But do not take fright. Wade through calmly."

At the same time, the sound of deep water splashing could be heard. It was different from the sound the men's feet and legs had been making in the water. But even the deep part was much shallower than they had expected. The water came up to only their lower waist. Bigger trouble was that their clothes were dripping wet and so were their heads and faces, which made them tremble from cold.

"Brrrr. It's cold!"

"A slap on the cold one!"

They slapped each other's backs and rubbed arms as they continued their march through the water and darkness. And somehow, the cold seemed to be forgotten.

When they went on like this for about an hour, they found that they had arrived at their destination. It was a spot in the waterway where bluish light came in through some sort of a hole or crevice overhead. Looking closely, one could see that there was a hall opening out to the ground level. Ariste went up the wall first with the help of a number of his followers. After pushing his head up outside the hole and peering, Ariste came down back. Everybody kept absolute silence while this went on.

"The guards awake at the Eastern Gate are only two and five are asleep. We will divide the party into three teams. One team will take care of the two guards that are awake and the second team will be in charge of the guards that are asleep and the third will open the Gate for the party of Commander Shaphan."

After giving this direction, he climbed up the stone wall

again with the iron stick and rope. He would use the iron stick as a lever when opening the stone lids. When he opened the stone lids that were in pair, he pulled his body up onto the ground and let the rope down. The men standing in the water caught the rope and started climbing up the stone wall in turn with the help of the rope. Two or three men used the rope at the same time.

After the Nabateans went up in this way, the men from the Blood Contract Corps followed. After landing on the ground level they went on toward the palace where Zilpah was supposed to be waiting while the men of the Remaining Faction were killing off the guards at the Eastern Gate. It had been arranged that Zilpah would be standing by the olive tree with two waiting women.

As they ran toward the palace, the men of the Remaining Faction could easily get rid of the seven guards and open the Gate for Shaphan's party. All went well up to this point. But it was a grave oversight on the part of Ariste not to have planned against the watchman on top of the rampart. Because as soon as Shaphan led his men into the open Gate, there was a clamour of the horn trumpet shrieking through the night air as if to rend the sky asunder. This was a signal of warning that the watchman on the rampart was making. The warning signal did not continue long, however, because one of the arrows that Shaphan shot hit the trumpeter on the chest. Then there was trumpet sound coming from the Northern Gate. This was a response to the signal the trumpeter of the Eastern Gate had sent. Following this, more trumpets gave signals from the Southern and then the Western Gate. But it was after the united forces (of the Shaphan's army and that of the Remaining Faction) had captured the Eastern Gate to the top of its rampart that the first cavalry appeared on the scene. The two cavalrymen that appeared first, therefore, soon fell from their horses hit by the arrows that came from up the rampart. Five more cavalry came but seeing the first one fall, the remaining four would not come near but turned back. But the trumpet was making as much noise as before.

It was about an hour after the invaders first came into the fort that an army consisted of twenty horses and one hundred infantry came upon the scene. They sent arrows at random in the direction of the Eastern Gate and the rampart. But compared with the united forces that were already stationed by the time the others came, they suffered far more severely in casualty.

"Bring all the men there are at the Southern Gate."

The one who shouted thus was the valiant warrior of Nabatea, Karhams.

Seeing who he was, someone shouted from the rampart:

"Karhams, are your wounds all healed, now?" It was Zechariah of Ophrah that had given Karhams a deep sword wound.

When Karhams heard this, he flared up and, raising his sword high on horseback, started shouting:

"Charge! Charge!"

But even he could not advance because as soon as he tried to push forward numerous arrows flew in as if it were a rain of arrows.

As the two camps were stalling in this way sending some arrows now and then toward each other, there came from the direction of the palace the trumpet muster call. All the Nabateans seemed to pause in alarm when they heard this call and then someone shouted:

"Traitor!" Then:

"General Dimon rose up in rebellion!"

"Who said that?" shouted Karhams but nobody answered.

"Saraknas!" Karhams called.

"He is at the Western Gate," answered one of Saraknas' men. Karhams seemed to guess something from this answer. Knitting his eyebrows in anger he said:

"Don't let any one of the enemy go alive!"

He then turned the horse and disappeared toward the palace. When he arrived at the palace, however, the king was already lying on the floor stabbed with a sword.

"Where is General Dimon?" He shouted shaking in anger. The soldiers that were gathered there were mostly Dimon's men.

"Where is the General, I say?"

"The General is at his residence."

Karhams went in with his sword drawn. As he came up to the spot where the king lay bleeding, he could see a few of king's favourite courtiers gathered around the lying body.

Karhams knelt before the dead body of the king and keened.

"Where is General Dimon?"

He asked again ceasing to keen.

"We sent a man to the General's residence. He will be here presently," answered one of the courtiers.

"Where is the murderer?"

Karhams was convinced that it was one of Dimon's faction that killed the king under Dimon's command.

"He put the queen on the wagon and escaped out of the Southern Gate."

"Then, he is not one of our soldiers?"

"We are not sure. It seems the Blood Contract Corps men and the Remaining Faction came in together and we cannot tell which of them killed the king."

Karhams was surprised when he heard this.

"How did they come in this deep?"

Exclaiming thus, he went out and getting on his horse ran in the direction of the Southern Gate. He meant to go after the enemy. But as he reached the Gate, the thought occurred to him that it would be foolish to chase after them by himself and besides what good would it do to kill a few of them, he thought. Therefore, he turned toward the Eastern Gate, but before he went halfway to the spot where his men were gathered, an arrow flew from nowhere and stuck in his back. As he jerked his back to see where the arrow came from, however, another arrow hit his side. He fell from the horse without even having had the chance to pull any of the arrows from his body. In half consciousness that was weakening quickly, he still did not guess that the arrows were shot by Saraknas. Although he had suspected Dimon at first, after hearing that the Blood Contract Corps and the Remaining Faction were into this thing, he had completely chased out any suspicion about Dimon and his faction.

Change of heart occurred with Saraknas, also. He had promised Ariste that he would not commit himself to anything more than abduction of Zilpah out of the palace. When the Remaining Faction killed the king breaking their contract with him, however, he quickly decided that rather than taking revenge on the betrayers, the best thing for him to do was to work toward pushing Dimon onto the throne. In order to do this, it was necessary to eliminate Karhams above anything, he thought.

The Remaining Faction too had experienced some contingency like this that night. When they went toward the palace with fourteen of Shaphan's men they had no intention of killing the king. Then they could not find Zilpah at the place she was supposed to be standing, and suspecting that their plan and contract had gone foul, they went on into the inner palace and killed the king.

All these accidental happenings of that night were explained soon enough, however. Also, the united forces that were confronting the Nabatean army at the Eastern Gate too learned how the situation stood within a short span of time. Because three men who had carried Zilpah in a wagon out of the palace went back to Shaphan and told him what had taken place. But none among them all that night knew the real reason why there had to be such an unforeseen tragedy (death of the king and blood-shedding that followed it). Most of them thought vaguely that it was because Zilpah was not found at the spot where she was supposed to be. But nobody knew that it was because Shaphan's circumstances forced the allies to hasten the undertaking by two days and Zilpah did not hear about this.

In any case, Shaphan ordered the allies to back out gradually when he was sure that they had got what they came there for.

Chapter 6

Galilee and Decapolis

From the time he met with 'the sinners' at the house of the tax-gatherer Matthew till the next spring, Jesus did not work many miracles. Part of the reason might have been that a rainy season occurred during this interval, but probably, a more significant reason was some psychological disturbance he experienced over this period.

To mention a few miracles of this period, he healed the man whose one arm was crippled on the Sabbath Day and again on the Sabbath Day during the feast of the Tabernacles, he healed a man who had been sick for thirty-eight years in Jerusalem, and then in the spring of next year, he healed a favorite slave of a centurion in Capernaum. And then there was that incident in the town of Nain to the south of Mt. Gilboa where Jesus had met with a bier in which he recognized a corpse of a boy he used to know, an only son of a widow. He had taken pity on the woman and said:

"Do not cry, woman," and then laying his hand on the corpse, said:

"Young man, rise from your bed."

The young man rose and called to his mother, and Jesus said:

"Woman, your son has risen. Go home with him."

These were markedly few compared with the numerous miracles he performed during the months before he met 'the sinners' at Matthew's house and also those of the period from about one and half a month after the incident of the widow's son through the autumn of that year.

He delivered many sermons, however, during this period of infertility in terms of miracle-working. There were perhaps three reasons to this change. The first was, as mentioned .before, the weather which made it inconvenient for him to move about actively. The second was that maybe his life wanted to take a rest along with his 'holy spirit.' The third reason seemed to be his encounter with 'the sinner' at the tax-gatherer Matthew's house.

Even after some time passed after the encounter, Jesus could not seem to forget the face of 'the sinner.' Even now, he seemed to see the broad shoulders, blood-shot eyes, prominent nose, and angry-looking beard of that man before his eyes. Also, he seemed to hear the husky, and yet, strangely endearing voice of the man which was also like the roaring of a wild animal. For a second, Jesus even had an illusion of him coming toward him pushing aside the crowd to his left and right. He was saying to him:

—Rabbi, we are on the earth. Let us fulfill what we bound ourselves with on the earth.

He had said to the man:

—Listen, son of man. Man is on the earth only so that he may bind himself with the Heaven. If man binds himself with man, he will perish with man, and if man binds himself with the earth, he will perish with the earth.

Truly, I tell you, man's life will be blessed with the eternal glory of God only by binding itself with the Heaven.

He had said these things to the man, but 'the sinner' had refused to listen to his words.

The reason why Jesus could not forget his encounter with this man was that unlike the Pharisees and the lawyers who only sought to test and put blame on Jesus, this 'sinner' clearly wanted Jesus to act the same way that Moses did in Egypt. That is, his reason to seek Jesus was clear and free from negative motivations. Although what he wanted was not what Jesus could give him, at least, it was something everybody wanted deep down in their heart except the Pharisees and their like whose wishes were always connected with their worldly interests. Maybe, what this sinner wants is what every Jew wants with a most pure heart, thought Jesus. And that is why he was now pained to think of 'the sinner.' He wanted to console him and many others who had his wish and whose heart was broken because this wish could not be granted.

It was, maybe, to explain things to these people and console their minds that Jesus decided to concentrate on his teaching rather than on miracle working during this period. And the prayers he taught his disciples during this time also seemed to have the mark of his encounter with 'the sinner.'

(Our Father who art in heaven. Thy name be hallowed; thy kingdom come; thy will be done on earth as it is done in heaven. . . .)

Jesus now repeated the phrase: Thy will be done on earth to himself thinking of all the hearts that were in pain and grief and which he wanted to console.

But his teaching drew more animosity from the Pharisees and the Sadducees than his miracles. It was because while the miracles could be taken by themselves as the work of God, his teachings and sermons could not be accepted quite so simply but offered many grounds for both refutation and bad feelings. From their point of view, the most objectionable part of his 'teaching' was that his words were not the same as the words of Moses or other prophets, and were unlike the teachings they had received from the teachers of the law. Since they had no idea about who this Jesus was, the fact that Jesus' teachings were different from those of the Pharisees, or the teachers of the law just because his teaching was more perfect than theirs did occur to their mind. They did not know yet that Jesus' teaching seemed different to them because it was not the superficial, hypocritical things that the Pharisees, and the lawyers taught them.

To mention a few more miracles that Jesus worked during this period, they were mostly performed on the Sabbath Day and for this reason aggravated even more animosity and anger than his teachings. According to their law, it was a sin to heal the sick on the Sabbath Day. It did not matter if healing the sick was the will of God or not. What mattered to them were their rules and laws only and they were the only truth and good they could understand. Therefore, when Jesus said to them:

"Which is right, to do the good or the evil, to save a life or to annihilate it, on the Day of the Sabbath?" They could not answer but only stared at him with discontent and enmity. It was because to them Jesus who talked of 'good' and 'life' apart from the rules and laws appeared to be no other than a heretic.

The Pharisees and the Levites were the ones who taught these rules and laws by profession. And so they were the mostly direct threat and danger to Jesus.

Jesus realized that the Pharisees and the Levites were spread all over the district of Galilee with an intent to trap him. It was in the midst of this tension and animosity that Jesus performed the miracle of 'scolding and calming' the wind and the water while sailing across the Sea of Galilee for Gadara. Gadara was a town in Decapolis (meaning ten towns) which was located to the southeast of the Sea of Galilee. Gadara was a town where the population was mostly Greek and its atmosphere was very liberal. The residents of this town did not follow various religious rules of the Jews and they even ignored Moses' Commandments. They bred pigs and gave themselves up to all sorts of loose enjoyments. Therefore, Jesus never liked or loved this town. The only reason he was headed for this town now was that he was being harassed by the Pharisees and the Levites (most of them, Sadducees and lawyers and teachers of the Law) and he wanted to be away from the district of

Galilee where there was much animosity directed toward him.

Jesus was extremely worn out at the time. As soon as he got aboard the boat, therefore, he took a seat and closed his eyes and soon fell asleep.

When the boat neared the center of the lake, however, a sudden wind rose and the water came into the boat. The boat nearly capsized because of the strong wind and high waves and more water came into the boat. And still Jesus continued to take his slumber. Philip went up to Jesus and shaking him by the shoulder said:

"Lord. We are about to drown."

Jesus opened his eyes. Water was leaping inside the boat and the wind and the waves were raging frantically.

"Why are the wind and the waves so violent as this?"

As Jesus scolded thus, the wind moved toward the horizon as if in a chase after a group of birds that were flying along the edge of the distant sky and the waves began to calm down. Jesus turned his face to Thomas and Philip who were standing beside him and said:

"Where is your faith?"

Philip looked at Jesus unable to speak because of the deep emotion he was experiencing.

From this time on, there was on the face of Jesus a certain vitality and energy that could only be defined as 'holy.' The two disciples could not tell at first whether this was because Jesus could rest for at least ten minutes before being waken up to scold the winds and the waves or because he had just done the wondrous job of calming the elemental things.

As Jesus and his party walked toward the town from the waterfront, a half naked man came down from the top of a hill by the road where there were tombs. His hair that came down to his neck was shevelled up and his two eyes were two bloody balls as if they had been poked at mercilessly by a carnivorous bird.

When this man took sight of Jesus, he hurried down and

kneeling before Jesus cried out:

"Son of God, what do you want with me? Why do you torment me? And why did you call me?"

"What is your name?"

"Legion."

". . . . ."

". . . . . ."

Jesus looked into his blood-filled eyes. He seemed to be having his dialogue with the devil that was inside the man. (According to Luke, the devil inside the man implored Jesus during this dialogue not to send him down the abyss.)

Finally Jesus raised his head and pointed to a group of pigs that were feeding on the hillside, whereupon all the pigs started as if they were surprised by something and then ran down the hillside toward the water where they all drowned.

In the meantime, the man fell on the spot and slept.

Thomas led Jesus and his party to the house of a friend of his.

Early next morning, the man who had been possessed by the devil visited Jesus in clean clothes. He said that he had for three years lived among the tombs half naked. His eyes that were so bloody too were clearing up.

The townspeople who heard this news, however, were seized with an uneasiness. It was because for the people who had no faith in God, Jesus' act of miracle which had the power of 'holy spirit' in it was nothing but a threat. There was nothing objectionable in healing the sick. But didn't he drive a whole horde of pigs into the lake? Wasn't this too great a price for healing one of his sickness? Now the Jews since they neither raised nor ate pigs would not have minded the loss of pigs but it was an entirely different matter with the people of Gadara. From their point of view, Jesus was a dangerous character to say the least who knew the way to use the power of this god who drowned so many of their valuable foodstock. They had no way of knowing what other great prices they would have to pay because of this man called Jesus who believed in Jehovah and not Zeus, Apollo, Dionysus and other Greek gods.

They, therefore, came to see Jesus in a big group and one of them said:

"Prophet of the Jews. Please leave this area with your disciples. We have been living in this place and we do not have anything to do with you."

Upon hearing this, Jesus looked at the man in silence and then said only after a long while:

"Man of an alien land! Do not take heed of me. One will not harvest blessing where it had not been planted."

Thus saying, Jesus left the place with his disciples and walked toward the waterfront. The Greeks seemed to feel triumphant about having made Jesus leave their district. They did not disperse but stayed on a long time watching Jesus and his followers leave by the boat.

As Jesus went to Magdala by boat from Gadara, he saw a great crowd who had been waiting for his arrival there. They had been especially impatient for his return there because the twelve year old only daughter of the president of their synagogue was dying from a fever. Jairus, the president of the synagogue, came up to Jesus and kneeling before him implored:

"Lord, my only daughter is about to die. Please come to my house with me."

As Jesus went to Jairus' house with him, the crowd followed him. This was when a woman suffering from hemorrhage had herself cured by merely touching the edge of the cloak Jesus wore.

Before Jesus arrived at Jairus' house, somebody from Jairus' house came toward them and said:

"Your daughter has already died. Do not trouble the Rabbi any further." Jesus said to him and Jairus:

"Do not be afraid. Only show faith and she will be well again."

Upon arriving at the house, Jesus allowed no one to go in with him except Peter, James, John and father of the girl.

When he heard the mother of the girl and other people weeping and lamenting for her, Jesus said to them:

"Weep no more; she is not dead: she is asleep." He then took hold of her hand and called her:

"Get up, my child."

The girl sat up and with a great surprise on her face with pointed chin, looked up at Jesus.

Jesus said in a very gentle voice:

"Give the child something to eat."

He told the girl's parents who were still not awake from their consternation never to tell of this to anyone and left their house.

It was the evening of the very day on which Jesus had revived the daughter of Jairus from death. One of the Pharisees in town prepared a feast at his house and invited Jesus to come. Peter, Andrew, John, James, Thomas, Judas were with Jesus when he went to this feast.

As they sat down at the table and prepared to eat the food, Philip, one of the twelve disciples, came in to join the party belatedly. Then the people at the table saw a woman who looked about twenty five or so coming in after Philip with a jade chest in her arms. She looked quite pale but beautiful in a pitiful way. She was walking fast with her head bent down.

At a glance, she did not look as if she came in company with Philip. Philip's attitude toward her was frankly indifferent and he did not try to introduce her to the company.

Without seeking permission from the host of the house for intrusion or excusing herself with the guests, the woman went toward Jesus and stationing herself by his feet began to shed tears. The tears were so sudden and profuse that it looked as if she were caught in some kind of paroxysm. Her tears made Jesus' feet completely wet. And her back and shoulders were twitching continuously as if they were things that lived apart from the rest of her body. At last, she brought her shiny black hair over her shoulder and started wiping his feet with her hair and then after kissing them opened the jade container. Out of it, she poured myrrh over Jesus' feet.

Simon, the Pharisee and the host of the house saw that the woman was Mary, 'the sinner' and the one possessed by 'seven demons' and wanted to see if Jesus could find this out through his wisdom of a prophet. Suddenly, however, Jesus called:

"Simon." And he continued:

"There are two debtors. One has a debt of five hundred silver pieces and the other fifty. As neither had anything to pay with, the money-lender let them both off. Now, which will love him most?"

"I think the one that was let off most," answered Simon.

"You are right," said Jesus and then pointing at the woman, he said again:

"You see this woman? I came to your house: you provided no water for my feet; but this woman has made my feet wet with her tears and wiped them with her hair. You gave me no kiss; but she has been kissing my feet ever since I came in. You did not anoint my head with oil; but she has anointed my feet with myrrh. And so, I tell you, her great love proves that her many sins have been forgiven; where little has been forgiven, little love is shown." Then he said to the woman:

"Your sins are forgiven. Your faith has saved you; go in peace."

The one who was most surprised by all this was Thomas. It was because the woman in question was no other than the mistress of Commander Shaphan, that is, Mary of Magdala. Thomas wondered what made her leave Shaphan and seek Jesus, or what had come out of her mission in Nabatea, or why she was pouring so much tear now.

Later, Thomas called Philip aside and asked him if he knew about Mary. Philip then told him that it was he himself that had led Mary to Simon's house the previous day. He explained how this came about.

It was two days ago that Mary had come back to Galilee. She had gone straight to Magdala to see her mother. Seeing that her daughter did not look well, the mother feared beforehand that something must have happened with her daughter again. And she was distressed because Mary had come home in that way a few times before and every time she had given a hard time to her mother.

"Mother!" Mary's voice was low when she called her mother first after seeing her. The mother looked at her daughter in silence. Then she saw that there was a strange gleam in her daughter's eyes which she had not seen there before.

". . . . . ."

"Mother, tell me, straight."

From this point on, Mary's voice trembled a little. Her mother, however, still did not know what it was that her daughter was driving at. And so she kept on looking at her daughter in silence.

"Mother, tell me quickly. Where did you pick me up?"

Mary's voice trembled harder now. And the mother's face had turned gray. And she too began to tremble staring at the fearful gleam in her daughter's eyes.

"Tell me, quickly, mother, tell me."

"In . . . in Chorazin. . . ."

"Chorazin?"

"Ye . . . yes. Chorazin."

"Whereabout in Chorazin?"

"By . . . by the Jordan River."

"How old was I?"

"Very . . . very young. Barely . . . barely three days old . . . ."

The mother acted as if she were a sinner standing on the platform for inquisition. Mary, however, did not ask her anything more but went out of the house hastily without even saying a word of leave-taking as if she had suddenly remembered something. When Mary heard the name Chorazin from the mother, she suddenly remembered Shaphan's mother who was in Chorazin and the fact that Shaphan's mother had once asked her how old she was. Mary had answered that she was twenty four years old and then Shaphan's mother had said in a sad voice: She would be the same age if she had lived. . . . She had said this as if to herself. But Mary had asked that time:

"Who is she, mother?"

But Shaphan's mother had merely said, pretending indifference:

"Oh, it's just somebody in my sister's house that is far away from here."

Since Mary had heard that Shaphan's mother had a sister somewhere, she had thought that maybe it was somebody related with this woman and had dropped the subject.

Shaphan's mother loved her more after this conversation, however. And, as mentioned before, Shaphan's mother had come to show more affection toward Mary than toward her rightful daughter-in-law Zilpah when the latter had come to pay a visit.

Since she had not known anything about her birthright then, Mary had merely thought that the reason Shaphan's mother loved her more than she loved Zilpah was that Zilpah was not from Galilee while Mary was. Never had Mary had an inkling of doubt about the woman in Magdala whom she had called mother all her life.

As soon as she left the house of her mother, Mary went straight to the waterfront and took a boat. She was being assailed by frightening thoughts as she sat in the boat. If Shaphan's mother were her real mother, what would she be to Shaphan? Oh, is Shaphan then her brother? Then, what would happen to Shaphan and herself? Oh, why didn't she remain as 'water ghost'? How can she face anyone, now?

When she thought about how she had to live without parent, Shaphan or any other relatives, she was so terrified that her hair stood up. But as her horror increased, her passion to find out the truth grew, too.

When she first saw Mary coming in, Shaphan's mother looked very glad.

"What a pleasant surprise! But why did you not come all together?" she said.

She seemed to think that Mary was coming from Nabatea.

"I came ahead by myself," answered Mary shortly.

"Are you sick? You don't look very well."

"No, I am not sick."

"Then?"

". . . . ."

Suddenly, Mary's face turned fierce and she stared at Shaphan's mother with this face. Somewhat taken aback, the older woman asked:

"Why do you look at me like that?"

"Mother!" called Mary in a very low voice and continued:

"Don't you think there is much similarity between you and me?"

"Why do you ask that?"

"I just wanted to know."

"I think there is similarity, to be sure. First of all, the neighbors have been commenting on the similarity of our voices. They say you and I and Shaphan have voices that are very similar. . . ."

But what Mary was thinking of at the moment was the words Shaphan had said on their first encounter about their voices both resembling the hooting sound of an owl. When she thought of this, she felt such acute sorrow that her spine ached.

"Maybe so," said Mary in a low voice. Suddenly, the older woman too seemed to feel something unordinary. She said:

"What do you mean?"

She opened her eyes wide beginning to look scared.

"It seems my mother found me somewhere as a baby. Somewhere here in Chorazin. . . ."

"In Chorazin, do you say?"

"By the Jordan River. . . . I wasn't four days old when I was found by her. . . ."

"What?"

Shaphan's mother stood up abruptly and took a couple of steps backwards. But then she came back forward and took hold of Mary's both hands and said:

"Was it so after all?"

She began to sob. When Mary saw her break into a sob, she was swept by a new sorrow and started to cry with abandon although she had resolved not to cry.

Before she ceased to cry, Mary ran out of the house in spite of the older woman's effort to detain her. There was nowhere for her to go, however. One comfort was that she was not afraid of anything now, even about people calling her a woman possessed by seven demons, or twice that number, for that matter. She walked toward the waterfront. Maybe she wanted unconsciously to see for herself the place where she was abandoned as a baby. She had forgotten, however, why she had come there once she arrived at the riverside. The first thought that came to her as she looked at the unclear water of the river was the thought of Shaphan. Shaphan, Shaphan, she called his name numberless times and she could well have thrown herself into the opaque water of the lake. She was drawing closer to the water thinking that was the only way to save her from this excruciating despair. Just then, Philip who was coming toward the waterfront on some business of his own caught sight of Mary who was just about to fall down into the water. Philip hurriedly ran up to her and caught her.

"What are you doing!" Exclaimed Philip. Mary, however, did not say anything. Philip could not get any answer or explanation from her although he tried in various ways to make her speak. He decided that she was not in a normal mental state and so leaving her in the custody of his family, went to Magdala and, there, found out the rough outline of the course of events. It was not until the next day, however, that Philip learned that Mary's real mother was no other than Shaphan's mother. He realized then the depth and darkness of Mary's tragedy for which he could find no words to console her with.

It was by chance that Philip mentioned the name of Jesus to Mary as she was sunken in this unfathomable despair. He had remembered the widowed woman who had followed the coffin of her only son in the town of Nain about a month ago. Philip happened to compare Mary's despair with the deep sorrow he had found that widow in, and then all of a sudden, the thought of mentioning what Jesus had done for that woman to Mary had occurred to him. He had witnessed with his own eyes how Jesus could save her from that bottomless despair. And from that he could easily imagine that there were many things Jesus could do for a person in despair.

"You had better go to him. Jesus, I believe, can solve all sorts of problems. In his hands, nothing remains unsolved. He can turn what has been happiness into misfortune and what has been unhappiness into blessing. There are things about him which we ordinary people cannot fathom."

When Mary heard this she said with a long sigh:

"You are the one who stopped me from seeking my salvation in death, so you had better take me to this Jesus."

From this time on, Mary became one of the women who went with Jesus wherever he went along with his disciples.

The crowd who followed Jesus were always over a thousand in number and half of it were women. But the ones who followed him along with the twelve chosen disciples of Jesus were the wife of Chuza Joannah, the widow who had her only son revived by Jesus, Salome, and Susannah. Especially, Joannah, Salome, and Susannah looked after Jesus and his disciples with their own money and for this were respected and envied by the crowd who followed Jesus.

And now Mary of Magdala became one of them. She had been called 'the woman possessed by seven demons' on account of her having lived with many men including the Roman centurion and this notorious person was now suddenly among this privileged entourage of Jesus. And moreover, she was the one who washed his feet with her hot tears and anointed them with myrrh and also spent her fortune for Jesus and his disciples with most generosity.

Joannah and other women found this situation awkward to say the least and they whispered among themselves:

"Wouldn't it be good if the Lord would place that woman separately from us?"

Just as they whispered like this, however, Jesus turned his clear blue eyes toward them and they all thought in their minds: The Lord has seen through our mind.

"Listen," said Jesus finally. "This woman is not the same as before. Do you still doubt the one who has been born again?"

As they were scolded by Jesus in this way, the women looked embarrassed and threw a surreptitious glance in Mary's direction. But Mary was indifferent to their glance or whispering. She was merely looking at Jesus with such intensity that she was completely immobile.

She had become wordless to the extent that she could have been taken as a dumb person after she began to follow Jesus. She neither talked to people nor answered them easily when talked to. When she was forced to speak, she spoke in very brief words. In spending her money for Jesus and his followers, Mary did not personally manage affairs but had Philip take care of everything for her.

Since Mary was so reluctant to speak, Thomas could not find out any more things from her aside from what he had heard from Philip. When he asked about the situation in Nabatea, also, she merely and reluctantly said, "Everything is fine, I think." When Thomas asked her about Shaphan, Blood Contract Corps, and Zilpah specifically, she did not give him any answer or explanation. In fact she was dumber than a real dumb from the point of view of the other people.

Thomas who knew about her more than anybody around, however, did not get angry with her or resent her for acting that way. Only he wanted to hear more about Shaphan, Blood Contract Corps and Zilpah but could do nothing about it.

After leaving the territory of Nabatea, the men of the Blood Contract Corps travelled divided into groups of five or seven. This was of course in order to hide their move and activities from the world. Shaphan was travelling in a carriage with Zilpah, and the carriage was guarded by the members of the Blood Contract Corps at the head and rear with some distance. When the party travelled past Mt. Nobo and reached the three-forked road of Heshbon, however, it was attacked by a gang of robbers of unidentifiable element. They were armed with arrows and bows and also with daggers, mostly. Only two of them had spear and sword. It was a dawn when a crescent in the shape and color of a sharp curved knife was hanging over Mt. Nobo. Shaphan and his party were asleep among the rocks when they received this attack, and the robbers came down on them from the top of the mountain.

It was Zechariah of Oprah that first caught sight of the assailants. Not knowing that the enemy was so large in number, Zechariah hid himself behind a rock and waited for the enemy to come down closer. He did not bother to wake Shaphan. At last, he saw a black silhouette emerge in the blue moonlight, and at the same time he shot an arrow and the enemy fell. Other shadows stopped moving and stayed among the olive trees, but all at once, a large number of men came down the mountain slope so quickly that they looked as if they were rolling down. Zechariah shot another arrow but now he had no time to ascertain its effect because there were too many continuing down the slope in a hurry. Zechariah called his partner Timeus: "Timeus, bring me a spear."

Even as he spoke he pulled his sword and ran out of his hiding behind the rocks and confronted the enemy. There were about seven or eight men facing him.

"I will cut whoever comes closer."

"Who are you?"

"I am one guarding this place."

"You move aside. We have no business with you. What we want is inside that carriage."

"It will be a better idea for you to turn back. That is, if you wish to keep your heads."

As soon as this was said, the robbers came down on him all at once. The one at the head threw a dagger at Zechariah but it only struck against Zechariah's sword and with a sharp noise fell on the ground. The robbers seemed to falter when they saw this. They seemed surprised that the dagger did not hit Zechariah on the chest or wrist making him drop his sword.

They moved forward again, however, this time in three groups. When he saw this, Zechariah was dismayed. While he was fighting against the three men who were approaching from the front, the rest of them came down on the right and the left.

By this time, however, Timeus had joined him along with some other Corps members with spears and swords. And they guarded the carriage so closely that the robbers could not even go near it and fled with two men seriously wounded and left behind.

Timeus himself had run to Zechariah to assist him. He found two bodies lying about where Zechariah was but it was not only the robbers that were wounded. Timeus saw that Zechariah himself was bleeding.

"Are you wounded?"

"It was this rascal that did it," said Zechariah and pointed to one of the bodies lying around his feet. He was the one who had come out first and thrown his dagger at Zechariah.

"This fellow was quite skillful with his dagger."

"You were wounded with a dagger?"

"The second dagger he threw. I could not meet it being busy fighting the others. And it was very dark, too, you know."

"But how could you get him like this?"

"I had to use my left hand. What else could I do?"

"Is he quite dead, then?"

"I don't think so."

"Are you going to finish him?"

"I will leave him as he is. He can go back alive if he desires it," said Zechariah and then added, "One that lies by your feet is not your enemy."

It was the belief of Zechariah that you should avoid any death if it is possible at all to do so. He was unusually skilled with weapons and was next to only Shaphan along with Jair in the Corps in military arts. He was an old friend and comrade of Jair's but he did not agree with Jair in the matter of killing. Jair believed that one should kill an enemy if one meets him in a battle.

"Why are you acting like a murder ghost?" Zechariah would say to Jair in a reprimanding tone. And then Jair would retort:

"I am not a sissy like you. Why do you carry sword if you don't wish to kill an enemy? Is it some kind of a toy to you?"

Even now, Zechariah seemed indifferent to taking the life of an enemy although he was lying at his feet completely powerless.

"Just as you wish," said Timeus because he thought that there was nothing to be done if Zechariah was acting out of his conviction.

Leaving behind the wounded robbers, therefore, they went down the slope to where the carriage was.

"Why did you not wake the people but fight the robbers all by yourself? Your ambition is unbelievable," said Shaphan jokingly.

"I did not know there were so many. I thought there were two or three at the most."

"Had they notified to you that they would come here only in two or three?" joked Shaphan again and they laughed together.

But in any case, it was not any problem for them to have a fight with gangs of robbers whether they be a gang of two or three or more than that. What was a real difficulty and danger to them was being pursued by the Roman army. From the letters sent by Ananias and Thomas lately, it was apparent that the Roman army was now concentrating on finding out the whereabouts of the Corps headquarters and Shaphan.

From Heshbon, therefore, Shaphan travelled only during the nights and spent the daytime either in shaded places along the valley or the houses of people who were connected with the Blood Contract Corps.

When Shaphan and his party arrived at Gadara, a man that belonged to Jair's section came up to them and reported that the Roman troops were spread throughout all important roads and towns around Gadara to the southeastern part of the Sea of Galilee. According to this man's report, it had been about a week since the Roman troops were positioned over this district. He also said that about three days ago, there was even an actual combat, although on a small scale, near the mountain slope of Gerasa where the Corps headquarters was located. It seemed there were only two casualties and that on only the Roman side in this confrontation. In the town of Gadara, too, one of the Roman soldiers had been killed by the Blood Contract Corps and therefore the Romans, he said, were afraid to go out in the night.

"Do you think, then, that they guess at the location of our headquarters?"

"I think they do, at least roughly."

"Why then did they not concentrate their force on Gerasa but scattered it all through the southeastern areas?"

"First of all, they do not know for sure that our headquarters is in Gerasa and then they seem to think that we have our bases in various places throughout the southeastern district."

Shaphan seemed to agree with this interpretation. Nodding his head, he said again:

"Also they are sure to have taken into consideration the fact that some of us were away in Nabatea."

After thus supplementing the man's report with his own comment, Shaphan asked again:

"How big is their force?"

"I think about two hundred men."

"They must be mostly searching squads and the advance guards."

That night, Shaphan sent Zilpah along with Zechariah to Chorazin and went to the headquarters with the falcon.

The mountain path on the cliff that one had to pass in order to reach the headquarters from Gerasa was very dangerous, more so than about ten years ago because of the increased number of traps that had been dug along the route.

In addition to the traps there were ditches, also, that had been dug in various places and even the rocks, trees, the hills, and the valleys were all mobilized as strategic tools by the Blood Contract Corps adding further danger to whoever tried to approach the headquarters. And all these were worked out by the Second and Third Members that belonged to Jair, Ananias, and Thomas. They had worked during the nights in order to provide the headquarters with all these various defence devices.

When he arrived at the headquarters, Shaphan found Hadad sitting as usual on his favorite rock in front of the cave. He was looking up at the stars in the sky.

"How are you, Corps Teacher?" Shaphan greeted.

"Oh, is that you, Commander? Have just come?" said Hadad with a voice that had more warmth than usual in it.

Shaphan told him what had happened so far and also mentioned how valuable a service the falcon had rendered during their struggle to rescue Zilpah.

Taking the falcon from Shaphan, Hadad said:

"So where is Zilpah, now?"

"I sent her to Chorazin because I judged it might be dangerous for her to stay here for the time being."

"Oh, no, Commander. It would not be dangerous for her here. It is your royal palace here."

"Examine my star for me, Corps Teacher."

"I have been examining it until now. You are on your way to becoming the king now. You need not heed anything as you follow this path. You need only to push on."

As he listened to these words of Hadad's, Shaphan felt a

burden lifting itself from his mind. Whether or not it was a realistic prophesying, Hadad's words gave him strength and comfort in the midst of the hard time he was going through.

That very night, he received report from Jair and also sent words to Thomas and Ananias to come to see him. Next night, Thomas and Ananias came to the headquarters. Ananias first reported to Shaphan that the Roman troops in the district of Galilee had from the first underestimated the strength of the Blood Contract Corps and seemed lately even to have begun to temper their suspicion of Shaphan. The reason why they had underestimated the strength of the Blood Contract Corps was that the Corps was smaller in scale than even the Zealots. They had considered the Corps as little more than a gang of bandits. In other words, they had not viewed the Blood Contract Corps as an anti-Roman organization but common armed bandits often seen along the valley areas. They had, therefore, thought they would be able to suppress the enemy quite easily with a force of thirty. When the thirty men whom they dispatched to Gadara failed to put an end to the rioting but rather resulted in the deaths of two men on their side, they sent sixty more men and had them cover the whole of the district of Galilee. When a couple more deaths occurred in a small scale battle near Gerasa, the Romans changed their tactics from an active search to a more passive operation.

The reason why the Romans had judged the suppression of the Blood Contract Corps force lightly and even after having a number of their men killed without any progress toward their goal still did not adopt any active tactics was that they still did not think the Corps as a real military threat, said Ananias.

"Didn't you say that the Roman force is now about two hundred men?"

"They seem to have increased the number after that."

"If so, they cannot be said to be passive in their strategy. Why would they have increased the number of men if they did not mean to take an active measure?"

"I think it was to prepare against emergency."

"What kind of emergency, do you mean?"

"Such emergency as our attacking them suddenly or the return of the Corps force that had been in Nabatea."

"It does not sound convincing. If they had thought, as you say, that we were no more than bandits, they could not have prepared against our giving them a sudden attack and neither could they have even imagined that we had gone as far as Nabatea with an intention to fight when we were mere gang of bandits."

"You have reason there, Commander. Maybe, then, the Romans changed their opinion about the nature of our organization after their initial confrontations with us. Come to think of it, even two days ago, there was a very lively movement among the Roman troops which could not be explained quite easily."

"What we should do, therefore, is to expect the worst possible situation from our point of view. Let us suppose, then, that after failing to defeat us with a force of about one hundred men, they decided that it would not be a simple task to put us down. The important part is what comes after that. The fact that they became less active after two attacks and some deaths on their part could be interpreted as a decision to change into a passive tactic. It could be supposed that they will remain quiet as long as we do not take an offensive attitude. On the other hand, however, they may be keeping themselves busy collecting information and making investigations."

"Conservatively, then, we should maybe rely on the second interpretation?" said Ananias. And here Thomas came into their conversation:

"If as you say there is a possibility that they would deal a sudden attack on us at a certain point of their present campaigning, what is your estimation of the time of that event?"

"What do you think is the factor that they are completely ignorant of at present?"

"The location of our headquarters. That we are protected by the water in the front and by the rocky hills on the sides and at the back, perhaps," spoke Jair for the first time since the conference started.

"In my opinion, although they may not be certain about it, they know the approximate location of our headquarters. It was in Gadara that they had stationed a force of thirty men at the start and then they had spread an army of sixty men along the southeastern coast of the Sea and finally had a battle, if on a small scale, near Gerasa. From all this, I think we may do wisely by judging that they have a pretty good idea about our position."

It was Thomas who made this remark and on this Shaphan commented:

"Yes, I think Thomas has a point."

Ananias seemed to agree on this point.

"If so?" said Shaphan.

"My feeling is that the Romans at least do not know the fact that we are trying to unite forces with Jesus," said Thomas. Shaphan nodded his head without saying anything and then spoke in a quiet voice:

"I think Thomas is right. What they do not know is our organization. They do not know that we are seven on the First Member level and forty-two on the Second Member level, two hundred and ninety-four on the Third, two thousand on the Fourth and then some of our sections have grown down to the Fifth Member level. As a result, over a hundred thousand of our Corps members are spread all over the country. They think that we are not such a political threat as the Zealots, for instance, and consider us bandits of some negligible scale. And we, on our part, have pretended to be just that. What we must remember is the fact that we should not rise up foolishly the way Judas, Theudas or Barabbas did but seize a moment when once we rise up we can really eliminate the entire Roman army from our land. We do not intend to ruin the Roman Empire but we must force them to make an exception of our country

Judaea that worships Jehovah. We will make them retreat somewhere, to Egypt, to Syria, or some other country. That is why we are trying to draw the Messiah to our side although we are equipped with fine armoury, formidable organization, and excellent military skill. In any case, what I want you to remember is never to lose your head. If our headquarters is attacked, we will move to our second base and then on to the third. There is no cause for alarm or confusion."

"We will remember well what you have just said, Commander," said Ananias and turned to Thomas and Jair in turn. Both of them nodded their heads in assent.

Shaphan next told Ananias to give full force to collecting information about the moves the Romans would be taking from then on and then to Jair he asked about the quantity of arms and food stored at the headquarters.

"We have enough to fight against a Roman army of three hundred for a year," said Jair confidently.

When the talk about the Romans and warfare roughly ended, Thomas began his report.

After reporting on the activities of Jesus since their last conference to this day, Thomas summarized what he had found out during the interval.

First, he made an analysis of the relationship between the so-called 'kingdom of heaven' that Jesus spoke about and the kingdom the Blood Contract Corps intended to found. He said that what Jesus called 'the kingdom of heaven' was essentially not a kingdom to be founded on earth and had nothing to do with flesh and material. But he did not seem to be entirely indifferent to the reality in which Judaea and Jewish people were situated in, said Thomas. It was clear when one thought about a phrase in the prayer Jesus taught the people, namely the phrase that ran: Thy will be done on earth as it is in heaven. Thomas added that he felt this particular phrase was the result of his conversation with Shaphan at tax-gatherer Matthew's house the previous year.

"I spoke to him again after that. If Israel is occupied by the

Romans and Jerusalem trampled with their feet, who would remain there to worship our God Jehovah?"

"What did he say to that?" asked Ananias.

"He said that the people of Israel did not forget to worship God even after they had been taken to Babylonia and told me to pray constantly so that the will of Jehovah would be realized on the earth. I asked him, then, if he thought, when the will of God would be realized on the earth, the Romans would move out of Judaea and, he gave me only an indirect answer by asking back how there could be suffering in the midst of the fulfillment of God's will."

"He avoided answering to your question directly," said Jair.

"It was clear, in any case, that Jesus wished to stay away from the Romans."

"Don't you think that it is because he is afraid of them?"

"I cannot tell because he never says anything definite about the Romans. As far as I could see, however, he did not seem to fear the Romans. Rather he seemed to ignore them."

"Why he ignores them is another question that needs an answer, don't you think?" asked Shaphan.

"Yes, I see your point. I will now tell you about another observation I made which perhaps would throw some light on the present question."

The other observation Thomas meant was the fact that the direct enemy Jesus was facing now were the Pharisees and the Levites rather than the Romans. But it was not because the Pharisees and the Levites were weaker as a force than the Romans, Thomas pointed out. He went on:

"It is absolutely clear that he hates the Pharisees and the Levites more than he hates the Romans. It is because the ones that hinder his propagation of the 'gospel of the kingdom of heaven' most are the Pharisees and the Levites. At first thought, this seems unlikely because the Pharisees and the Levites are the people who, like Jesus, worship Jehovah, the only God of Jewish people while the Romans are not. But the reality is that since the Romans do not know anything about

Jehovah or care anything about Him, for that matter, they are almost entirely indifferent to the work Jesus is doing whereas the Levites and the Pharisees are not in a position to be indifferent to it. Jesus calls Jehovah his father and claims that it was He that sent him to the earth. He also says that all the power he had came from Him and that his power included the power to forgive sins. He also thinks nothing of healing sicknesses on the Sabbath. From the point of view of the Pharisees and the Levites this is blasphemy to God Jehovah whom they worship and a traitorous act against Moses who is the founder of the Law Jesus breaks, and also since Jesus criticizes and condemns them in front of the people, Jesus was their personal enemy."

"Is the conflict very sharp at present?" asked Jair.

"Yes. The Levites and the Pharisees set their minds on trapping Jesus at first chance. And Jesus is determined to go on with his work of spreading the gospel of the kingdom of heaven even if he would have to confront them directly. To Jesus, it seems more important to spread more news about his kingdom in heaven than fighting the Romans."

Shaphan spoke again:

"You have just said that it is more important to Jesus to spread the gospel than fighting against the Romans. But I am not sure if you are quite right. The bases of my doubt are first maybe Jesus thinks he could make the Romans go by spreading his news of the kingdom of heaven and second he may think that when the kingdom of heaven is established on earth through his effort, the conflicts between the Romans and the Jewish people or between any other parties would automatically disappear. If the former is the case with Jesus, Ananias' suspicion that Jesus may be preoccupied with this spreading of the gospel because he wishes to avoid direct confrontation with the Romans for fear may be right. If the second is the right guess, however, Jesus is one harder for us to grasp than we have thought up to now."

"If I dare to insist on my own personal opinion, I think the second is the right interpretation. I am convinced myself that it is not to avoid direct confrontation with the Romans or to settle with a less formidable enemy that Jesus chooses to fight against the Pharisees and the Levites before the Romans."

"Don't you then think Jesus is the Messiah?"

"I do not know. My hesitation to believe him to be the Messiah is based on the doubt why Jesus does not wish to chase the Romans out of this land if he is the Messiah. And then, on the other hand, if he is not the Messiah how could he talk as if he were descended directly from heaven and how could he work such wonderful miracles? The solution I found for this question is to build my hope on his admonishment about our praying that the will of Jehovah be realized on earth as it was realized in heaven."

"Do you mean to say there are no other ways except praying?"

"I asked him that, and he said what method there could be besides praying in bringing about the realization of the will of God."

"Even so, if that will is to be realized on this earth, it seems there would be other means of bringing it about besides prayers. For instance, Moses relied only on the prayers at first but later he stood up and went out to fight the Egyptians from the front, didn't he?"

"But Jesus is different. I don't think he has any intention of confronting the Romans for the time being."

"If we take the lead?"

"He will leave us to our fate as he left Baptist John to his."

"If the Romans interfere with the activities of Jesus?"

"I don't know what he will do in that case."

Before Thomas finished speaking, Ananias opened his mouth:

"We cannot stand and watch him forever speak about the kingdom of heaven not minding what happens here on the earth. Thomas, Judas, and Philip should try all means to connect the power of Jesus with our work without any further delay. Do you not think so?"

"You are right in saying that and in fact I am at a loss what to do. Seeing his power work miracles, I cannot possibly declare he is not the Messiah, but hearing him speak about things too distant from our goal, it is hard to believe that he is really the Messiah."

Thomas spoke in a candid tone. All looked at Shaphan who after a long while said in a thoughtful but sad voice:

"He will support us when the time comes. What we should do is push on according to the plan."

"We understand the meaning of your words roughly, but do tell us in more concrete terms," said Thomas. Since he was following Jesus with a mission to connect the Corps and Jesus, he was not in a position to let Shaphan's words go only half understood.

"All right," said Shaphan. And he disclosed a plan he had in mind. It was letting one of the Corps members kill a Roman soldier and put the blame on Jesus and his followers.

"We will take care of all the necessary actions. And your job is to stay closely by Jesus and watch his reactions merely. And without his sensing anything, try to lead him into taking the steps Moses had taken. Do you understand what I mean, now?"

"Yes."

"Do you think Peter and John and their brothers will also cooperate?"

"They too wish Jesus to become a more realistic Messiah. But they will not cooperate if they found out that it was through intentional intrigue of the Corps that Jesus is forced into taking that position."

At last, Thomas made a brief report on what happened with Mary of Magdala. (Detailed report on her had been made to Shaphan before the conference began.)

He told the group about how she had been led to Jesus by Philip and how she was saved out of despair and how ardent a follower of Jesus she had become.

None of the men present had any comment to make on this report because it was not in the nature of a Corps meeting to discuss this affair in any seriousness or detail.

Shaphan too kept silence. But his face was shadowed by a deep sadness and agony.

Chapter 7

Disappearing Stars

It was during the most active teaching period of Jesus that Mary of Magdala came to Jesus. He did not seem to have any hesitation or fear about his work, at this time. He was filled with purpose, passion and courage. He was also most active in demonstrating his power as the son of Jehovah. It was during this period that he fed five thousand men with five loaves of bread and two fish and yet had twelve baskets of remnants afterwards, and this was also the period when he walked over the lake between three and six in the morning and during this interval he also made a blind man 'see everything clearly' in Bethsaida.

His accusations and denunciations of the Pharisees and Levites also had reached the peak. He said, for instance:

"Alas for you Pharisees! You pay tithe of mint and rue and every garden-herb, but have no care for justice and the love of God. It is these you should have practised, without neglecting the others. Alas for you Pharisees! You love the seats of honor in synagogues, and salutations in the market-places."

Listening to this, one Pharisee lawyer protested:

"Why do you insult us, Master?" And Jesus said:

"Alas for you lawyers! For you load men with intolerable

burdens, and will not put a single finger to the load. Alas, you build the tombs of the prophets whom your fathers murdered, and so testify that you approve of the deeds your fathers did; they committed the murders and you provided the tombs."

To the chief priest and elders he said:

"Truly I say to you; the tax-gatherers and prostitutes will enter the Kingdom of Heaven sooner than you will."

The Pharisees and the Sadducees at first planned to dispose of him by using force, but they feared his disciples and the great crowds that followed. (This was when Jesus went to Gadara to avoid them.) They next tried to get rid of him with help of King Herod (Antipas). They, therefore, went to Herod and told him that Jesus called himself 'the Messiah' and had a plan to rise up against the Romans or that Jesus was Baptist John come back to life. These reports touched Herod on the sore places just as the Pharisees and the Sadducees had counted on.

Herod sent men along with the Pharisees to check on the situation. So they went to Jesus.

The Pharisees who had gone to Jesus with the messengers of King Herod said to Jesus:

"Master," he said, "we know that what you speak and teach is sound; you pay deference to no one, but teach in all honesty the way of life that God requires."

The manner of the Pharisees with Jesus was perfectly polite and humble. The reason for this was that they wanted to earn sympathy of the people by acting that way. They now asked Jesus:

"We have a question. Are we or are we not permitted to pay taxes to the Roman Emperor?"

There was a triumphant smile on their faces as they put this question to Jesus. They felt sure that Jesus would not tell them to pay the taxes to the Roman Emperor who was the greatest enemy of Jewish people. And if Jesus told them not to pay the taxes, it would be an act of rebellion toward Roman Empire, which was an offence grave enough to receive a capital punishment if reported to the Roman governor. In short, the Pharisees were convinced that whichever answer Jesus might give them, they would be sure to catch him this time.

Jesus knew what was in their mind and after fixing his glance on his interlocutors a while, opened his mouth:

"What kind of money do you use to pay your tax with? Show it to me."

One of the Pharisees took a silver piece from an agent of Herod's and handed it to Jesus.

"Whose head is this, and whose inscription?"

They answered:

"Caesar's."

"Very well, then," said Jesus, "pay Caesar what is due to Caesar, and pay God what is due to God."

They did not understand the meaning of what Jesus told them clearly. But they felt that they could no longer carry on the interlocution on the subject. And the crowd was shouting in triumph when they heard Jesus' answer to the Pharisees. It was not that the crowd understood Jesus any better than the Pharisees. They were only happy that Jesus did not tell the Pharisees either to pay the taxes or not to pay them and instead stopped their mouths so that they could not ask any further questions. This was enough for them because they knew from the first it was really not the question of paying or not paying the taxes to the Roman Emperor as long as Judaea was under his rule but a matter of how Jesus could escape their conspiracy to trap him by a skillful manipulation of words. And Jesus could not only escape their trap but also made it impossible for them to continue their chase. And this feeling was shared by the closest followers of Jesus, also. Thomas was the only exception. He was sorry when he saw the Pharisees retreat without being able to question Jesus any further. That evening, he went up to Jesus as he was resting under fig tree. He said:

"Lord, you spoke very well this afternoon. But there is one thing I could not understand. That is why I come here like this."

Jesus turned his head slowly and looked at Thomas. After a long while, Jesus said in a very low voice:

"Speak, Thomas."

He looked very tired and seemed reluctant to speak. But at the same time, he seemed to feel duty-bound to answer a question a follower of his wanted to ask.

"You said, Lord, that we should pay what is due to Caesar to Caesar and what is due to God to Him. I know that the silver piece we use is Caesar's, but whose are the Jews and the land where they live on?"

Thomas was thinking this was a question the Pharisees of that afternoon ought to have asked Jesus as he put this question to Jesus.

Jesus was silent with his eyes closed. It was not clear whether he was thinking what to answer or just taking some more rest. And Thomas watched his face with anticipation. When quite a long moment passed in this way, Jesus opened his eyes and said:

"Thomas."

It was a low and gentle voice that Thomas finally heard from his mouth.

"Yes, Lord, I am here."

"Which side are you closer to, the side of the sinners you were with that time at the house of tax-gatherer Matthew's or the Pharisees of this afternoon?"

Jesus was asking Thomas this question remembering the fact that Thomas was with the Blood Contract Corps head members such as Shaphan, Ananias, and Judas when they had gone to Matthew's house with a secret intention to meet Jesus and he was also reminding Thomas that the question Thomas had just put to Jesus was being asked from the point of view of those 'sinners' rather than from that of the Pharisees.

"Lord, the Pharisees can take their consolation from the Law. But the 'sinners' you have just mentioned believe that if Judaea continued to be trampled under the feet of the Roman rulers, there would be no Law, or property that could give consolation to the Jews. I myself was one of the 'sinners' before I followed you, Lord."

"Thomas, your words are in the right. Therefore, I will say this to you: The Jews and the land they live on belong to God."

"If so, Lord, why is Pilate who is one of Caesar's people the master of this land and its people?"

"Listen, Thomas, it is not all of Jewish people and their land that Pilate is the master over. He rules only the flesh of Jewish people and the silver pieces in their hands, not their minds. Therefore, Thomas, what you should do is to worship with the mind God gave you and strive to earn the eternal life and glory of His Kingdom."

There was strength in the voice with which Jesus said these words which Thomas could not have imagined there would be looking at his tired face when he first found him under the fig tree.

"O my Lord, how can there be mind where there is no flesh? The house of mind is body and the house of body is land. Let our mind be with our body and our land."

"Thomas, you do not know yet the meaning of the words that your mind belongs to God. What you need now is not words, therefore, but prayers. Go and pray."

Jesus' voice was still gentle as he concluded their conversation thus.

The question remained in Thomas' mind even after he had this conversation with Jesus in which Jesus explained things to him in such a kind and patient way. What he could not understand above all was why there should be a division between the flesh and the mind. It was as unclear to Thomas just as the concept of heaven and land as two separate and incompatible things was difficult for him to grasp.

Next evening, Jesus and his followers went back to Capernaum. Shaphan and quite a few of the Corps members were also in Capernaum. In fact, they had been waiting for Jesus' return there.

On the second day after his return, a group of Sadducees came to Jesus in early hours. The Sadducees were a privileged class consisted of the learned and the wealthy of Jewish society and on account of their background were inclined to Greek ways. Many of them, therefore, did not believe in the eternal life but claimed to have higher culture and the more progressive mind than most of their countrymen. They also thought that if there were to be the Messiah among the Jews, he would be born from their own class and, therefore, did not have any reverence toward Jesus. The only reason they did not make themselves direct opponents of Jesus the way the Pharisees did was that their power did not have much footing in the common populace. In other words, the people did not belong to the Sadducees but to the Pharisees.

Geographically also, the Sadducees were in the most part residing in Jerusalem quite a distance away from the Galilee district where most of Jesus' activities so far were based. Galilee was not only quite remote from Jerusalem but also was considered less accommodating in its living conditions than the district of Judaea to the Jewish of higher classes. It was only in such bigger towns of Galilee as Tiberias or Capernaum, therefore, that Jesus had any chance of running into the Sadducees.

Now the Sadducees who came to see Jesus early on that day asked him this question:

"Master, Moses laid it down for us that if there are brothers, and one dies leaving a wife but no child, then the next should marry the widow and carry on his brother's family. Now, there were seven brothers: the first took a wife and died childless; then the second married her, then the third. In this way the seven of them died leaving no children. Afterwards the woman also died. At the resurrection whose wife is she to be, since all seven had married her?"

The reason they asked this question was to put Jesus in a difficult position, Jesus who saw through their minds said in a severe tone:

"You do not understand the Bible or the might of your God. At resurrection, one does not marry. Men and women who have been judged worthy of a place in the other world and of the resurrection from the dead become like angels of the Heaven. You talk of resurrection of the dead but talk as if you have not read in the Bible how God called Himself 'The God of Abraham, Isaac, and Jacob.' God is not God of the dead but of the living; for him all are alive."

Even the Sadducees who boasted of their learning could not find any word to say to these words. That at resurrection nobody would marry was something they had never heard before and was an entirely new interpretation of the text. But as long as they could not deny the words written in genesis, they could not possibly denounce the words of Jesus that they had just heard. They went away having only proved their own ignorance and lack of learning.

The Pharisees and the Sadducees were all put to shame in this way although their intention in approaching Jesus was in leading him into a trap so that they might lay their hands on him. The crowd that followed Jesus were very much moved by this victory of Jesus over his difficult inquisitors and revered him even more. At the same time, they whispered among themselves that this might result in something serious.

It was that very night.

About a hundred men who seemed to belong to the crowd that had been following Jesus attacked the barracks of the Roman army stationed in Capernaum and, after setting a fire on them and killing and wounding six soldiers, disappeared. This happened a little after midnight.

The Romans who were extremely alarmed put down the fire on the one hand and chased after the ruffians, on the other. They had completely disappeared, however, by the time the Romans recovered enough sense to go after them. The only thing they could guess was that some of them ran in the direction of the quay but a greater number went in the direction of the mountain foot where the tents of Jesus' followers were pitched.

The Roman army surrounded the area where the tents were. They were the more convinced about their action because they seemed to have heard at the time of the attack, some mentioning of Jesus and the Messiah from the mouths of the ruffians.

The followers of Jesus were peacefully asleep when the Roman soldiers surrounded them. Only when the soldiers had nearly finished their siege, they began to waken up.

"What happened? Surely the rascals ran this way...." muttered the Roman centurion who had led the chase.

The centurion had some of the men search among the people in the tents for weapons. And the result of the search was more disappointment because there was hardly anything among the possessions of the crowd which one could call a weapon. The soldiers, therefore, decided to arrest the ones with as much as a walking stick or a pocket knife. They amounted to two hundred men.

The two hundred captives were taken to the camp of the Roman army and were questioned. The Roman inquisitors insisted that among the two hundred were the culprits who had attacked their barracks. They threatened the men that they would execute them by nailing them on the cross if they do not produce the ruffians who had set fire on the barracks and killed their soldiers.

But how could any of the men that were there as captives know anything about what they were being questioned about? About a dozen of them said something about having heard some noise coming from where the barracks were or having seen flames rising in that direction but none of the rest had heard or seen anything.

"All right, then. You will all be crucified tomorrow," said the commander of the army.

It was not, however, as if there were none among the Romans who did not share the general feeling about the captives. One of them was the centurion whose favourite slave

Jesus had saved from death.

"In my view, Jesus has never acted against the Roman army. He has never said any bad word about the Romans and has never incited anyone to use violence on no matter whom. We saw for ourselves that the ones we have here were sound in sleep until they were caught, didn't we?"

"Didn't the ruffians say the name of Jesus, though? Some of our men say that they heard the word 'our Lord Jesus.' Let's bring Jesus here and question him."

"The army of great Roman Empire should refrain from careless acts at all times. If we were to put our hand on one who is receiving so much attention and respect without sure evidence, we don't know what kind of a fix we will be driven into. My opinion is that we carry our investigation in a different way."

Nobody refuted these words. It was a fact that although there really were some of them who claimed to have heard the name of Jesus uttered by the invaders, this did not prove anything because it could be an enemy as much as a friend who called the name of Jesus. Also, the fact that the chase was undertaken only in the direction of the foot of the mountain when it was evident that some of the invaders had fled to the waterfront was another factor to reconsider.

While there was this conflict of opinions about the method of investigation, a report which disproved the opinion that insisted Jesus' involvement in the attack came in from the Roman army stationed in Gadara. It was that on the night of the disturbance, a number of men who might be the men of the Blood Contract Corps took two boats at the waterfront of Capernaum and dispersed one party in the direction of Bethsaida and the other to Gadara vicinity. The reason they guessed these men to be the Blood Contract Corps members was just that there was no other underground organization in or near Galilee that had that much capacity for a collective action.

"See that? Maybe they are the true culprits."

This time, nobody objected. That night, all the men that had been taken from the tents were released.

The number of Romans stationed in Gadara increased daily. In the beginning, about two hundred were transferred from Tiberias and Capernaum making it a force of three hundred men in total. Later, another two hundred were brought in from the posts in Samaria.

About five hundred soldiers as a result surrounded Gadara on three sides, ready to attack during the day and lying low during the night but always alert.

The Blood Contract Corps in the meantime were only seventy in number as they took their position for fighting at the headquarters. Since they were to fight a force seven times their number, they were obliged to use the characteristics of the terrain to their advantage and also rely on other factors such as the traps, or some such other handicaps for the approaching enemy. At all events, they could not afford to have a face to face fight with the Romans. There were also the intricate signal system they had cultivated and excellent military skills of most of the members to count on. Although they could easily mobilize about three hundred Third Members that resided along on the shores of the lake, Shaphan and other First Members as well as the seventy men who were with them at the headquarters did not think it necessary or wise. Their firm belief was that with their geographical advantages, military skill, and discipline, they could fight not only against five hundred enemy soldiers but also against fifteen hundred.

The core of the matter was not in whether or not the Blood Contract Corps would be able to defend their headquarters but in forcing the Roman army to pull out of Galilee and Judaea altogether. It was, therefore, meaningless for them to come out victorious in a fight against a Roman force of five hundred in defence of their headquarters, unless it was conducive to the retreat of the Romans from the country. In other words, the headquarters did not need be the cave on the eastern shore of the Sea of Galilee. It could be moved to any other of the auxiliary centers of the Corps such as Mt. Tabor or Mt. Gilboa. What was important was that they ought to be reasonably confident about their ability to bring about a general retreat of the Roman army from all districts of Judaea before they could expose their force and the nature of their organization fully to the Romans and to the world.

The fight became more violent day by day and the Romans lost a force of forty men either in deaths or severe wounds after only three days' fighting. Still, they showed no intention of pulling out. The Commander-in-chief of the Roman army said:

"He must put an end to this even if five hundred more of Roman soldiers would have to be called in here. This is the order of the higher offices and also our duty."

His voice was pathetic as he announced this determination.

Although it was a three-sided confrontation, the main fighting was on the southern front. Every night, there was a threat of a sudden attack on either camp and Jair himself led a number of attacks and counter-attacks during the night. These were made by seven or eight men squad and all of them fought as if they were prepared to die. They went right into the midst of the Roman camp with their swords and spears ready to cut and kill. The least move to keep them off could end in a severe loss on the Roman side. Although the men of this shock party were especially fast and outstanding in military arts, it was the squad of strong bowmen at their back that played a greater role in wounding and killing the enemy. What was striking was the fact that the shock party rarely left their dead bodies behind after their charge.

In the southern front, the Roman army found only three of the enemy dead compared with sixty casualties on their side in the same area.

"Do we have to continue this war in this state?"

"Well. What a bad luck it is that we are to fight a war against a gang of bandits of all possible opponents!" The Roman soldiers grumbled. Although the cliff where the Blood

Contract Corps headquarters was was not a real fortress, it was indeed harder to capture than a real stone fortress.

Zechariah of Ophrah that was in charge of the eastern front, had dug deep ditch in the middle of the hill making it very difficult to climb up further once a man falls in this ditch. And the Romans who were in the lower terrain could not count on an effective fight when they should try shooting their arrows up the hill. This only chance was in a sudden attack but Zechariah never gave them any such opportunity. The Romans tried to fill up the ditch two times but failed every time.

On the northern side, there was a cliff that stretched on to the western front and the Romans were in a very dangerous situation along these parts because even a rock rolled down from the top of the hill could be a threat enough for the Romans who were at the foot of the hill.

In view of the various handicaps they faced because of the peculiarity of the terrain, the Roman Commander-in-chief gave up the fast-attack-and-fast-conclusion tactic that he had decided on in the beginning of the war and adopted a long-term strategy with a focus on the siege. With this intent, the Romans began to build a camp that was half permanent in the terrain they had secured. At the same time, they stopped attacks altogether.

The Romans seemed to calculate that if they continued the siege in this way, the enemy on top of the cliff would perish automatically for want of food.

This was, however, his miscalculation. The Romans could not cut the supply route of the enemy unless they could keep a watch over the entire area on and near Galilee day and night. There were two hundred and fifty Third Members of the Corps along the lake shore and the lake was just like their front yard. There was almost no chance to stop them from supplying food to the ones that were fighting on the cliff.

In this way, the war fell into a standstill.

Zilpah's falcon had been taken to the headquarters after the return from Nabatea but it was sent to Zilpah in care of Ananias when he came to the headquarters for their conference after the return. From next day on, the falcon came every day to the rock in front of the cave—the one Hadad sat on when he watched the stars at night—and perched itself on it.

It was the next day of the outbreak of the warfare. The falcon came to Hadad with Shaphan's letter on its leg as in Nabatea.

I am now at Ananias' house and am planning to go to Chorazin tonight. About last night, we were successful in setting the fire on the Roman barracks and escaping from there but are not sure how the Romans are going to take it. Show this letter to Jair and have him contact Zechariah and others and let them know of this also.

The Twenty First of August
Shaphan

Under the Feet of Corps Teacher Hadad

Hadad had Jair write an answer to this letter. When Jair said, "It would be better if you wrote it, Corps Teacher," Hadad had said:

"No, you know the circumstances here better than I do."

Jair picked up the writing brush and wrote as follows:

The Corps Teacher showed me your letter. From it we could learn about how things stand there and informed other Members accordingly. We will wait to hear about what happened afterwards.

The Twenty First of August

Under the Feet of Commander Shaphan

And next day Shaphan wrote:

Over two hundred followers of Jesus were at first taken by the Roman soldiers to their camp but most of them were released by evening. It seems they have heard some new reports from the Roman army stationed in Gerasa. The content of the report, as we found it out, was that several dozens of suspicious looking men crossed the lake and disappeared in the area of our headquarters and Bethsaida. Consequently, Jesus and his followers who had been strong suspects up to then which would have been most convenient to us stand differently at present.

From this all, it would be sensible to think that Romans will increase in number in your area and we can also foresee an open fighting.

The Twenty Second of August
Shaphan

Under the Feet of Corps Teacher Hadad

The next day, Shaphan wrote:

I have moved back to the house of Ananias in Capernaum along with Zilpah and her falcon. Ananias has a good foundation in this area and has many friends and information network that is most wide and intricate. I hear through him news of everything that happens. And besides, I think it is safest to stay here for the time being. From what I hear through Ananias, the Roman army has opened an emergency meeting and has made a decision to bring in one hundred more men from the Galilee district and another hundred from Gadara to be joined to the force in Gerasa. We must admit the fact that they have the power to bring in one thousand more men to fortify the present force. If so, it would not be possible for us to defeat them. And besides, unless the special power of Jesus is brought to our side, we could not have an open warfare with the Romans. We must, therefore, make a run through their boundary line and reach Dariqueyea and get together in Mt. Tabor before the Roman forces gather in Gerasa. I have let

one of our men get in touch with our headquarters in
Dariqueyea and Mt. Tabor.

The Twenty Fourth of August
Shaphan

Under the Feet of Corps Teacher Hadad

The reason why Shaphan did not take an authoritative tone
in writing these letters but merely gave hint to the general
outline of their strategy was that first of all he did not know
concrete circumstances at the Corps headquarters in Gerasa
and the Romans that gathered there. Secondly, even while he
planned general tactics, he could not help hoping that Jesus
would perhaps join forces with the Corps very soon. Maybe
there was some other motivation for his unusually passive
attitude but Shaphan himself was in no mood to analyze the
matter any further. The reason why he suggested their getting
together in Mt. Tabor was that Mt. Tabor was one of their
auxiliary headquarters next to the main headquarters in
Gerasa in importance. At the time, the Blood Contract Corps
decided on the cave in Gerasa as their headquarters, they had
also decided on two auxiliary headquarters one in Mt. Tabor
and the other in Mt. Gilboa.

On this day, the falcon came to the cave a little later than on
the previous day. It was around noon that the bird came to
perch on the rock in front of the cave. And the Romans had
started an attack early in the morning. The opinions of Jair
and Zechariah on the situation coincided, and they decided to
fight back as well as they could. But Jair asked Hadad:

"Corps Teacher, how do our stars appear? Do we have to
leave this front behind and go to Mt. Tabor?"

"Oh, Master Jair, our stars have already put on their
helmets and taken their spears. But only the enemy is bleeding,
not we," said Hadad as if he had been waiting for Jair to ask
that question.

"If so, there is no need for us to move to Mt. Tabor?"

"Oh, Master Jair, this is our headquarters. The falcon will have to fly from Mt. Tabor to this place."

Jair did not understand what Hadad meant by this but he was used to hearing Hadad give an answer that was quite off the mark of a question asked him or an answer that seemed to have no relation with the question asked. Asking him again in these cases was no use because he would only repeat the words he had already said. Jair did not ask him again this time, either. Instead he decided to write to Shaphan what Hadad had said:

By the time the falcon came to the cave, we had already been surrounded by the Romans on three sides. And besides, it does not seem right that we give our headquarters up before we can have a fight even. If our original plan was to forsake the headquarters and make our run through the enemy camp, we can do it any time. It won't be too late even if we fight back as long as we can and then, in case we are convinced that we can never win, act according to the original plan. Also, Corps Teacher's reading of the stars shows us as having put on our helmets and picked up our spears already. He also told us that it is the enemy that is bleeding and not us. We wish that you direct us as to what we should do next.

The Twenty Fourth of August
Jair

Under the Feet of Commander Shaphan

As he read Jair's letter, he felt a strange trepidation in his heart. His immediate thought was how he wished to be with them in their cave! All of a sudden, he felt an acute longing toward his comrades that were there. At the same time, the thought of his first discovery of the cave at the age of eighteen came back to his mind as clearly as it had been an affair of two days ago. It was then that he had first met Hadad. He had tried to kill Hadad with his dagger that time but was succumbed by his superior arts of magic. And it was from this time on that they had been bound with a tie that connot be broken throughout life.

(So then, is it war, at last?)

He mumbled to himself but as yet he could not think of anything in the way of acting up against the situation. He could not think of anything much at the moment, for that matter. He did not understand why he was so excited. He asked Ananias to let him have a jarful of wine. From earlier time, Shaphan had had a habit of getting drunken and sinking himself in debauchery when he was put to making an important decision. In other words, he got his answer through an intuitive conviction that rose up to his mind in the midst of a sensual gratification rather than through any intense thinking. After drinking up the wine that Ananias had brought to him, he began a wild feast of body with Zilpah. He seemed more drunk with the sight of the feast than with wine.

"Why are you so cold? Are you a woman, or are you a star that came down from the sky, what?" Shaphan talked as if to himself even while he frolicked wildly. It was because Zilpah did not open her mouth at all, although she never refused to do anything Shaphan asked her to do. She would take off her clothes if Shaphan asked it, and raised her arms if that was what Shaphan wanted. But she kept her mouth tightly shut from the first to the end. Only when the first rooster crowed Shaphan subsided the angry waves in his heart and then soon he started snoring.

Early next morning, Shaphan opened eyes that were bigger and more blood-shot than other mornings. All at once, he felt a happiness in his mind. It was because he now had a conviction that once he would get up from the bed, he would be able to go into action immediately.

First of all, he needed to let the Romans know that he did not stay at the headquarters but was away from it. And at the same time, he needed to make the Romans realize that the headquarters was where the Commander was and not the top of a cliff in Gerasa. In order to do this, he had to take up his position in Mt. Tabor and think up a way of challenging the Romans from this position. He was glad that he had drunk and had his debauchery because as always he was getting his reward for it. He turned to Zilpah and asked:

"Wasn't I too rough last night?"

". . . . ."

Zilpah did not answer.

"Did I say something awkward to you?"

". . . . ."

Zilpha looked at Shaphan with eyes that seemed to ask Shaphan why he was asking these questions as if he were a stranger.

"What's the matter? Why don't you answer?"

As Shaphan urged her to give an answer, Zilpah finally opened her mouth and said in a very demure voice:

"I am your only wife."

Shaphan could not say anything more. The meaning of Zilpah's words seemed to be that 'wife' was something that did whatever the husband told her to.

From her tone of voice, however, Shaphan could tell that she was not vexed with Shaphan's behavior of the previous night. All through last night, he had talked about Mary but Zilpah acted as if she were indifferent to it. Shaphan remembered how Mary had acted when Shaphan talked about Zilpah in front of Mary after Zilpah had been taken into the Nabatean palace. Although Mary's attitude may be said to have gone over the limit in its intensity, Zilpah's indifference also seemed somewhat unnatural. It could of course be a matter of background and upbringing, he said to himself, but perhaps there was something uncanny in her character that knew nothing of jealousy.

"Zilpah, don't you miss Mary?" Shaphan had asked, and Zilpah had raised her head for the first time to look at Shaphan. On her face was a hint of interest and sympathy now.

"Madam Mary gave the falcon to me."

"She had gone to Nabatea with us to rescue you."

"Where is she now?"

"Why? To send the falcon after her?"

". . . . . ."

"Zilpah, haven't you heard the word that Mary is my sister?"

"Who said that?"

Zilpah seemed ignorant of it.

"That is why she ran away from my side. She went to this man called Jesus. . . ."

"I don't understand. I think Madam Mary is a good person."

"Zilpah, I have only you now, and we will transfer our headquarters to Mt. Tabor in the near future. We will go there all together."

At the same time that he transferred the headquarters to Mt. Tabor, Shaphan fortified the force on the southern shore of the lake. It was because that was the entry they would use in going back and forth between Mt. Tabor and the Sea of Galilee.

Thomas had been in charge of Dariqueyea and its vicinity. After Thomas began to go around Jesus along with his fellow Corps members such as Judas and others, however, Timeus who was a Second Member took his place. Timeus was the one who had distinguished himself with his outstanding skill in the use of weapons in the rescue operation of the Blood Contract Corps at Nabatea, along with Zechariah. Shaphan had special feelings toward Timeus because he too was versed in military arts and the use of weapon.

That was why Shaphan entrusted Timeus with such a heavy duty. Also, he was the most trusted of Thomas' seven Second Members, too. In a sense, he was somewhat like Jair in his present relationship with Shaphan.

Shaphan was intent on letting the Romans believe that Mt. Tabor was the present headquarters of the Blood Contract Corps so that the enemy would not concentrate their force in

Gerasa, and in fact Mt. Tabor was becoming the main strategic center in that Shaphan himself posted himself there. His plan was to make the force in Gerasa move to Mt. Tabor as soon as Jair, Zechariah and the rest of the Corps members in Gerasa would have succeeded in giving a substantial loss to the Romans.

In case Mt. Tabor would become their main center of action and strategy, however, Dariqueyea could but be the sole passageway for the Blood Contract Corps members to make their moves in and out of the Lake of Galilee. And Timeus would accordingly be in the responsible position that Jair had been in up to the time of the beginning of this warfare.

As Timeus took care of various businesses that concerned the Corps and the Corps Commander with responsibility, the Second Members of the Corps who had served under Jair along with Timeus, were placed in the position of receiving commands from Timeus. They accepted this situation and moreover agreed among themselves to be as loyal to Timeus as they had been to Jair. As a result, Timeus had under his command the seven Third Members that had been under his command originally plus the six Second Members that had been under Jair with Timeus himself. Under the circumstances, some conflict of delicate nature arose between the Third Members and the Second Members that excepted Timeus.

When Timeus confided in Shaphan this new trouble of his that arose on account of his promotion to a higher state, Shaphan gave a few taps on his shoulder and said:

"You don't need to worry about it."

Right away, he made the following resolutions. He decided that out of the Second Members that had gone to Nabatea last time, he would send Uzzah and another to Gadara where they could work at the armoury or rather manufacturing plant of weapons. As for the remaining four, Shaphan decided that the two who got along with Timeus remain in Dariqueyea in the capacities of Timeus' senior adjutants, while ordering the remaining two to join the force at Mt. Tabor and guard the headquarters there.

Becher and Liberdinus, the two Second Members that were ordered to guard the headquarters at Mt. Tabor, went to their new post along with the seven Third Members that belonged to each of them. Ten out of them set about digging the cave deeper and installing the rooms, hanging up a cage for Zilpah's falcon, making traps between Mt. Tabor and Dariqueyea, preparing secret refuge, and so on. The four remaining ones went on a secret mission of Commander Shaphan to various districts of Samaria and Judaea, along with the two Third Members under Timeus. To Galilee and Decapolis, five Second Members under the leadership of Ananias were sent in order to convey Shaphan's order about preparing a guerrilla warfare against the Romans.

The concrete contents of Shaphan's order were as follows:

One. That in view of the fact that the day of the Messiah was near, the Corps members attack Roman barracks or armoury under the command of their regional leader and set fire on their housings and plunder their arms.

Two. That they apply themselves to mainly surprise attacks and guerrilla tactic but not fight the enemy from the front.

Three. That they should know that this was a war that would continue until the Roman Army should withdraw out of the country and so the Members must not rely on any horizontal contact until the Messiah should join forces with them.

Lastly, Shaphan had added, they should not take any reckless actions until good opportunities should present themselves.

The above message of Shaphan's was received with tension and excitement by the Corps members that were in Galilee, Judaea, Samaria, and even in some parts of Decapolis. The words 'the day of the Messiah was near' gave them much courage and enthusiasm.

"The Messiah has come."

"The Messiah has been seen."

They were all somewhat afloat with expectation and exhilaration. And it was no wonder because they had focused their lives on the final emergence of the Messiah in their midst to help them with their mission. Right now was the time they should prove their solidarity and faith in their mission, they thought. This was one time when one should burn one's life, they felt, and then all at one they remembered the name of Jesus. It was because to their minds, Jesus was either the Messiah or one who was closest to the Messiah. Even if he was not himself the Messiah, his appearance on the scene must have something to do with the immediate arrival of the Messiah, they thought.

Another factor in Shaphan's order that excited them was that he had told them to avoid a direct confrontation with the enemy until Jesus should join forces with them. They had through experiences with Judas of Galilee, Barabbas, and Theudas, learned the fact that the open rebellion of the Jewish people against the Roman army would end in 'sacrifice of blood' and in this view, Shaphan's order that they should not fight their enemy openly until the Messiah should be on their side moved their heart with its penetrating perception of the reality they were situated in. For this sagacity and consideration, they could act up to the situation with an absolute trust toward their commander and their organization. Gallio of Jobba was the first to rise up in action.

Gallio, who had more love and respect for Shaphan than any other head members of the Corps in spite of the distance between the Corps headquarters and his post, and who also longed for the arrival of the Messiah more ardently than most, was overwhelmed with emotion when he heard about Shaphan's command.

"Ah, this is an act of destiny!" he said and even trembled from deep emotion. This was the next day of the coming-in of Roman arms at Jobba quay through Alexandria. The arms were to be carried into the warehouse by the quay within that night. Since there were among the hired hands working at the waterfront many Corps members including some Second Members under his personal command and many Third Members, setting a fire on the warehouse or even the ship itself was no problem. What Gallio had meant by 'an act of destiny' referred to the fact that the arms and other supplies brought by the ship were right at the moment piled up in the warehouse ready to plunder or set fire on.

The only problem was how to go about it without letting the enemy find out the identity of its intruders. In order to find an answer to this question, he consumed a great deal of time thinking and experimenting. As a result of this long study, he alotted the work of setting fire to only a very few of choice members. In order to make it look like an accidental fire, they decided to set the lumberyard that was next to the warehouse on fire and let the fire move onto the warehouse with help of the wind. In order to make their plan work, they utilized the rather strong wind that blew in from the Great Sea (Mediterranean). Four days after the order was conveyed to him, Gallio succeeded in setting fire on the quay. The flame rose high in the sea wind.

The fire at first stayed on the warehouse but gradually spread wider, and, finally, by midnight, covered the entire area of the quay in flames. Wind was only one element instrumental to this spreading of fire. The other factors that helped the fire to spread were the lumber imported from Phoenicia and oil to be sent to Rome, which were all piled up at the quay. That night, while the red flames of the fire were still rising, Gallio hid the six members that were connected with this incident in a secret hiding place which nobody but himself knew.

The next day of the big fire at Jobba, there occurred a surprise attack on the Roman barracks stationed in Ophrah. A party of unidentified men, about two dozens in number, killed a Roman guard and penetrated into the barracks and after killing about a dozen sleeping soldiers set fire on the barracks and ran away with some arms belonging to the Roman army. Although the fire was soon put out, there were over a dozen casualties on the Roman side which instantly contacted Roman stationaries in Tiberias and Gerasa and other places. It was supposed by the Romans that it was the same party — the Blood Contract Corps — that was the culprit of this new offence just as in the similar happening that had taken place in Capernaum some time ago. Then on the seventh and tenth day after the incident in Ophrah, there occurred clashes between the Blood Contract Corps army and the Roman army.

Small scale incidents such as assassination of one or two Romans or infliction of wounds on some such small numbers were common throughout all areas.

The Roman authorities at first had thought of only the Ophrah incident as having any connection with the incident of Capernaum and judged the other incidents such as surprise attacks, murders, plunders, and armed collisions that took place in various spots as the deed of the Zealots.

As the reasons for thinking these other acts not as those of the Blood Contract Corps, the Roman investigation authorities pointed out the fact that the Blood Contract Corps forces were at the moment on the point of annihilation under a siege by the Roman army and, therefore, could not operate a wide-ranged strategy such as could be surmised by the nature of recent happenings in various areas throughout the entire land. Next, the Romans insisted that since the leaders of the Corps were nothing but bandits that chiefly aimed at plundering of goods, they could not be interested in such organized rebellion such as had been tried by such Zealots as Judas of Galilee or Barabbas. Another reason why they did not connect the incidents with the Blood Contract Corps was that they could not imagine that the Corps had a network that stretched not only through Judaea and Samaria but also Jerusalem and its vicinity. (Since the Jews in latter district had a habit of looking down on the residents of Galilee, it was, as a matter of fact, rather difficult to guess at a close connection between the two areas.)

What convinced the Roman authorities in their guess was the incident of the arrest of Barabbas, leader of the Zealots in Ephraim about two weeks ago. He was Theudas' direct successor and had many supporters throughout Jerusalem and Samaria. With these, he had planned an open rebellion but was betrayed by one of his own followers and captured alive. The Romans anticipated a retaliation by his followers and kept a close watch over the area comprising Arimathea, Ramah, El-bethel, Zorah, Nezib and Shechem and Thebez of Samaria. Even about the incident at Jobba, therefore, they had at first suspected no organized plan but had decided it to be a violence inflicted by the waterfront laborers either by accident or random disorderliness common among the waterfront gangsters. The Ophrah incident was the only happening that they had established any connection about with the Blood Contract Corps. When more incidents happened in other places including Jericho, Shechem and Arimathea, they began to suspect a large-scale planned rebellion, and yet, they only connected the incidents with the Zealots and left the Blood Contract Corps from even the scope of their imagination. It was only two weeks after these incidents that the Romans began to change their outlook on the situation. What made them have this changed perspective was the fact that contrary to their expectation that the Blood Contract Corps would be completely put down once the Romans captured their headquarters in the cliff at Gerasa, the Corps forces were active in their new headquarters between Galilee and Samaria led by their Commander and also the fact that some military tactics similar to those used by Shaphan could be detected in smaller collisions Romans had in Galilee, Judaea, Samaria, and part of Decapolis. The characteristics of their strategy were surprise attack, setting fire, killing, and plunder of arms. In all these clashes, the excellency of their skill with weapons, agility of movement were noted and they all used similar looking daggers and arrows and in similar style, too.

At this time, Jesus was spending his days in distant port towns Tyre and Sidon in Phoenicia. He had come out to these distant places in order to take a refuge from Galilee where he had many complicated relationships and Jerusalem and Judaea as a whole which had much enmity toward him. This was an act similar to the one he took when several months ago, he had gone to Gadara of Decapolis to rest. He had wanted to stay longer in Gadara but had been pressed to leave by the Greeks of that place. But it was about this time that his passion for teaching reached its highest peak and as a consequence there grew as much and acute enmity toward him as there were love and adoration by his followers.

What made his position more delicate was his relationship with the Blood Contract Corps. Although Jesus himself did not even know the Corps very well, he was the object of intense interest for the Blood Contract Corps members who wanted to mobilize his Messianic power and bring his huge crowds into their anti-Roman struggle. They did not hate Jesus the way the Pharisees and the Sadducees did but they too tried to pull Jesus into a trap. As the matters stood, Jesus had no political power to back him up. The Pharisees, the Sadducees, the Herod Faction, the Blood Contract Corps, the Roman army, and the Greeks in Decapolis, they all wanted to trap or kill him, or at the least, to chase him away from them like the Greeks. The rest were the people, the people who had no power or money but were only hungry and sick. And then they were the ones who always asked him to use his 'power' to heal their various diseases. Of course, they had no intention of harming him, but they were a cause of perpetual fatigue for him because prayers such as were required to satisfy them were a consumption of so much life energy on his part.

So he had come to Tyre and Sidon in order to get away from the kind of tense, complicated and energy-exhausting situation as mentioned above. He had wanted to talk to his disciples about the Kingdom of Heaven in this strange port town where nobody knew him.

The rumour about Jesus, however, had spread even to this remote area, and as a result, he could not rest even here. Soon a woman who was Phoenician by nationality came to him and cried in a loud voice:

"Lord, take pity on me. My daughter is possessed by an evil spirit." It was regretful for him to meet someone who knew him and wanted him to work a miracle and he wanted to pass by pretending not to have heard.

He said reluctantly:

"I was only sent to find the lamb of the house of Israel."

Saying so, he walked on without turning back. But the woman came up to his side and throwing herself at his feet implored:

"Lord, save me."

Jesus turned a face that showed displeasure to her and said:

"It is not fair to take the children's bread and throw it to the dogs."

It was too severe a comparison to call the Jews 'children' and the Gentiles 'dogs.' But 'children' was, of course, the same as 'the lamb' which he had mentioned when he first talked to her and so it was rather a comparison between 'the lamb' and 'the dogs' rather than 'children' and 'the dogs.' The meaning of his words was that he could not possibly save the Gentiles when he was not able to find the missing children of Israel.

But the woman was undaunted. She said:

"What you say is right, Lord. But even the dogs under the table eat the children's scraps." And she looked up at Jesus. In her eyes, Jesus saw the same thirsty longing that he had seen in so many faces that had implored him to save them and he felt an uncontrollable pity for her. And it had been always in this way that he performed the miracles, that is, he could not help looking at these pitiable faces without doing something for them. The moment he recognized the face of a life in despair in front of his eyes, Jesus could not differentiate 'the lamb of Israel' from 'the dog of the Gentile.'

"Woman. For saying that, you may go home content; the unclean spirit has gone out of your daughter."

The woman bowed to him many times and went back to her house.

He had, however, no intention to meet many more people, teach the gospel, or perform miracles in this area. He, therefore, went on to Sidon and then going around the upper stream of the Jordan River, went to Decapolis. He decided to go there instead of returning to Galilee because as yet he did not wish to expose himself to the dangerous and complex atmosphere that would surround him there.

In Decapolis, too, however, he was visited by the lame, the deaf, the blind, the paralyzed, the possessed who called Lord, Lord and surrounded him. He felt that he could not get away this time.

He began to pour the fresh water of Heaven on those imploring faces and cured them all.

Jesus could not stay in Decapolis for long, however, because a fight had started over the entire area of Gerasa. It was said that the Romans were fighting a punitive war to suppress a bandit uprising. Andrew was the first to hear this news and convey it to Jesus. Jesus and his disciples at once took boat and started for Galilee. Andrew and John wanted to go back by the road they had taken to come there and Thomas and Judas insisted on taking a shorter route, the one that went along the eastern shore of the lake. The two insisted on this route because they wanted to find out about the progress of the war and then also wanted to make Jesus get aroused by the scene of the fight to feel righteous anger toward the Romans.

When they were near Hippos, however, they were halted by the Roman cavalry. Jesus and his disciples were questioned by the commander of the cavalry who was tall and had a long face.

"Your name?" He asked Jesus.

"Jesus," answered Jesus calmly. At the same time, the commander smiled faintly. He had seen Jesus in Capernaum many times and also had heard from his colleague, a centurion, that Jesus had saved his slave from death. From other people too, he had heard of his teachings and the various miracles that Jesus was supposed to have worked. He, therefore, did not harbor any ill will or intention to harm him from the first but only wished to keep him off the battle zone.

"Your hometown?"

"Nazareth of Galilee."

"Where are you headed for now?"

"Galilee."

"And who are these people?"

"My beloved lamb."

"And the crowd outside?"

"The lamb that are looking for their shepherd."

"What is your occupation?"

"That of a shepherd."

"What do you feed those with?"

"I feed them the water of life from Heaven."

Kaska, the commander of the cavalry, tilted his head as if he could not understand what Jesus meant. He repeated, "The water of life," in perplexity.

Jesus, however, did not explain any further.

"Do you know there is a fight within thirty *ri* (= 7.5 miles) from this place?"

"No."

"Would that crowd not join in the war?"

"I don't think so."

Then Kaska asked the disciples:

"You, too, would you not join in the fighting?"

"We will only follow our Lord's footsteps," answered Peter.

Judas looked at Thomas which Thomas could feel without looking. But the latter did not know how to bring out the question. He had for nearly two years followed Jesus around. He had soon realized that he could not, as had been planned in advance, trick him into a trap—like the one which had been dug to force him to have a clash with the Romans—and yet he could still not leave the side of Jesus. The reason for this was the attraction he felt about the personality, thought, and power of Jesus. One more reason, perhaps, was that he wanted to believe Jesus to be the Messiah. Thomas thought that if Jesus was the Messiah, he would be one even if he would not act as they, the Blood Contract Corps, wanted him to. He also thought that even if what Jesus was trying to achieve now was remote from their own goal, in the future their separate goals would come together as long as he was the Messiah.

It was too much of a pity, however, that he should let a good opportunity such as the one that presented itself to him now pass by. He, therefore, stood up and opened his mouth as if to supplement the answer Peter offered.

"But we are very tired because we have travelled a long time. We would appreciate it very much, therefore, if we could go by the eastern coast from here."

Kaska hesitated a moment and then said:

"All right."

He seemed to decide that as long as Jesus and his followers had no intention of participating in the fight, he would do best by avoiding any clash with them over trivial disagreement.

The questioning of the Romans was over quickly in this way. But Kaska added as they were leaving:

"Your safety is secured if you will go straight along the eastern coast. If you would linger near Gerasa, however, you will be halted again or even arrested by the Roman army."

When they had gone out of the Kaska's quarters, Judas came up to Thomas and said:

"We will be acting too disloyal to the Corps if we cannot work up some good method to achieve our end."

"Isn't that why I talked the Roman commander into letting us take this route?"

"But we will be at the lake by this evening and so if we

cannot start something, right away, even your trouble to get us this route will serve no end, you know."

"But what could we do? I try but there is not good enough thought in my head, it seems."

Hearing Thomas speak thus, Judas smiled merrily and then said:

"I will tell you one idea I have. Will you hear?"

Thomas looked at him with a twinkle in his eyes. He seemed happy to hear Judas had an idea however good or bad it may be. Judas continued still smiling, "You know, the Romans are very fond of women."

"So?"

"What I mean is Mary of Magdala who is with us is an outstandingly beautiful woman. She would be enough to captivate any Roman soldier's mind at first glance, I think."

"So?"

"My idea is that we let her be caught by something like a centurion. Then, our Lord who loves her so would not stand by and do nothing, don't you think?" said Judas with a triumphant smile on his face.

"It is some idea, but hard to put into practice, I think."

"In what sense?"

"First of all, it is not possible to make Mary get arrested by the Roman army, quite apart from the question of how the Lord would act up to the situation. . . ."

"You are always full of questions and doubts. How come?"

"You had better have your try, then. I will talk to the Lord about rescuing Mary after you have done your part. . . ."

"All right, that suits me. But you must help me when I talked to the Romans since you know Greek and Roman better than I do."

Judas called Philip who was walking about twenty steps ahead of them. He was talking with Matthew when Judas called him. He halted and waited for Judas to catch up with him while Philip went on with his way alongside Batholomew.

"I have something to talk with your sister Mary. Won't you

arrange it for me?"

Philip agreed to do so without having a second thought about it. He merely thought that it was about one of those things Mary was involved in on account of her complex background that Judas wanted to see her about.

Mary who came with Philip to where Judas was standing kept her kerchief over her head and did not even look up at Judas.

"I will see you later, then," said Philip and walked away from them.

"The reason I wanted to see you was," began Judas after a while. "...By the way, have you heard about Romans surrounding our headquarters and attacking the Members?"

"No," answered Mary in a low voice.

"Commander Shaphan, Corps Teacher Hadad, Jair, and Zechariah are all locked up in the cave under the siege, you know."

After saying this in a grave and confidential tone, Judas threw a glance at Mary to see her reaction. Mary, however, did not say anything. So Judas was obliged to speak again.

"So, I thought of asking for your cooperation to rescue Commander Shaphan."

"......"

Still Mary did not say anything.

"You and Commander Shaphan are sister and brother, aren't you? And in the past you were lovers, too. I pray you help me with my plan for this one time."

"How can I help you?" said Mary in a barely audible voice.

"It is just that you meet some Roman in the rank of centurion."

Mary was silent again.

"Will you do it?"

"What good would it do?"

Mary's voice trembled a little when she asked this question.

Judas was embarrassed. He could not possibly say that she could be a help because she was so beautiful or that it wouldn't be too much to ask of her since she had the kind of background that she had.

"Isn't Commander Shaphan your own brother, Mary? Or, rather, something more than that, I should say...."

"I don't have a brother or anything else. I have forgotten every name I had ever known. And I don't want you to call me by my name."

Mary's voice was more resolute now.

"I cannot believe it. No, I cannot. You have a duty to rescue somebody who is your brother and was in such a special relationship with you in the past."

"......"

"Would you forsake your duty?"

"My duty has gone away when the names of people went away from my memory."

"That means a suicide for you. That means you are a corpse, do you realize it?"

Judas adopted a threatening tone of voice as he said this. But Mary kept her calm and said:

"No, it is not true. I have a different life, now."

Judas was even more upset by this reply. To him, this only meant that she now loved Jesus in place of Shaphan.

"You mean you replaced Commander Shaphan with Jesus?"

"Yes. The Lord gave me a new life, a different life. I have forgotten my former life altogether. All of it has disappeared. Do not blame me. In my mind, there is only a clear breeze that cannot be a burden on anyone. My past life was always just tears, sighs, and weeping...."

"That's where you are wrong. You fall in love with one man and then you possess him whole and forget all other things and then you move on to another man and the same thing happens...."

Judas seemed ready to inflict her any pains. But Mary seemed indifferent to it.

"The Lord has given me a new life. He told me so when I shed tears at his feet. Now I have no other wish than to listen to his words, and look up at his face and the robe he wears. Other than that I find no meaning in my life," said Mary and, turning, walked away from Judas.

"What, no other meaning in your life? Then, do you also deny the fact that you caused the death of a Roman centurion four years ago? Don't you know Shaphan is involved in it as much as you are? Who is Shaphan that you think so little of leaving him to annihilation?" Judas shot words at the back of Mary's head as she walked away.

"......"

Mary seemed unperturbed even by this. Without as much as turning back, she went to join other women.

Judas went to Thomas and after pouring curses and insults directed toward Mary, said:

"I will inform this woman to the Roman army."

"Inform her to the Roman army?"

Thomas looked at Judas unable to understand what was in his mind. He could not even understand why Judas was so upset with Mary of Magdala, in fact.

"Do you have any pity left for a woman who has betrayed us?" asked Judas sharply.

"Judas, you and I seem to have different ways of looking at things. From my point of view, she was not one of us to start with. It is up to her, therefore, to or not to render service to our Commander or our Corps. We cannot impose it on her, you see."

"That she was not one of us is only a play of words. Even if she was not formally a member, she was more than a member, to tell the truth, wasn't she?"

"It was through her personal relationship with the Commander that she was so. It may be a different story if she had taken advantage of such a relationship, but that is not what she has done. And besides, you say she herself said she has forgotten her past, that it has disappeared from her. Under the circumstances, it is not right for us to ask her to do anything for us."

"Your trouble is always your theory. Especially since it is always one that inflicts a loss on you. Do you, in short, think that she doesn't have a duty to rescue Commander Shaphan?"

"......"

Thomas seemed to find it hard to make an answer to this question. He kept silent with knit brows.

"She thinks the Commander is under siege at our Gerasa headquarters. I told her so. I won't care if she does not feel duty-bound toward the Corps itself. But what about the Commander? Does she or does she not have a duty toward Commander Shaphan? Just tell me this."

"Judas, in my opinion, it is something that must be settled between the two of them."

Thomas spoke in a voice which was lower and softer than before. And he continued:

"And Judas, you must remember what an unhappy woman Mary is. Isn't it rather natural for her to wish to forget even the name of Shaphan? I think it is perfectly understandable and we are in no position to blame her."

"Do you really think so?" Judas said in anger. He continued excitedly:

"Do you really find it so understandable for a woman to deny her duty toward one who was her lover, husband, and also a brother? Thomas, have you lost your head just like Mary?" said Judas and glared at Thomas with his peculiarly yellow eyes.

"My guess is she has forgotten him just because he was her lover, husband and brother. If he had been just one of them to her, she would probably not have forgotten him. It was precisely because he was those different things to her that she is denying all. Why don't you try to understand her feeling?" asked Thomas fixing his grey eyes which were deep-set contrasting with Judas' protruding eyes on the latter.

"I say that's just you game with words. If you add one to one, you get two; you don't lose both. I will take seven steps backward and accept it that maybe she replaced Commander

Shaphan with Jesus as lover. Still, would there not be her tie as a sister to him? If she forgets all other human ties just because she has found a new one, what does that make her . . . except a woman possessed with seven demons."

"Do you think Mary feels that way about Jesus?" asked Thomas. But he did not wait for Judas to answer his question. He continued:

"All right, let's suppose she does, that doesn't make much difference. But as you can see, she has no intention of making Jesus her husband. From this, couldn't we say that she is probably intoxicated by the deep comfort and new hope that she could receive from Jesus?"

"Where does she get this 'deep comfort and new hope' as you put it, then?"

"That is a question to which I am not sure I can give an answer easily. But before we consider that question seriously, let us admit once and for all, the fact that Mary has reached the most profound despair that any human being possibly could. She is known by the world as a woman possessed by seven demons as you pointed out, and then, she has lost any chance of continuing a natural relationship with Commander Shaphan, and then also, she cannot even go back to her mother for support and consolation now. In short, there is no human relationship in this world on which she could sustain her life. It was the same as being pushed over the edge of a cliff. There was no hope whatsoever left for her, do you understand? It was just at this desperate point in her life that she met Jesus. And how did Jesus receive her? You saw it as well as I did. Did he treat her as a sinful woman possessed by seven demons? Did he stop her from coming near him? No, he didn't, right? He acted contrary to any expectation. He made the heaven become the earth and earth the heaven. Didn't he speak more highly of her than he did Simon who was the Pharisee and the master of the house? Didn't he cleanse her from all the contempt, hate, and curses of the world, at once? That's how it all began, isn't it?"

"That does not explain anything except the motivation of Mary's involvement with Jesus."

"Exactly so. And what I am trying to say is that since her motivation for involving herself with Jesus was different from her other involvements with men, her goal and result have also been different. Judas, you supply an answer to this question: why is it that Jesus treated Mary in a way different from any attitude we have hitherto observed in the people of the world? It was in view of this difference that I hesitated to express an opinion about where the comfort and hope came for Mary. I could not quite understand why Jesus negated what was considered good by the world such as money, power and prestige and why it was that Jesus had only contempt for the Pharisees and the lawyers whom the whole world think so highly of, and then, he befriends the harlots, tax-gatherers, and the lepers whom the world would do anything to keep away from and only hates and despises. Why? Why is everything upside down in his order?"

Thomas sounded as if he were talking to himself rather than asking Judas to answer as he said these words slightly rolling his deep-set grey eyes.

"Isn't it what Jesus talks about when he tries to describe the Heaven to us? Isn't it how things will be ordered in the new country Jesus is going to found after the Romans are chased out of this land? What you meant by the 'deep comfort and new hope' that Mary received also is connected with this. I mean, those things have connections with each other and also with this prayer Jesus has taught us that has these parts in it: 'Your kingdom come' and 'your will be done on the earth.' A person such as Mary who experienced an utter defeat in this life would be bound to be comforted and cheered by the thought of such a thing as this new country Jesus is talking about founding. But Thomas, Mary would, you must listen to this very carefully, very likely try to have Jesus as her husband once he becomes the king of this new kingdom he is going to establish and I think this is where you are wrong about her. Or at least, she is planning on becoming a high-standing waiting woman on Jesus and this is where her 'profound comfort and new hope' comes from. That is, she has high hopes about becoming a queen in the future kingdom. It is the same hope that our Corps Teacher Hadad had as he offered his beautiful daughter up to Shaphan to be the queen of the future kingdom Commander Shaphan would found with the help of his Blood Contract Corps. And it is not very different from the brothers of Peter and John aiming to become the chief ministers. And I also have an answer to the question you threw at me, that is, why Jesus treated Mary in a way different from the attitudes of all other people. I think the answer is simple. That is, he treated her in that way for the same reason that you and I are interested in her. I mean it is because she has good looks."

Judas seemed to get excited more and more as he talked on and as a result he said things that he had never dreamed of saying since he was born. Thomas seemed not a little disgusted by the last of his remarks. He looked at Judas with his deep-set grey eyes and then said in a low but clear voice:

"Judas, you are a strange person. You seem to have a strangely-formed mind."

"About that I know better than any other person."

"......"

Thomas just looked at the face of Judas with its protruding yellow eyes.

Judas spoke again:

"There is no camouflage of pretty fog in my mind. Many people deceive themselves and others because of this camouflaging fog so that everything might look pretty and good. But I am not like them. All I am interested in is looking at things as they really are, in their true nature and essence. The reason why people tend to have a complicated ideas of things is that they are blinded at least partially by the thick fog that dominate their minds' eyes. If they can only chase away this fog that camouflages and blinds, they would see things and affairs of the world far more clearly than they ever have.

If you see me as a strange person, it is because I don't have this kind of a fog in my mind or sight. Nobody can deceive me. Look at my eyes; they have a special faculty that can see through the fog that covers people's minds and look at the true nature and essence of a thing."

Judas was still excited but there was self-confidence in the way he spoke these words.

"Judas, maybe, your mind is a treasure to you but I must say I cannot agree with all its perceptions. You seem to think you are able to penetrate into a person's mind better than any other person, but in fact, you seem to have a shallower and narrower understanding for it than any next person. You know that Commander Shaphan had not met Mary before several years had passed after the incident at Gadara and if you were to frame a case against Mary making it up that she and Commander Shaphan had conspired to kill the Roman centurion, it would be nothing but a false accusation. Don't you realize that?"

"Thomas, if I accuse Mary on false grounds, it is not because I lack the judgement but because maybe I consider it necessary for the good of the Corps and my own personal interest to take that action. I don't care if it is false accusation. The only thing that matters is, perhaps, that I am acting upon the true understanding of things as they stand."

When the two men reached the eastern hill, the others of their party had prepared boats, and they got aboard after Jesus.

The boat that had Jesus and his direct followers aboard arrived at the northern end of Dariqueyea, whereupon Thomas led Jesus and his disciples to the house of a friend of his. It was the house of the wife of Timeus who had taken over the command of the district from Thomas.

That night, Shaphan visited this place upon words of Thomas of their arrival there. He met Thomas first.

Thomas was as glad as a younger brother would be upon meeting his older brother in a strange town.

"I have so wished to see you, Commander!" he said unable to conceal his feeling. Then he reported to Shaphan about their activities during the time of mutual absence from each other. Shaphan told him about what was happening at Gerasa and also at various other places in the way of the Corps' collision against the Roman army. From Shaphan he learned of the lack of food and weapon at the Gerasa headquarters on account of the siege.

"Isn't there some way of supplying them with those things?" asked Thomas.

"Since they are surrounded on three sides, there is only one way to do it, that of climbing up the cliff directly from the lake," said Shaphan.

"Then, it is not impossible. Although it depends on how closely the Romans watch the lake. . . ."

"Yes, you are right. It is not impossible. But do we have to take that risky course is the question, you know. Wouldn't it a better tactic to make the Romans exhaust their energy in reaching what they believe to be the main hiding place of this Blood Contract Corps and then realize after a loss of several hundred of lives on their side that it had been for nothing they had fought all those days or months depending on how long it would take altogether. I mean they are bound to find out that the real headquarters of their enemy was elsewhere. Wouldn't they be somewhat dissettled by this aspect? Tell me what you think, Thomas."

"Would it be possible for the men at Gerasa headquarters to make their retreat without blood-shedding?" asked Thomas.

"I think so, if they manage well. Although there may be some casualties within a negligible degree."

"Wouldn't the Romans come down on us at Mt. Tabor?"

"I don't think so. Because they would have learned by that time that it would be no use. They would have learned their lesson at Gerasa. And on our part, we are free to move our headquarters to any place any time. . . ."

Shaphan looked at Thomas with his blood-shot eyes that

were somewhat deep-set like those of Thomas'. The expression he had on his face was such as he assumed when asking someone to do something for him or when asking someone to trust him.

What Thomas could learn from this all was, however, merely that Shaphan had some ideas of his own about whatever had happened. He therefore brought up another question.

"How is Jerusalem after they took in Barabbas," he asked.

"Not too active. The Romans and the Jews in Jerusalem seem to think some guerrilla works over there as something attempted by the remaining faction of Barabbas. There seemed to be some dissension about this point but lately they seem to have got back to their original suspicion about the true culprits of the harrassments in their area."

"That was fortunate from the view point of our Corps, wasn't it?" said Thomas.

"Not harmful to us, anyway, I think," answered Shaphan with an expression that seemed to say he didn't much care either way.

Their conversation ended here, for the time being, because just then Judas came to them. Shaphan had asked Judas to arrange for another meeting between him and Jesus.

"Where is Jesus?" asked Thomas in place of Shaphan.

"He has not come down from the hill. He seems to be praying under an olive tree. But I think he will be down soon," said Judas.

"Then we had better climb the hill and wait for him to finish praying," said Thomas. And Shaphan got up from his seat without a word of protest.

There were stars in the sky and sea gulls squeaking over the lake.

As Shaphan went up the hill with Thomas and Judas, he saw John and his brother and Matthew and Philip sitting on a rock waiting for Jesus to finish his prayers and come down to them. He could see Jesus, their master, praying under the shade of an olive tree standing about twenty steps away from them. Shaphan said to Matthew as he came up to the rock where Matthew and others were sitting on.

"How have you been, friend?" he said.

Matthew seemed somewhat embarrassed by this greeting but, as Thomas told him in a low voice who it was that was accosting him, said:

"We haven't seen each other for long, it seems, Commander Shaphan."

Although he was one of the men that belonged to Ananias once, he had become an ardent follower of Jesus once he was called by the latter along with Peter and John and his brother.

But it seemed he had not forgotten his loyalty toward the Blood Contract Corps and this was ascertained in his attitude toward Thomas when the latter mentioned the Commander's name.

Judas turned to John and his brother and whispered in a low voice:

"This is our Commander Shaphan who were with you at the house of tax-gatherer Matthew's to share food and drink with our Lord. . . ."

Then Thomas took over the conversation from Judas and said:

"The Commander has come here because he has business with Jesus."

The disciples of Jesus who were at the rock could not possibly refuse the new comers their request because they were all old acquaintances.

When Jesus came down from his higher place on the top of the hill, John ran up to him and said:

"Lord, an acquaintance of Thomas' wishes to see you."

". . . . . ."

Jesus did not say anything as if he had not heard what John said to him. He only turned his head up to the heaven as if he wished to look at the stars.

Then, John spoke to him again:

"Lord, this man has been with us at the rock over there."
And he pointed at the rock. Jesus walked to the rock he
pointed at.

Shaphan rose and went to Jesus saying:

"Rabbi, I am here because a difficult thing has happened to
me and to the people of Judaea."

His tone was polite. But Jesus did not say anything. He
merely turned his head toward Shaphan and looked at his
face. Judas came forward, then, and said:

"Lord, shall we let him sit on this rock and ask you questions
or shall we make him go over to the shade of that tree over
there?"

Jesus looked at Shaphan's face again and then said:

"Speak to me here, son of man."

Shaphan spoke at once:

"Rabbi, we know that you are different from all other
prophets, and all other teachers of the Law. Save us from the
trouble and suffering we are in, Rabbi."

"Son of man, why did you not listen when I told you what
you should do but come here to me at this time with your
complaints?"

"The Romans are out to capture me."

"What did you do to the Romans that they try to capture
you now?"

"I have killed, plundered, and set fire in order to make them
go out of this land."

"Those who have killed cannot enter the Kingdom of
Heaven. And those who killed the Romans would be killed by
the Romans."

The attitude of Jesus was calm to the degree of
inhumanness. But Shaphan did not seem to be disconcerted by
this. He said:

"Rabbi, Moses killed many Egyptians so that he might
rescue the Israelites from their land. It is, therefore, following
Moses' example to kill or chase those who do not worship
Jehovah. Do you not think so?"

To this, Jesus replied in a tone more heated than before:

"Son of man, do you think that what Moses achieved is perfect? Do you not realize that the Israelites were invaded by the Gentiles even after they were settled in Canaan and also how many of them were killed or taken by them. Even if you say you killed the Romans for the peace of Jews, an eternal peace of the Israelites could not be won in that way. The blood calls only for blood and the men will only sink deeper in calamities."

"But Rabbi, how can we live without chasing Romans out of the land? They do not worship Jehovah and try to close our temples and make us their slaves although they collect many taxes from us. Rabbi, save us from this suffering and death. Save the Jews. Become our king. Establish an eternally peaceful Israel which even Moses or Solomon could not establish. We have prepared everything against your coming. If only you give us the word, we will rise up in all places."

"Listen, son of man. I have for long prayed to my Father to grant me that dream. Would not my Father have given it to me if he had wanted me to have it. Truly I tell you that there cannot be an eternal peace in any country on the earth. If I were to establish a kingdom on earth, it would not prosper long in glory just as the kingdom of Solomon could not. Son of man, do you not see with your own eyes that nothing remains long on this earth? Neither money, nor power, nor glory.... Everything goes away just as our body goes away. I tell you truly, therefore, that there is nothing eternal for man unless his life is reborn in Heaven."

"Rabbi, life of man stays with his body and his body stays with the land. If the Romans take our body away from us, how can our life look for the kingdom of heaven or be reborn in it?"

"Listen, son of man, our ancestors were taken to Babylonia and yet their minds came back to Jerusalem and erected the holy temple. I tell you truly that the temple in Jerusalem is not as big as the temple in heaven. The temple in Jerusalem can be pulled down by the Babylonians or the Romans because it is a thing erected on the earth but the temple of Jehovah that is built in heaven cannot be pulled down to eternity. Son of man, listen. You asked me to become the king of your kingdom on earth but I have already established a kingdom in heaven that will not perish forever. If man binds his life to this kingdom of mine, he will have eternal happiness with me."

"Rabbi, the kingdom you have erected is a place where we go only after our death. Our life that is alive wishes to see your kingdom erected on earth as it is in heaven. Even now our beloved brothers are being killed in their struggle against the Romans at the top of a cliff in Gerasa so that they might receive your kingdom on earth. Do lift up the siege the Romans threw on them and rescue them. Lead them with us into your kingdom."

"Son of man, you worry about the deaths of your brothers across the water and yet you do not realize that you too are dying. You think you are alive but your life is no better than death. Your ears along with your mind are closed to the gospel of the kingdom of heaven. And your mind along with your body are sunk in the sins of this earth."

The voice of Jesus sounded full of anger. After stepping down from the rock, he went straight down to the foot of the hill. John and his brother followed him down with Matthew and Philip.

Shaphan remained on the rock even after Jesus went down, looking across at the distant mountains of Gerasa which was enveloped in darkness.

The falcon flew up every day even after they moved to Mt. Tabor but came down again as if it could not make its way to Gerasa.

Shaphan told Timeus to take the falcon to the middle of the lake and fly it from there. He had judged that it was the route between the lake and Mt. Tabor that the bird was not familiar with yet. When Timeus flew it from the lake, the falcon finally disappeared in the direction of Gerasa. It came back and perched itself on the sail after about two hours. Then Timeus went back to Shaphan with the falcon. It was, however, not an easy job to travel like this with the falcon. For one thing, there was no telling when Timeus' boat would be found by the Romans.

Another thing they could do was taking the bird to Ananias in Capernaum and let it travel from there to Gerasa, and they tried this way too.

In any case, the falcon made several trips to Gerasa by these different routes.

Three days before the Festival of Tabernacles, Jair sent the following note through the falcon:

> We have decided to use the 'path of the cliff' following your direction. The night before the Feast of Tabernacles, we will make a torchlight. We will extinguish it soon and then make it burn again when the work is done.

On the eve of the Feast of Tabernacles, Shaphan sent seven boats to the foot of the cliff in Gerasa. In three of them were Timeus' men all armed and seventeen in number. The rest of the boats were empty except for the boatmen. The seventeen armed men were there in preparation against emergency.

Shaphan also ordered Jeremoth who was in charge of Gadara district to take seven or eight armed men to the southeast of Gerasa. He told Jeremoth to lie in wait until he should see a torchlight in the direction of the headquarters around midnight. He was to burn a torchlight to divert the attention of the Romans.

"You should, of course, avoid fighting the Romans from the front when you are so outnumbered. All you need to do is just draw their attention to your side. You do not even need to disrupt the Roman force. It is because although Jair would take a formal offensive move toward the Romans, he has no plan to make a charge through them. You and your men had better move to the place we have already talked about after the torchlight. If the enemy does not come after you, burn another torchlight. But don't let any be wounded or killed on your side."

That night, Jair burned the torchlight around midnight and shot more arrows than he had done recently toward the Roman camp.

At the same time, the men started their climb down the cliff with the help of a rope. One end of the rope was fixed around a big rock in front of the cave and the Corps members could safely get down to the surface of the water where the boats were waiting thanks to this rope.

The ones that went down first were the fourteen-men team that had been fighting on the northern side, and the next were twenty-one from the eastern encampment, and the last to climb down were the twenty-five men from the southern front.

All sixty members went down in this way. Now there were only Corps Teacher Hadad, Jair and two closest to Jair.

Hadad would not listen when they told him to go down beforehand.

"I am all right. I don't even have any reason to fear the Romans. They will kill me? I don't think they will. Besides, what matters if they do? I have lived long enough as it is. Look at my arms. Do you think I could hold the rope with these? I might try, though, if I were afraid to die. But I am not."

He talked to the men in this way at first, but as they urged repeatedly, he did not even argue with them as if it were too tiring for him to do so. But he told them he would go down when Jair would. Jair was supposed to climb down the rope after burning the last torchlight. But he was still not back at the cave from the encampment.

Jair was shooting the last of the arrows and sending an answer to Jeremoth who was burning the torchlight in the south. One of his two men came back from the cave where he had been sent to see about the escape of the men by the rope.

"All sixty of them went down," said he.

"What about Corps Teacher?"

"He said he would make up his mind when you should come back to the cliff."

"You two had better go down, then."

"We will go with you."

"I have to take care of the signals yet. Someone has to stay here until our boats should be safely on their way toward Dariqueyea."

"How could you leave here if the boats are safely on their way?"

"I can swim across; don't worry."

"But what about the Corps Teacher?"

"You two had better take him with you."

"He says he won't move until you come back."

"......"

Jair looked at the two men in silence.

"Go, now. It will be helping the Corps."

The two men looked at each other but did not make a move.

"Please, go," urged Jair.

"We two have sworn to fight by your side to the last. We won't go away before you do."

Again, Jair looked at their faces without saying anything. In his eyes were tears that looked like blood. He pointed to the Roman camp with his chin and said:

"I am going to go down that way."

His voice sounded husky and a little shaky as he said this.

"We too will go that way," answered the two men all together. Jair again looked at them a long while and said:

"I thank you for your loyalty."

And he burned the last torch.

"You had better go up to the cliff and unbind the rope. Throw it into the water," he said to one of the men. Then, along with the other of his men, he began to shoot the remaining arrows toward the Roman camp.

Chapter 8

The Cross of Shaphan

It was next morning, many hours after the last of the Blood Contract Corps troops went down the rope from their headquarters on the top of the cliff that the Romans captured the cave. Jair and his two men threw themselves into the middle of the enemy camp with their daggers and spears. One of the two men fell in front of the Roman encampment shot by an arrow, but Jair and the other man could make a dash into their camp and swishing their daggers and spears in all directions could wound and kill many dozens of the enemy. When Jair and the last of his soldiers fell, covered with blood and wounds, in the middle of the Roman encampment no longer able to move, the Romans were in such a frightened state of mind that they only wished that this night of horrible nightmare would quickly pass away. Even when Jair and his last man fell, the Romans could not make themselves come forward but kept their defensive position behind the rocks. They did not take as much action as rising from their hiding place and look around to see if there were more enemies in their midst. They were that much frightened by the few bandits that rushed in. They seemed to be wondering if those were not devils instead of men.

285

It was only after the sun rose high next morning that the Romans found out the fact that the enemy camp had been evacuated. Still, they did not have the courage to go over and check. They shot many arrows in that direction and called out to the enemy to see if there would be any response from the other side. Only then could they approach that side slowly.

"All gone!"

"There's nobody here!"

Their shouts were a mixture of shock and relief.

"It could be some more of their trickery," said somebody. And perhaps this was what went through the mind of every other Roman there. But there seemed to be no doubt this time.

"Nobody is here."

"The bandits are gone."

They rushed to the cave.

It was when the first of them went up within ten steps of the spot where the big rock was. The two foremost suddenly fell into the ground. They fell into one of the traps the Corps members had dug around their cave. The rest of them scattered backwards in fright emitting strange sounds of fear. They did not know at first that it was just a trap. Soon finding out about the truth of the situation, they recovered their composure.

"Bring a rope," one of them shouted.

Since the trap was made utilizing a small valley, the two fallen men could climb up with no difficulty when the rope was let down for them. One of them could not stand up straight because he had a sprain on his side and the other was bleeding from a long cut he received on the forehead.

"The bandits are a tenacious lot. They would leave traps behind them!"

"We have our first wounded of the day."

The soldiers chattered at random. And the two men went down the hill assisted by their comrades.

The rest of them finally reached the entrance to the cave. Some of them climbed up on the top of the rock. They all tried to look into the cave through the narrow opening.

"Don't go in!" ordered the centurion. And nobody seemed especially eager to go in, anyway.

"What is that object in the cave?" asked the centurion.

"It's a man," one of the soldiers answered.

The centurion pushed aside the men standing closest to the entrance and pulling his sword went up to the mouth of the cave.

He saw sitting in the cave an old man with eyebrows and hair entirely white and a strange gleam in his eyes.

"Who are you?" asked the centurion.

". . . . . ."

The centurion asked once in Greek and another time in Roman, but the old man did not answer. The centurion went in closer to where he was sitting. Tapping the old man with the tip of his sword on one shoulder, the centurion asked:

"What is this? Why don't you answer?"

He said this in Greek. Still the old man kept perfectly calm. But this time he opened his mouth and said:

"Who are you?"

He spoke in Arabic and sounded as if he were offended by the rudeness of the men. The Romans decided that maybe the old man did not answer the centurion's questions because he did not understand them and so one of the soldiers who knew a little Arabic was chosen to interpret.

"Who are you, old man?" the soldier asked in Arabic.

"I am one who have been living here," answered the old man.

"You too belong to the Blood Contract Corps, don't you?"

"I said I am one who have been living here."

"Where are all the bandits that were here?"

". . . . . ."

The old man pointed at the cliff meaning they disappeared that way.

"You lived with them, didn't you?"

"I was here before they came."

"What is there inside the cave?"

"This is my house."

"Is there no bandits in there?"

"I don't think there are any."

"What about the arms?"

"I do not know."

The centurion had the men examine the cliff and the inside of the cave. The examination was over soon. A long rope was found at the foot of the cliff and inside the cave there were some kitchen utensils, a set of leather bed things and a couple of empty sacks. There was not so much as a scrap of metal left in it.

The remaining problem was just the old man. They had to decide whether or not they should kill him, and if they were to let him leave, whether they should leave him here so that he could live as he had hitherto or send him on to Capernaum. They ended up concluding the matter by deciding to wait until their commander-in-chief should come on the scene. When commander-in-chief Titus heard out the report, he said:

"You had better leave him just as he is. You can merely keep an eye on him. Maybe we could harvest something good from this. Observe all his activities including his manner of eating. About sending him on, we can do that any time afterward."

Shaphan heard from Zechariah and Timeus about the procedure of the retreat. Except Hadad, Jair and his two men, everybody had come to Mt. Tabor without the Romans so much as suspecting anything. When Zechariah told him about Hadad, suddenly Shaphan cried out:

"What? Isn't Hadad come, then?"

Shaphan opened his big eyes wider and clenched his teeth. He looked nearly maniacal at that moment. Zechariah thought that he had never seen Shaphan in this way before, but he felt he should finish his report. He told Shaphan what happened to Jair and his two men, that is, the fact that they did not come with them.

"What? Jair, too? O. . . ."

Shaphan seemed to be moaning.

"After the last torchlight, we heard the sound of a violent clash in the direction of the Roman encampment. From it, we surmised that the three of them made a dash into their camp."

"What, Jair went into the Roman camp . . . you mean Jair killed himself?"

Shaphan was thrown into sobbing after shouting thus. It was unthinkable that he should break down like this and Zechariah felt as if Shaphan had turned into a different man.

"I think it was thanks to them that the rest of us could make our retreat safely."

"Ah, what should I do?" said Shaphan and looked at Zechariah and Timeus with fearfully bloody eyes.

". . . . . ."

". . . . . ."

The two men did not know what to say. Zechariah was thinking that Shaphan was not normal this evening. He could not understand why Shaphan was taking the matter which was not so extraordinary under such circumstances in such an unusual way. Why would he plunge himself into a despair and sorrow so deep and strange, he asked himself. He thought that this was a side he had not even suspected to see in Shaphan.

Timeus who could not stand it any longer spoke.

"We are all ready to sacrifice our lives for the Corps. It was only that Jair was the first to practice it."

"That's another matter. We have all sworn to die in order to recover our country from Rome. But what we really meant was we would live happily together after we take our land back from the trespassers. It was not to die that we have got together. I do not want to see you die one by one in front of my eyes."

Shaphan's voice trembled with sorrow and emotion.

Then Zechariah opened his mouth.

"Jair once said to me that the headquarters was his life. I

think he decided to kill as many enemies as possible if he were obliged to give away the headquarters."

Zechariah spoke calmly and placatingly, almost.

Shaphan sat with his head bent without speaking for a long time and then raised his head and said:

"Yes, Jair died and we are alive. Since we are alive, we must do some work. Our first job is to find the body of Jair."

Timeus opened his mouth again:

"I will send some people over and let them look for his body even today."

"Yes, do that. We will bury him in Mt. Tabor. We will all be buried in Mt. Tabor. Let them find the bodies of the two men who died with Jair, too."

"I have someone under my command who is acting something like the Roman agent. I will send him along to find the bodies."

Shaphan seemed to find strength in what Timeus said.

"Yes, that sounds like a good idea," he said with more composure. Then he turned to Zechariah and asked:

"Zechariah, what happened to the Corps Teacher? Clearly, he is not here."

He sounded as if he were blaming the two men for the absence of Hadad. Zechariah found it somewhat disagreeable that Shaphan should question him as if he were responsible for every aspect of the retreat. He swallowed his bad feeling, however, and said:

He remained at the headquarters. He would not listen to the entreaties of the messengers Jair sent to persuade him to leave with the others. He said that he would go away with Jair when he should come back to the cave."

"You mean neither you nor Jair talked to him in person?"

"I guess Jair had to act the way he did according to his own judgement. But for my part, I was ignorant of the fact that Hadad was not leaving. We were all obliged to keep ourselves busy with our respective duties so that we did not have any chance to see about other things under the special circum-

stances of the retreat we made. You must understand that."
Zechariah's voice was so calm that it sounded nearly cold.

"The truth is...." said Timeus. "I don't think the Corps
Teacher really meant it when he said that he would leave
when Jair should come back to the cave. The reason I think so
is that the Corps Teacher is said to have asked the men how
he could hold the rope with the kind of arms he had and I
think he was right in doubting it because the climb down was
not an easy job even for the young and the strong. I think,
therefore, that he only told the men that he would go away
with Jair only so that they would leave him alone."

"Is that really what you think?" said Shaphan as if he were
out to find fault with Timeus.

The two men did not say anything further because there
was not anything more they could say now.

"Hadad should have tried even if he would have failed on
the rope. What can we do without Hadad?"

"Take heart, Commander. As long as he is alive, Corps
Teacher will surely come back to us some time."

"He will come back some time? Of course he will. He will
be buried here some time. But the question is he is not with us
here now when we are fighting a whole-scale war against the
Romans. Who will now read the stars for us? We have no hope
of getting help of Jesus now, and we have even lost Hadad who
would have told us what to do or what not to do according to
what the stars will tell him. We cannot defeat our over-
numbered enemy with just our daggers and arrows. Why do
they all leave me at this critical moment?"

Shaphan's voice sounded so forlorn that it was almost like
some kind of chanting he was memorizing. Zechariah was
bothered by all this. How could Shaphan who was like a tight
knot of courage and will power turn to this soft-minded self-
pitying person! There must be some strong reason here,
thought Zechariah. Is it because his second confrontation with
Jesus ended in failure? But it was too early for despair
notwithstanding Jesus' stubbornness. Thomas and Judas are

still trying to make the joint of forces work out. Is it then because of Mary? But he had Zilpah who was many times more beautiful than Mary. Then what is it? Suddenly it occurred to Zechariah that maybe it was all these things put together that drove Shaphan into the strangely depressed state of mind they were now witnessing. In order for him to rise out of this deep gloom, there ought to be something really hope-generating and new, thought Zechariah. What can be such a thing, however, asked he. He could not find anything that could do such a work on Shaphan. Except maybe trying Jesus again....

"Maybe, Jesus has changed His mind, by now. Let us try seeing Him again," said he as if to change the subject. Although it may not be something on which one should build much hope, still it was something that might give some comfort to Shaphan in his depression.

Shaphan looked at him as if he did not understand what he was saying.

"I think Zechariah has sense, Commander. Do as he suggests. I too think it quite likely that Jesus has a different mind about your proposal by now. Because he is sure to realize that the Pharisees and the Sadducees are out to get him at the moment. He too would need us to protect him."

Timeus who guessed that Zechariah's suggestion was an improvisation to console Shaphan and to draw him out of his despair talked on at random.

Shaphan turned his face to Timeus without a word and Timeus continued:

"We hear that Corps Teacher taught how to read the stars and how to train the falcon to his daughter Madam Zilpah. I suggest, therefore, that you appoint Madam Zilpah the Corps Teacher until he himself should come back to us. And we on our part will make a new contact with Jesus."

"......"

Shaphan silently nodded. He seemed to like Timeus' suggestions. Seeing this, Zechariah thought he would give some more stimulation. He said:

"The death of Jair was a great loss to us but to be frank it is not as though we lacked honest and courageous warriors in our Corps. Until our last expedition to Nabatea, we did not even know that there was such a fine warrior under Thomas as this Timeus proved himself to be, did we? From this we may safely assume that there are outstanding men who are now hidden in the shadow. There may be someone under Ananias and there may be some good soldier even among my own men, don't you think? Jair was your most loyal helper and he was also our comrade and friend. But if we were to abandon ourselves to a sorrow over the death of one man, however valuable he might have been to each of us, what would happen to our duty toward countless men of our Corps who are now struggling all over the land?"

Shaphan seemed to accept his argument. He nodded his head a few times as before and then looked up.

"Zechariah, and Timeus, I have regained my strength thanks to you two. I am sorry. I would have liked to get utterly drunk to forget my pain but I will refrain from it to show my thanks to you. Not just today but for seven days I will abstain from wine," said Shaphan in his characteristically husky voice.

After parting from Shaphan, Jesus tried to pay a visit to Nazareth but sensing the atmosphere of tension there because both the Pharisees and Sadducees, and now even the Blood Contract Corps were waiting to get their hands on Him — He headed north instead, as He did before. Although many days had passed since His meeting with Shaphan, the worldly demands of the man kept coming back to His mind. He remembered especially these words of Shaphan:

— Rabbi, we know that you are different from all other prophets and teachers of Law.

or

— Become our king. Establish a kingdom that neither Moses nor Solomon could establish on this earth.

He seemed to hear his voice saying these words even now.

(Yes. That's what he thought I was, the Messiah. But one who has the worldly aims and ambitions. The Messiah who will be the king to a kingdom on this earth which neither Moses nor Solomon could found there. This is what the man and his followers want me to be. No, that is not it. Not only they but the whole Israel wants it. A worldly Messiah! The victor of the earth! The Messiah of their dreams! But it is impossible for such to exist. They are asking the God in Heaven to come down to earth to become their king. What they want is to enjoy the privileges of being the Jew in the kingdom that is ruled by such a Messiah. They have this wish because they do not know their God. They confuse the God with Caesar. They do not know that in order for the God to be God, He cannot become the Caesar. They do not know the Kingdom of God is different from the Kingdom of Caesar. They do not know that they have to give up the earthly kingdom if they wanted to live forever in the Kingdom of Heaven. They do not realize that they have to let go of one thing to gain the other, that they have to give up all the good things of the earth such as money, power, and prestige, in order to enjoy the eternal happiness of the Kingdom of Heaven. Even James and his brother do not seem to understand this. They are asking me to give them the positions of the two highest ministers on the day I become the king. They do not know that it is not the kingdom of earth but that of the Heaven that I am going to be the king of. This is sad. If my beloved disciples do not understand my position, who will?)

Jesus had these thoughts in his mind as he passed a village in Caesarea Philippi. Only nine of his twelve disciples followed him, the remaining three staying behind.

Jesus was glad that only his disciples were following him instead of a big crowd. It was very relieving for a change. There was a hill by the roadside and on the hill stood several olive trees. He decided to go uphill and rest under the olive trees with his disciples.

After looking over his disciples, Jesus opened his mouth

slowly:

"Who do the people say I am?"

This was a question he had been thinking about for some time.

John who was standing with one hand touching the trunk of an olive tree said:

"Some said you were Baptist John, some said you were the Elijah and others called you Jeremiah and still others say you are one of the prophets."

This was what other disciples have often heard people say, too.

"Who do you think I am?" asked Jesus. Then Peter who was sitting on one side with his knees pressed to the ground said:

"Lord, you are Christ and living Son of God."

He used the Greek word Christ instead of the Hebrew word Messiah. In fact, he had a debate over this question with Thomas a few days ago. They agreed with each other on the point that Jesus was the Messiah. But what they disagreed on was whether or not Jesus was sent to rescue Judaea from the Roman bondage and establish an eternal kingdom of peace as prophesied by the prophets. Thomas was of this opinion while Peter had a different view about it. The ground of his dissention was the fact that Jesus distinctly differentiated what belonged to Caesar from what belonged to God. If so, Jesus was perhaps a different Messiah but not the Messiah they had been waiting for, retorted Thomas and put Peter in a logical dilemma from which he could not get out easily. Peter had said in improvisation that if he was the Messiah anyway, it was wrong for them to have any doubt about him just because he did not fit in the prophesy to the letter. And in this sense, he could very well be called Christ, he said. Upon this, Thomas could not help smiling and asked Peter if he thought there was difference between the Sea of Tiberia and the Lake of Gennesaret.

Peter used the appellation Christ thinking of this argument with Thomas but inside his mind he was somewhat uneasy that his Master might reprimand him for it.

But Jesus smiled suddenly and said:

"Blessed are you, Simon, son of John, because it was not flesh and blood that revealed this to you but My Heavenly Father."

Peter felt a strange sensation go through his whole body as he heard Jesus say this and the next moment he felt a self-confidence which he had never felt before. Jesus opened his mouth again:

"I will give you the keys of the Kingdom of Heaven; whatever you bind on earth will be bound in heaven, and whatever you allow on earth will be allowed in heaven."

With this pronouncement of Jesus, Peter became the first of the twelve disciples. The rest of them remained somewhat confused as this procedure between Jesus and Peter continued. Most of them had thought that Jesus probably was the Messiah but this was the first time that they knew it for sure. If he is the Messiah, they thought busily, we are in something serious. What would it be? How would it happen? They all asked this same question.

And Jesus knew what was in their minds and said:

"Do you not realize that the glory of the Son of Man will bear fruit in the Kingdom of Heaven? Do you think that the glory of the Son of Man will bear fruit on the earth just as that of those stubborn-hearted Pharisees or the Zealots (he meant Shaphan and his followers by this)?"

After he clarified himself to be Christ, Jesus seemed to put more emphasis on this appellation: Son of Man. He seemed to use it interchangeably with 'the Messiah.'

As the disciples remained silent not knowing what answer to give him for his question, he continued:

"The Son of Man will be nailed on the cross so that the glory of heaven may be accomplished. This is because what the Son of Man seeks is the same as what the Pharisees, the Sadducees, and the rest of the world are seeking. Just as the Kingdom of Heaven belongs to the Father, everything on earth belongs to them. After three days, however, they will see that the glory of the Son of Man is accomplished in heaven."

Thus saying Jesus climbed down the hill quietly.

Peter who was following directly after him, said, taking hold of his sleeve:

"Mercy on you, Lord; This must never happen to you!" He did not dare mouth the word 'cross,' and so used the word 'this' in its place.

All at once, the expression on the face of Jesus turned stern and he said severely:

"Get behind Me, Satan, you are a snare to me; for you are not taking the divine view but the man's."

Jesus seemed very angry with Peter as if he had forgotten how he had praised Peter a while ago. Was it possible for Peter to become such a commendable person and then such an evil one almost at the same moment? Or rather, was Jesus really such a generous-minded person as the disciples had thought him to be? The disciples who had by now all caught up with Jesus and Peter wondered. Or, was Jesus Man, at all, for that matter? If so, how could he talk about men apart from their earth?

But Jesus looked them over with eyes filled with sorrow this time and said:

"A true Messiah would not come to accomplish the work of the earth. If anyone wants to walk after Me, he must deny himself, take up his cross and follow Me; for whoever wants to save his life shall lose it, but whoever loses his life for Me shall find it."

Jesus and his disciples turned south again at Caesarea Philippi. They returned to Capernaum first, and then after bidding farewell to their beloved Sea of Galilee, they progressed toward south.

Jesus was aware that his time came and so was heading for Jerusalem.

He travelled through Samaria and reached Bethany which was only about 10 ri (= 2.5 miles) from Jerusalem. In Bethany, he went to the house of Martha. Martha and her sister Mary were cousins of Glovah of Jericho and were related with Judas, too, on his wife's side. Judas made himself free to visit or utilize their house because of the special relationship between Glovah and Judas (that of comrades and friends) and also because of the relationship of Judas with the sisters. Besides, Judas was secretly in love with the younger of the sisters, Mary. Martha was a housewife of twenty-four in age and Mary was a girl of sixteen. Both of them were ardent worshippers of Jesus after they met him urged by Judas.

For these reasons, the sisters took it for granted that Jesus and his party would take lodging at their house when he came to Bethany.

When Jesus and his disciples went into their house on that day, Martha and Mary ran out to meet them leaving off their respective jobs.

But Martha was too busy to sit down and listen to the Master's words for long this day since they were in the midst of the Festival of Tabernacles then. There were many things to do including the preparation of food for Jesus and the disciples. Mary, however, did not help her but stayed by the side of Jesus listening to him talk. Martha was piqued at this and asked Jesus:

"Lord, is it right for my sister to sit there doing nothing when I have so many things to do? Tell her to come out and help me, my Lord."

But Jesus did not tell this to Mary, but said to Martha:

"Martha, Martha, you are anxious and bothered about many matters, when there is need of but one thing. Mary has selected the good portion which will not be taken away from her."

Next day, Jesus took his disciples, Martha and Mary's brother Lazarus and went into Jerusalem.

The ruling class of Jerusalem — mostly chief priests and the Pharisees — remembered the incident that Jesus healed a man who had been crippled for thirty eight years on the Sabbath

Day and also the number of occasions after the incident on which Jesus denounced them publicly. They made up their mind to lay their bands on Jesus this time. But like before, they could not trust the crowds because although some of them hated Jesus and cursed him, most of them respected and loved him even if not all of them believed him to be the Messiah.

Jesus walked through the crowd and went up to the holy temple. Then, standing in front of the huge crowd that gathered there, he started asking questions:

"Moses gave you the Law but you neither understood nor observed it. Yet, are you now trying to kill me?"

Someone in the crowd shouted:

"You are possessed, Rabbi. Who is seeking to kill you?"

"The one who says it thinks everybody is like himself. If you circumcise on the Sabbath, why are you indignant with me for giving health on the Sabbath to the whole of a man's body?"

The crowd then whispered among themselves asking each other who the person was that had said the words. There were some among them who shouted: Who is killing the Prophet? Or some that said: Even if the Messiah would come, he could not show more signs than this man. Listening to these words, the agents of the high priests and the Pharisees that had mixed themselves with the crowd took fright. When later they were reprimanded by their superiors for not laying their hands on Jesus, they said:

"Nobody has ever spoken as he does." And they confessed to having been moved by his words instead of desiring to kill him.

In this way, three days passed without any serious trouble. The eighth day of the Festival of the Tabernacles was the last day of the season. On this day, it was a custom to offer an ox on the altar but it was the biggest of all days during the Festival which originally lasted for seven days. On the first day, they offered thirteen oxen, on the second, twelve, on the third eleven, and so on making it seventy in all by the seventh day. In the course of time, however, one more day was added, and on this day only one ox was sacrificed. And this eighth day

of the Festival came to be called the biggest day of the entire
Festival time. The idea was that the seventy oxen that they
sacrificed during the seven preceding days were an offering
made for the entire people of the world while the one ox that
was offered on the last day was a sacrifice made for only the
people of Israel. Also the seven preceding days were kept in
order for the dew to descend but on the eighth day they prayed
for the rain.

On this eighth day of the Festival, Jesus went up to the
temple early in the morning and cried out:

"If anyone is thirsty, let him come to me; whoever believes
in me, let him drink."

Hearing these words, some people in the crowd said to
themselves that "This must certainly be the expected
prophet," some that "This is the Messiah," and others that
"Surely the Messiah is not to come from Galilee? Does not
Scripture say that the Messiah is to be of the family of David,
from David's village of Bethlehem?"

One day after the Festival of the Tabernacles, the Pharisees
and the lawyers brought a woman to Jesus who had gone to
the temple in the morning.

They said:

"Rabbi, this woman was caught in the very act of adultery.
Now Moses ordered in the Law to stone such as she, so what do
You say?"

This was, of course, a question they were asking to test
Jesus. And it was a question to which an answer could not be
found quite too easily. Perhaps, one could say: do as the Law
says. But giving a violent punishment to such a woman, though
adequate at Moses' time when order was maintained only
through such a heavy punishment, could be considered too
severe unless it were dealt by ones closely related to the person
such as her wronged husband or father. Apart from this
aspect, Jesus had been known to take the side of one who was
driven into a difficult position in life either through sinning,
bodily defects, or social ostracization.

The Pharisees and the lawyers, therefore, knew very well that Jesus could not tell them to just go ahead with their stoning. But he could neither excuse her simply because then it would be like justifying the act. And, moreover, it could be condemned as breaking the Law.

Jesus did not answer them at once but squatting on the ground wrote something with his finger on the dust for a while. Unable to withstand the tension any longer, however, he stood up and said:

"Let the sinless one among you throw the first stones at her."

After saying this he stooped down again and resumed writing in the dust. But nobody threw stones at her and they went away conscience-stricken. Jesus turned his eyes to the woman and asked her:

"Woman, where are your accusers? Has no one condemned you?"

The woman answered:

"No one, Lord."

"Then I will not condemn you either. Go, and from now on do not sin any more."

For these things, Jesus gained new respect and love from the crowds, and more envy and hate from the chief priests and the Pharisees. The latter were vexed because it was dangerous for them to kill Jesus in the midst of all that love and respect he enjoyed from the common people. They felt that they had to downgrade Jesus in the eyes of the people somehow before they could lay their hands on him. But they had failed in everything they had tried in the way of setting a trap for Jesus.

The agents of the chief priests and the Pharisees continued to move among the crowd looking every minute for an excuse to get at Jesus.

One day, Jesus spoke to the crowd:

"If you adhere to my teaching, you will never die."

Then the agents of the Pharisees laughed at him and said:

"Now we are certain that you are possessed by a devil. We

know that all the progeny of Abraham have died, too. And do you claim to be bigger than Abraham, then? Who are you?"

"I do not belong to this world with you but receive my glory from my Father whom you call your God. Your forefather Abraham longed to see my time and he was pleased with me."

And his accusers were very angry to hear this:

"You are still not even fifty, and how can you claim to have seen Abraham."

Jesus, however, answered calmly:

"I was before Abraham came."

Hearing this, they picked up stones and were about to throw them at Jesus and this once even the crowd who loved Jesus could not accept what he said. To begin with, they did not know the meaning of his words, and secondly, they felt that there was no need for Jesus to degenerate their ancestor at such a time of tension as this and aggravate the conflict.

Jesus left the temple while people were busy finding stones or debating or throwing insults at him.

Coming back to the new headquarters at Mt. Tabor, Shaphan flew the falcon early next morning, in the direction of Gerasa.

(Hadad, where are you?)

was all the message he sent by the falcon. The falcon did not come back. It could mean that the bird was caught by the Romans or met death by some other way.

Shaphan's gloom came back after they came to Mt. Tabor and especially after the falcon became missing. He became more taciturn than before and spent much time looking up at the stars at night. Zilpah tried to console him saying:

"Father will come back."

And he opened his mouth only because it was not often that Zilpah talked to him.

"Oh, Zilpah. You know how to read the stars, don't you?

You must have learned it from your father. Won't you read the stars for us?"

Shaphan spoke these words looking with his blood-shot big eyes at the jewel-clear eyes of Zilpah. He sounded somewhat like a small boy who was nagging his mother to give him something he coveted.

"My father is alive. He is with the Roman soldiers," said Zilpah without any hesitation. Her voice was as cool and clear as always. In contrast with Shaphan's sorrowful and gloomy attitude, she showed no uneasiness or suffering on her white clear face.

"What, you mean Hadad is really alive? Zilpah you must know. Tell me. Where is he now, where is he?"

Zilpah did not answer this question, however. Of course, she would have told him if she could, but then if she didn't know, why did she not say so?

"How can you stay so cool and comfortable when I am so agonized and frustrated as this? Hadad is my teacher but he is also your father. Why don't you tell me what you know? Is Hadad really alive? How can I be sure of that?"

". . . . ."

Zilpah was no different from a dumb. She merely looked endlessly at Shaphan's face. Her face was as impenetrable as that of a stone statue.

"Zilpah, I feel you too know how to read the stars. Read the stars for me now. Tell me where Hadad is and what happened to the falcon."

"I only watch the stars while you are sleeping."

"So what did you read? Tell me all about it."

"I am not as good at it as my father was. But as I watch them for a long time, they seem to open their mouths for me."

"What is it that they told you?"

"They told me that my father is alive and that he is with the Romans. This is what the stars told me."

"When did they say that he would come here?"

"I have not heard anything about it yet."

"Do ask them about it for me. And also about when Jesus is going to join hands with me."

". . . . . ."

Zilpah did not say anything. It was not because she found it difficult to ask those questions to the stars but because she felt she might not be able to receive answers to them.

"Zilpah, if you won't ask them, I will leave. I will go after Hadad."

Shaphan's voice sounded threatening. But Zilpah only said calmly:

"Don't go."

Next day, before Shaphan had time to leave, Ananias arrived from Capernaum. He had been staying in Capernaum even after Shaphan had moved to Mt. Tabor collecting information and making contacts. After Shaphan's second conference with Jesus ended without any positive results, except that Jesus was colder to his proposals than before, Ananias was not disappointed as much as Shaphan, Thomas, or Judas but went on about his duties with poise and faithfulness. He came up to Shaphan, a tall man with fair complexion and a neck on which veins stood out.

"It has been a long time, Commander," he boomed good-naturedly.

Shaphan looked worn out because of his worry and irritation. And the first words he uttered to Ananias was:

"Where is Hadad?"

"He is at Capernaum," said Ananias in his sonorous voice.

"Ananias, are you telling me the truth? Is he really at Capernaum?"

"Absolutely, Commander. Aquila gave me a detailed report on him."

"Aquila?" Shaphan asked in surprise.

According to Ananias, Aquila who had abducted Zilpah to Nabatea when the Blood Contract Corps did not keep its promise with him and had been locked up by the Corps for it had been set free at the same time that Zilpah made her safe return to Galilee and was now staying around in Capernaum. While the Blood Contract Corps had been away in Nabatea, Aquila had been again suspected of incriminating the Corps by presenting the arrow with which the Roman centurion had been shot many years ago (claiming it to have been shot by Shaphan), but the suspicion was proved groundless and as a consequence Aquila was released after promising to cooperate with the Corps after the release.

It was a truth that Aquila had been as helpful as he could afford to be to the Corps through his services to Ananias. Besides, he had no friend in Nabatea now that the Remaining Faction of the deceased King and the faction of the First Queen took power and spreading the word that Aquila was the one who caused all the trouble by bringing the questionable arrow and Zilpah into the Nabatean court so that all Nabateans hated Aquila. In short, he did not wish to return to his country under the circumstances. He decided, instead, to start some sort of a business in Capernaum and while making a living that way help Ananias with his work on the side. But he was fearing that the Nabatean court might send an assassin or something over to remove him.

"Is all this true, do you think?" asked Shaphan.

"I make it a rule not to believe him entirely. But so far, he has proved himself to be reliable. Since he realizes that his life is in our hands, partly, at least, I don't think he will do anything foolish."

Shaphan knew that Ananias who had been doing the intelligence work of the Corps for a long time would easily let himself be tricked by one as infamous as Aquila.

"What kind of business is he thinking of opening?"

"He says he will bring in jewels from Arabia and sell them to the Roman soldiers. He says it will serve two purposes, that of making living for him, and earning information for us."

"Have you checked on the route through which he plans to import the jewels from Arabia?"

"Aquila claims to know quite a few merchants along the

coastal line of the Sea of Galilee, and he means to get hold of the jewels through them. I have not checked on this point thoroughly, yet. But I have him tailed in all his actions so far, I have not caught him in any deceit. I think it is all right for us to let him go loose for a while as along as we keep our eye on him."

As an example of Aquila's newly cultivated reliability, Ananias mentioned the fact that over the last siege of the Gerasa headquarters, Aquila had informed him of a number of moves Romans were planning to make and they all proved to be valid as a result.

"To what extent do you trust him, Ananias?" asked Shaphan.

"I don't trust him."

Ananias' answer was final.

"You mean you don't trust him as a person but think his informations are reliable, right?"

"Yes."

"I see. Just don't relax your watch is all I could advise you since he is an unusually cunning person."

"I understand, Commander."

"All right, then. Now, is it absolutely certain that Hadad is in Capernaum?"

"Yes, Commander. I know it is because I had that information from another source, also."

Shaphan seemed to be turning some thought over in his mind and then he said to Ananias:

"Ananias, which would be easier, for us to rescue Hadad by cunning or by force?"

"I don't know which method would actually be the easier, but I suggest that we try the former method in the first place."

"If it fails?"

"There's too much risk in trying it by force. After our retreat from Gerasa, the Roman main force has moved to Capernaum leaving only about a hundred men in Gadara and its vicinity. It seems they are abiding time until they are ready to make their attack on Mt. Tabor."

"It would not be difficult for us to fight against a Roman force of several hundred with a little fortification, but the bigger problem would be to transferring the headquarters to Mt. Gilboa this time."

Shaphan seemed reluctant to move the headquarters to Samaria.

"But they will capture Dariqueyea and blocking all access to and from the Sea Galilee cause us to lose of our Galilean territory plus most of our base in Decapolis, which is a lot for us to bear, I feel."

"Even so, we could manage if only we had Hadad back with us," said Shaphan and gazed at Ananias as if in reflection. At this moment, Ananias felt that there was some change in Shaphan and with this thought in mind, he looked him straight in the face.

Four days after Ananias' visit to Mt. Tabor, Thomas came unexpectedly. He said that he had gone up to Capernaum from Jerusalem on a business and then decided to drop in at the new headquarters before he would go back to Jerusalem. He also said that 'the business' he went to Capernaum about concerned Mary and that the reason he decided to pay a visit to Mt. Tabor was to give a report to Shaphan on Jesus and other things connected with him and the needs of the Blood Contract Corps.

He told Shaphan the following:

First. That Jesus declared that He was the Messiah at Caesarea Phillipi last autumn but that He did not say anything about rescuing Israel from her bondage to Rome or chasing the Romans out of the country. Thomas specified that what Jesus mentioned as His mission as the Messiah was helping the people, to seek an eternal life and enable them to escape death.

"How can He enable the people to escape death?" asked Thomas and then continued, "He said that we could escape our death by throwing away our body that belongs to the earth and get born again in the Kingdom of Heaven. He also said that He did not belong to the earth but to heaven, and therefore whoever wishes to enjoy the glory of the Kingdom of Heaven would do well by forsaking their body that belongs to the earth and many interests that are bound to their body but prepare themselves to bear the cross like Jesus himself.

"Later, Jesus went up to Jerusalem and tried to participate in the observances of the Festival of the Tabernacles as if He felt some special mission to perform, and the chief priests, the Pharisees, and the Sadducees tried to test Him with hard questions so that He would fall into their traps, but Jesus defeated them and also the crowds acclaimed and supported Him most zealously so that His enemies could not do anything more to waylay Him. And up to now, the plan of His enemies to kill Him has not succeeded, and Jesus was now staying in Jericho."

The above was the essence of Thomas' report to Shaphan.

"Doesn't He have any plan to come down to Galilee?" asked Shaphan.

"It won't be easy even if He had such a plan. After your last conference with Him, He gained more enemies all over the country, and He seems to feel that if He were to be surrounded by danger, anyway, He is better off in Jerusalem."

Next, Thomas talked about Mary or rather 'the business that concerned Mary.'

"Some time ago, as we were travelling back from Tyre to Decapolis by way of the upper stream of the Jordan River, Judas tried to persuade Mary to get caught by the Romans so that Jesus might feel enough angry to stand up against the Romans but this scheme failed. Judas was vexed by her unwillingness to cooperate and even threatened her that he would inform on her to the Roman army but I dissuaded him."

But Judas did not give up on her all together. This time he tried to take advantage of her while they were travelling in Jericho and as Mary rejected him flatly, he was so chagrined that he sold her to the Romans anyway.

Thomas had gone to Capernaum to see a centurion with whom he had an acquaintance (it was the centurion whose beloved slave Jesus had cured) and have him testify to the Romans to the fact that it was quite a long time after the incident at Gadara that Mary met Shaphan. But he unexpectedly ran into Aquila in Capernaum who said that since he knew more about the incident in question than any other person he would clarify things for Mary and then he went to the Roman commander-in-chief and obtained from him a certificate testifying to Mary's innocence. And so, Mary was likely to be released very soon, added Thomas.

When Thomas finished speaking, Zilpah who was present said:

"Where is Madam Mary now?"

"She is kept in a shack in Jerusalem but will be released upon my return."

"You are going to see her?"

"Yes."

"Would you please tell her that I miss her?"

"I will, Madam."

Two days after Thomas left Mt. Tabor, Roman attack on Dariqueyea started finally. The main part of the force was supplied by the men that had been collected in Capernaum and some came from Gadara in a side attack.

Shaphan judged that with the small army he had at hand, he could not possibly fight an enemy seven times as big as his. He ordered the troops that were in Dariqueyea to fight discreetly until the enemy should reach there, and then they should retreat to Mt. Tabor on their first chance after inflicting minor injuries on the enemy.

Early on the morning of the Roman attack on Dariqueyea, Aquila paid an unexpected visit to Mt. Tabor.

"How have you been, Respected Commander?" greeted Aquila.

"Oh, how are you?" Shaphan answered. His greeting sounded amiably but inside his mind Shaphan was somewhat uneasy about his coming like this.

"I have come because of some urgent matter. I felt I had better report to you at once," said Aquila but he did not seem to be in any hurry to make his report on what he called 'some urgent matter' but instead proceeded to tell Shaphan how it came about that he came to Mt. Tabor rather than any other person who was member to the Corps and then also he seemed eager to tell Shaphan about various things and difficulties he experienced on the way. As to the reason why he, rather than another person closer to the Corps by formal affiliation, happened to be the messenger of the news he came to disclose, he explained that when he who happened to be the first to receive this important news, went to the house of Ananias to convey what he heard, Ananias had gone to Chorazin or was it Bethsaida? In any case, he was not home and so Aquila decided to wait for him, but seeing that Ananias did not return by as late as ten o'clock in the night, Aquila had decided that he would not wait any longer but would at once be on his way considering the grave nature of the mission. He could not travel along the coastal areas because they were occupied by the Roman soldiers and so was obliged to travel by way of Albera which seemed to have caused his quick arrest by the Blood Contract Corps patrols which after all proved beneficial to everybody concerned since it hastened the process of Aquila's search for the Mt. Tabor headquarters of the Corps.

"Please accept my thanks for your pains. But what is this matter which you call 'urgent'?" said Shaphan.

"Well, since you seem rather in a hurry to hear it, I will disclose the matter to you," said Aquila and then lowering his voice by a pitch continued:

"The Romans are taking your Corps Teacher Hadad to Jerusalem."

"When?"

"I am not sure when they made this decision but it was

yesterday evening that the news reached my ears. And I had gone hurriedly to your honored subject Master Ananias in perplexity. Why? It was because I had arranged with Ananias to help the Corps Teacher to escape and here I was confronted with the surprising news of the Romans taking him away to Jerusalem."

"When is this going to take place?"

"I think they already took him this morning to make the trip to Jerusalem from Capernaum."

". . . . . ."

Shaphan watched Aquila's face with an expression that showed that he too did not understand the situation fully. And Aquila continued his 'report.'

"Corps Teacher will travel by a carriage pulled by two horses. And the soldiers that would escort him are forty in number among which thirty-six are to return to Capernaum while the rest of the troops, that is, four remaining men will follow him as far as Jerusalem."

Aquila sent a glance in the direction of Shaphan and then as if determined to supplement his own interpretations, he said:

"The reason why as many as forty men follow the Corps Teacher in his transfer to Jerusalem was that they knew there was a chance for a surprise attack by the Corps along the Sea of Galilee," he said.

Shaphan just nodded his head in silence. If Aquila were telling him the truth as he seemed to be to Shaphan they needed to take an action immediately. Even if it were a false report, it could not be ignored considering its nature, as long as there was no counter-evidence. One thing, however, was amiss. It was that there were not enough men to mobilize at the moment. Although Aquila said that once the party would have crossed the boundary line to Samaria, the carriage would be escorted only by four horsemen, it would be reckless to go in too small a number and the number that could be gathered right away was only eight not counting himself because all the rest were gone to Dariqueyea where a combat was expected.

He could neither call them back under the circumstances nor was there time to do so. Yes, he could not afford to lose any time. Especially since he had to pursue the enemy before they cross over the Samaritan boundary.

"Aquila, will you help me?" asked Shaphan.

"No, Commander. Because the Romans will find me out then. I don't think it is wise for me to show up there."

(What is the meaning of this?)

Shaphan wondered. He thought fast. He could not let him go back where he came from because there were a number of contingencies to be taken into consideration. He had to keep Aquila at Mt. Tabor, at least.

"Then do this for me. We are somewhat underhanded right now. If you will stay here at the headquarters and keep an eye on things, it will be a big help to me."

"I can easily do that. And I wish you a luck. . . ."

Shaphan left Mt. Tabor with four men setting his direction at Ginnea to start with. Before he left, he called Becher and warned him:

"Watch Aquila closely. You should never let him get away. And if it should become necessary, you know what to do."

From Mt. Tabor to the boundary line of Samaria was about fifty *ri* (= 12.5 miles) and Shaphan and his men had to cover this distance in a run. They were, of course, all good horsemen. Still, it would not be an easy journey, thought Shaphan.

Just before they crossed the borderline, Shaphan and his men ate breakfast by taking turns. After that they went over the line slowly. They took their station on a hill from which they could look out at the village of Ginnea and with their arrows ready at the bows, they watched the northern road.

"We will shoot our first arrows at the cavalry. After we can get rid of them, it won't be any problem to capture the wagon," said Shaphan to his four men.

"What if there are too many on the horse?" One of the men asked.

"If what Aquila told me is correct, there will be four, but if there are many more, I will make a run at the wagon after the first shooting and in that case I want you to keep them busy while I rescue the Teacher."

The rain started again and it was cold on their skin.

"Rain is early this year. . . ." One of the men said.

"It's better for us to have the rain although I can't say for sure how Romans will like it," another said.

When two hours passed, one of the men said breathlessly:

"Look, something's coming!"

And he pointed with his finger.

"Ah, at last! It's a wagon. And there are the horsemen, too," said another.

"How many horses?" asked Shaphan.

"Four."

"No, six!"

"Look carefully," said Shaphan in a reprimanding tone.

The wagon turned the bend and was now coming toward them.

"Shoot!" said Shaphan and all at once five arrows flew. Two horsemen fell and one horse stood up on its hind legs as result of the first shooting. The second shooting of five arrows threw one more man on the ground and caused one horse to collapse. But now the Romans were shooting back.

"You take care of the cavalry now," said Shaphan and ran single-handed toward the wagon, which had not stopped when the fighting started but went on toward the village of Ginnea. Shaphan could overtake it when it had just passed through the village and he could do so only because he could shoot one of the drivers down to the ground with his arrow which slowed down the wagon. But just then a group of Roman soldiers—about two dozens—who must have been ambushed came rushing toward where Shaphan and the wagon were. That second, Shaphan thought maybe he was dreaming or was having a hallucination. He, therefore, looked once more in that direction. There was no doubt about it.

Shaphan was not afraid to fight against an enemy of that number. He had done that before, killing about half and forcing the rest to run away. But, of course, there was no surety that it would turn out like that this time, also. A lot depended on how good his enemy were with their weapons. To rush into a battle against them was not advisable, therefore. Shaphan did some fast thinking and what he came out with was that he would do one of the three things. The first was fighting against the whole of his enemy right away and see what happens, the second was not paying any attention to them but rescuing Hadad out of the wagon first and then act according to the situation as it arises, that is, try to run away or do the fighting, and the third was not doing any of these things but pulling out of there immediately. But even as he was thinking, he knew that the third option was impossible. Then there remained just the two choices. Suddenly, a thought darted in his mind. It was the thought that if he were to take up the first choice of action, that of starting a fight against the two dozens of enemy soldiers, the wagon would be gone too far ahead for him to catch up again even in the event of his coming out of the fight victorious. He decided, therefore, to stop the wagon first at all events and then see about the oncoming enemy.

Shaphan felt like congratulating himself for having been able to see the situation correctly at the last minute and told himself that it came from long training in calm thinking at crises even as he ran up to the wagon, stuck the dagger into the back of the remaining driver with rein in one hand and whip in the other, and tore the door open.

"Hadad! Hadad!"

Shaphan's voice as he called his old Teacher sounded gentle, courageous, and happy all at the same time. But Hadad who should have pushed his head out from inside the wagon was not there. Instead of his white head, a dagger shot out of the wagon and struck Shaphan on the face. Shaphan felt he lost his sight. He could not tell whether he could not open his eyes for some reason or he had lost them. Or rather, whether he was dying or just not able to see. He just experienced something like an evening glow envelope him bodily mixed with some strange soreness of feeling.

At this same hour, Aquila was talking to Zilpah.

"I will convey your father Hadad's message to you, Madam. It was that in case of your husband's death during the battle with the Romans, you were to return immediately to Aroer."

"I will stay here," said Zilpah.

"Of course, you will, Madam. But the Commander is right now fighting against the Romans as you too know, Madam. Although by right, your husband ought to win the Romans and come back victorious, you cannot tell anything for sure about a war until you see the result. I think that is why your father sent you that kind of message. Nobody has won the Roman army, they say. And although we are hoping for the best, even Commander Shaphan may not be completely immune to contingency. Your father's order is based just on that point, I think."

"I will stay with my husband." Zilpah was adamant.

"I wish you could, too, Madam. And I am sure that is your father's wish, also."

Aquila looked at the crystal clear eyes of Zilpah that shone like the rarest jewel, and thought anyone would stake his life ten times in order to own them. At the same time he thought about Shaphan who would by now be either dead or captured by the Romans, and thought about how even such a clever man as Shaphan got caught in the trap he Aquila set, and said to himself inwardly that a really well-set trap can catch almost anyone if only the trapper had some patience.

This was the second time Aquila stretched his scheming hand toward Zilpah. The first time was when he abducted Zilpah to be offered to King Aretas to cover up his failure with the Blood Contract Corps, but this time he wanted Zilpah for his own use.

But it was not his plan from the first to sell the Blood

Contract Corps to the Romans or lay his hand on Zilpah. His original plan was to make money and then go back to Nabatea to lead a comfortable life in his old age. However, he happened to hear that Hadad was moved from Gerasa to Capernaum and then through Ananias, he heard about how Shaphan fretted to rescue Hadad. And these two things gave him the idea of ruining the Blood Contract Corps once and for all and then taking Zilpah for himself.

What enabled him to bring his plan to success was his access to some of the Corps' inner secrets. When he first met Shaphan on the water of the Sea of Galilee carrying the letter and presents from King Aretas, he had something like a premonition that maybe things would not work out quite well. Until he met Shaphan, to suggest the collaboration between Nabatea and the Blood Contract Corps, he had not known much about the organization except that he had heard from people such as the disciples of Baptist John, for instance, that although the Blood Contract Corps was known as a group of bandits by most people, their real purpose was in saving Judaea from the bondage of the Roman Empire. He had also heard that the Corps members were polite and valued loyalty very highly. That they never did anything cowardly was also what he heard about the Blood Contract Corps. But when he actually met Shaphan, and spent some time as his guest, he could not help doubting the validity of what he had heard about the Corps. First of all, Aquila could not understand the way he was treated. He had expected that the Commander would take him to his place and spend the night telling him his plans and talking over the Nabatean proposals. Also he should have acknowledged his receit of the royal letter and gifts either in a written document or orally but he did not do any such thing. And then, didn't they chase him to some house of somebody unknown that was in another part of the coastal region, which turned out to be the house of Ananias in Capernaum. Of course, even though Aquila had visited them as their friend, it was perhaps rather natural that they did not open their heart to him all in one night. But they should at least have been courteous. Besides, what other people except a gang of bandits would receive letter and gifts from a king and not acknowledge it in any formal way? That is, by fulfilling the promise for which the gifts were given? He could not possibly ask them to return what they received. And yet if he were to go to his king and tell him what had happened, he would appear like a fool who had gotten swindled by a bunch of robbers. There was no other way besides paying them first and wait for the action as their request went. And so he brought them a chunk of gold in advance payment for their participation in Nabatean plan. But the result was the same. They only promised that they would take action when an appropriate time arrives. He then had to stake all he had, not only his political career but far more than that, on the deal with the Blood Contract Corps. To be sure he won a point over them by successfully abducting Zilpah to Nabatea. But hadn't he become their prisoner as a result?

After Zilpah returned to Galilee, Aquila had been released. But it was not a real release. Everywhere he went, he was followed by an agent of the Blood Contract Corps. If he had madè a least slip, he would be in the deep of the water as a corpse by now. In order to keep his life, and in order to take revenge, he pretended to have turned a loyal servant to Ananias and have been providing him with news and information which could be verified every time. Although at times, there were incorrect factors in his reports, it was not an intentional misrepresentation but some imprecision caused in the process of circulation. In any case his service was good enough to earn him a trust of Ananias and through him that of Shaphan as well. And this made it possible for him to learn a little about their underground organization. More than anything, he learned the fact that Ananias of Capernaum was a chief member of the Blood Contract Corps which had a large and complex underground network. He also learned the fact that if the Corps were to lose Ananias, it would be like losing one arm.

But he did not inform on Ananias right away. He wanted to have a clearer evidence, but even more than that, he could not overcome a temptation to overturn the Corps totally at the same time that Ananias would be ruined. He had three reasons for wanting it. First of all, he saw that the chance of his possessing Zilpah would become greatest when the Corps would be overturned entirely. Secondly, unless the Corps is not broken up, his passage back to his country would not be clear. The third reason was that he could be paid a fat reward by the Romans.

He, therefore, had been waiting for a good time to put his long-planned scheme to practice and when he heard about the Corps' plan to rescue Hadad and Shaphan's impatience for action, he decided that his time had come.

He requested an interview with the Roman commander-in-chief through a Roman sergeant he was acquainted with and when he was led to the commander-in-chief, he gave him the following two facts. That Ananias was the one through whom all information about the Roman army was being conveyed to Shaphan and that he was also the head of the underground network of the Blood Contract Corps in Capernaum. Therefore, Aquila suggested, the Roman army would do better by arresting Ananias and his subordinates than trying to capture their headquarters. (And yet Aquila did not know the fact that Thomas and his successor Timeus had another large network in Dariqueyea and also the fact that the Blood Contract Corps was a highly complex and pervasive organization that covered the whole country.) Another tip Aquila gave the Roman commander-in-chief was that spreading a news about transferring Hadad to Jerusalem would be a sure way of arresting Shaphan. If Shaphan hears of the news he would try to rescue Hadad at all costs. But if the Romans would follow his suggestions, they would be able to capture Shaphan alive without too much casualty on their side. If these two schemes would work out, Aquila said, the Blood Contract Corps would become as good and dead and this was a result one could not hope to get even at the expense of the thousand lives of Roman soldiers. If these plans succeed, therefore, Aquila would like to receive fifty thousand silver pieces plus Zilpah as recompense.

The Roman commander-in-chief at once replied that he would accept the conditions as a rule except that the condition about Zilpah would hold only so far as she would remain alive and under Roman custody. He also said that about Ananias, the Romans also had had their suspicions. And then in conclusion, the commander-in-chief declared that he would pay Aquila no less than he asked for in silver pieces.

Aquila was satisfied. Straight from there he went to Mr. Tabor and then the rest followed. The promise with the Romans was that Aquila would send Shaphan to a certain place the Romans would designate and the rest was to be taken care of by the Romans. When Shaphan believed his words and left Mt. Tabor for Samaritan border, therefore, Aquila's work was over and he only needed to wait for the fifty thousand silver pieces to be handed over by the Romans. And now, all that remained was for him to take possession of Zilpah.

He looked at Zilpah with a face that shone with a sense of triumph and said:

"I hear you come from Aroer, is that right, Madam?"

". . . . . ."

"I wonder if you too remember. I mean to trip we took together, you and I and Master Thomas. You know my home is not far from Aroer."

He wanted to draw some attention from Zilpah if he could not win her heart. But she did not show any sign of interest. He spoke again:

"Your father is now with the Romans in Capernaum. On this account, he seems to know quite well about the circumstances of the Roman army. If by any chance something should happen to Commander Shaphan he wants you to go right back to Aroer without delay. He expressly asked me to convey the message to you. And he also asked me to accompany you to Aroer since my home is nearby."

"......"

"If you, Madam, should ever decide to leave for Aroer or to go to Capernaum to see your father, please look me up. When I leave here, I will be back in Capernaum by your father's side."

When Zilpah heard these words which sounded like a farewell, she opened her mouth quietly keeping her eyes down:

"Mr. Aquila, I have made no promises with you. I am now regretting not having detained my husband when he left here upon your prompting."

Zilpah's voice sounded cold like the spring water. Just then Becher came up to them having eavesdropped their conversation nearby.

"Master Becher, isn't it strange that Commander Shaphan has not come back yet? What if you, Master Becher, ride out and take a look? And if you would rather stay here, I will be glad to go and see," said Aquila looking at Becher's face.

"I cannot leave here until Commander returns," answered Becher.

"I will go and see, in that case. Good Bye, Madam. And don't forget your father's message. And you, too, Master Becher, I humbly bid you farewell...."

Aquila started walking out of the cave as he finished his farewell greetings.

"Wait, Mr. Aquila," said Becher.

Aquila turned back slowly.

"You must stay here until the Commander should come back," said Becher in a dry tone.

"You don't know, Master Becher, what kind of relationship there is between the Commander and myself," said Aquila in a very calm voice.

Becher did not say anything to that but merely stared at Aquila.

"I have come here to convey an important news because of

my special friendship and loyalty toward Master Ananias and
your Commander. And I had not done it for recompense
either. Therefore, my coming and going is absolutely my own
choice."

After saying thus in a voice which sounded almost gentle,
Aquila again turned to go with a smile on his face.

"Mr. Aquila!" called Becher again.

Aquila stopped for a moment but went on toward the
opening of the cave.

"Mr. Aquila!" Becher called him again this time a little
more loudly than before.

Becher had raised his bow and arrow ready to shoot and was
aiming the top of an olive tree on the hill. It looked as if he
were aiming to hit a bird that sat on an olive branch.

"Did you call me, Master Becher?"

Becher separated the bow and arrow in his two hands and
faced Aquila. But he did not say anything. He merely stared
at Aquila.

"Did you call me, Master Becher?"

When Aquila asked him again, Becher said in an irritated
voice:

"You must stay here until our Commander comes back."
Aquila who did not know what else to do walked up to Becher
and asked:

"What is the matter, Master Becher?" Aquila tried to
suppress an anger as he said this and as a result his voice came
out low.

"......"

Becher did not answer.

"Isn't this going too far if you are joking?"

"I am not joking."

"Then what is it you're doing?"

"I am performing my duty."

"Your duty? What does that have to do with me?"

"It is my duty to guard this place. While the Commander is
away, people's coming in here and going out of it becomes my

direct responsibility."

"So I explained to you how things stand with me. I told you that the sole reason I came here was to help the Commander and that it was an act I voluntarily performed, which means that I can go back when I want to. Do you find anything wrong in this?"

". . . . . ."

"I have to see Master Ananias within the night, and this, too, is to do him favour only."

As Aquila said as much as this, Becher smiled faintly because he had just a while ago received a report that Ananias had been arrested by the Romans.

Aquila did not seem to know yet it was under Shaphan's orders that Becher was keeping him from going and he said testily:

"In case I don't go back in a hurry, something bad may happen to Master Ananias. As to the Commander, I can come back even tomorrow and see him. You understand, don't you, Master Becher. Then. . . ."

With this last word, Aquila turned back without even looking in the direction of Becher. And he looked determined this time never to look back even if he would be called repeatedly.

Becher seemed to feel his determination also and before he called out to Aquila, he picked up the bow and arrow he had laid by his side and held them ready to shoot.

"Mr. Aquila," Becher said with the bow and arrow still ready. Aquila did not turn back. At the same time the arrow flew with a swish in noise. Aquila fell with the arrow in his back.

It was on the nineteenth of March, that is, ten days before the Passover, that Shaphan was transferred from Capernaum to Jerusalem. At that time, Jesus was resting in a small village called Ephraim which was about twelve miles to the north of Jerusalem. The rest was a preparation for the big tasks he was going to perform soon. He had already told his disciples that he would be crucified in a near future but he wished to make it more meaningful if it were an unavoidable burden for him. He was thinking that the time of consummation of his mission would be about the Passover and the place Jerusalem. Although there could be no alternative in the choice of place, the time seemed to allow for some margin. The Festival of the Tabernacles or the Day of the Pentecost appeared as good as the Passover. The only condition required here was that it be a day of sufficient importance. He only thought it would be best if he could make it over the Pentecost. It was because he liked spring. Under the warm spring sun, the pain at the cross would be easier to bear, he thought to himself. And so he decided to take a good rest until the Pentecost in a secluded place.

Six days before the Passover, Jesus left Ephraim for Bethany. It was Saturday. At Bethany, he stayed at Simon's house as usual and Martha, Mary and Lazarus prepared a good table for him. Also at the feast in this house were many other people including Cleopas of Jericho who was a Blood Contract Corps member and also a relative to Simon and also many others. Some of them were those who came from Jerusalem in order to look at Lazarus whom Jesus had revived from death.

Mary, sister of Martha, brought out about a pound of expensive oil and just as Mary of Magdala did that time poured it on the feet of Jesus and wiped them with her hair.

Seeing this Judas thought it a great waste. Since he was the one who did accounting for the group, he was quick in calculating.

"You should have sold the oil for three hundred denarii and distributed it to the poor," he said. But of course it was not because his heart was with the poor.

Jesus said when he heard what Judas said:

"You always will have the poor with you, but you will not always have Me." Therefore, let her do it for the day of my burial."

When Judas after being rebuked thus by Jesus came out of the room where he had been with Jesus and others, Cleopas also came out after him. He had come here from Jericho as soon as he heard the news of Shaphan's transfer to Jerusalem. He was still hoping that something might happen at their last meeting in Jerusalem between Jesus and Shaphan in spite of the fact that their last meeting seemed even more disastrous than the one before that. He was thinking that maybe Jesus would work some miracle which would solve all their problems at once. The reason Cleopas had this hope was that he felt something would happen in Jerusalem which would force Jesus to take some decisive and drastic action. Cleopas was well aware of the fact that the ruling class of Jerusalem, that is, the chief priests and the Pharisees were trying to kill Jesus under any pretext whatsoever.

If Jesus would die here because of that conspiracy, the Blood Contract Corps would have to close down much of their activities until the time should come for the real Messiah to arrive. Or if Jesus proves himself to be the Messiah on this occasion, and takes some action against the high priests, the Pharisees, and the Romans, the Blood Contract Corps would have to respond to it at once, he thought. He, therefore, pulled Judas by the sleeve now and said:

"Jesus talks as if he knew he were going to die soon. What do you think of it?"

"I don't know. He talks in that strange way often. And so I am not sure if he really means what he is saying. . . . Did you see Shaphan, though?"

"I have tried since yesterday to obtain a meeting with him along with Gallio and some others but there seems no hope for the time being anyway. If things continue in this way, our only hope would be what Jesus would do at the last moment."

"What he would do at the last moment?"

"If he goes into Jerusalem this time, he will be caught by the high priest, do you not think so? If this happens, Jesus would have to make some decision about his attitude, that is, whether he would let himself be caught up by them and die, or make them bow before him by showing them his might as the Messiah."

"You mean once he shows himself to be capable of the might of the Messiah, the Commander would be automatically rescued? If that is what you mean, I won't build hope on it much. He has for many times declared himself to be the Christ and yet nothing has changed for us so far. And then what more do we have to hope for in that line?"

"That is why I mention his last attitude. Everyone discloses his real self when facing death."

"Would they then arrest him for sure this time?"

"That's certain. I heard it directly from one of the servants of Caiaphas."

Caiaphas was the name of the high priest. And if the news had spread to the servants of his house, it must be a thing decided among themselves (Annas, father-in-law of Caiaphas and other chief priests), thought Judas.

"Then what is it we should do?" asked Judas looking into Cleopas' eyes.

"That is what I have been meaning to talk over with you. My opinion is that we should tone down on our activities from now on. If we don't wise up, we are likely to end up on the cross for being his disciples."

Hearing this, Judas changed color and there was a sudden fear in his protruded yellow eyes.

"You . . . you mean they will get us, too?"

His voice trembled when he said this. At that moment his head seemed filled up with the fear for the cross and he could not help a violent trembling in his heart.

"I don't mean it has been decided but that it may happen because from what I hear they seem to be considering it as a possibility."

"C . . . Cleopas, what shall I do, then? Tell me. Tell me what it is I should do. You and I are not merely fellow members but close friends, aren't we? So, tell me."

"Well, what I can suggest is that you just take it easy and play cool."

"What about getting out of the party in advance?"

"I do not think there is need for that. Especially since we have duty toward our Commander, too. I think we should still follow him along with the others and see what happens."

"Al... all right, we will do that, then. But remember, I trust you to help me. You know as well as I do that I was not his disciple from the first. I was only a member of the Blood Contract Corps just like you were. And you and I are very close friends, aren't we?"

Judas seemed to feel a desperate need to stress the fact that Cleopas and himself were 'very close' friends. And that night, he came to Cleopas with a bottle of wine as if he could not rest his mind unless he did not make sure about Cleopas' loyalty in some other way and said:

"Don't forget that you and I are very special friends. Because we are, aren't we? By the way, is this servant of the high priest good friend of yours? All right, I will trust you, just you, in any case."

Judas slept the night at Cleopas' quarters.

The next day was Sunday and the twentieth of March. Jesus and his followers went up to Jerusalem early in the morning. Jesus had his disciples go to the opposite village and bring a colt which nobody had yet ridden and if anyone should say anything to them they were to answer:

"The Lord needs it."

He then rode the colt into Jerusalem.

Seeing him riding the colt into the city, the crowds who had gathered there to celebrate the Passover, welcomed him happily. Especially the Blood Contract Corps members and young people took off their outer garments and spreading them on the road sang out:

"Hosanna, to the Son of David! Blessed is He who comes in the name of the Lord! Hosanna in the highest."

The reason the Blood Contract Corps people showed so much enthusiasm on this occasion was that they looked toward the 'last moment' in which Jesus might perform some tremendous miracle so that their commander Shaphan may be safely rescued and their long dreamed hopes realized. They cheered the more loudly and eagerly so that they might help Jesus to make his ultimate decision.

And their plan seemed to work.

Jesus became more outspoken and condemning in his words and attitude and looked as if he would begin to denounce and condemn his other enemy besides the Pharisees and the chief priests, namely the Romans, in no times. But at the same time that this was happening, the chief priests and the Pharisees who had been aggravated to a point of explosion, anyway, did break out in great fury by his severity and boldness. Up to then, high priest Caiaphas had tried not to arrest him in his name, but on this day, he changed his mind suddenly and gave up the thought of maneuvering so that it would look like a spontaneous happening brought about by the mob. This was not possible under the circumstances which was that the crowds were absolutely rapturous about Jesus sending him acclamations and words of devotion. Caiapha went to his father-in-law Annas at once, therefore, and obtained his permission to arrest Jesus.

That night Malchus, the said servant of Caiaphas secretly met Cleopas. Since Cleopas was impatient to see how Jesus acts in his last moments, he cooperated with Caiaphas — although it was through Malchus — all he could.

When Malchus saw Cleopas, he said:

"Did you see, Master Cleopas how people were carried away and raved when Jesus came into the city today?"

"Yes, I did."

"That's why my master gave up on arresting him in his name in public."

"And?"

"So he intends to arrest him when he is not with the

crowds."

"About when?"

"It would have to be night, don't you think?"

"Do you know on which day?"

"They have not set the date yet, it seems. But it may be over the feast of the Passover, I think. And, of course, you will have to help us in everything."

"I am trying my best. It so happens, I have a friend among Jesus' disciples and through this friend I am keeping a close watch on Jesus."

"You will have your friend report to you about everything Jesus says or does, won't you Master Cleopas? Above all, He must not get away from us without our knowing."

"It's a lot of work, though, and expenses, too, to tell the truth, what with having to meet him often and occasionally treating him to some good things to eat or drink, you know."

"In fact the high priest gave me ten silver pieces to hand over to you. He wanted to hear something more definite from you today and also promised to pay you in bigger sum maybe about tomorrow, he means after you let him hear something more certain than what you have been telling us."

Cleopas received ten silver pieces from Malchus and told him about the recent affairs and activities of Jesus.

Next day, that is, the twenty-fifth of March, Malchus met with Cleopas again and handed him thirty pieces of silver.

"The ten pieces that you received yesterday apart, these thirty pieces may be given to your friend or you make them your own as you think fit. And my master thinks the date will be about day after tomorrow."

Cleopas understood what was meant by that. If he thinks he can buy Judas with that money, it was better to do so, but if he wanted to have the money himself, he would have to take the responsibility of the entire affair until it should succeed or fail.

"I understand your position. All right, then. I will see you tomorrow." said Cleopas and parted from Malchus carrying the thirty pieces of silver with him.

In the meantime, Jesus had made a routine of entering the city of Jerusalem in the morning and going back to the Mount of Olives at night praying while he spent some afternoon hours in Bethany and also ate supper there. The Mount of Olives was situated about five *ri* (= 1.25 miles) north of Bethany.

Cleopas had at first planned to be Caiaphas' agent himself and tailed Jesus and his disciples for three nights on end from Sunday through Tuesday. But as time went, he had doubts about the plan. Since he was not himself a disciple of Jesus, he could not hope to go very near him and so in case he pointed his finger from some distance at Jesus, Malchus, to whom he had told to arrest the one he would point with his finger, could misread it as meaning someone else. He, therefore, decided belatedly to give the job and money to Judas and instead he took over for himself the job of leading the soldiers of Caiaphas to the foot of the Mount of Olives where Jesus and his disciples spent the nights.

Judas was paying nightly visits to Cleopas to find out the progress on the part of Caiaphas and his friends of the arrest of Jesus. What he wanted to know was whether the disciples also would be arrested along with Jesus or not. He wanted to hear the news of each day so that he would not be caught unawares. But Cleopas told him the same thing each day:

"We don't know yet. They are going to decide after Jesus is arrested."

"I just wondered if they did not suddenly change their plan. . . ." said Judas.

"Didn't I say that I would vouch for you in case anything should happen?"

"But I couldn't be sure that you were still in the position to do so, I mean if circumstances have not changed after I last saw you."

Like Cleopas, Judas also said the same words every time. Although Judas was a very clever man and he believed himself to be so, once he is caught with fear he could not function normally and became stupid. Also, his principles of life were valuing life of all things and not trusting another person under any circumstances.

"If you can really not trust me, why don't you join in and help them do their job? Wouldn't your problem solve itself, then?"

"How can I help them?"

"It's simple, I will go to the Mount of Olives, even tomorrow night, leading the soldiers of Caiaphas and you go up to Jesus when you see us with our torchlights and kiss him."

"Is that all? Will I be safe, then?"

Judas seemed not reassured.

"Of course, you will be safe. And besides, you will get the prize money."

"Prize money?"

"Don't you believe me? Look. . . ."

Cleopas threw the bag of thirty silver pieces to Judas.

"What's this? Is this, is this. . . ."

Judas' yellow eyes bulged out further as he ascertained the contents of the bag.

"That's what came from the high priest. I was going to earn the money myself instead of giving the job over to you, but seeing you so distrustful of me and also considering the fact that you are in a better position to do the job than I am, I think it's better for you to keep the money."

It was finally decided that they would arrest Jesus on Thursday, one day later than the originally planned Wednesday.

Jesus seemed to be aware of the fact that his final moment came. He prayed:

"I cannot speak because my heart is trembling. Father, let me avoid this fate. But as I came for this, let me glorify my Father's name."

The Passover feast began on Friday. And Thursday, the day before the first day of the Passover feast, was the twenty eighth of March. As in the present time, people started the celebration of holiday one day ahead.

That afternoon, Jesus called Peter and John to his side and said to them:

"Go and have them prepare for us to eat the Passover."

When they asked Him where they would prepare the feast for Him, He said:

"Go into the city and a man will meet you, carrying a water pitcher; follow him. And wherever he enters, say to the proprietor, 'The Master says: Where is the room reserved for me to eat the Passover with my disciples?' He will show you a large room upstairs, set out in readiness. Make the preparations for us there."

As in the case of the colt, Jesus gave them directions as if he had already seen everything with his mind's eye. But why was it that his mind's eye had become clearer and more penetrating than heretofore? One reason may have been that he had for the past several days not performed any miracles such as healing or reviving people and on that account his mind had not been exhausted but rather was pretty well stocked with holy power. Another reason was that Jesus knew that his time was really near and so he wanted to speak and act becomingly for the Messiah.

When Peter and John went into the city, they saw that things were just as Jesus had told them.

Jesus and his disciples went to the large room upstairs. And this was where the last supper took place.

The surprising fact of his washing his disciples' feet occurred also in this room.

Jesus seemed satisfied in spite of the oncoming hardship and sorrow in his heart.

"How much I have wanted to eat this Passover with you!"

He took the cup of wine somebody had poured for him and gave it back to the disciples.

"Divide this among you. Truly I tell you that from now to the day when the Kingdom of Heaven should come I will not drink anything that had been gotten from the vine."

He did the same thing with the bread. He broke it first and

then distributed it among the crowds.

Every word he spoke stung the heart of each disciple.

It was a most moving farewell scene. And yet, Jesus could not keep from saying one thing which he had meant to keep silence about to the end.

"I tell you this: one of you will betray me."

When his disciples heard this, they whispered among themselves asking each other who it could be.

Just then John who had been sitting close to Jesus asked Him urged by Peter with eyes:

"Tell us who it is, Master," he said.

Peter and John were not totally ignorant about the truth. They had heard from Philip only that morning that Judas, Cleopas, and Malchus, a servant to the high priest Caiaphas, held a secret meeting in some obscure place. It was Philip that informed this to Thomas first, and he also asked the latter to do what he could to prevent whatever those three were plotting. Thomas turned the request down, upon which Philip protested:

"I am a member of the Corps and a disciple of our Lord Jesus just as Thomas is. And I think it is unthinkable to let our Lord die by a plot in which we had any hand."

But Thomas felt differently about it.

"I also have heard a detailed report from Cleopas, and it is my honest feeling that only if our Commander had not been in such a critical situation, we would never agree to use any such drastic method. As it is, however, we don't have any such reprieve. The execution of our Commander could take place even tomorrow. And it seems a natural impulse on our part to want to push this Jesus to the very edge of a cliff and see if he will fly up instead of falling down. If he flies up at the end of the cliff, our Commander also will fly up with him and our hope will have chance to bear its fruit, but if things turn out differently, we will have to find a new way for ourselves."

"Do you not love our Lord, Thomas?"

"I do. I love him and respect him. But I have complaints

about his establishing his kingdom in heaven instead of on the earth. I cannot accept his attitude of letting our homeland Judaea remain under the fetters of imperial Rome and merely seeking eternal life and happiness in this kingdom which he says he is establishing in heaven. I want to see him join hands with our Commander even if I would need to push him all the way to the very edge of a cliff."

"I don't know about things as well as you do, Thomas, but I cannot let Judas sell our master just like that," said Philip and went on to Peter to consult with him.

This seems to have reached the ear of Jesus in its course of circulation, or maybe it was his 'holy eye' that made him see what was happening. As things turned out it was neither meaningful nor possible to clarify how Jesus came to have an insight into the truth of the situation. Once Jesus alluded to the 'one' that was going to sell him, it was most natural that someone among his hearers should ask him 'who' it was that would betray him.

Jesus answered very calmly:

"The one to whom I will give a piece of bread dipped in honey is he." Judas who sat at the end of the table did not hear what Jesus said very clearly.

There was such silence in the room that one could hear another breathing.

Jesus broke a piece of bread from a loaf and then dipped it in the honey. He then handed it to Judas while everybody watched it in high suspense.

Judas looked at Jesus with his protruded yellow eyes. The face of Jesus he looked at was completely devoid of expression. Judas extended a trembling hand and received the piece of bread. He, however, did not take it to his mouth but put it on his plate and rose from the table.

The supper was almost finished and the disciples looked from one to another in silence.

Jesus stood up.

The disciples who followed him out of the room were all

seized by a most painful emotion and their steps as they
followed Jesus were very heavy. They walked toward the
Mount of Olives as usual but Judas was nowhere to be seen.
Thomas who took up the rear tapped Philip who was walking
in his front on one shoulder and said:

"From whom did you hear about Judas selling Jesus?"

Philip did not answer at once but ended up by answering:

"I heard it from Cleopas."

"You mean there was no such thing as a rumor before
then?"

"I don't think so," said Philip and then after a moment he
said:

"I heard about it from Mary the first time."

"From Mary?"

"Yes."

"And how could she learn about it?"

"It seems she heard it from somebody who was close with
the wife of Cleopas."

"So?"

"Mary said she would find out from Cleopas if it was true
and if it is, do whatever she could to prevent it."

"Did you then tell Peter and others about it?"

"No. Apart from Mary, I have done my best to dissuade
Judas from his treacherous act. I had half a mind to tell Jesus
all about it but I dissented from it and merely told it to Peter
and some others. Although I may be doing wrong to you,
Thomas, I have not changed my mind about that."

"Philip, toward you, I have always felt like toward a
younger brother and that is exactly how I feel toward you
now," said Thomas.

The place which Jesus frequented during his last nights was
the hill of Gethsemane which was along the western foot of the
Mount of Olives. This was a place where Jesus seemed to find
some refuge from the turmoils of the human world among
olive and fig trees.

On this night, also Jesus went to Gethsemane and when He and His disciples reached there He told His disciples to keep awake until He should come back and removed Himself to a ground which was as far as a fling of stone could reach. It seemed He had some premonition on this night because He usually did not tell His disciples who were apt to fall into sleep before He finished His prayers to wait up for Him.

Although He had prepared Himself for the cross, He seemed to be in agony about the impending event. He prayed that if it was possible 'this cup' removed from Him. He qualified His request, however, with: "Not, however, what I will but what you will."

After the prayers, He seemed to feel more reassured. He looked up at the crescent moon that was just disappearing over the crest of Mt. Seil.

It was at the same time that the crescent completed its descent over the crest of the mountain that Cleopas and Malchus came up to Jesus with the guards of the temple, the Pharisees and their servants with weapons and torchlights following. After them came the Roman soldiers who carried the spears and the swords.

Cleopas pointed to Judas for the benefit of Malchus and the guards and said:

"Jesus is the one whom that fellow would go up to and kiss. Watch him closely, therefore, and arrest the one whom he would kiss."

They all looked at Judas. Judas went to the side of Jesus and putting one hand on His shoulder and made a move to kiss Jesus.

"Whom are you looking for?" Jesus asked at that instant.

The chief of the guards said that they were looking for Jesus of Nazareth.

"It is I," said Jesus.

Malchus stepped out then and together with the guards tried to lay his hand on Jesus. Peter who was by His side at the moment, however, struck him on the right ear and cleft it.

Jesus ordered Peter to put away his sword and picking up
the fallen ear of Malchus put it back on his head. The guards,
the Pharisees, and their servants rushed on and tried to bind
up Jesus.

Jesus did not resist. He let himself be bound by them and
lying on the ground said as if to himself: "It is your time now
and the darkness is the power that rules."

Shaphan was in prison at this time. It was the ninth night
after he had been transferred to Jerusalem. He was making a
hole in the wall of his prison room using chisel and hammer.
The chisel had been supplied by Gallio of Jobba and the
hammer by Zechariah after much difficulty.

It was almost dawn when he finished making a hole which
was barely big enough for a human head to go through. But
outside was not the street or a field but only backyard of the
prison and so the hole was soon discovered by a guard who was
passing by.

Although it was a very early hour, a great commotion was
created in the prison. Shaphan was dragged out and was not
only flogged severely but had his right arm broken at the
wrist.The soldiers who did the job was surprised at the tough-
ness of his bone and commented among themselves that this
man had bones that were either those of a horse or a lion.

As soon as Jesus was arrested at Gethsemane, most of his
disciples took fright and hurried away in search of hiding
places. Only Peter and John remained and mixing themselves
among the crowds followed after their Master.

Jesus was first taken to Annas, the father-in-law of the high
priest Caiaphas. Although Annas was no longer active as a
high priest, he still ruled over all important affairs of
priesthood. Therefore, people still referred to his house as 'the
house of the high priest.'

Peter had followed Jesus as far as the high priest's courtyard
and sat among the attendants, warming himself at the fire

they made in the yard. One of the serving women of that house pointed to him and said that he was with Jesus. But Peter said, "I know nothing." Peter was questioned in this way three times that night but only when he heard the rooster crow did he remember what Jesus had said:

"Before the cock crows twice you will disown me three times."

Peter left the place and finding a corner he cried over what he had done.

Annas looked down at Jesus who was bound and placed under his feet. He said:

"Tell me about your teachings and your disciples." He was an old man but on his eyebrows and in his eyes that glared fiercely, one could still see much energy.

"I have spoken openly before the world and have taught in the synagogues and the temples. Therefore, do not ask me about my teachings but ask those who have heard me," answered Jesus.

This was an unforgivable attitude to show toward one as eminent and feared as Annas was. A servant standing by hit Jesus on one cheek and said:

"How dare you speak in that way to the High Priest?"

Jesus said to him:

"If I spoke amiss, state it in evidence; if I spoke well, why strike me?"

The one who hit Him did not say anything but looked at Annas. He seemed to be waiting for his order.

Annas, however, seemed to have remembered the fact that he could gain nothing from a quarrel with such a one as Jesus and so he sent Jesus onto Caiaphas.

Caiaphas immediately took legal procedures and condemned him. His offence was 'delusion.' And as evidence his saying: that he would rebuild the temple he destroyed within three days. According to him, this was a blasphemy against the temple and a blasphemy against the temple was blasphemy against God.

Since the High Priest did not have the power to put someone to death, however, Jesus had to spend that night in all kinds of difficulties.

When the daylight came, they dragged Jesus to the quarters of Pilate, the Roman governor. It was Friday the twenty ninth of March and the first day of the Passover. The Jews themselves stayed outside the governor's headquarters to avoid defilement so that they could eat the Passover meal.

Pilate who was tired of the Jews making a great trouble of themselves with their quarrels over their religious questions seemed to feel no interest in the case. After giving a brief reading to the letter of accusation sent by the synagogue, Pilate asked Jesus:

"Are you the King of the Jews?"

Caiaphas had accused Jesus of deluding the Jews in that name. To this Jesus said:

"Is that your own idea, or have others suggested it to you?"

And Pilate asked him again:

"What! Am I a Jew? Your own nation and their chief priests have brought you before me. What have you done?"

And Jesus said:

"My kingdom does not belong to this world."

"Are you a king, then?"

"'King' is your word. But my kingdom is that of heaven, not that of the earth."

Pilate could not understand Jesus at all, but did not think that Jesus looked like an evil man. He did not want to kill a man who was not guilty of any real offence in the legal sense of the word. Especially, his wife had told him how Jesus was respected and loved by the Jewish people and how the High Priest and his faction wanted to kill him out of jealousy and hate. No, Pilate did not want to kill an innocent man and earn resentment and hatred from the people whom he was to rule.

What he came out with here was the idea of granting a special pardon in honor of the Passover of which there had been precedents, too. He went out to the people and asked them if they would like him to just give him some flogging and let him go on the Passover pardon since he could not find the man guilty of any real offence. But the people to whom Pilate talked to were mostly of the High Priest and from Jerusalem, the Galileans and the people close to Jesus being only a small fraction among them. And Pilate's question drew an unexpected reaction from them. They cried out that if the governor was to pardon one person to commemorate the holiday, they wanted him to release Barabbas. Cleopas and a number of Blood Contract Corps members called out the name Shaphan but people knew too little of this person who led an underground organization in Galilee and was transferred to this part of the country only ten days ago. And it was entirely hopeless for his followers to get him a pardon. Besides, the Pharisees and the Sadducees were inciting the people to ask for the release of Barabbas by spreading the news among the people that Barabbas was a Zealot of Jerusalem.

But Pilate still wanted to save Jesus and with this intent he asked more questions to Jesus. Jesus, however, hardly answered him. In the meantime, the crowds were shouting for the release of Barabbas more loudly than before and threatened Pilate by saying that if he released Jesus it would be acting against the Emperor Caesar. And Pilate felt he had to give Jesus away to the people.

The Roman soldiers dressed Jesus in purple, and a crown of thorns on his head. Then they slapped him shouting, "Hail, King of the Jews!"

The Roman centurion who was in charge of crucifying Jesus brought two robbers from the cells of the prison. One of them was Shaphan and the other was one whose name was unknown. The three of them were made to bear each his own cross to the place of execution. The place where they were supposed to be crucified was a mound about a dozen feet raised from the ground called Golgotha.

Although Shaphan and the other robber could walk under their crosses, it was not so with Jesus who had not been eating properly for many months and had been flogged and beaten, moreover. He fell many times as he walked toward Golgotha. Although at first the soldiers whipped him every time he fell, later they had Simon, a farmer who was coming back from the country, carry his cross.

At first, Shaphan did not know that the man was Jesus. One of his eyes which were bloody originally had turned into a ball of blood after being stuck with the dagger. This made him a one-eyed man. And with the sweat coming down the face, he saw very little at the moment. And although he felt that large crowd had gathered, he just vaguely thought they were there for his sake. It was only when he saw the man who was walking in front of him fall that he could see that it was Jesus himself. He felt at once that it gave him a considerable consolement to know that the one who was going to be crucified with him had not been a sinner but Jesus. And he seemed to see better than before. And a hope raised itself up in his mind for the last time. If he had really been the Messiah? This thought made his heart pound hard. How many times had he felt his heart pounding at this thought up to now? And how many times had he been disappointed and experienced the sense of failure? And yet now again he found himself getting all excited over the thought. It was because he felt that both he and Jesus had arrived at the last line of life together. Shaphan had hoped that maybe Jesus would show some of his miracles when he realize that he reached this last line.

From a long time ago, Shaphan was almost convinced that Jesus was the Messiah, and so he now believed that Jesus would in these last moments show to all the world some definite sign of being the Messiah. When that is done, the cross of Shaphan or of Jesus, too, for that matter, and all the big and small troubles of the Jewish people would disappear at once, thought Shaphan and he fervently longed to see the sign.

But if he should not show any sign? Ah, what then? But that was impossible, said Shaphan to himself with emphasis. He who revived a dead person, calmed the angry winds, and healed countless sick people just by willing it cannot but be the Messiah. And that he was caught by the Pharisees and sent over to Pilate to be sentenced to crucifixion and now was carrying his own cross like that was also so that what he would do at last would be the more overwhelming and surprising to the ones who witnessed it. With these thoughts, doubts, and hopes, Shaphan walked on carrying his own cross.

When they reached Golgotha, it was some time before noon. While the soldiers built three execution stands on the ground in line, Shaphan looked up at the sky. He felt the brightness of the sun on his one remaining eye. And he could see thousands of crowds watching from down the valleys and the slopes of opposite hills making some indistinct noises. Suddenly Shaphan seemed to see a woman's face among them that was sunken in sorrow and the thought that maybe Mary of Magdala would be watching among them occurred to Shaphan. And then, he saw Zilpah's face that came to his head out of nowhere.

(Oh, beautiful Zilpah! Why didn't I listen to your words on that morning when I lost one eye? Why was I so stupid? Why didn't I make you my Teacher in place of Hadad? Oh, my beloved Zilpah, my own Zilpah!)

Shaphan cried out in his mind.

Although he was aware that he would probably die very soon, Shaphan was not afraid or sad for it. And it was not entirely because he was excited with curiosity and hope about what Jesus would do at the last moment. He felt that he would feel the same about his personal death even if his expectation in Jesus would again be betrayed the way it had been betrayed many times before.

(I don't know why, but the thought of death seems so natural to me. It feels almost pleasant.)

Shaphan mumbled to himself. He had enjoyed women, wine, and cultivating military skills. But all these pleasures of his life had been too little compared with the deep sadness and fury he felt in himself at all times. The sadness and fury came,

of course from his awareness of the state of things his country
and fellow countrymen were subjected to, namely the usur-
pation by the imperial Romans of their land and rights. In
the midst of his enjoyment of women and wine, therefore, his
pain and thirst that was caused by the misery of his country
and the Jewish people never left him. And now, standing
before death, he seemed to feel relieved thinking he would be
freed from that pain and thirst in no time now.

(Death? What is death? Why should I be afraid of it? Have
I not sent to it Jair, Hadad, and many more of my beloved
friends?I am only going where they have gone already. And,
think of how many more friends I have on this earth. I am
only sorry not to be able to see them any more and to be going
before I have done anything to make life happier for them.
Good bye, Ananias, Thomas, Zechariah, Gallio, Timeus, and
oh, good bye, my Zilpah. . . .)

As he thought in this way, his cross seemed to get lighter on
his back.

When he finally stood on the mound where the stands had
been erected, he looked up at the cross on which Jesus was to
be crucified. At the same time, he felt a strange sense of
contentment.

(Yes, that's it. I am lucky to be able to see the last before I
die. What a fate, that I am to die on the same ground in the
same manner as Jesus! And if he lives, I will live, too. But if he
does not live, then, I, too, will die, and gladly, too. Why not?)

He still believed that Jesus would show a sign at the last
moment and, if he does, both Jesus and Shaphan would be
saved, but if he does not show a sign and ends up by being
executed on the cross, Shaphan was glad to be a companion to
him in death.

The cross of Jesus stood in the center which was the right
side of Shaphan's cross. The face that Shaphan saw just before
they were crucified was the color of ashes. Seeing that,
Shaphan thought that maybe Jesus was after all not the
Messiah. Otherwise, why would his face be so filled with great

suffering and covered with such piteously abundant sweat? To Shaphan's eyes the face of Jesus already looked like the mask of death. What Shaphan did not think of at this moment was the fact that Jesus had been exhausted to the point of physical death after dragging the heavy cross over such a distance. Shaphan kept on wondering about Jesus. He wondered about his miracles, now. Why did he work so many miracles and give such teachings if he too was to die in this ignominious way?

The soldiers finished erecting the execution stands and they started taking the clothes off the three to be crucified. Then they dragged them to the stands. The stands were low and in front of them were stepping blocks about two feet high. All the soldiers needed to do was to stand the three on these stepping blocks, make them spread their arms, nail them by the wrists, and then remove the stepping blocks from under them. Sometimes the feet were bound together and fixed on the stand by a rope but on this day they decided to put nails on them also. It was about noon that the three were finally put up on the cross. It was Jesus that they crucified first. They made him spread his arms and put nails on his wrists. Jesus could not seem to bear the pain that penetrated into the deep of his inside, and he cried out:

"Oh, Father!"

Shaphan who was standing on the stepping block looked at Jesus with displeasure at hearing the moan. Shaphan made his body lean back on the stand and spread his arms wide as the soldiers wanted him to. He ground his teeth unawares when the nails went into his wrists but instantly recovered his spirits and told himself that pain and early death were a thing of natural fate for one who was born into a country like Judaea. When the nails went into his feet, he felt as if ice water had been poured into his veins and the unbearable chill seemed to come up to his chest.

Blood began to flow from the wrists and feet of all three men on the cross.

Shaphan turned his head toward Jesus and said:
"Jesus."
". . . . ."
Jesus did not answer.
"Are you not the Messiah?"
Shaphan's voice trembled as he asked this.
". . . . ."
Again, there was no answer.
"Why don't you show the sign, the sign of the Messiah?"
"Have you not seen the sign yet?" Jesus answered him in a barely audible voice.
"This is the time! You must show the power you brought from heaven!"
"I cannot test the power of Heaven because of the affairs of the earth."
"Jesus, are you going to forsake Judaea along with yourself?"
"I do not forsake it but I am trying to save it."
"All right, save it! Save it in the midst of this pain!"
"The pain of the body will go away with the body."
Their conversation was carried on in a very low voice intermixed with moans that escaped their mouths.
The Roman soldiers cast lots to divide Jesus' clothes among them and then they began to deride him reading out the label that was put up on his execution stand. It said: the King of Jews. The Jews complained about the labelling and had asked Pilate to change the words to: Self-appointed King of Jews, but Pilate would not concede and the words stood as they were.
Cleopas and Gallio were among the crowds and they now shouted:
"Jesus, if you are the Son of God, come down from the cross!"
For them, this was an appeal made in desperation to save Shaphan, too.
As he heard voices that sounded familiar to him and which

he seemed to be able to identify as those of some of his Corps members, he stared at Jesus again in anger and desperation. But the face he saw had no life in it. Ashen and covered with cold sweat, eyes closed tight and mouth half open, it was the face of a man who was dying if not already dead. Shaphan realized that he could no longer expect the man to work any miracle of the Messiah, and at the same time as he realized this, he was assailed by an overwhelming despair and his eyelids came down of their own accord.

(Death, take me quickly. For there is no land I wish to tread, now.)

He mumbled these words almost unconsciously. It seemed like a relief to him to give himself up to death forgetting everything else, as long as things turned out the way they did. He felt that now at last he would be released from an unending pain and agony and attain some comfort. But what he actually remembered at this last moment was not all the pains and agonies he had experienced but the enjoyments he had had.

Just then, someone in the crowd shouted:

"Son of God, come down from the cross."

To Shaphan this voice sounded like that of someone in the Blood Contract Corps again, and when he thought this, he felt sorry that he was giving himself up to death and the forgetfulness it assured and leaving them all behind on this earth.

(Hadad!)

He called the name without even realizing that he did. And all at once, the faces of Jair, Thomas, Ananias, Zechariah, and the face of Zilpah in Mt. Tabor and the face of his mother in Chorazin appeared in his mind's eye.

(Ah, the faces that are so dear to me! I wish you all the best there can be as you remain on this earth with that sunshine!)

He mumbled almost unawares.

"King of the Jews, come down from the cross," somebody cried out again from among the crowds. Since those who loved

Jesus were silent by now, it could be only someone among the chief priests, the Pharisees, or someone of the Blood Contract Corps.

At this moment, the robber who was being crucified on the left of Jesus spoke as if he felt all this reviling of Jesus was too unjust:

"We suffer because we have sinned but this man suffers for nothing he has done."

But nobody said anything in response to his sympathetic words. Shaphan would have liked to say something but he was by now too weak to wish to open his mouth unless he had to.

The robber too fell into silence after that. All three of them seemed to have taken one step over the threshold of the house of death. When silence continued in that way for some time, however, the robber opened his mouth again and said to Jesus:

"Wh.... When you go to you... your k... kingdom in heaven, re... remember me, pl... please...."

When Jesus heard this, he said although he, too, was near his end:

"I assure you, today you will be with Me in paradise."

In spite of the fact that Jesus said these words very faintly, they were said loudly enough for Shaphan to hear, and Shaphan felt an anger even in the midst of his pains and exhaustion. So he said as if in his last strengths:

"Coward, where are you seeking your paradise? Have you not forsaken Judaea and her people as well as your own life?"

"......"

Jesus did not make any reply to his scolding. It was not that Jesus was without consciousness at this time. And perhaps in his last consciousness, he still hoped that his Father in heaven would do something to show the whole world the glory of His Kingdom other than what He had shown already. But this was of such a nature that Jesus himself could not speak of it beforehand. The robber who had entrusted Jesus with his soul in his last moments was motionless, now. Maybe he was dead. And Shaphan too closed his eyes.

About three o'clock in the afternoon, the sky was covered with sheets of black clouds and suddenly Jesus cried out as if in a spasm:

"Eli, Eli, lama sabachthani?" that is, "My God, My God, why have You forsaken Me?"

Then he was no more. With that, the lamplight that was alight in his consciousness died, also.

Shaphan, however, was still wide awake. And if he were left in this way, his suffering would have continued endlessly. But fortunately, if it could be called that, there was a custom among the Jews not to leave anyone on the cross over the Sabbath day. And it was on Friday that Jesus and the other two had been crucified. The execution had to be over within that day. The chief priests and the lawyers requested Pilate that he put an end to the criminals by the method that had been used traditionally by the Jews, that of cutting the last breaths of the criminals by breaking their knees. Shaphan was put to his end by this method.

The news that Shaphan had lost one eye and was captured by the Roman army all through an intrigue maneuvered by Aquila had reached within that night the ear of Timeus who was in charge of defense in Dariqueyea. A little before this news arrived, Timeus had also heard the report that their secret armoury in Gadara had been invaded by the Romans and the members that had been guarding the armoury including Uzziah had been arrested. And they also learned that both events were caused by intriguing and treacherous Aquila.

Timeus sent these unhappy news on to Zechariah, who then went to Mt. Tabor taking with him Timeus and Lucius. Now that Shaphan had been captured and all his chief assistants arrested, Zechariah had to take the leadership of the Corps upon himself. If Thomas had been in Dariqueyea, he would have been urged to take over at once, but as it was, Thomas and Judas were with Jesus as their responsibility imposed on them. The reason that Thomas was considered the first choice for the leadership was first that Mt. Tabor was within the boundary line of his jurisdiction; secondly, if one compared the military art of Zechariah and wisdom of Thomas, one would choose Thomas for his wisdom because brain was a prerequisite more valued than military excellence in a leader. Although Zechariah had earned trust and respect of the Corps members through his courageous act and firm loyalty during their Nabatean excursion, and Shaphan too had shown special appreciation for his service, still Thomas would have been a natural choice by all concerned if only he had not been away with Jesus.

There were only seven members gathered at Mt. Tabor. And of the First Members, there was only Zechariah. Although Timeus was now doing the jobs of Thomas and Jair put together, still in priority he came below Zechariah because he was a Second Member after all.

Zechariah led the meeting giving a brief report on the happenings and activities of the Corps during recent weeks.

"I regret that Thomas and Ananias cannot be here with us today. As to Thomas, we know that he is doing an important work for the Corps although he is away from us. Our only hope at this point depends on how Thomas is going to lead Jesus to cooperate with us."

Timeus made a proposal first.

"Master Zechariah, I think we need to elect somebody to give orders for the Corps. My suggestion is that Master Zechariah act as the commander until Commander Shaphan should come back."

As soon as Timeus made this suggestion, the remaining five acclaimed it.

Zechariah, however, did not accept the election at once.

"We cannot think of our Corps without Commander Shaphan. My opinion is that until we should rescue the Commander from his confinement, we should take orders from Madam Zilpah."

A silence fell in the room as Zechariah said this. They seemed a little confused and not to know what it was they ought to say.

Timeus spoke again:

"Master Zechariah, you made a good suggestion, but from the point of view of those who have to take orders at all times, what you suggest does not seem quite practicable. I have no objections to electing Madam Zilpah to the position of the commander, but I feel that somebody should act as her aide, at least. And I think you should be that person."

"I think you speak sensibly except that there is one important reason why I cannot accept the suggestion that concerns me. It is that I have to leave here at once and go to Jerusalem. I am going to rescue Commander Shaphan even if I die for it. Therefore, you Timeus must help Madam Zilpah to lead the Corps."

Nobody said anything to this.

"I am not being modest or anything like that. I am just doing what I think is the best for the Corps. Accept the nomination, Timeus, you must."

It was almost an order.

Timeus said from his seat:

"If it is the best for the Corps, I will obey it."

They now looked for Zilpah.

"Madam Zilpah, we want you to take the place of Commander Shaphan until he comes back," said Zechariah briefly.

Zilpah showed no sign of surprise or embarrassment. She said in her crystal clear voice:

"I am sure all of you will help me and there will not be any difficulty."

But the Blood Contract Corps that had Zilpah as acting commander and Timeus as her aide was not to continue long. The Romans were attacking Dariqueyea with more ferocity every day. From the first, Dariqueyea was not fit to fight against such a large army as the Romans. There was not even a proper fortress. Timeus and Uzziah decided, on the third day of great battle, that it would be better for them all to retreat to Mt. Tabor since it would be impossible to continue fighting so unmatched a war.

The Romans did not attack Mt. Tabor at once. Maybe they did not want to repeat the experience of the battle at Gerasa. Since the fort at Mt. Tabor was stronger and larger in scale, the Romans seemed to think that they needed a larger army to attack it. Besides, they seemed to think also that now that Shaphan was taken away from them, the Blood Contract Corps would die away even if they did not fight to suppress them. Most of the Roman army, therefore, retreated to Gadara and Capernaum.

The people at Mt. Tabor headquarters, therefore, no longer had anything to do.

Three days after the Blood Contract Corps army made their retreat to Mt. Tabor, Timeus went to Zilpah and said:

"Commander Zilpah, give me permission to go to Jerusalem."

Zilpah looked at his face a long while and then said:

"I thought you promised to guard Mt. Tabor headquarters."

"I did, but we face a different situation, now. The Romans have given up their intention to attack us at Mt. Tabor and are gone back to their original posts leaving only a small detachment in Dariqueyea. Under the circumstances, I think it is better for some of us to go and try rescuing the Commander instead of spending useless days here in an unnecessarily large number."

Timeus explained in some length so that Zilpah would understand his position.

"What are you going to do about this place, then?"

"There's Becher. And all twelve men under him are all fine soldiers."

"Do as you think best, then. Since it is important that our members now in Jerusalem come back as soon as possible."

"Yes, it is so, and that is why I am going to leave here. I shall see you when I come back, then, Commander."

Timeus took his leave and came out of her presence.

When Timeus reached Jerusalem with three of his men, however, Shaphan had already been crucified. He called Shaphan by the name until he lost his voice in the evening light at the foot of Golgotha and did not leave the place even after the evening light was gone.

Then, what happened to the corpses of the three on the cross?

First of all, that the body of Jesus was taken over by two upright men is what is written in the record. The two upright men were Joseph of the village of Arimathaea and the Pharisee Nicodemeus. They were both members of the council. The former was a very rich man and the latter an outstanding scholar. Without such background, indeed, one could not even think of interfering in the disposition of the bodies. Joseph went first to Pilate and asked him to give him permission to bury the body of Jesus. Pilate confirmed the death of Jesus with the Roman centurion that had been in charge of the execution and then gave Joseph his permission. When he went to Golgotha for the body, and prepared to carry away the body, he was met with Nicodemus who came with a mixture of aloe and myrrh in great amount. The two of them wrapped the body of Jesus with spices in the linen according to the burial custom of the Jews and laid him in 'a new tomb in which none had ever yet been laid' which belonged to Joseph. They rolled a large stone in front of the opening of the tomb.

This was, of course, not a formal burial. Since it was the preparation day with the Sabbath coming up, they could not continue with the burial work any further. Their plan was to finish the burial on the next day after the Sabbath.

When women (Mary of Magdala, Mary the mother of James, and Salome, mother of John and James and also aunt to Jesus) came to the tomb at dawn of the Sabbath day, however, the large stone that had blocked the opening of the tomb had rolled out and the body was gone. Perplexed, they went to the disciples of Jesus and told them what had happened. John and Peter were the first to run to the tomb. It was just as the women had said. Peter went inside the tomb but he could not find the body. In its place, there was the linen in which the body had been wrapped and a little away from it Peter saw the cloth with which His head had been wrapped. They searched for some more time but the body was nowhere to be seen. Only then did they begin to think that maybe Jesus had risen from death just as he had told them he would.

The first people to believe this prophecy of Jesus about his resurrection were the three women and Peter and John.

The bodies of Shaphan and the other one were dumped in a hole near the ground of execution after they were taken down from the cross. It was where the bodies of the executed criminals were customarily disposed.

When it was dark, Timeus had his three men go to the hole and remove the body of Shaphan from it.

Although Thomas, Gallio, Cleopas, Zechariah, and Timeus were all nearby, they did not dare approach the hole because their faces were known among the Roman soldiers and there was a possibility of their getting arrested once they were seen by any that could recognize them. That was why they sent the three men who were not yet known as members of the Blood Contract Corps for the job of removing the body. And in case they get caught removing the body, they were supposed to tell the soldiers that they were the dead man's relatives.

The body carried away by the three men was placed in a carriage that had been prepared by Cleopas and ran toward Galilee. Thomas was against this undertaking at first. The reason was that there was chance of being searched on the way from there to Galilee. In case the search should take place, the Romans would not only take away the body but also would punish the men in charge of transport with utmost severity.

Cleopas and Timeus were of different opinion, however. Although there indeed was the chance of being searched by the Roman soldiers on the way, how many of them would recognize Shaphan, especially now that he had turned into a corpse, they argued. Zechariah and Gallio took the side of the two men on the following condition.

The condition was that in case Roman soldiers were seen on the road or if such news should reach them, they were to hide in a nearby village or if this was impossible they were to bury the body temporarily, to be transported again later.

The body of Shaphan arrived at Mt. Tabor early next morning and the wagon with Zechariah and the rest arrived in early afternoon. Next day, many more members gathered.

On the third day, they buried Shaphan in a most secret part of Mt. Tabor and decided to bury there the bodies of Jair and Hadad, and other members also, as they would be found.

They also decided to hold the activities of the Corps for the time being except trying to obtain release of Ananias from his imprisonment. After he should be released, they could continue with normal activities as before, they agreed.

Lastly, there was the problem of Zilpah.

Thomas asked Zechariah what he thought of taking Zilpah to Ophrah but Zechariah said it would be better to ask Zilpah about her preference first.

So Thomas saw Zilpah and asked her:

"Commander, we have decided to disperse for the time being and take a rest, for a change. Zechariah thinks he could make you comfortable in Ophrah. What do you think of it?"

Zilpah never showed surprise or confusion no matter what she was told. And she now answered in her calm, cool voice:

"Thank you, Master Zechariah. But I followed Master Thomas when I left and came to the Corps headquarters. So I wish Master Thomas could now take me back to Aroer."

Zilpah's voice was shakier than any other time that she spoke, however.

Thomas felt perplexed. Although it was under the command of Shaphan that he had become Jesus' disciple, he had become much influenced by his teachings in the course of time. And since Jesus had prophesied resurrection, he could not stay away from Jerusalem for long. Besides, he had a lot to think about now that both Jesus and Shaphan were dead and the teachings he had received from them were left unsorted.

"I understand your wish perfectly and I will be willing to wait on you if you do not have to go back to Aroer right away. The only problem is I still have to take care of some matters for the Corps which includes, among other things, confirming Jesus' prophecy about resurrection. In fact, I intend to go back to Jerusalem without delay."

"I will wait for you at a place you decide for me until you should be free from your responsibilities. You realize, of course, that affairs of the Corps is also my affairs."

It was agreed by all then that Thomas would look after Zilpah until she should be back with her family in Aroer and that all the rest of the members would be tending their own affairs until they should receive words. Zilpah brought out a bottle of wine saying:

"This is what Commander Shaphan left in my charge. I want you to drink this together for farewell."

Zilpah poured the wine for everybody present. When she had finished pouring the wine, Thomas raised his cup and said:

"To Commander Shaphan, Madam Zilpah and to all of us! That we all may be tomorrow's victors!"

Everybody repeated the toast and put down their cups.

What happened to Jesus after he was laid in the tomb?

Joseph of Arimathaea locked himself in his house after he returned from the tomb of Jesus. When it was night he could not sleep. Although he had succeeded through an entreaty with Pilate in laying the body of Jesus in the tomb that he had hewn out for himself, he still did not believe that Jesus would remain dead in the tomb because he had a belief in Jesus' prophecy about resurrection. There was another reason besides Jesus' prophesying why he believed in resurrection. It was what came about with his uncle who had been an astrologist. While he was living, his uncle ate only about half the amount of food that other people ate; then, in the year he became forty years old, he said that he would die within the year but that they were not to bury him until a week would have passed. It so happened he died in April of that year and his family according to his will left him unburied. On the third day after his death, he opened his eyes again and began to breathe again. All his family gathered and waited on him and a doctor was called in, too. In any case, he revived completely and lived like before and died after three more years of normal life.

Joseph believed in the possibility of Jesus' resurrection all the more when he remembered what had happened to his uncle. So he kept awake until very late that night and only when the cock crowed for the second time did he lie down. Next day was the Sabbath and he spent the day wholly in prayers. It was the hour of the cock's first crowing that night. Joseph was sitting on his bed with his eyes closed when suddenly he saw Jesus before his eyes.

"Joseph, I am awake like this."

"Oh, Lord."

When Joseph opened his eyes, Jesus had already disappeared.

Joseph had a carriage waiting in his yard with two servants aboard it. Now he prepared ten silver pieces to bribe the Roman soldiers that might be guarding the tomb.

When he arrived at the tomb, the cock had crowed for the third time. Two Roman soldiers were asleep nearby. Joseph got off from the carriage with his two servants. He was going to take Jesus home even if he was lying there as a dead body. It was because he believed that Jesus would revive. But Jesus was awake when he entered the tomb. And Joseph could feel his heart pounding uncontrollably. Everything was just as he had expected and dreamed of. He went up to Jesus.

"Lord, I came to take you home because I knew you would be awake."

When Joseph said this, Jesus moved his left arm a little but with difficulty.

Joseph turned to his servants and said:

"Carry the Lord to the carriage. And be very careful."

Thus saying he handed the outer garment made of thin cotton that he had taken with him to the servants.

The servants wrapped Jesus with the fine cotton garment and lifting him in their arms, carried him out of the tomb. And Joseph who was left behind, cleared the kerchief and the linen sheet at random and came outside.

He was still holding the ten silver pieces which he had brought to bribe the Roman soldiers in case of need. But the soldiers were still asleep.

As to how long Jesus stayed at Joseph's house after he was taken there in the carriage, what he told Joseph, where he went from there, or what he did afterwards and with whom, we will leave them all as eternal enigma.

Although Hadad had been taken to the Roman camp in Capernaum, it was testified by Aquila that he was not a member of the Corps but an astrologer. Consequently, he did not receive a harsh treatment from the Romans and enjoyed considerable freedom in half confinement.

When Aquila did not come back from Mt. Tabor whence he had gone to trap Shaphan, however, the Romans began to build a plan on Hadad. That is, they thought of exchanging Hadad for Aquila. They consulted Ananias who had been imprisoned by them about the matter and Ananias readily said that it could be arranged if they released him so that he could go to Mt. Tabor and talk to his comrades there.

The Roman army did not put this idea to practice because seeing that Aquila did not come back after playing false with Shaphan, they suspected that Aquila was already dead. Also they did not wish to let such an important enemy as Ananias go loose for uncertain reward.

They decided to hold an interview with Hadad himself.

"What is your wish, old man?"

"It is to return to my cave with my daughter."

"Will you listen to us if we let you do so?"

"What are your words?"

"That you go to Mt. Tabor and take Aquila back to us."

"Is he at Mt. Tabor?"

"Yes."

"Since Commander Shaphan is said to have been executed, I would think Aquila, too, is dead by now."

"It is not certain. We want you to go and find out. If Aquila is alive, take him to us on the condition that we would release Ananias in return. And take your daughter back with you."

"I will try."

When Hadad went to Mt. Tabor, however, the Corps had been disbanded already and Aquila's body had been buried in a temporary burial.

Hadad could hear from a Second Member who was guarding the cave about what had happened up to then.

"Ask Master Thomas to take my daughter back to Aroer for me. And as to Aquila's body, I may be able to arrange its exchange with Ananias."

Liberdinus, the Second Member guarding the cave who was also a soldier under Zechariah at the time of the battle of Gerasa was overjoyed at hearing this.

"Please make it work, Corps Teacher!" he said.

Hadad returned to Mt. Tabor after five days. He said that the release of Ananias was likely to be materialized. He added that although he had intended to go back to the cave in Gerasa, now he wanted to come to Mt. Tabor when Commander Shaphan was buried and become the tomb-keeper.

Liberdinus embraced Hadad and exclaimed:

"I thank you, Corps Teacher."

Within that night Liberdinus conveyed this news to Thomas and all the other chief members.

Next, we will find out in what form the resurrection of Jesus took place for Thomas who had been a faithful disciple of Jesus at the same time that he was a loyal head member of the Blood Contract Corps.

When people were excited about the resurrection of Jesus, Thomas said to himself: Unless I see the marks of nails on his hands and feet and put my hand on the wound on his side, I will not believe it. Four days after this, he was sitting in his room alone when suddenly Jesus appeared before him.

"Oh, Lord!" he said and was about to get up. But Jesus put out one hand before him and said:

"Feel the nail mark on my hand with yours. And put your hand to my side."

The reason he said this was that Thomas had said to the other disciples that he would not believe his resurrection until he could feel his wounds with his own hand. Thomas took the hand held out before him with his both hands and exclaimed:

"Where will you stay from now on, Lord?"

"Would you believe me only when you can see me?" said Jesus without making any reply to what Thomas had asked.

"Lord, be with me. I will lead you to a place where you can stay."

Thomas was thinking of the cave at Mt. Tabor where Jesus would be seen by nobody.

But Jesus again did not pay any attention to what Thomas said.

"Thomas, do not become one without faith." He said and then next moment he was gone.

Thomas fell into a new doubt. Although he had seen Jesus with his own eyes and felt him with his own hand, he could not be sure how he had come in and how he had gone out of his room. Also, Jesus had not answered him when he brought up the question of his lodging. Thomas had believed himself to be a man of solid thinking and it was for this reason that he had felt Jesus with his own hand. But about his coming and going, he knew next to nothing. And this was bothering him.

As he was thus sunken in doubt and confusion, he was

visited by Cleopas who at once asked Thomas if he had heard the news about Jesus' resurrection. When Thomas had told him of his experience, Cleopas said:

"I met Joseph of Arimathaea yesterday. As you know, he is one of the Third Members in my unit. And he insists that he saw Jesus resurrected. But he said he could not tell me where and when he saw him. He also said that he waited on Jesus for one full day and night."

"I, too, I saw him clearly and felt his wounds with my hand. When I offered to take him to some place where he can stay, he scolded me for my lack of faith and then disappeared. You know, I had thought of taking him to Mt. Tabor. And now I don't know what to think of all this."

"I think then that he really resurrected. If he appears again, we will take him to Mt. Tabor if we have to use force. And Madam Zilpah, too. . . ."

Cleopas stopped talking when he noticed a surprised look on Thomas' face.

"What were you going to say, Cleopas?"

". . . . . ."

"When I thought of taking Jesus to Mt. Tabor, I only wanted to offer him some place where he could rest in peace out of the way of the world. And what you seem to suggest is. . . ."

"I will be frank with you if you will promise not to misunderstand me. Although it is certain that Jesus resurrected, he cannot come out in the world and engage in any activities as he had done before. If so, he could become our new leader, something like Hadad and Commander Shaphan put together, you might say, and then I thought it won't be amiss if we would have Madam Zilpah back here by his side. . . ."

Thomas felt that it was all because Cleopas wanted to revive the Corps and was moved in his heart. Therefore, he said to Cleopas in a voice more gentle than before:

"Cleopas, I am going to take Madam Zilpah back to Aroer

before long. And in my opinion, Jesus will not take over the leadership of our Corps although as to where he will go or with whom he will affiliate himself, we can say nothing at this moment."

Jesus did not appear to Thomas again.

"Is there no other news from Jerusalem?" asked Thomas.

Cleopas told him about the robber that had been crucified along with Jesus and Shaphan that day and also of what happened to Judas.

The man who had been blessed by Jesus in his last moments on the cross had been taken into the hands of his family four days after he died.

As to Judas, he was not miserable or unhappy contrary to the rumor. He had at first expected that Jesus and Shaphan would join hands and achieve something grandiose. But when Jesus repeatedly and forcibly rejected the approach from the Blood Contract Corps, Judas knew that there was no hope. From the time Jesus began to be seriously persecuted by the Jewish ruling class he began to be afraid for his own safety. When people started talking about the possibility of Jesus' dying at the hands of the Roman governor and also the possibility that his disciples could be taken in at the same time of his arrest, he decided to take the way he had taken. But afterwards, he could not bear to be stared at and hated by the world and especially he could not bear the resentment and ostracization of his one-time friends of the Corps. And so he decided that he would take leave of people and live by himself somewhere on the money he had received for betraying Jesus. And he seemed content enough with the life as it has been shaped for him, said Cleopas.

"It was a mistake on the part of the Corps to have put Judas in charge of Jerusalem."

Cleopas seemed to feel as if Thomas were blaming him.

"To tell the truth, I nearly received the money myself."

He then got up to leave.

Thomas was aware of the fact that Cleopas and Judas had

gone around together much about the time of Judas' betrayal and so he was not very surprised when Cleopas made that confession to him.

Next day, Thomas went to Mt. Tabor in order to ask Hadad's opinion about Zilpah.

Lastly, Mary of Magdala went back to Galilee with the mother of John. But three days after her return, she disappeared. At first, people thought she had maybe gone to see her mother in Magdala, but they learned that Mary had stayed only one night at Magdala and then went on again. Philip who knew about her history, went to Chorazin to see if she had gone to see her real mother. But when he got there he was told that she had not even appeared there.

"She was a strange woman, anyway."

"Maybe, she drowned herself in the sea."

People said what they liked about her disappearance.